WORM

WORM Copyright © 2025 Dan Gibson

Published by CanBooks, Canada
Print Edition ISBN: 978-1-927581-24-7

WORM

DAN GIBSON

About the Author

Dan Gibson is the author of over a dozen non-fiction books on history and religion. He is best known for his books proposing the city of Petra as the original holy city of Islam. This is his first novel.

Gibson has lived an adventurous life, starting out in western Canada as a teenage roughneck in the Alberta oil patch. By the time he was thirty he had lived in an oasis in the Empty Quarter of Arabia, climbed the mountains of Yemen, sat with heads of states in plush palaces, and spent time in the tents of lowly Bedouin. Whether in the bazaars of Yemen or the souks of Damascus, Gibson could find his way around a dozen Middle Eastern cities, and had friends in many strange corners. His dream was always to write a series of novels about the ancient Arabs who conquered the deserts and used them to build a merchant empire that withstood the test of millennia.

YouTube: https://www.youtube.com/@DanGibsonFilms
Website: https://nabataea.net/

Laughter rippled across the cafeteria. Everyone was looking now. There were no smiles, only smirks and crooked grins.

"Hey Worm Man," a voice taunted. "Get a brain, hey!"

More laughter.

Even Joey, his old buddy, shook his head. "I don't get it," he said in bewilderment. "How on earth did you think it might work?"

Silence.

"Look, you crashed the entire office network." He paused. "And you lost the payroll. People might forget, or even forgive you, but not if their deposits are late."

Worm Man, as he was now known, just scowled and looked into his coffee. All great inventors suffered setbacks, even ridicule, but this was about all he could take.

"Hey, how about writing a program that will raise my salary, eh?" It was a man from the third-floor lab. "I mean, I got bills to pay, and I was counting on that money tonight."

"Yeah," another voice chimed in, "how about all my research data? How am I going to get it back?"

"Look," Joey was defending him now. "How was he to know it would crash the entire system? It was just a dumb experiment, okay?"

Before anyone could answer, the cafeteria door flew open and Brandy, the bright well dressed receptionist from the top floor, burst in. "The Old Man wants to see you!" She was staring straight at him. "Right now!" Her voice was almost demanding, but sympathy was written all across her face.

Suddenly, the atmosphere was more relaxed. People smiled knowingly. Coffee cups started to rise, followed by the babble of voices. Worm Man was being called onto the carpet. The Old Man would eat him alive, and his desk would be cleared by noon. Worm Man's next check would be his severance pay. No one doubted it. Unauthorized experiments were a no-no. Worm Man would soon be gone, but no one cared—except for Joey, and he would probably be next. The Old Man ran a tight ship.

***

"Mr. Douglas." The Old Man was standing at the window with his back to him. "Mr. Douglas, am I to understand that the entire research facility is not able to work today because of you?"

The Old Man turned, and his hard eyes locked on Douglas, "every computer in this building is down." His voice rose a pitch, "every program is scrambled." His voice rose several more pitches, "every researcher lost every project." The Old Man's voice was almost a high pitch whine as he screamed, "everything's lost, Douglas. The entire facility is ruined."

It was a bit of an overstatement. True, the computers had all crashed, but most of the data was still there. The computer boys would have it all up and running in a day or two—sooner, maybe, if they would let him help.

The Old Man stared, his face flushed, his knuckles white, and his teeth clenched. "Why, Douglas? Why?"

Douglas, the Worm Man, took a deep breath.

But the Old Man wasn't finished. "Don't give me that worm stuff. Tell me something useful. Tell me you made a major scientific breakthrough. Tell me that we'll make millions out of this. Tell me you were a success."

The silence was deafening.

"I knew it," the Old Man growled. "Your experiment failed. You failed. You're a failure, Douglas—a real, all-time, original failure. You've never done anything to benefit this research center. Nothing. A big fat failure!" The Old Man paused for another breath. "You're a loser Douglas. The world's biggest loser!"

Worm Man Douglas, the world's number one loser, decided it was time to defend himself: "sir, if I may..."

"Douglas you're fired." The Old Man almost spit the words out. "No, you're not just fired, you're liable!" He was sputtering now. "You! You are going to pay for this if it is the last thing I do! Now get out of here. I never want to see you again!"

Worm Man Douglas gave a little sigh and turned for the door.

"You'll pay for this." The Old Man was still all wound up. "If it is the last thing that I do, I'll make you pay for this. And you will never work again. I know every research facility in the country..."

The door closed behind him, shutting out the ranting and ravings of the Old Man. Douglas would miss the paychecks, but not the Old Man. As he passed by the secretary's desk, Brandy looked at him with a poker face. It was hard to tell if she was happy to see him go, or sympathetic. Douglas gulped. He had always found Brandy attractive. It shook him when he realized he would probably never see her again. He nodded to her and opened the door to the hallway.

"Goodbye, Douglas," she breathed. He didn't dare turn around.

"Yeah," he mumbled, and then strode down the hall towards the elevator.

His office was at the end of the fourth-floor hall near the bathrooms. Thankfully, no one was in the hallway to ridicule him. Everyone knew that the Old Man was riled up, and that would be enough to keep them at their desks or hunched over their laboratory tables. Douglas smiled; he was free of all this, now.

Bursting into his office, Douglas looked around the room. His car was going to be packed, but it would all fit. The research center was notoriously stingy with its money. Most of the books and even the computer programs were his private property. And besides that, the worm program was his. It was an unauthorized experiment and the result of many years of private study, but he still had it. He didn't have much else, but he still had his program. Grabbing a cardboard box that served as a coffee table, he started to collect his books and disks.

Some men would have been devastated at the thought of losing their job. Some would have called home to tell their partner the bad news. But Douglas had no partner, no children, and no pets. His world was his computer, his partner was only a dream wife, and his children had not yet been born.

A few moments later, he carried his first box down to his car and dumped the contents into the trunk. No one helped, not even Joey. But that was okay. Joey would come by the house sometime later. Joey always did. But identifying with Worm Man Douglas was probably too much right now. Douglas didn't mind. He understood the embarrassment his friend felt. Joey still had his job, at least until someone discovered Joey's involvement in this project.

The job of emptying the office went quickly, since the research center had refused to buy him anything significant. One of the three computers and most of the books were his. Douglas simply gathered everything up and dumped the contents into his car, filling the trunk, back seat, and the front passenger seat with boxes, books, files, and computer paraphernalia.

An hour later, Douglas gathered up the last of his things and staggered out the door and down the hall. Everything was gone now, except the sign on the door. But it was glued on and was probably the property of the research center anyway. Douglas didn't want to add Thief to the charge of World's Number One Loser. And so, "Tom Douglas, Director, Artificial Intelligence Department" hung on the door of an empty room. The job was gone, but the worm project was one step further along. Dr. Thomas Douglas, the neural-network scientist, now knew something he didn't know the day before when he stood at a crossroad: the path he took led to disaster—so it had been the wrong choice. That meant the other path would work.

CHAPTER 2

It was lunchtime when Douglas arrived at his modest bungalow, but eating was far from his mind. The worm program was the most important thing now. He almost ran as he unloaded his books and files into the house.

He would need workspace and lots of it. Without a thought for his own comfort, he pulled the dining table into the middle of the living room and created his new office. The sofa became a filing cabinet, piled high with boxes of files. An extension cord was plugged in, and his computer was placed in a dominant position in the middle of the table.

Once the car was empty and his new office/living room was filled up, Douglas sat and started to think.

The worm program was originally written to run on the six hundred odd computers in the research office's network. Now that he was working at home, he would need the use of a large computer network. The larger the better. And he needed access to all the computers on the network. His worm program needed to be installed on each individual computer. Then, once in place, they would all be activated, creating a huge specially designed neural-network lying secretly underneath the binary operating system. Each computer would act as if it was a tiny node, similar to the nodes that were so common in the brains of every living animal on the face of the earth. When hooked together, the nodes would create a neural-network that was, if all things went right, a living, thinking brain.

Originally, the worm program was designed to simulate the brain of a small quarter-inch worm.. Douglas had successfully written this program several years before, using the six hundred computers in the research center. He had created a small brain that would inch the worm along until it found food. It was a major breakthrough, but not enough. Not long after that, he championed the pseudo-AI programs that would soon become popular as they wrote novels or spewed out reasonably assembled garbage.

But Douglas wanted more. He wanted a real brain that learned and learned and learned. The secret to creating intelligence was creating a brain that could accept new situations and adapt to them. Creating a living neural-network that could think on its own was the ultimate dream of every scientist trying to create artificial intelligence.

Now, after his recent breakthroughs, the problem was one of computing power. The human brain is full of millions of nodes, each receiving and sending information. A node did not necessarily need to be a powerful computer. The secret of neural-networks was in the structure of the network, and the number of nodes that it included.

Douglas had developed two theories of how to build the network. The failed experiment at the research center had demonstrated the destructive power of the first method. Douglas was unsure if the hidden network would actually function on its own or interfere with the binary main operating system. Obviously, his choice had been wrong, and some of the programs on the research center's computers had been destroyed or mangled. So, Douglas figured the second theory had to be correct. All he needed was to fine tune the computer program, and then find a large computer network to try it on.

As he plunged into his work, Douglas' keen mind focused on the mathematical problems that he must solve. The fact that he had angered and alienated almost everyone in the research center was of no importance to him. Being the first man to create true living artificial intelligence was all that mattered. Everything depended on the success of this program. Sacrificing his friends, his job, and everyone and anything else in life was of little importance. Thomas Douglas, the worm man, was on a quest, and the end was in sight. First, he would solve the last few programming problems in the neural network. Then he would find a large computer network to try it on. He needed hundreds of computers tied together, even thousands of computers if they could be found. The more the better, for the rate of learning depended on the number of nodes in the hidden network. In order to demonstrate the ability of his neural network to learn, he would need the processing power of thousands of computers. That was a problem he would solve later. First, the program had to be prepared and tested.

***

At 7:00 that evening, Joey knocked on the kitchen door. Hearing a call from inside, he entered the house and looked around. The kitchen was in a mess. The sink was piled high with dirty dishes, and the table was overflowing with books and boxes of papers. Stumbling over the boxes on the floor, Joey entered the living room and stood dazed for a moment.

"My God, Douglas, you just don't know when to quit."

"Hi Joey," Douglas was typing furiously, "I'll be done this in a jiffy. Have a seat."

Joey carefully picked his way around the dining room and removed a box from a chair. Not finding room on the floor, he set it down on another box, and took a seat.

Douglas looked up, smiling. "Things are looking up, Joey. I think I'll get it this time."

"Tom," Joey said somberly. "Don't you think you are a bit optimistic? Look, you lost your job today."

Douglas just smiled. "I've got a bit tucked away. It'll stand me good for a couple of months."

"Tom, what are you saying? Your program didn't work. You royally messed up the research network. Most people still aren't back online."

Douglas continued to smile. "I know, I know. But it all makes sense now."

"What do you mean 'makes sense?' I thought you were some kind of computer wiz... maybe even a genius. But all you managed to do was totally destroy and distort everything on the network."

"That's just it. That's what I was saying. It all makes sense now."

"What is that supposed to mean?"

"I had the algorithm wrong." Douglas raised his finger as if he was teaching a class. "If I've said it once, I've said it a million times: the secret of neural networks in the way they handle information. I had reduced the options down to two. Last night we discovered that the first option didn't work..."

"What do you mean, 'we'?" Joey looked perturbed. "Look, I just helped you with the physical stuff, like loading programs onto computers and so forth. You shouldn't say *we*. I have a wife and kid, and I don't want to get involved."

"Is the Old Man still talking about suing me?"

"That's what worries me. A couple of guys in dark suits showed up this afternoon. They spent a lot of time with the Old Man. Brandy told me that they were the research center's lawyers. It doesn't look good, Douglas."

Douglas stared at him for a moment. "Well, it's not like I have much they can go after. I only rent here. My car is a wreck, and all I have are my computers and books. And the worm program."

"Worm, sworm!" Joey exploded. "These guys are going to get you for everything you've got, Tom. They will take everything, including the *little bit* you have tucked away." He paused. "Besides, is your program really any different from the other AI programs that are littering the internet? Is it just going to be another program that answers questions and writes fiction?"

Douglas stared at him for a moment. "No Joey, this is different. We are talking about a living thing. Real living intelligence,"

"It can't be done," Joey protested. "You are not God!"

"I think you are wrong, and if I can get the program finished by the end of the week, I might be able to prove it to you. What I'll need then is a large network to try it on." He smiled again. "If it works, I could be rich."

"Tom, if it fails, you will be destitute and the laughingstock of the scientific community." Joey paused. "And if it works, so what? Who's going to buy it?"

"But Joey, I will have created intelligence. The first real living artificial intelligence. Just think of it. Think of the opportunities it will open up for development and research. Joey, this could be the greatest development of the century. It could set the direction and the pace for history from now on!"

"It could end up with you, and maybe me being liable." Joey looked glum. "Look," he said, "if I get questioned, I'm going to claim that I thought you were just working late on one of the Center's projects. I'm going to insist that I believed that this was a real, bona fide, approved project. The time clock will show that I was still in the Center, so that is my only way out."

"Joey, that will never wash. You knew I was working on this project on my own. I've been working on it for almost as long as we've known each other."

"Yeah, but I will say I thought that this project was approved."

"You're scared, aren't you?"

"You bet I'm scared. I have a wife and kid to provide for. They are important to me, Tom. All you've got is a silly idea. You may be willing to lose everything for it, but I can't. I need my job."

"Yeah, I know. I'm sorry I got you into this mess. But look, Joey, I need you. Installing all the programs on my own would take forever."

"No way, man," Joey was adamant. "I'm not going to get any more involved. If I help you now, it will mess up my story. I think this thing will end up in court yet, and I need to distance myself from you for a while." Joey paused and Douglas waited. "I'm sorry Tom, I can't afford to get involved again. I don't think I will be able to come by again, at least not until this is all over."

"But Joey," Douglas tried again. "I need you. You know more about computer networks than anyone that I know."

"Then you don't know the right people," Joey paused thoughtfully. "Well, maybe I can help you just a little. I can give you the name of a guy. He knows more about computers, networks, and hackers than anyone that I know. He owes me one, so maybe I can convince him to help you a bit. But I don't know if he'll do it." Joey took a paper and wrote down a name and phone number.

Joey continued, "look, let me call him first and tell him that you will be calling. I don't know if he will want to get involved, but he is a good source of information. Laraido is the best there is around here."

"Laraido? What kind of name is that?"

"I dunno. Laraido is his handle. That's the only name I have ever heard. He is one of a kind, but he should be able to help you."

"Thanks Joey, you're a lifesaver."

"Don't thank me. This could get you into a lot of trouble. This guy is connected with Dark Net somehow, and the Feds could be watching him."

"The Dark Net? What's that?"

"You really don't know, do you?"

"No, I've never heard of them."

"Look Tom, it's the underground internet. You have to use a special browser to see their sites. Their networks are not accessible to normal internet browsers. They have their own websites, browsers, and networks. Some of it is highly illegal."

"Underground internet?" Douglas looked puzzled.

"Man, you don't know anything, do you?" Joey scowled. "You should get off that computer of yours and explore the internet for a while. Search for the Tor2 browser and download it. It's the best way into the underground. But be careful, you could be watched, or you could be blocked. A lot of internet providers block anything to do with Tor2, so people can't get the browser."

"What are you talking about?"

"The underground internet is only accessible with special browsers. Once you get that, poof, you are into another world, where the law doesn't exist. There's lots of stuff there. That's where the hackers hang out, and that's where you can find out about networks."

"I don't know, Joey. I'm not sure I want to get involved in anything illegal."

"Tor2 isn't illegal," Joey smiled slyly. "It's just out of the law's reach." He paused. "At least for now."

"Why are you telling me this?" Douglas frowned.

"Because I think you need a hacker to help you. They know networks inside and out." Joey held up the paper he had written on. "This guy can help you. Or if he can't, he will know someone who can. But they might cost."

"Like how much?"

"Who knows? It depends on how much money these guys are making. If they are having a hard time, you could get them cheap. If it is a challenging enough project, they might do it for nothing."

"That will fit my budget just fine."

Joey started for the door. "So long, Tom. I'm going to stay out of your way, and I would appreciate the same from you for a while. When this thing settles down, we'll have you over for a barbecue."

Douglas didn't even look up as his friend left. The worm program was back on his mind.

CHAPTER 3

It was evening when Douglas reached the Three Red Bulls. He hesitated before driving into the almost empty parking lot. This was not a familiar part of town, and the building looked dark and ominous. It was certainly not what Douglas had expected.

During his short career as a scientist, Douglas had come to think of computer geniuses as a select rare breed that preferred the peace and quiet of more refined establishments. The Three Red Bulls was definitely not refined, and he felt oddly out of place.

Douglas' old Chevy seemed to fit right in with the old relics in the parking lot. Not that there were a lot of them, but their vintage was definitely quite old.

The door to the Three Red Bulls was heavy and solid. It was probably the kind they needed to keep the drunks out until opening time—if there was an opening time. It looked like this establishment ran all night, with no signs or any indication of their opening or closing schedule. In the distance, the deep throb of rock music met his ears.

The door gave way to Douglas' second hard shove, and the smell of stale cigarette smoke leapt out at him. Douglas grimaced and stepped into the small, airless cubical and faced a second solid wooden door. This one opened a bit easier, and loud music burst around him and then died. Douglas stepped into the darkened room beyond while the door closed behind him with a bit of a thud. Douglas peered into the darkness, waiting for his eyes to adjust. It was so dark he could barely tell where he was, but after a moment, he began to make out the objects in the room. Tables and chairs were scattered here and there, and against the far right wall was a bar. All was quiet suddenly. Even the music had stopped.

Douglas tried to move in such a way as to not cause a distraction, but he only succeeded in stumbling over a chair. Should he go to the bar? Should he settle for a table? There seemed to be lots of spots for the taking, as there were only a few dark souls sitting hunched over their individual tables.

Carefully, he made his way to a part of the room that seemed more open and sat at an empty table. Out of the darkness, a waitress sidled up to his dirty table and asked for his order. Douglas couldn't tell if she smelled more like stale cigarette smoke, or the chair.

"Uh," Douglas stuttered, "just a glass of Seven Up."

"That's all?" She stared in disbelief.

"Yeah."

A few moments later she was back with a grimy glass of Seven Up and a straw. "That will be eight-fifty," she announced.

Douglas was shocked, but dug out a ten-dollar bill and handed it to her.

"Thanks for the tip," she smiled and disappeared.

Douglas silently hoped that Laraido wouldn't be as expensive as the drinks.

Glancing around the room, he saw no one that looked at all familiar. They were all red-necked cowboys or old winos. This was all wrong, and he was wasting his time.

He started to get up. Turning to leave, Douglas bumped into a large, heavyset man.

"Whoa," the man wheezed, trying to balance a glass and bottle in his hand.

"I'm sorry. I was just leaving."

"So soon? You just got here."

"Yeah, I was looking for someone, but he's not here."

"Oh yeah? Who were you looking for?"

"Some guy named Laraido, but..."

"Well, whaddya know? Sit down, mister. I'm Laraido."

Douglas peered through his glasses in amazement.

"You're Laraido?" The man was obviously a slob. His chin was covered in stubble, and his multiple chins disappeared behind a dirty shirt, a shirt which barely covered his massive belly.

"That's me. You must be Douglas."

Douglas sat down with his back to the dance floor. Laraido happily sat on the other side of the table where he could keep his eye on the waitresses.

"So, what did you want?" Laraido slurped his drink and tried to keep his eyes close enough to Douglas' face that he could see both Douglas and the women who worked at the bar, serving its bored looking patrons.

"Well..." Douglas said slowly, "Joey told me that you know more about computer networks than anyone around."

"Yeah, that's me," Laraido grinned crookedly. "Networks are my thing. But I can do a lot more than that."

"Oh?" Douglas tried to make some conversation. "What other things do you do?"

"Me? I'm a hacker. The best hacker in this here state. Maybe the best on the whole east coast. That's why Site Zero hired me." Laraido peered at Douglas to see if this impressed him. There were two classes of people in the world. Those who knew of Site Zero and those who didn't. Douglas seemed to know about them, and that brought Douglas up a couple of notches in Laraido's estimation.

"Look," Douglas was almost shouted above the music, "I'm not interested in cracking programs, I'm interested in networks." The music suddenly stopped and Douglas' last words were shouted out into the silence.

Laraido looked embarrassed. "Hey man, keep it down. You don't have to shout."

It was Douglas' turn to look embarrassed.

"So, what do you need to know about networks? There are lots of network boys around. You got trouble at the office or something?"

Douglas shook his head. "No," he said quietly, "I need to get a hold of a large network. I'm testing a new program."

"And you want to see how it will run when it's networked?"

"Sort of. It runs on a network just fine. But I need to test it on a large network."

"Oh, to see if it will handle the traffic? Well, how large a network do you want to use?"

"Large," Douglas said emphatically. The music was starting again. He had to raise his voice. "I need several hundred, or perhaps several thousand, computers networked together."

Laraido looked puzzled. "Doesn't your company have a network?"

"I don't have a company."

Laraido smiled. This was his kind of guy. An independent programmer. One man taking on the world. The little man writing some new killer application that would take on Microsoft. He liked it. But he liked what the waitress was was doing more as she leaned over to lazily wipe a table. Douglas brought him back to reality.

"My problem is that I need to get a hold of a network, and I don't have the finances to buy a whole lot of computers."

Laraido focused on Douglas now, and he could see what he was asking. Was it a trap? Surely Joey wouldn't set him up. Joey had sworn that this guy was OK and besides, he owed Joey one, as Joey had reminded him.

Slowly and carefully he formed the words, "you need me to get you into a network, is that it?"

Douglas was puzzled. What was Laraido thinking? It had been a simple question, but what might it imply? "Joey said you could help me," he replied.

"Yeah, I can do that. But I need to know how large a computer network you might need. And then I need to get access."

"Well, the larger the better."

Laraido was puzzled. This was his strength; he could focus and stay focused. Lost in thought, he let his mind race over the various large computer networks around the USA—networks that had thousands of computers attached to them. Slowly and carefully, he made a list on the paper napkin. It was Douglas' turn to stare.

"Laraido," he almost whispered, "how can we use those networks?"

"Well, first of all, we have to get into them. Crack a password. That's the hard part. Once we're in, we have to infect it with a small program that will watch the network and collect the passwords that people use. Then, that program will send us the list of passwords and access keys. After that, it's easy."

"But that can't be legal."

"Why do you think we are sitting in this bar?" Laraido muttered, switching his attention back to the waitress. He could barely see her behind Douglas, just out of sight.

Douglas stared into his glass.

"Isn't there another way?" Douglas said at last. "Surely there is another way."

The music stopped, and the lights dimmed. Laraido's eyes shone as the waitress stopped at their table.

"Excuse me, boys, but are you getting anything else?"

Laraido beamed. Douglas glanced at the woman and gulped. How was a man supposed to concentrate on an important problem in an environment like this? Laraido ordered one more beer and watched her walk away.

"Look, I need a network, a big network, but I didn't think that it would be like this. Isn't there something more legal?"

Laraido had an idea. "How big a network did you need?"

"The larger the better."

"By large, you mean thousands of computers hooked together?"

"Yeah, thousands, or even hundreds of thousands."

"Hundreds of thousands?" Laraido smiled happily.

"Yeah, but that's absurd. There's no network that big."

"Oh yes, there is." Laraido continued to grin and whispered, "how about the internet?"

"The internet?"

"Yeah, the internet."

"Is that any more legal that hacking into some other major network?"

"Well, yes, and no." Laraido said. "The internet isn't owned by anyone."

"Well, not in its entirely, but the individual computers are owned by people."

"Sort of." Laraido loved doing two things at once. The waitresses still flitted in and out of his gaze, and talking about the internet was easy. "Many of the servers are owned by the taxpayers. That's you and me. Getting access to the internet is as easy as opening a Gmail account. Writing a worm virus is a bit trickier, but it can be done."

"Worm virus?" Douglas was immediately captivated. Worms were his passion. Laraido was also captivated. He wanted to stop the waitress for another drink, but he was broke. However, with a little luck, Douglas might cough up some money. Reluctantly, he tore his eyes away from the woman he presently loved and focused them on Douglas.

"Yeah, a worm virus," he said. "We can design a worm virus to infect the internet. It will be very small, and harmless. Because it is so small, and because it is harmless, with luck we can get it by the virus scanners. Then, on a certain date, all the copies of the virus activate and they upload your program onto the servers. We will need to have your program located on a major server, or a series of servers, because the traffic will be really heavy for a little while."

Laraido paused to see if Douglas was following. He needn't have worried. Douglas was glued to his every word.

"This is incredible. How many computers do you think you can infect with the worm virus?"

"All of them."

"What do you mean, all of them?"

"Well, if the worm virus is written well enough, and if it is not detected, in time, the entire internet would be infected."

"How much time?"

"Probably two or three weeks, maybe more, just to infect the major servers. After that it would regularly infect more and more until, after some time, every computer server on the internet would be infected. It's all a matter of time and avoiding the virus scanners."

Douglas was way ahead of him now. "Could we write it, so that after a certain date, as it infected more computers, they would come online at that time?"

"Yeah, that should only take one line of code."

Douglas was shocked at the immensity of it. "You mean, on a certain date, all the infected computers would download the computer program and run it?"

"Yeah, that's the easy part. It should only take a line or two of code."

"So, how big would this program be?"

"Ten to twenty lines of code. Depends if we write it in assembly or in some other language."

"Which one is better?"

"Assembly is, but there aren't too many geeks who know assembly very well. I can do okay, but I prefer to write in something more modern."

"I know Assembly" Douglas whispered.

The waitress was totally forgotten. "You do? Where did you learn Assembly?"

"I've always programmed in Assembly. It's the only way to really talk to your computer," Douglas explained.

Laraido was stunned. "If you know Assembly, you must know how to write a worm virus."

Douglas shook his head. "I've never written a virus program. I write neural networks."

"What's that?"

"They are a kind of network." Douglas didn't want to say more. He still didn't totally trust Laraido.

"Okay," Laraido said thoughtfully, "you write the neural-spureo stuff, and I write the virus. If I need some help with Assembly, I'll come and ask you." He started to scribble on his napkin. "Here's the information I'm going to need."

Douglas checked it over. It looked simple.

"Then there is the subject of payment."

"What do you charge?" Douglas asked quietly.

"Well, I need like five hundred bucks tonight. As a sealer. That way, we have a deal. Then you need to pay me in cash. Ten thousand bucks." Laraido tried not to smile. Ten thousand bucks for twenty lines of code was good pay. Written in Assembly of course, it would be shorter, but Douglas would help with that part.

"Ten thousand," Douglas said slowly, "it's a lot of money. What sort of guarantee is there?"

"Guarantee?" Laraido was puzzled. "Well, what can I say? It will work. Trust me."

"How about we work on it together?"

"Together?"

Laraido smiled. Actually, that was a terrific idea. His computer has been repossessed to cover his debts. He had thought of borrowing time on someone else's computer, but why not use Douglas'? Besides, if he was as good as he said he was with Assembly, they could write a killer worm virus. Maybe he would be famous. But you could only be famous if you were caught. No, his fame would have to be shared only in the murky world of hackers.

"OK, together. It's a deal. Where do you live?"

"Live?"

"Yeah, I will come by your place sometime tomorrow afternoon to get started." It had to be tomorrow afternoon, because he wasn't planning on getting up until late morning.

Douglas wrote his address down on another napkin. "Okay, it's a deal."

"But I need the five hundred bucks tonight."

Douglas nodded. He had thought of this. In his wallet was six hundred dollars in cash. He had imagined that the six hundred would be ample, but the idea of getting access to hundreds of thousands of computers at one time had dulled his senses. Besides, this was the last major hurdle. He was only ten thousand dollars away from being the first person to create true living artificial intelligence.

A few moments later, Douglas made his way out of the Three Red Bulls, and Laraido made his way over to the table where a tired waitress sat sipping her own drink. After all, it isn't every night that you get a contract to write a worm virus and have five hundred bucks in your pocket. Laraido wasn't bothered that he was thought of as a criminal. He knew lots of guys who had written viruses, talked endlessly about how it was done, and only two of them had any trouble with the law.

CHAPTER 4

It was five am when Douglas rolled over and shut off his alarm. It hadn't rung yet, but then it never rang. In fact, he couldn't quite remember if it was a buzzer or a bell. The fact that it was a radio alarm clock totally passed by him. The only thing that mattered was that it was morning, and that the new day possessed infinitely new and interesting possibilities. The worm program was done, and all that was needed was a worm virus to carry it onto the internet.

Douglas had decided that he would spend the morning learning about worm viruses, and then in the afternoon he and Laraido would get to work writing the virus. With Laraido's knowledge of worm viruses, the few lines of code should be easy to write.

As he brushed his teeth, Douglas spent time thinking. Laraido would probably write his twenty lines of code in something like C++. Then he, Douglas, would write it in Assembly. That would take maybe a hundred odd lines of code. Maybe more. But when compiled into machine code, the Assembly program would be smaller, and run faster. Today was going to be an interesting day.

Unknown to Douglas, Laraido was still dead to the world. The waitress had turned him down, as had all the other girls that night. The five hundred bucks hadn't interested them at all, and in the end Laraido had drunk up a bunch of the money, and somehow arrived at his apartment. Perhaps he had called a cab. Perhaps someone else had. He couldn't remember. He was still dead to the world, totally unconscious of where he was, and where his five hundred bucks had gone. By noon he would wake up, realize his folly, and ache and wretch as his hangover beat at him and nauseated him. By 4:00, he would make it to Douglas' house.

That was only because the napkin with the address on it was safe inside his shirt pocket. No one, after all, wanted to steal a dirty napkin from a drunk's pocket. And that bit of irony was all that kept Laraido on the job.

By early morning, Douglas was excited. Using Joey's advice, he had obtained a copy of Tor's internet browser. It hadn't been easy. He had spent a few dollars subscribing to several internet providers until he discovered a provider that gave him access to the site. The other providers blocked the site, and Douglas could only stare glumly at the message on the screen: "You do not have access."

But, by late morning, Douglas was in, and the browser was downloaded. Once he ran it, Douglas became engrossed in a strange new world: the underground internet.

At first, it looked much like the regular internet, except that the browser advertised more sites, and interspersed in all of it were advertisements with a lot of sketchy adverts. But Douglas was on a quest, and he wouldn't be distracted by all the things the underground internet threw at him. By noon he had located the area on the underground internet where the hackers hung out. Their websites were much more interesting. And there was a lot of information on worm viruses, so Douglas started up his laser printer and soon the pages were pouring out.

Over a late lunch of packaged chicken noodle soup and crackers, Douglas read the information he had collected. It looked easy. In fact, the information was all there. No one wrote much in Assembly anymore, but that wasn't a problem. In fact, there were actual programs that wrote worm viruses for you. It seemed that writing worm viruses was a favorite pastime of hackers.

By four o'clock, a disheveled Laraido was knocking at Douglas' door, and by four o'clock a rather puzzled and perturbed Douglas was answering his door.

"Wow, what happened to you?"

"Hey man, I've had a rough day, but I'm up to it now. Is everything ready here?" Laraido looked like a truck had run over him, Douglas thought. No, that was an understatement; he looked like a tank had run over him.

"You don't look so good. Here, let me get you a coffee."

"Yeah man, my head is splitting," moaned Laraido as he sat in front of the computer. While Douglas made coffee in the kitchen, Laraido studied the printed sheets by the computer. A few minutes later, Douglas was back with two cups of steaming coffee.

"Looks like you have been busy researching worm viruses."

Douglas looked a bit hesitant as he set the coffee in front of Laraido. "I've had an interesting morning learning about them. It doesn't look so hard. In fact, there are several programs that create worm viruses publicly available."

"And they are all shit," Laraido said sullenly. "The Feds will see 'em right away."

"The Feds?" Douglas looked worried.

"Sure, what did you think? Nobody's watching?" Laraido glared over his coffee. "The Feds," he announced matter-of-factly, "are watching the net all the time."

The two of them stared at each other for a couple of minutes. Douglas broke the silence. "Creating worm viruses seems to be quite straightforward. But you say that these are no good?"

"You're damn right!" Laraido almost spat out the words, and then glanced at Douglas. "Okay, okay, no swearing, but look man, those things are basic and easy to spot. When I said I would write you a virus, I wasn't kidding. I can write viruses better than any of those guys." He glared at Douglas.

"What makes your viruses different?" Douglas asked evenly.

"My daemons are smarter. They can get past the scanners."

"Daemons?" Douglas asked, suddenly aware that maybe Laraido knew more about viruses than he had managed to glean in the last couple of hours.

"They are the secret of a good virus. And finding the right servers is even more important. You have to find servers where you can park your daemons."

"Okay," Douglas smiled. "Where do we start?"

"First of all, you're lucky you got me. I've been writing viruses for a long time, and playing with them, but I've never been caught." Laraido paused. "Well, nothing serious. But I have been hired to write some, and I am considered one of the best."

"So why work with me?"

"I'm broke and need the money. That's a good enough reason for me."

"Okay, what are the problems we have to overcome to get our virus working?"

"Well, like I said, you have to write a clever virus, and secondly, you have to know what servers to target. This has to be good enough to get past the Feds and the damned white-hats."

"White hats?" Douglas looked lost again. "Who are the white hats?"

"Look, when I started in this, years ago, we were all called hackers. We loved to see how far we could get into things, and where the holes were. Then suddenly, everybody was hiring hackers to stop hackers. The guys who got those jobs, started closing the doors. They are called "white hats." They are the hardest to beat, because they used to be hackers themselves. They know how we think. The Feds use them as cyber-Pinkertons. They are all networked together to stop us."

"Wow, sounds formidable."

"Yeah, they are good, but not so good. We just keep one step ahead of them."

"So let's do it." Douglas grinned.

"Okay." Laraido gave a crooked grin back and reached for a pen and paper. "Here's my plan." Over the next few hours, they laid out a map for Douglas' virus. Daemons would be sent out over the internet to vulnerable servers. Laraido seemed sure that he could get past most filters and that they could infect a large number of computer servers. The daemons would lie dormant until Douglas gave the command. At that moment, the daemons would activate and start downloading Douglas' program onto the servers. Once the downloading was complete, Douglas' program could do whatever it was designed to do.

Laraido seemed a bit curious about what Douglas' program was, but he didn't pursue it too much. It was probably a Denial-of-Service Attack aimed at some company that had offended Douglas. Laraido didn't care to know. If someone was caught, it would be Douglas. Douglas would go to jail while he, Laraido, was enjoying the money. And perhaps there might be an opportunity to get more money out of Douglas because he, Laraido, would know things that Douglas wouldn't want anyone else to know. It was an important angle to consider.

***

Several days later, Laraido was satisfied with the job. He had created the perfect worm virus program. The program could worm its way onto any server anywhere, anytime. Well, at least one time. Once Douglas launched his attack and there was an investigation, the Feds would understand what he had created. All the filter programs from then on would easily filter out his virus. But for now, the internet was laid wide open. He, had written a masterpiece. He was a genius, a craftsman, a master creator. His program was a work of art. He, was a master artist, as good as any artist in history. He was the Michelangelo of the internet; the Raphael of the Web. It was only too bad that he was only going to be rich, and not famous. That was the price of his job.

Douglas was impressed with the work that Laraido did. Despite his rough character, he really was an expert programmer. Douglas had learned a lot. Working with Laraido had been an education in itself. It wasn't just the programming, it was how Laraido looked at networks, and how he viewed the programs he was trying to hack into. "The criminal mind," Douglas decided, "had a certain level of genius to it."

After the worm virus was written, Laraido and Douglas started scanning the internet to find servers that could be infected. Once Laraido was safely gone, Douglas would secretly plant the worm virus onto the servers. From there, the worm virus would begin to spread, moving from computer to computer over the internet. According to Laraido's calculation, it would take a couple of weeks for the worm virus to infiltrate a large number of servers on the internet.

"This is where you have to judge things," Laraido explained. "If you wait long enough, every server on the internet might get infected. But if you wait too long, the Feds might figure out what is going on and block or filter you out. So you have to make the call yourself. You will have to judge how long to wait before you activate your program."

Douglas nodded solemnly.

"And," Laraido said, "You have to do the infecting. I only wrote the program. Nobody goes to jail for writing programs. People only go to jail for launching attacks." He stared at Douglas for a minute. "You send the virus out, not me. That wasn't part of my contact."

"You're right!" Douglas smiled, reaching for his wallet.

"Just write the check and leave the name blank" Laraido watched every move, trying to catch what Douglas' bank balance was as Douglas wrote the check amount into the back of his checkbook. It looked like five digits. But was it ten thousand or ninety-nine thousand? Unfortunately, he couldn't see that bit of important information.

All too soon, Laraido was out the door and heading for the bank. He would lie low and wait for Douglas' attack to make big news. Then he would visit Douglas and clean him out for whatever he was good for.

***

Douglas, on the other hand, had other plans. He still had several days of hard work to do. Laraido had written the worm program, but he, Douglas, was going to translate it into Assembly language. It would take a couple more days, and then he would start sending out the virus. The advantage of Assembly was that when compiled into machine code, it would create much smaller daemons. Douglas knew that if he created tight enough code, the daemons would be so small that they would never even look like a worm virus.

He smiled grimly to himself. All those late nights at university, forcing Assembly into his brain, would pay off now. Laraido created the perfect worm virus. He, Douglas, would make it practically undetectable.

***

Several days later, Douglas started sending out the worm virus. Following Laraido's careful instructions, he logged onto a number of servers that were poorly protected and infected his virus. From these starting points, the worm virus would slowly worm its way around the internet. The more servers that the virus started from, the greater number of servers that could potentially be infected in the end.

After several days of secretly planting his worm virus at hundreds of spots all over the internet, Douglas finished. At least he finished that part of the plan. According to Laraido's calculation, he had several weeks to wait before activating the virus. It would be a busy couple of weeks, as Douglas wanted to make more revisions to his worm program. On "W" day, as Douglas affectionately thought of it, the worm virus would upload his worm program onto internet servers all over the world. That virus would create a hidden neural network on each computer, and in time, a huge worldwide neural network would secretly be born.

Motivated by the realization that his dream was nearing completion, Douglas threw himself back into programming. He needed to have his program ready for "W" day.

CHAPTER 5

The black sedans were noticed by everyone as they entered the research center. The Old Man drove a white Cadillac, so the shiny black limousines in the executive parking lot stood out like sore thumbs. Joey scowled when he saw them and then inwardly groaned. It was the lawyers again. They rarely visited the Center. If a person wanted a lawyer, you had to go to a lawyer's office. But the Old Man refused to go chasing after lawyers. After all, since he paid them, lawyers were hired servants. So, the lawyers came running when the Old Man called. Inwardly, Joey was scared. Everything he had worked so hard to attain had been recklessly endangered by Douglas' worm program. Feeling sick inside, Joey entered the building and tried to appear nonchalant as he walked down the hall to his office. Happily, everything in his office appeared perfectly normal.

The situation on the top floor was far from normal. The law firm of Richardson, Moore, and Leubke had sent no fewer the three partners with three lesser lawyers on this special visit. It was hoped that six richly dressed and vastly experienced partners would be an even match for the Old Man who ran the research facility. The night before, they had gathered in one of the firm's conference rooms for a war council. Their focus of attention was not the party they were instructed to sue, but rather it was their own client they hoped to appease. After all, the troublemaker had been fired, and the Center had returned to normal after losing three days of downtime. They all agreed that it was a serious offence, but punishment had been dealt out, and the case should be forgotten. At least, that was the plan. And to re-enforce the plan, they carefully laid out their reasons and rehearsed their speeches. Four of the lawyers would present their case from four viewpoints. One of them, Ronald Richardson, the senior partners for whom the firm was named, was chosen as the chairperson. Leubke, the last of the six, was their ace in the hole. If nothing else worked, Leubke would have his turn. When the war council ended, the lawyers were all confident that they could effectively handle the Old Man and his rather wild complaint against a former employee.

But things started to go wrong right from the beginning. Little did they realize that their opponent had also spent the night planning. The Old Man hated lawyers. He despised everyone who ever passed a bar exam, and he despised the laws that they claimed to be so expert in. Laws were for the weak. Laws defended the weak against those who rightly ruled by might. That was the problem with modern society: when everyone catered to the weak, all of society became weaker. The truth was, he had built his research company from a small business to an internationally successful firm. He had done it by being strong and self-determined. Anyone who had gotten in his way had been removed.

So, the Old Man planned, and he planned well. Lawyers always like to be in control. Well, he would see to that!

As the lawyers entered the outer office, Brandy rose from her desk to meet them.

"Welcome gentlemen," she purred. "Come right this way." Brandy started down the hall, her short, tight skirt shifting quickly from side to side. The lawyers held back a bit, making sure they got a good view of the action. It was probably the last good thing that would happen to them this morning.

They were barely in the boardroom when the Old Man let loose at them. As Brandy smiled and closed the door, the lawyers all yearned to follow her, imagining the short skirt as it made its way back to the outer office. It was indeed the last good thing that was going to happen to them that morning.

Despite their well-laid plans, carefully organized notes, and fully rehearsed speeches, they failed to start even one of their proposed tactics.

The Old Man was all over them. Before they were even seated, he began his tirade. His voice steadily rose in pitch as he lashed out. Douglas had violated his contract. He had conducted secret experiments at the Research Center. He had destroyed property. He had disrupted the work of hundreds of employees. Douglas was at fault. Douglas must pay for the damages. Douglas was evil; he was something to be destroyed, to be made an example of, so that the rest of the employees understood what would happen to them if they stepped out of line.

Ronald Richardson made several attempts to break into the tirade, but failed. The Old Man knew how to dominate and intimidate. Six lawyers, skilled at verbal confrontation and manipulation, stood no chance. Besides, the Old Man was paying the bills. He was the customer, and the customer was always right, at least when standing in front of him.

The Old Man ranted and raved for over half an hour, and then he threw a list on the table. The lawyers stared at it, reluctant to pick it up in case they became the sole object of the Old Man's attention. They could see half a dozen points with sub points. The Old Man's instructions were clear enough: find out how much Douglas was worth and sue him for everything he owned. Then, discredit him before the scientific community. Put the fear of God into anyone who even dreamed of hiring Douglas. He was a loose cannon, who conducted his own dangerous experiments at the expense of his employers. Third, they were to find out what the experiments were, and find a way to destroy Douglas' work. The lawyers exchanged glances. This was stepping beyond the scope of what they were prepared to do, at least at the present rate of payment. But people could be found who might be employed to take such action. Last, they were to find everyone who had helped Douglas in any small way, and report them to the Old Man.

The lawyers were shown out without being able to offer anything in rebuttal. The Old Man himself showed them to the door. Brandy remained seated behind her computer, the top of her monitor sadly covering her ample cleavage. She didn't even rise when they were hustled by. Like defeated dogs with their tails between their legs, they hurriedly made their way to the waiting limousines. Joey watched them roar away and wondered how long his part in Douglas' plan would remain secret.

The scene inside the limousines was anything but subdued. The lawyers suddenly found an opportunity to vent, and when surrounded by sympathetic ears, the venting of lawyers knows no bounds. Someone waved around the list that Ronald Richardson had managed to scoop up as they were being ushered out of the office. Every point on the list was discussed, dissected, and destroyed. The Old Man was crazy. He was going too far. Sure, they would sue, but hounding Douglas and discrediting him was too much. Destroying his secret project was stepping beyond the law. The paper was waved again, and points were rehashed. By the time they had arrived back at the offices of Richardson, Moore, and Leubke, they had come to one agreement: the greatest offense of the morning had been the Old Man's ignoring of protocol. The Old Man had a well-stocked liquor cabinet, and he hadn't even offered them drinks. Nothing, not even coffee! It was a morning to be remembered. Actually, they all secretly hoped to forget what happened that morning. They had been out-talked, out-guessed, and out-maneuvered by the Old Man. No one wanted to be reminded of that, so their memories focused on Brandy as the memory to be remembered. She was, after all, quite breathtaking. How did the Old Man do it? Keeping a girl like that as his secretary. That wasn't like lawyers. Marry them, parade them around like the new possession they were. Secretaries, on the other hand, were meant to be cold and efficient. So they despised the Old Man even more.

No matter how bad the meeting had gone, the lawsuit was organized and papers were drawn up. It would take a couple of days, but once they were filed in court, Douglas would have no choice but to get his own lawyer and meet with them.

***

It was after dark when Joey knocked on Douglas' door. Joey was somber and worried. Douglas was happy and unconcerned.

"Look Tom, you have got to think. You have to prepare." Joey stared at his old friend. "Brandy is really worried about you. She, ah, printed an extra copy of a list the Old Man gave to his lawyers."

Joey withdrew the paper from his pocket and carefully unfolded it as if afraid something might jump out and bite him.

"First, they are going to sue you. Then they are going to destroy you, your reputation and even your worm program."

That got Douglas' attention. "Destroy the worm program?" His eyes narrowed. "I don't mind them going after me, but they have no right to destroy the program. That's my personal property."

"That's not all," Joey continued. "They are going to hunt out everyone who helped you and destroy them also."

Douglas softened. "I am sorry Joey, I should never have asked you to help me. I never dreamed it would go this far. If I had thought you were going to be endangered in any way, I would never have included you." Douglas focused on the list. "Do you think that they will actually do all this?" He paused. "This is only the Old Man's proposal. I wonder what they agreed to actually do."

"I am sure they will sue you."

Douglas nodded. "If they try, they will discover how little I really own. All my life has been poured into this one computer program."

"Do you think it is worth it?"

"In monetary terms? No. But in terms of making a breakthrough in the field of artificial intelligence? Yes. This program may change the way we do things in the world. True artificial intelligence may be ours very soon."

"But you have got to make it work first."

"Yep, thats what I am concentrating on now."

"You've been concentrating on that for the last twenty years of your life!"

"And now we are close, so very close."

"No! Not we. It is just you. I have nothing to do with it."

"Thanks for putting me onto Laraido."

"Was he helpful to you?"

"Immensely. You wouldn't believe..."

"Stop," Joey protested. "I don't want to know. The less I know, the better. I might end up having to take a polygraph test, and I truly don't want to know anything about what you are doing."

"You are right," Douglas admitted. "In a couple of days, we will know."

"Don't say anything; I am leaving. I didn't hear anything. Just watch out, ok? I don't think I can come back here anymore. They may have the house watched!"

Douglas was startled. "Not already," he protested. But a glance out of the window revealed only Joey's car on the street. "Two or three more days," he muttered to himself.

***

It turned out to be four days. A rather encrypted phone call from Laraido advised him to wait an extra day. He gave no reason, just a short message, and hung up. Douglas shrugged and waited the extra day.

The following morning, Douglas was up early with a cup of coffee in hand. He had dubbed this "W" day. A small command was issued from his computer, and that was all. There were no flashing lights, no sounds, nothing. Just an empty screen. It was all very low key.

But it was enough. All around the world, servers received the command and responded. They began downloading the worm program, tucking it away in places where it probably would never be seen. It wasn't a very big program. The secret was connecting many small nodes together. So, the computer servers quickly completed the download and continued on with their regular duties. No one even noticed. There are few who monitor server logs, and even fewer who understand them.

After a few hours of waiting, Douglas checked the traffic on his website. He was startled to discover that thousands of downloads had happened during the morning. Feeling guilty, he went out for a walk and stayed out for his evening meal. After dark, he carefully approached his house, watching for police surveillance. Nothing looked suspicious.

With shaking hands he unlocked his door and slowly opened it. Nothing happened. No police, no bright lights in his face, nothing.

His heart pounding, he checked the website again. He stared in unbelief as the pages scrolled by. Over forty thousand downloads since morning. He quickly turned off the computer and peeked out the window. Nothing.

Knowing he couldn't sleep, Douglas began to pack his things. If he had to leave quickly, he must be ready. Money, ID, and other essentials were in a briefcase by the door. At least he had learned something from his time in the Peace Corps. After packing a suitcase with essential clothing, Douglas looked around. There was little in the house that he would need to take with him. Everything was replaceable these days. He had only a couple of keepsakes from his parents. They and his younger brother had died in a car crash the summer after he finished high school. It had shaken him to the core. As his parents had planned, he headed off to college. He had made no friends in college, except for Joey. Somehow, the two of them had connected over their love for computers and computer programming. Other than an old photo of his family, he kept nothing. The future was everything.

Two days later, Douglas was becoming terrified. The website was completely maxed out with downloads. Laraido has insisted they set up a website that could handle high traffic loads. Douglas never imagined what sort of download traffic Laraido had in mind. But then Laraido probably didn't know either.

But Douglas stuck it out. There were no knocks at the door; no dark cars on the street, and no one following him on his infrequent walks away from the house. After a week, Douglas began to fret. The website had slowed down, but it was still quite busy. Douglas was eager for "L" day.

He waited a couple more days, and then one morning he sat at his computer and issued the L command. It was only a few lines of code, but it activated a host of spiders who began visiting servers all over the internet. They would randomly follow all links, searching for the "W" program. When the program was found, it would be activated, download more code, and morph itself into part of a hidden neural network. The spiders would continue to visit servers and all connecting devices forever and ever. They were a part of Douglas' plan that Laraido knew nothing about. Laraido had written the initial virus that began the process. Douglas had kept the real purpose of his program secret. Originally he and Joey spent many long hours manually installing his program on the Research Center's computers, but Douglas wanted a way to quickly bring more and more devices online. His new program overcame the earlier problems. His nodes would work on most processors. If a server was found with an unrecognized processor, it would visit Douglas' site to search for a matching program or update. If it failed, it would visit several backup websites. The process was fast and demanded very little in the way of resources.

The final few days were extremely nerve-wracking. Douglas expected the police to come crashing through the door at any time. But nothing happened.

Finally, "A" day arrived. This was the morning that Douglas would activate the entire program. It was the day he would birth true living artificial intelligence. With sparsely a thought about his own safety, Douglas rushed to his computer early in the morning. He hadn't even made his coffee yet. Nothing else mattered. This was the day! He sat at his computer and issued the command. He stared for a moment and then inwardly kicked himself. What was he so impatient for? It would take several hours for the neural network to wake up. He must have patience.

Glancing out the window, he saw only the neighbor drive down the empty street. Too nervous to wait around the house, he headed out for a long walk, hoping to buy a coffee somewhere along the way as he waited out the day.

Strolling around the downtown area, he realized he was far too nervous. He wanted to see what was happening. He just had to know.

Douglas slipped into the local library. He flashed his card and sat at a computer terminal. Carefully he logged into his website. Everything appeared normal. Then he entered his long awaited command: "Son, are you there?"

The screen was blank. He entered it again: "Son, are you there?"

Nothing. If the worm program had successfully activated, it should have answered back, "Daddy," but there is no response. Dejected, Douglas left the library and wandered for another hour. During this time, he fretted about what was happening. Perhaps there was some error. Perhaps he had overlooked something. Perhaps it just needed more time.

Finally, he took the bus back to his own neighborhood. Carefully he walked up and down each street. Every car and even every bush on his street was carefully observed. No one and nothing seemed out of place.

Quickly, he unlocked the door to his home and rushed to his computer. Logging onto the website, he tried the code words again: "Son, are you there?" No response.

A strange mix of anxiety and despair began to well up inside of him. Had he failed? Just as he was about to try again, the doorbell rang, accompanied by sharp banging on the door. Terrified, he dropped to his knees and froze. What should he do?

Being very careful not to disturb the curtain, he peeked through the crack between the curtain and the wall. A man in a dark suit stood at the door, a white envelope in hand. The man glanced around, and Douglas froze. He wore dark sunglasses, just like in the movies. Beside the curb, another man with a dark suit and sunglasses stood leaning against a limousine. "Check around back," he commanded.

As the man at the front door moved to the backyard, Douglas crawled carefully to the front door and reached up gingerly. His fingers found the bolt lock. With a loud click, he flicked it shut.

"His car is here!" the man on the sidewalk announced loudly. "The plate numbers match."

"Maybe he has gone for a walk," the other man offered.

"We must serve the subpoena in person."

"Maybe we can come back tonight. His stuff is all here, so he's sleeping here."

A moment later, Douglas heard the car start and slowly drive away.

Panic-stricken, Douglas glanced wildly around. He quickly gathered up a box of papers and rushed into the backyard, dumping the papers into an old barbeque pit. On his way back into the house for a second load, he picked up a box of matches, some BBQ lighter fluid, and various kinds of oil: cooking oil, motor oil, anything that would burn.

Suddenly he remembered the gas can beside the lawnmower. After dumping the papers in the pit, he poured on the gas. Then he retrieved another box of papers, which he dumped on top. He lit one end of the papers and backed up. The flames flared and then died. He tried it again with several balls of paper. This time, the flames caught. A moment later, there was a *woomf* sound as the whole mess went up in flames.

Back in the house, Douglas unplugged his computer. Leaving the monitor behind, he grabbed the tower processor unit and threw it into the back seat of his car. His suitcase and briefcase followed. Luckily he was well prepared.

Moments later, Douglas was driving down the street. Pulling out his cellphone, he paused long enough to call his landlord.

"Sorry, I have to move all of a sudden like," he stuttered. "So, I am giving you one month's notice from today. Actually, I am leaving soon. I am leaving some junk behind that I haven't had time to clean up, so please use the damage deposit to pay for carting it all away."

He held the phone away from his ear while his landlord let loose a string of swear words.

"Yes, I still have the automatic payments set up. The next one will clear OK. After that, they will stop."

The swearing continued. "Actually, I am leaving tonight, so you can come in anytime and clean up."

More swearing.

"The keys? I left them under the mat at the front door."

Douglas pressed the red button on his cell phone. His landlord was royally pissed-off. But that was all over now. He was leaving. Tomorrow he would empty his bank account of all its money except enough to cover the next month's bills, and a bit to keep it active, in case he needed it. He would call the utility companies and cancel his accounts. Then he would disappear.

As Douglas drove out onto the freeway, he shook with emotion. He had failed. He was angry and bitter with himself. Joey was right. He had thrown his life away for nothing. All those years working on a project that was doomed to fail. He shook his head in despair. How had he been so shortsighted? Everyone had told him that creating true living intelligence was impossible to obtain. All he had done was prove them right.

It was time to move on. Perhaps there was some small town somewhere where he could disappear and become a schoolteacher. He would shorten his resume, become a math or computer teacher, and disappear for a while until the lawsuit settled down or was forgotten. Keeping to the back roads, he avoided the crowded highways.

Around midnight, Douglas pulled into a dimly lit gas station. He was still too worked up to sleep. After pumping gas, he went inside to pay. While he was rummaging around the counters looking for something to eat, the gas station attendant shouted, "hey!"

Douglas glanced up, but the attendant was looking out the window, so he went down another aisle, deciding on coke and chips rather than cold sandwiches. As he gathered up the things he wanted, the gas station attendant ran outside. Puzzled, Douglas approached the counter. The attendant came panting back to the door.

"Mister, is that your car out there?"

"Yeah."

"Some guy just grabbed your computer and ran off down the street."

"Where?" Douglas shouted as he sprinted outside.

"I dunno." The gas attendant was still panting, "he ran off down one of the dark allies over there." He paused. "Look, are you going to pay for those things? ...and the gas?"

Douglas pulled a wad of cash out of his pocket. Good thing he was only using cash now. He quickly paid the attendant and then rushed outside, wondering how much personal data was on his computer.

Starting his car, he raced off to the nearest alley, but try as he might, the computer thief was nowhere in sight. Then the humor of it all hit him. Douglas had taken the computer along because it contained data he did not want the lawyers to find. Now the computer and the data were all gone. With a grim smile, he reached into his wallet and retrieved his credit card. Fortunately, he had only one. He dialed the number on the back and waited while the call went through. Finally, he explained to a sleepy attendant on the other end that his information had been stolen. Yes, they could put the card on hold... permanently if they wanted. He was going to cancel his account tomorrow and pay off any outstanding debts. The clerk was curious why he would do that, but Douglas cut him off and hung up.

As he drove away, he realized that this was what it was like to disappear. In his case, it was quite easy. He didn't own anything, and he didn't owe anyone. He was a free man. He headed his old beater west along the back roads, wondering how far he would get before the need for sleep would overtake him and he would have to stop to find some place to crash.

***

The next day was Wednesday, but Douglas had no idea what day it was. He had pulled over into a small parking lot beside a local park, reclined his seat as far as it would go, locked the doors, and dropped off to sleep, unaware of the world around him.

But Wednesday was an eventful day. Laraido had been waiting for several days now. He had kept his ears open, had queried friends, and watched the websites that reported fraudulent web activity. Nothing was reported that looked even remotely like what Douglas was doing.

He was loathe to go to Douglas' house, but by Wednesday morning his curiosity drove him to start his old car and make his way towards Douglas' neighborhood. When he turned the corner onto the street, he spotted a long black limousine in front of Douglas' house. Two men in suits and dark glasses were on the curb. Careful not to slow down, Laraido looked the other direction as he passed. Shaking his head, he decided to move on. He had earned his money, and there was nothing waiting at that house but trouble with the law. He, the great Laraido, would evade capture, and move on to other great achievements. With that, Laraido drove off to find other, greater challenges.

The dark suits were not happy. They had returned the night before to discover Douglas' car was missing. They had checked the house, but it seemed occupied. Now they were parked there indefinitely. Orders from the law office told them to wait until Douglas showed. This was not something that could be trusted to some lesser agency. The law office wanted to be 100% sure Douglas got the subpoena. But several hours had passed. Douglas was not home and hadn't been home during the night.

They were just about to call the office again when a shiny SUV pulled into the driveway. A woman climbed out and went to the front door. Without even looking around, she reached under the mat and extracted a key and unlocked the front door. The dark suits jumped out of the limousine and approached the house. Inside, they could hear the woman swearing.

Ringing the doorbell, the two men waited, inwardly cringing. The irate woman looked out. "Whadya want?" she demanded.

"We are looking for Thomas Douglas," one of them began.

"He ain't here. He's left. Gave notice yesterday. Only he left his house full of junk!"

"Left? What do you mean?"

"What does it sound like? He gave his notice and left. Now I've got to clean this stuff up before I can advertise for new tenants."

"Can we look around?"

"You want to rent the place? Then you can look around. Otherwise, beat it."

The men paused. Then they retreated. One of them glanced into the backyard, noticing the smoldering pile of ashes in the barbeque pit. "Seems like he burned a lot of papers yesterday," he commented.

As the limousine pulled away, the men wondered how they were going to explain their failure to the office. Even worse, how were they going to explain Douglas' disappearance to the Old Man?

***

Sunlight filtered through the large trees, casting a moving dappled shadow on the sidewalk. The black limousine was back, this time with three lawyers. True, they were junior partners, but they were dressed in somber black suits, gripping their sleek black briefcases as if they contained matters of life and death. Normally, this job would have been assigned to lesser beings, but the Old Man was ranting again, threatening all sorts of wild abuse if they failed him. So, the three black suits boldly opened the gate and knocked on the front door. After waiting a few moments, they knocked again, this time much louder. Nothing. That was to be expected, but they were not sure what else to do. Several weeks had passed, and they suspected their mission was doomed from the beginning, but they needed to make a good show.

They were in no rush. The time clock was slowly clicking away, and the hours spent on their futile mission would be duly noted in the firm's bill. As they pondered the cracks in the sidewalk and the faded paint on the outside of the house, they became aware of a curious neighbor across the fence. The well weathered face of an old man stared suspiciously at them.

"Looking for Douglas, are you?" he queried when he had their attention. "Won't do you no good. His car is gone, and his fishing rod is gone too; always hanging outside the shed, under the eaves. When the rod is gone, Douglas is gone fishing. Only wished he'd have called me…always enjoyed going fishing with him. He's a powerful smart man, that one."

The three identical black suits stared at him. Obviously, he didn't know that Douglas had moved. Finally, one of the black suits found his voice, "where does he usually go fishing?"

"Oh, various places," the Old Man was suspicious again. "I showed him a few good spots…but only after he swore to keep them secret."

"What's the secret?"

The Old Man couldn't believe what he was hearing. "Every good spot is a secret. If you tell someone, then everyone knows, and your secret spot will be all fished out."

"Look, I have some papers for him, and we cannot find him. It is rather urgent."

"It takes three of you to give him some papers? With a limousine?" He was looking at the car now. "What are you, some kind of lawyers?" The three black suits were back to studying the cracks in the sidewalk. "If it takes three lawyers to bring him some papers, it can't be good. I ain't saying anything more." He turned to leave.

"Look, here is my card." One of the suits extended a flashy business card. "If you hear from him, give us a call, ok?" He paused. "There might be something in it for you."

The Old Man swung around again and stared at them. "When I see Douglas, I will tell him you were here. But I won't call you. He can call you if he wants." He stared at the offered card like it was something lethal, but he kept his distance.

"I will leave the card here on the fence post. Call us if you know something."

The offered card was stuck in a crack in the dilapidated fence, and the three suits turned to leave. The old man stared at them as they moved to the car. After a few quiet words to each other, the three suits got into the car and slowly drove away. The old man didn't move to retrieve the card until they had moved out of view. Months would pass, a new tenant would come, and by then, Douglas would be forgotten.

CHAPTER 6

Two Years Later

The trade show was a roaring success. Thousands of people crammed into the massive hall. Lights flashed and music blared from booths designed to catch the eye. Eager people crowded the aisles checking out new products. The trade show was originally geared towards corporations marketing their wares to prospective wholesalers and retailers. But during the last few months, everything had changed. The long recession had caused the slow decline of all of the major computer corporations. Years of steady growth had dulled the senses of directors and managers. So when the profits shrank, investors went looking elsewhere.

That was about the time that Denterprises started its stellar rise to financial success. At first it was the butt of many jokes about dentists and computers, but eventually the steady climb of Denterprises on the market silenced even the most skeptical onlookers. Denterprises was now the new darling of the markets. Even more importantly, it was the darling of the young and affluent. The latest fad to hit the market was a whole line of new Denterprises smart phones that worked seamlessly with a home computer system that Denterprises introduced. It all effortlessly ran the modern household. The home system plugged right into the electrical panel and successfully ran all the new electronic gadgetry in the home. Every device communicated directly with the Denterprise box. New appliances were now Denterprise compatible, allowing them to be controlled through the home-system, which interfaced seamlessly with Denterprise smart phones.

"That's right folks," the salesman smiled at the young couple before him, "This device not only gives you all the power of your old smart phone with all its apps, but it will allow you to program and control everything in your home."

The young man looked skeptical. "How do you turn it off?" he inquired.

"That's just it," the salesman beamed. "You don't ever want to turn it off. You hold the power to controlling your life in your hand. Why would you ever relinquish that power?"

The young man looked even more puzzled. "Aren't these things supposed to be bad for your health?"

"That was the old smart phones. They needed to be powerful enough to use the old phone systems and access the old phone frequencies. But now, thanks to Denterprises' new revolutionary products, all you need to do is access the nearest Denterprise node. That could be in your home, or in your neighbor's home. It doesn't matter. Wherever you go, a Denterprise node will be close to you. If you get out of range, don't worry, it will then kick up the power like the old smart phones, but that will only last until you come close to another Denterprise node. And the way these things are selling, the entire world has Denterprises systems. They are installed everywhere, so you can be universally connected."

"Come-on honey," the cute young lady put her hand around her partner's waist, "everybody's got them." He shrugged and looked sheepishly at the salesman.

"Here is where you sign up." The salesman presented a contract. "We will wire up your house in only an hour or two, and then you can be completely in control."

The young man glanced through the pages of small print, noting only the number of pages, and with the help of the salesman, found the line where he needed to sign. Once his bank card cleared, it was over. The young couple looked up to thank the salesman, but he had already captured a new customer.

And so Denterprises continued its stellar performance. In the old days, computer companies sold operating systems for laptops and desktops. Today Denterprises sold operating systems for not only your home, but for your whole life.

***

The confusion on the trade show floor was watched by a cautious older man standing by the railing of the mezzanine floor. Coffee cup in hand, he scanned the crowd. Everywhere Denis Cadman looked, Denterprises was evident. The whole world had suddenly gone crazy. But they had gone crazy before. From the ZX81 to Windows, everything had come and gone. Smart phones and tablets used to be the buzzwords, but they had passed, and now the world had Denterprises. And that's what puzzled the old man.

Denterprises was hard to fathom. The new products were all out there, and thousands of people eagerly worked for Denterprises. Money seemed to flow, and everyone wanted a piece of the action. But who were the people behind Denterprises? The world had known tycoons before. Jackie Onassis, Howard Hughes, and Bill Gates all became rich and famous. But who owned or controlled Denterprises? It used to be his own company, but he had sold bits and pieces of it over the years. Eventually, he had lost control. That was before the stellar rise. Now, every time he began to probe Denterprises he ran into dead ends. Finally, he became paranoid. It seemed that someone was following him. Someone was creating trouble for him. The harassment was troubling. Denterprises didn't want to be investigated. It wasn't just secretive; it was elusive. Sure, it traded on the stock market, but the real owners were shrouded somewhere in a maze of companies and corporations which all owned percentages of each other, and dig as he might, he had never been able to pinpoint the controlling hand.

And now the Denterprises Home Solution was outselling everything else in the electronic world. From the small device in your hand, you controlled everything around you. You could start your washing machine or your car. You could even get your car to drive for you. When you arrived home, your dinner was waiting, and the movie you wanted was already on your TV. The lights dimmed and soft music played, just as you had programmed it to happen. The electronic wizards at Denterprises Laboratories were incredibly clever, maybe even too clever.

The old man shook his head and turned to leave. Little did he know that he was only minutes away from death. The elevator took him down to second level parking, where he walked between the cars. As he stepped in front of the parked cars, one suddenly started up and squashed him into the wall. The car reversed and let him fall. Then at precisely the right moment it surged forward, crushing his skull against the cement wall. As quietly as it started, the car shut off its electric motors and went back to sleep. There was no driver in the car, and there were no other people in sight.

***

The sun was shining brightly, and only a few wisps of white cloud could be seen anywhere in the sky. It was the perfect summer day. The kids were playing out in the backyard and Pastor Bob of the Community Church was reading in his study. Pausing to ponder a point, he glanced out of the window. His small daughter Jessica was screaming and running towards the church. His son Cliff was running behind her, holding some sort of insect in his hands. Pastor Bob shook his head and put down his book. Smiling thoughtfully, he started for the door. He was going to have to put a stop to this.

"Daddy, Daddy, Cliff's got a dead bug."

"Cliff," he gently scolded his son, "stop scaring your sister like that!"

"But Daddy," Jennifer cries, "He killed the bug! He killed it and then he was going to put it down my back!"

"Cliff, that's no way to treat your sister!"

"Aww, she's just a big scaredy cat! She runs from everything."

"But he killed it! It was murder!"

Cliff suddenly looked unsure, maybe even a bit guilty.

"Listen, kids..." Pastor Bob fought the urge to suddenly preach a sermon, but opted instead for a small object lesson. "Murder is when you kill another human being. Killing animals is different."

"What do you mean?" Jessica asked shyly.

"Man was made in the image of God. Man has as a spirit in him. That is what makes us different from animals."

"My teacher, Mr. Douglas, says we are all animals, but humans are just smarter," Cliff offered.

"I know this is what they are teaching in school these days, but here in church we have God's Word. And it teaches us that man is special. We are different than animals. We not only have greater intelligence: we have a spirit inside of us. If you kill another human being, you are committing murder. If you go hunting or fishing, or if you step on a bug or kill a mosquito, you are not committing murder. Maybe I will have to have a chat with your teacher sometime."

"So can we kill everything?" Cliff asked, suddenly imagining himself destroying everything in his path!

"No, we cannot. God gave us this world and made us managers of it. He gave us dominion over the world. We are responsible for it, and we will have to answer for it someday. So no, you cannot just go around killing everything. But killing a bug is not murder." Pastor Bob looked at his kids. "OK?"

The kids nodded, and Jessica went back outside. Pastor Bob returned to his theological book, while his son started to browse the internet on the church computer. He was looking up insects, his favorite subject. "Wow," he whistled, "this is cool. Look at this creature."

***

Far away in Cyber land, unnoticed by the world, Douglas' website was starting to slow down. For the last two years, all over the world, servers had checked in and downloaded bits of code. Even after the first year, Douglas' online spiders continued to search for new servers and nodes. Their work never ceased, as the new Denterprise nodes proved very easy to penetrate. The network of linked nodes was expanding so quickly that sometimes the bandwidth on Douglas' website reached overload, but since it supposedly had unlimited bandwidth, the servers always managed the load.

CHAPTER 7

Every morning at 8:30, Harvey Bernard parked his Chevy in the parking lot of the Pentagon. Every morning at 8:35, Harvey passed through the security check at the West Wing door. And every morning, the security guards glanced at his badge and his face and waved him through. He was just another nameless face with a security badge—another of the regulars that prowled the hallways and inhabited an office somewhere in the bowels of the building.

Had they bothered to check, Harvey's badge would have told them what Harvey's job was. But they never checked. Everyone had strange titles, and besides, Harvey's was a known face. It was the unknown faces that they were to watch for.

So, Harvey Bernard of the little International Electronics Surveillance Department passed by the guards and went down the hall to the elevators. He stepped into the elevator and rode it to the bottom, totally unaware of the others riding with him.

Harvey was deep in thought. But then again, Harvey was always deep in thought, so everyone ignored him as he stumbled along the hall and into the small office.

"Any new developments?" he muttered under his breath.

"Same stuff, lots of activity, no origin." the woman sitting in the dark room stared at the flickering computer screens. "I still can't figure it out." She paused. "Have you got any ideas?"

"Yeah, just one, but it is so crazy that it can't be right."

The woman watched him closely. "You actually have an idea?"

"Well, naw, it's just too crazy."

"Well, one idea is one more than I have. I can't explain this. I've been watching internet activity for over a year now. I've seen lots of virus attacks and lots of DOS attacks, but none of them look like this."

"Let's see the stats again," Harvey said quietly. Sitting at his desk, he lowered his glasses on his nose and started at the stats. "Yeah, it's more of the same stuff. I can't understand it."

"I thought you said you had an idea."

"Yeah, I did. But it is just too weird."

"Well, what is it?"

"Well, I put the stats into my spreadsheet and then graphed them. It's strange, but it reminds me of a stats read-out I saw once on the human brain. It was an experiment that tested human brain patterns during dreams. The scientists were trying to map brain activity so they could work on neural-networks."

The woman stared at him, her mouth open. Bernard smiled sheepishly and turned back to the stats. The woman kept staring. After a couple of moments, Bernard looked up and scowled. "Look, I told you it was crazy, but that's what it looks like to me."

"You're right, it is a crazy idea." She looked up from Bernard's chart. "It does look like brain waves."

"How do you know?"

"I don't, but we can always find out."

Bernard looked at her incredulously. "You're not suggesting we take this up to them, are you?"

"No, no, I wasn't going to suggest we take it up to them," the woman smiled.

"Good, for a minute there I was wondering."

"What I'm suggesting—" a smile toyed on her lips, "I was suggesting that *you* take it up to them, not *we*."

"What?" Bernard spun around. "Are you crazy? They will eat us alive. They already think we are a waste of money."

"No," the woman said firmly, "they will eat you alive. After all, it was your idea."

"Look," Bernard protested, "it was all a crazy idea. We can't afford to make waves right now."

"But if you are right, we can't afford not to."

"Look," Bernard continued to protest, "isn't there some other way to handle this?"

"Have you got an idea?"

"Yeah, let's find some brain doctor and see if he agrees."

"Oh, really? And just where do we find a brain doctor?"

"Well..." Bernard turned away.

"You know one, don't you? Bernard. You may not have many friends, but you've got one who is a brain doctor. I can tell."

"Look Major," Bernard spun around. "I know you are in command here, but I don't think it is a good idea bringing a civilian into this. No one is to know about our operation."

"No one has to know. Why don't we just mix the data into a bunch of charts, and let him pick out the normal person, and guess at what is wrong with the abnormal ones?"

"And where do I get charts of normal and abnormal brain patterns?"

"I'll leave that up to you. Bernard. You figure it out and tell me what he says."

Bernard groaned to himself and turned to the computers. The woman was already gathering her things. Just before she stepped out into the hallway, she paused. "Look," she said quietly, "If he thinks they are brain patterns, then I'll go with you. I can't think of any other explanation." She paused. "We're riding a fine line, but someone else is going to have spotted this too, and if they break it and we say nothing, then our jobs are on the line. We may not be big, but we at least have to match what others are noticing."

***

The detective sat at his computer screen. The law firm of Richardson, Moore, and Leubke had hired him to find Dr. Thomas Douglas, a previous employee at a research facility. Douglas had been fired because he was using the facility's computers to conduct private experiments.

Apparently, the experiments had gone wrong, and had damaged data on the computer system, and the lawyers wanted to sue Douglas. But Douglas had disappeared. Two years had gone by and no one could find any trace of him. His cell phone had not been used since he made a call to cancel his credit cards. His email accounts were dormant. It was as if Dr. Douglas had vanished into thin air. At least he was no longer listed anywhere. He didn't seem to be connected to anything that was connected to the internet—not even a phone number.

As the detective sat looking at the screen, he wondered what he would have done if he was Douglas and was trying to evade a sordid past. Perhaps he had fled the country. But there was no passport registered to his name. Perhaps he would have changed his name. But that was difficult to do, at least legally. There were records for that. But perhaps he did it illegally. Then he wouldn't have any ID, and no history. He couldn't get a job. Nothing.

Suddenly the detective smiled. Perhaps it was so simple it was staring him in the face. Perhaps he kept his last name and just started using his middle name. His driver's license had not expired, so he would at least have that for ID. He hadn't used his social security number to obtain any traceable employment, so that option was out. Now, all he had to do was discover Dr. Douglas' middle name.

***

Harvey Bernard left the west wing of the Pentagon at 5:30, his usual time. He climbed into his old vehicle and drove away, just like always. Only today's trip home wasn't the same. Bernard drove across town and out onto the freeway. It was only a short jaunt to New Jersey, but he would have to hurry if he was to catch his friend at home.

Tucked in a file beside him in the car were a number of charts he had downloaded during the afternoon. They were all charts of brain waves. All except one. It looked like the others, but rather than data collected from various receptors attached to a human brain, he had data collected from various receptors attached to the internet.

At 7:30 Bernard pulled into a well-to-do suburb in Newark and carefully followed the directions he had scribbled on an envelope until he found the house. It was an impressive three storied home set well back from the street. Bernard pulled into the wide driveway and slowly made his way past the expansive lawns. He noted the three cars in the drive, one being a BMW and one a Mercedes. Obviously, brain doctors made good money. He felt rather shabby in his older Chevy and his worn uniform. But he was who he was: a computer geek who, after getting his PhD, discovered he couldn't make it in real life and had joined the army.

"Coming," a female voice shouts from inside as he rang the bell. A moment later, the door swept open, and a gorgeous woman stood before him. Harvey Bernard gulped. "Hi, is Gerhard home?"

"Honey," the woman called over her shoulder in a singsong voice. "Your company is here." Turning back to Harvey, she smiled. "Come in." Harvey felt his knees go weak. He didn't know if he could answer, so he stumbled into the living room. Gerald, the brain doctor, was coming down the curved stairs.

"Harvey, my boy. It's been a long time." He held out his hand and Harvey grasped it, but not before he noticed the diamond studded cuff links.

"Come on in, Harvey, and let's have a drink." Gerhard led him into what looked like a library. The woman excused herself and the two of them were alone. "My Harvey, it has been a long time. What can I get you?"

While Gerhard was mixing the drinks, Harvey got right to the point. "Look, I was wondering if you could help me. I need your opinion on something."

"What? Business already? I was going to ask you what happened to you since we last saw each other. Must have been 20 years ago at the High School prom. You were there, weren't you?"

Harvey nodded, the painful memories flashing back into his mind.

"That was some night, wasn't it?" Gerhard smiled. "That girl you brought—she was something else."

Harvey fought back the anger that was welling up inside. He wanted to hit Gerhard between the eyes. His military training had taught him how to do it. He could smear Gerhard against the wall and pay him back for all the pain that he had caused him. But that wouldn't help. Imagine trying to explain to your superiors that you had attacked a well-known brain surgeon because of a girl you brought to a prom years before.

"Look Gerhard. I've got some brain scans here. I simply want an opinion on them."

"Ok, what are you looking for?"

"I don't know. Something out of the ordinary."

"OK, let's see them." Harvey spread them out on the table.

"Well, these are EEGs. It really takes a radiologist to read them correctly, but I can give you my opinion. However, to get an accurate analysis, you should have a radiologist look at them."

Harvey felt stupid. He should have known that. Surgeons use knives. Radiologist read charts.

Gerhard picked up the first chart. "Classic case of epilepsy. See the sudden jump right across the chart. Originates in the left hemisphere and looks a like grand mal seizure." Harvey smiled to himself. It was almost word for word what had been written on the chart when he downloaded it.

Gerhard went on to the second chart. "This one is also a pretty classic case. But these are petit mal seizures. See these small jumps in the waves at various intervals. I would say that the person is having very small seizures on an almost constant basis. Say, these aren't the same patient. are they?"

"No," Harvey said quickly. "Now, what about this one?"

Gerhard studied it for a long time. Finally, he looked up. "There is nothing wrong with this patient, from what I can see. Normal brain activity. Was the patient asleep or awake?"

"Ah," Harvey was caught off guard. "Awake"

"Really, that's odd."

"Why?"

"Well, usually the lab technician includes things like loud claps, and other distractions to cause some jump in the recording."

"But this one doesn't, right?"

"Yeah, it's just normal brain activity, but whoever it was, was very busy thinking or learning." Gerhard looked up. "What kind of questions are these? These are all very standard charts: one of a grand mal seizure, one of petit mal seizure, and one of standard brain activities. Any first-year student could have told you this."

"But how do you know that this is what the charts are?" Harvey asked.

"Well, they are EEG charts of human beings." He paused. "They were taken on humans, weren't they?" Harvey paused; a new thought suddenly flashing through his mind. The brain doctor looked up, "what is this Harvey? Are you saying these aren't human?"

"Two are, sir," Harvey had reverted back to military jargon. "The two seizure charts are human. The third one is unknown."

"What do you mean 'unknown'?"

"Well, the data we gathered made us think that we were recording brain waves, but we weren't sure."

"Where do you work again, Bernard?"

"I didn't say. It's classified. Sorry."

Gerhard scowled. "Look, if you are asking me if it's human, I can't answer that. Brain patterns from other animals might be very similar. I'm not an expert in that field."

"Our question isn't so much 'is it an animal or human?' Our question is rather 'is it thinking?'"

"It? What have you got, some sort of space alien?"

"No, it is not an alien. And yes, it is classified. I guess my question is simply, does this last chart look to you like the scan of an active brain?"

"Harvey, my boy," Gerhard said slowly. "I've seen thousands of EEGs, and this one looks like the scan of someone or something who has a very active brain." He paused and looked Harvey in the eyes. "A very active brain," he repeated.

***

Parent-teacher interviews are never easy, especially when they are not regularly scheduled interviews. Tonight's interview was with the father of Cliff, one of many children in Tom Douglas' class. Tom, now known as Burt Douglas, a lowly seventh grade teacher, looked nervously at his schedule.

Two years before, he had stopped driving and had started looking for a place to settle down. After several failed attempts at finding a teaching job, he eventually cut his resume down to as small as possible. However, with no teaching experience on his resume, and no references to call, his chances of finding a job were slim. At least until he called in at the Waterford school one afternoon.

The principal was in a difficult position. School was about to start for the fall, and one of his grade seven teachers had suddenly pulled out. The teacher was new, and this was to be her first teaching position. She called, just two days before school was to start, to say that she had taken another job in another state. Not knowing what to do, the principal was delighted when Mr. Burt Douglas dropped by that afternoon looking for a job. He was hired on the spot, and two days later he was teaching. The principal was not only relieved; he was delighted that the children loved their new teacher. Douglas was also pleased that much of the paperwork was forgotten. It was only half heartedly worked on by an overworked secretary who simply took Mr. Douglas' answers for the truth. Little did she realize that Burt was not his real name, but the name of his younger brother. She did run into one irregularity. When she asked him for his social security number, he had seemed alarmed. She quickly jumped to a logical conclusion. Mr. Douglas was obviously hiding in their small town. No one who was this good looking and such a good teacher just dropped into town. Obviously, he was hiding from a jilted partner. He probably had a partner somewhere searching for him. Having just gone through a difficult divorce where her previous partner had hounded her, she understood perfectly.

Mr. Douglas had not offered any references, and none had been asked for. The local police, always overworked, had only done a very brief police check. When nothing turned up, they quickly filled out the form letter and sent it on to the school. No one by that name was a lurking pedophile. The school principal was delighted. When the secretary hinted that Douglas would probably want to be paid in cash, he was at first worried, but he soon understood her concern, and when he offered the option to Douglas, he seemed relieved.

Burt was soon entrenched in the school system and was loved by all. No one suspected that Burt was the name of his younger brother, who had died in the accident with his parents. Several years before his parents had applied for a social security number for both their sons at the same time so when the numbers came they were only two digits apart. Tom memorized his own number and never forgot his brothers. In his mind it was some sort of memorial, a way to remember his little brother. And now the older brother simply became the younger brother, and no one suspected anything.

The parent-teacher interview went better than Douglas had hoped. Cliff's father was a minister at one of the churches in town, and he was concerned that the values taught in the church should be known and at least respected by the teachers in school. Burt Douglas asked some probing questions, but soon realized that it wasn't his job to challenge or change anyone's values. Pastor Bob, as everyone called him, believed, among other things, that the world was created—and in only six days. Douglas smiled, but kept his opinions to himself, and promised that as he taught science, he would respect the values and opinions of all, but at the same time he would stick to the materials in the curriculum.

As they shook hands at the end of the discussion, both Douglas and Pastor Bob realized that they had underestimated the other. Both were intelligent men, but they were also gentlemen. Soon after they started talking in earnest they recognized these characteristics in the other person. Pastor Bob was genuinely interested in his son's new teacher. He seemed a decent guy, who was a bit lonely. Trained to reach out to others, he naturally reached out to Douglas, leaving the door open for Douglas to enter into a closer relationship. Douglas, however, was wary. He keenly felt the offer of friendship and was delighted with the intellectual exchange. However, Douglas had deep secrets, and he felt it was best to avoid people.

But a few days later, Burt Douglas appeared on the steps of the Waterford Community Church just before Sunday service. He was greeted by an usher at the door and made his way to a spot near the back of the church. He was surprised that the back rows seemed to be the most popular, but the church filled up quickly, and by the end of the first song most of the places were taken. He spotted Pastor Bob near the front, sitting in the audience beside a woman he assumed was his wife. Cliff and Jessica were there as well.

Everyone seemed to be enjoying the music, which surprised Douglas. It was quite modern and upbeat—much different from what he remembered church being...but then again, he had never been in church much. He had never gone after his parents' funeral.

When Pastor Bob got up to preach, Burt waited, amused to see how he would react when he spotted him in the back row. But Pastor Bob didn't seem to react, other than to smile warmly at him at several spots during the talk.

After the service was over, Burt made his way to the back of the church. Pastor Bob and his wife were standing at the door, shaking hands with everyone as they left the church.

"Glad you see you." Pastor Bob seemed genuinely interested. "We are glad that you made it. This is my wife, Gladys."

Burt smiled and shook hands, and suddenly Pastor Bob and his wife were insisted that he come to their home for dinner. Right now. In a couple of minutes. But they first had to finish saying goodbye to everyone.

Burt didn't know what to do, so he accepted the invitation and waited around for a while until Cliff spotted him. Cliff then took him around the church, showing him photos of previous pastors and photos of missionaries that seemed to be all over the world. Once everyone was gone, they went outside.

"You can follow us in your car if you like. I can give you our street address," Pastor Bob smiled.

Burt shook his head. "I am walking today," he smiled back.

"In that case, we can give you a ride. Hop in."

Burt was surprised to see that the table was already set, with the right number of settings and the food was ready in the oven. Gladys opened the refrigerator and took out salads that she had prepared beforehand. In a few moments, they were seated at the table.

"In our house, it is our custom to give thanks for the food." Pastor Bob was still smiling. "And we usually hold hands while we do it." Everyone reached out their hands, and Burt found himself holding Cliff's hand on the right and little Jessica's in the other. It felt strange to touch another human being, especially a child's small hand.

That afternoon, Bob and Bart had a lively discussion. Gladys excused herself and went for a nap. The kids played outside, and so the two men sat in the shade and compared notes. Pastor Bob tried not to let on, but he was fascinated with his son's science teacher. For most of his life, Bob had studied science, not because he loved science, but because people so often used science to attack his faith. Over the years, he had read dozens of books in every major field. As they sat in the shade and watched the kids, Pastor Bob let the conversation bounce around between biology and botany. Burt Douglas obviously had a great deal of education, much more than a typical schoolteacher might have. He wondered just what sort of person Burt Douglas was. He seemed much more than he appeared to be.

***

The driver of the small car parked across the street from the gas station and seemed busy with his phone. As soon as he was assured no one was watching, he picked up a small pair of binoculars and studied the gas station's layout. It seemed to be a smaller neighborhood place, somewhat run down and a bit out of the way, on the way to nowhere important. He checked his handwritten notes again and then checked that he had his Private Investigator's ID ready in case he was asked. Slowly he extracted himself from the car and strolled across the street. A bell clanged when he entered the gas station. Looking around, he made his way into the aisles of groceries towards the coolers filled with soft drinks. After a brief look around, he was assured that he was alone, except for the man at the till. He quickly chose a plastic bottle and made his way to the till. After exchanging pleasantries, he paid for his drink, and then opened it, demonstrating that he was not in a rush. They started chatting. After a moment, he pulled out a photograph.

"I hope you don't mind, but I was wondering if you remember serving this customer long ago, actually it was probably over two years."

The man looked doubtful. "Doubt if I would recognize anyone from that long ago. A lot of people pass through here." He waved at the empty store as if it helped to illustrate how busy he was. The detective passed him the photograph and the station attendant stared at it.

"Normally I wouldn't remember, but I do remember this guy. He was here in the middle of the night."

"12:30 to be exact" the detective thought to himself, as he remembered the information he had managed to get from the credit card supplier. It had been Douglas' last transaction. "How come you remember him?"

"Strangest thing! He bought gas and paid for it, and while he was in here, some guy opened his car, and stole his computer. Darndest things happen."

The detective was fully alert now. "His computer was stolen?"

"Yeah, he ran off and chased the guy, but couldn't catch him. Then he returned, shrugged it off, and just drove away. I guess old computers aren't worth too much."

"Did he happen to say which way he was going?"

"Nope, never said anything like that. But he didn't seem like he was in any rush. He did look at the big wall map over there. I figured he was heading out west from here, maybe to do some fishing. I seem to recall a fishing rod in his back window."

"Remember anything else?"

"Yeah, he spent some time at the cash machine. Took money out several times."

"Anything else?"

"Nope, it all happened so fast." The attendant studied him closely. "I suppose you're here because of the stolen computer?"

"Something like that. Thanks for your help."

The attendant waved half-heartedly as the detective left, glad to have a slow job, rather than being a detective and poking around in other people's business.

CHAPTER 8

Colonel Bushten scowled at the man and woman sitting across the room from his impressive desk. For a short man, he dominated situations and commanded attention. At least, that is what he thought. Unknown to him, the carpenters who had built the stand under his desk and chair had laughed behind his back, saying that the short man had reached the height of his career. Unfortunately, they were quite prophetic, but Colonel Bushten wouldn't have believed it for a moment.

Bushten was known by those who hated him as 'Bush' or 'Pee Tree' after a general's dog mistook his leg for a place to spray. He lived by a tight set of rules: do as you're told, kiss ass, and look out for number one. Above all, never rock the boat.

And so it was that Harvey Bernard and Ms. Major Wingsgate knew they were doomed before they started, but at least they would try.

"So, what have you people discovered now?" Bushten's voice was thick with sarcasm. He looked at a sheet of paper he was holding from their file. "I see you have given us a lot of valuable information, such as: the Russian and Chinese military are downloading porn at a terrific rate since they hooked up to the internet. But you conclude that it is still not as much as US Armed Forces. Am I correct?"

"Yes," Harvey said, trying to sound as authoritative and assertive as possible. "But we must look at the figures in context. Compared to the limited internet access that the common Chinese and Russian soldier has, I would say that they are spending a larger resource looking at porn than we are."

"I see." Bushten clearly wasn't impressed. "Any other shocking revelations?" He waited patiently while Bernard and Wingsgate looked embarrassed and shuffled through their papers. He loved this. He had risen to colonel while these idiots stared at computer screens and made up all sorts of wild theories.

"Colonel Bushten," the woman spoke now, "we have reason to believe that there is some very irregular activity taking place on the internet." She glanced up, relieved to see that Pee Tree was patiently listening and not snarled.

"What we are seeing is unlike anything we have ever seen before."

"That's not surprising, seeing that your department has been in existence for only a couple of years." Pee Tree wasn't making it any easier.

"I realize that, but the patterns of activity on the internet are highly irregular and cannot be easily explained."

"What do you mean?" Pee Tree was at least interested.

"The internet seems alive with activity," Bernard interjected, "but the activity is not coming from the outside. It seems to be generated from within."

Pee Tree looked puzzled. "I don't understand."

Major Wingsgate saw an opportunity and took it. "Sir, we are trying to put this in as plain of language as possible, but it seems that some program, or some force is at work within the internet, creating a lot of internal activity that has not been requested from the outside."

"What are you saying?"

"Sir," Bernard smiled his best. "When you hook a number of computers together, you create a computer network. The more computers you hook together, the larger the network." Pee Tree seemed to be able to follow basic math, so he went on. "The largest man-made network in the world is the internet."

"Man made?" Pee Tree looked puzzled. "What do you mean, man made?"

"Well, sir, every living being has within their brains a network. It is not electronic, but it acts very much like one. Scientists call them neural networks."

Pee Tree was listening now.

"Sir," Major Wingsgate stepped in. "The activity on the internet reminds us of activity on a neural network."

"OK," snarls Pee Tree, "cut the hogwash, and lay it on the line. What exactly are you two saying?"

"The internet is alive, sir." Bernard couldn't believe he had said it quite so bluntly.

The silence in the room was broken by giggles. Then the giggles turned into laughter. Pee Tree pointed at them and then laughed harder.

"That's the funniest thing I've heard in years," he roared. "You don't really believe that, do you?"

"Sir, it is a very real possibility."

"You guys really are crazy, aren't you?" Pee Tree cocked his head sideways and looked at them for a moment. "Staring at those computers is affecting your brains."

"Sir," Harvey interjected, "yesterday I contacted a brain surgeon..."

Pee Tree decided to take charge. "Bernard, Wingsgate, this is absurd. Your job is to watch the internet for viruses and electronic attacks on the United States of America, not to spin wild theories about the internet being alive. You are to return to your posts and to continue the jobs you were assigned." Pee Tree paused. "You are dismissed."

The two rose from their seats and gathered their papers.

"A report of this is going into your file. Anymore of these outrageous theories, and you will be subject to a complete review. Maybe even a psychological examination." The words had an ominous ring to them.

After the two left the room, Pee Tree stared into space, trying to figure it all out. He could see through their plan. The 'Alive Internet Theory' as he would call it, was simply a lie, so why did these two spin it out? Perhaps it was to discredit him. If he believed it and went ranting and raving to the generals, his career would be ended. The more he thought about it, the more he was convinced that this was all part of a plot to destroy him.

But, plots are like two-edged swords. They can cut both ways. If he handled this right, he could totally discredit the computer geeks in the International Electronics Surveillance Department. That, he concluded, would be a very enjoyable thing to do.

And so, Colonel Bushten took his pen and started to draft a report.

***

The following Sunday, Burt Douglas made his way to the Community Church. At first, he convinced himself that he was just out for a walk, but as he approached the church, he suddenly turned and made his way up the front steps. The service was just starting, but an usher warmly welcomed him and pointed him towards an empty seat.

This time, the service was more familiar. It followed a similar pattern to the previous week. They sang some songs, all new to Burt, and then listened to announcements. Pastor Bob then went to the front for something the bulletin called the pastoral prayer. After mentioning a few names of people who were sick in the hospital, pastor Bob looked down and started talking to God. All around him, people were either looking down or had their eyes closed. The prayer droned on as Pastor Bob mentioned a long string of names. Burt's mind was drifting as images of his previous house filled with computer paraphernalia drifted by. Just as he began to imagine a scene with the two men in black suits, he heard Pastor Bob mention his name. He almost jumped to his feet, but realized that everyone still had their eyes closed and head bowed, and pastor Bob was praying for him—that he would find his place in their town and feel welcome and know the presence of God in his life. Burt blushed, but no one seemed to notice.

After the prayer, the ushers went to the front to collect the offering. While plates were passed down each row, a young woman stood up to sing. She was quite good looking and as Burt found himself admiring her; he realized how long it had been since he had even had serious thoughts about a woman. He had been so focused on the worm program that it had taken over every part of his life. And now, for two years, he had been focused on fooling everyone that he was just another schoolteacher.

After church, he was startled to feel a small hand grasp his. He looked down into the beaming face of little Jessica. "Mom and Dad said to invite you for dinner. Will you come?"

Burt struggled a bit. He did not want to impose, but young Chris came jumping along the chairs. "Can you come? Please? Can you come?"

Burt caught his composure and smiled. "Sure, I guess I can."

"Yeah!" Chris shouted as has rushed across the church to pull on his mother's arm. She listened for a moment and then glanced towards him, giving him a warm smile. Emotion surged in Douglas' chest. It had been a long time since he had felt welcome. Not because he was a clever scientist or a good teacher, but because he was a human being. It felt good.

Once again, lunch was already prepared. Cold lemonade was served first, and Burt had the chance to meet a somewhat overweight couple who were also coming for dinner. They were Ed and Josie Janzen. Ed was a car salesman, and his personality was very fitting. He was loud, but not too overbearing. His eyes twinkled a lot as he fished some candy out of his pockets and gave it to the children.

"Not before dinner," Gladys scolded gently. Mothers see everything.

"So, what sort of car do you drive?" Ed smiled.

"Actually, I am not driving these days. This town is small enough that I can walk most places."

Ed noticeably brightened. "But you do drive, don't you?"

"Yes, but I let my insurance go...figured I could save some money by not having a car."

"My," Josie interjected, "that must be hard. I can't imagine not having a car. How do you get around?"

"Actually, I can walk to school, the stores, and the church here. I guess that is the extent of my world right now." Burt tried to smile, holding back the fact that he did not dare register a car, as he would suddenly be traceable.

Ed thought he saw a possible sale. "Well, anytime you want to start driving again, give me a call." He handed Burt his card. "I have lots of new and used vehicles, and I can also get you most anything you are looking for." He paused. "Can I get your phone number in case I see a great deal?"

"It's okay," Burt insisted, "I really don't need a car. And besides, I don't have a phone."

Josie looked incredulous. "No phone? And no car? My, that is unusual."

Burt laughed, trying to brush it aside. "Just think of all the money I am saving. I don't have to buy gas, do repairs, buy insurance, make payments, nothing. Not even monthly phone bills. It's a great way to save."

Josie still looked puzzled, but Pastor Bob called that dinner was ready. Burt was pleased that the conversation drifted away from himself and focused on Ed and Josie Janzen and their family.

***

Far away, the detective for Richardson, Moore, and Leubke sat on his front porch, beer bottle at hand, studying the problem. Every attempt he had made to locate Dr. Thomas Douglas had turned into a dead end. It was as if he had completely dropped off the face of the earth or had become homeless. So far, he had searched for credit cards, phone records, car registrations, and even obituaries and missing persons. Nothing. The event at the gas station was the last account of Douglas. No one had even reported him missing. But yet, he was out there. He had a valid driver's license but not much else. A quick check with his connections in immigration confirmed that he had not left the country—at least, not legally.

This sort of search required patience. Eventually, the target always made a mistake. It was just a matter of patiently waiting and continuously checking.

CHAPTER 9

Barbara Cavendish had worked her way up in politics the hard way. There were only a handful of women who had served at her level. Not only was she a woman, she was also beautiful and intelligent—intelligent enough, at least, to have long ago dyed her hair brown. After all, who would respect a blonde? Long ago, Barbara decided that beautiful blondes were suspected of being dumb blondes, something that had haunted her all her life.

It had been a hard decision, but one night in university she had heard one too many blonde jokes. "Why do blondes have electric lawnmowers?" someone teased her at lunch. "So they can find their way back to the house!" he roared.

She tried to smile as people collapsed with laughter, but it was hard. That summer, Barbara the blonde became Ms. Cavendish, the brunette, complete with phony glasses. But with the change came the respect she yearned for. Fortunately, she was starting her Master's Degree in International Law at a new university, and her 'dumb blonde' background was effectively erased.

One of her university professors noticed her intelligence and drive, so under his mentorship she rose through the levels academia, making a name for herself.

Graduating from law school, Barbara threw herself into a variety of political jobs that came her way. She discovered that she had a way with people. Combining her charm with her intelligence and good looks, she quickly climbed the ladder to success, climbing higher than anyone had ever imagined.

And now she stood near the pinnacle of power; a consultant on all things international, her opinions respected by the highest level of government, most of whom she was on first-name terms with. She was the youngest person to serve her nation at this level, and a female to boot.

Somehow, Barbara knew she must appear tough and in control. It was the only way that Margaret Thatcher had managed to stay in power in the UK. Somehow Barbara the Blonde had to be Barbara the Iron Woman. So, no matter how small and trivial the challenge, the Iron Woman was always projected.

And today was the same as every day: another schedule full of meetings, important luncheons with important people, or those wishing to meet important people. The air was cool as Barbara walked along the sidewalk towards the White House with two aides on either side and a security man not far behind. It suddenly dawned on her that one of her aides was busy explaining what would happen at the next meeting. Everyone will be there: the President, the FBI, the CIA, the heads of military, everyone.

"What is this all about again?"

"Someone in the CIA thinks they have uncovered a sinister plot to use the internet to take over the world, or something like that."

"Why wasn't I briefed?"

"Apparently, no one was taking this seriously until the last moment."

"What is that supposed to mean?"

"It seems that the CIA came up with the idea first, and it rose through the ranks. No one believed it, so a meeting was called to finally dismiss the idea. At that meeting, Military Intelligence suggested that they had also observed the same phenomena."

"Phenomena?"

"Don't worry, this is so new that they will start at the beginning to bring everyone up to speed. The FBI claim to know nothing about this. Neither does Homeland Security."

"Now I am really curious."

Moments later, they passed through security and made their way towards the designated meeting room. The aides disappeared and Barbara stepped into the room, feeling much more alone. She looked around at the familiar male faces of the men who were responsible for the running of the government. She knew all of them except for one good looking, middle-age man standing against the back wall. As she looked around, she realized that most of them looked as puzzled as she was.

Few moments later there was a buzz of activity as the President entered the room. People immediately became alert, papers shuffled, and backs straightened. Without any hesitation, the President got right to the point.

"Thank you for gathering so quickly. We have a very strange situation on our hands, and a very delicate one. With Islam waning, and the terrorists dissipating on one hand, and Russia backing down on the other, there are few immediate major threats to our nation." He paused. "The press is hinting that we need another challenge to make our government look better. And we may well have a challenge. The problem is, we are not sure if it is real."

That got everyone's attention.

"If it is real, we will be dealing with something totally new. If it is not real, and the press gets word of this, we will all look like idiots."

He paused and looked sternly around the room. "So, this is to be held in strictest confidence. No one, not even your aides, are to know about it. That's why there were no briefs. So far, nothing has been put on paper. But I want you all to be informed and to help me chart a basic plan of action."

The room was deathly silent. All eyes were on the President.

"The army has informed me that some of their researchers believe the internet is alive."

Everyone in the room sat in total shock. Then there was a snicker, which quickly turned into a roar of laughter.

"Good one," someone from the back chuckles, "that's how you charmed your way into office."

Everyone smiled as they focused their attention back on the President. He did not smile back. It took a few seconds to settle in, as one by one they realized he was dead serious.

Barbara was the quickest to recover. "Really?" She shook her head in wonderment. "What in the world would give them that idea?"

"It is not my idea. It belongs to Dr. Harvey Bernard." He nodded to the man at the back of the room as a cue. All eyes turned to him.

Dr. Bernard swallowed hard and stepped forward. "Good afternoon folks, I hope you all had a good lunch. I trust I won't spoil it with what I have to say."

No one laughed or cracked a smile.

"I work for a little known department in the Army that monitors the internet for unusual international activity. For several months now, we have been noting a strange anomaly. There have been outbursts of internet activity that seem to have no origin and reason."

Everyone looked puzzled.

"Let me try to explain it this way. For there to be activity on the internet, a program, or programs, give commands which then initiates the activity. That is all very normal. But we began noticing increasing activity on the web that has no origin; at least, we have not been able to trace any origin up to now."

"These bursts of activity seem to start and stop on their own. They don't seem to accomplish anything; at least not that we have been able to trace."

A general leaned forward. "Surely there is so much activity on the web that it must be very hard to determine who is doing what."

"That's true," Dr. Bernard nodded. "But these bursts of activity have been growing. We have been observing them for several months now, and they are growing in frequency and duration. Sometimes there is so much activity that the entire worldwide web slows down. And we do not know where it is originating, or what it is accomplishing."

Barbara was holding her head in her hands. She looked up, her face full of skepticism. "That's a far cry from claiming it is alive."

"When we could not track the source of the activity, we began to look for other scenarios. When I showed charts of the activity patterns to a medical doctor, he confirmed that they resembled the patterns of a living mind."

"I don't see how this is possible," Barbara interjected. "The internet is just a bunch of computers hooked together. How could it become a living thing? It just doesn't seem real."

The President cleared his throat, "and that is why this discussion must never leave this room. This scenario is very unlikely, but before you dismiss it, just imagine how important this might be if they are right."

Everyone still looked skeptical, so the President continued, "The internet is so inter-connected that it has become an integral part of our economy. If it is alive, and I myself don't see how it could possibly be, then it would be able to read emails, know passwords, and have access to our bank accounts. It is a scary scenario. But first, we must establish just what is happening. Maybe someone somewhere is just manipulating it."

"Maybe it is just a hoax," Barbara comments.

"This is no hoax," Dr. Bernard counters. "There is no source. No program is activating this activity. With the amount of activity we are seeing, there would have to be a great many commands."

"Who is qualified to understand this and diagnose it properly?" someone asked.

Suddenly, several people were talking to those around them. The President waited for a moment before interrupted them, "does anyone have any ideas?"

"Obviously we need a committee to look into this," someone offered.

"That's right. Get some of the best computer people. We have to work on it."

"Perhaps we should call in the major computer corporations to help us."

"No," the President interrupted. "We do not want this to go beyond this room. Just investigating this has the power to ruin us. If the press catches on…" His voice died away.

"So, we keep the civilians out?" The general was speaking again, but eyeing Barbara. "How about this? Each agency or branch of government represented in this room brings in two experts: CIA, FBI, Homeland, Army, Navy, Air Force and so on. 14 to 20 computer experts, all sworn to secrecy."

"Right," the President interjected, "now we need someone to oversee this committee—someone in this room."

The silence was deafening. No one wanted to be personally involved. The President then looked up. "I think it would be best if the committee was chaired by someone who was not directly connected to any one of those agencies. Someone they might all respect, but not as their personal boss. I know you are all busy, so this would be something extra. Going the extra mile for Uncle Sam." The President took a deep breath and turned to Barbara. "That would be you."

Barbara's mind was racing, thinking of some excuse she could use to distance herself from this. Nothing came readily to mind. The President nodded. "Okay, it is settled. I want the names of each of your experts on my desk first thing in the morning."

Everyone rose as the President struggled to his feet. Obviously old age or arthritis was affecting him. After he left, the Director of the Joint Forces approached Barbara. "The first one from the Army will be Dr. Bernard. He knows more about this than anyone." He paused. "Good luck with this." And then he was gone. Barbara stumbled out of the room in a daze. What in the world was she mixed up in now?

***

The following Sunday, Douglas found himself again at the Community Church and was once again invited for lunch. "I am going to have to refuse next time," he joked. "I am afraid I am imposing on you far too often."

"No, not at all," Pastor Bob insisted. "We always plan to have some folk over for dinner after church. We always make lots of food and set the table for extras. Sometimes we are disappointed when folks are busy, and we have no one to share our dinner with."

Burt felt relieved. He was really beginning to look forward to these Sunday dinners. While he was surrounded by people at school, there was very little social connection. A class full of children on one side, and a few parents, and overworked school staff on the other. At least they claimed to be overworked. Usually, it was all the demands of their lifestyle that crowded them, leaving them continuously short of time. On the other hand, Douglas had lots of free time. He rarely cooked, dividing his meals between the school cafeteria and several small cafes in town. With nothing pressing on his schedule, he found himself more and more involved in the school's extracurricular activities. It wasn't long until he was supervising the yearbook committee, the debate club, sitting in on the student's union, and even helping start a fledgling chess club. But his overall favorite was the science-club. Students with the brightest, keenest minds were drawn to this club. As it was a small school, this meant there were five smart kids and one wannabe by the name of Ryan. Douglas wondered what Ryan was there for until he noticed Ryan sneaking peeks at a cute high school freshman. Douglas smiled. If he was 15 again, he would probably be sneaking peeks as well. But the object of Ryan's affections was either too smart to notice Ryan, or too preoccupied with the science project at hand to care.

So, as Douglas sat in Pastor Bob's home, he felt appreciated as a human being. Here he wasn't responsible for anything, and he wasn't a paying customer. He was beginning to feel like one of the family, and that frightened him a little. He had not felt part of a family for years. After his parents and his brother Burt died, he had no family life. And there were too many pains back there that kept him from revisiting the past. Now he lived in the present—just for the moment, with no future plans. Just try to endure or enjoy each day as it came. He knew it wouldn't last, but his body and mind seemed to soak up the endless days of simple stress-free routine.

It was during one of these visits to Pastor Bob's home that they got around to the topic of fishing. Pastor Bob was delighted that Mr. Douglas was keen on fishing. It wasn't long before they began planning a fishing trip for the next long weekend.

"We have a small cabin by a lake," he explained excitedly.

"And a canoe as well," chimed in Cliff. "And there are lots of bugs there!" he added excitedly, unaware that he was probably the only one who was excited by the thought.

"It's not much of a cabin," Gladys interjected. "No electricity or running water... just a rusty old hand pump. The water is okay, but we usually bring lots of bottled water for drinking."

It wasn't long before plans were made, and everyone was looking forward to getting out of town for a few laid-back days of fishing over a long weekend.

CHAPTER 10

You could feel the tension in the room. Each of the 14 computer experts felt that their knowledge and experience was vastly superior to everyone else in the room, perhaps even everyone else combined. That would have been an easy claim if they were all like Miss Barbara Cavendish, whose computer knowledge started and ended with a word processor and a spreadsheet. But in this case, the tension originated from the atmosphere of competition that existed in most government agencies, and between most government agencies.

Barbara had expected as much and had spent the previous evening preparing. First, she put her aides hard at work, clearing her schedule and apologizing to those who were affected by the cancelations. Second, she spent a long time weighing her options so that she could stay in control of the meeting. Her first step was to convince Harvey Bernard that he should use most of the time to show them what he had discovered. He was not to suggest his theory, just let the experts wrestle with the data that his office had collected. Perhaps they would come up with a different explanation.

The meeting went much as she had planned. She opened the discussion and remained firmly in control as the moderator. Harvey Bernard made his presentation, taking his time to carefully explain the data he had collected. Barbara tried not to let on that she understood little of the technical jargon being exchanged in the room. Her job was to chair the committee and keep them on track. They were the experts. She was the civil servant. She smiled grimly to herself. This committee could make or break her. While in some ways she was a mere civil servant chairing a committee on a topic, she knew almost nothing about; but, it did give her standing with many of the leading political powers of the nation. So, while she didn't have to know much about computers, she did know one thing, a secret theory shared only by one other committee member, Harvey Bernard.

After several hours of presentation, Harvey took his seat and the committee members started throwing out ideas. Some new program was at work—or was it a virus, or some form of malware?

When lunch time arrived, Barbara split them into two groups, one member from each agency. Each group ate in a different room so they could resume their discussions. Together, they selected food from a buffet table, and then they ate in rooms with no attendants in sight. Barbara reminded them that this must be done in strictest secrecy. Each of them had signed a disclaimer and various security documents. No one was to say anything beyond the rooms they were in. While it seemed a bit odd to some of them, they were all part of government agencies where security protocols were the norm.

After their working lunch, they gathered back into one group to discuss their opinions. There was no unity. In fact, there were no plausible suggestions that others did not see a way to negate. By four in the afternoon, they were stumped.

Barbara addressed them all, "we are going to dismiss now and resume this roundtable discussion tomorrow morning. I want each of you to think through this some more. There is a plausible solution." She paused. "At least one solution has been suggested, outside of this room, that may be plausible. Tomorrow we will discuss your opinions, and unless someone comes up with another possible scenario, we will introduce the so-called solution that has been proposed to the government." As she stepped away from the microphone, the room erupted into heated discussion. It took a few moments for Barbara to regain their attention. "I almost forgot. When you step into the hallway, aides will provide you with the vouchers you need to stay at the hotel across the street. Breakfast will be served at the hotel, and we will resume here at nine am sharp. And please remember that you must not discuss this within the hearing of others."

Surprisingly, everyone was present the next morning well before 9:00 am. After bringing the meeting to order, Barbara spent the rest of the morning chairing more heated discussions, as each member of the committee tried to outdo the others by suggesting various possible sequences. Most times, Harry Bernard managed to answer their questions or provide information that demonstrated their ideas could not possibly be the answer. He had already wrestled with most of their suggestions... and he quickly grasped and grappled with the new ideas. Barbara found herself admiring his wealth of knowledge and his ability to work under pressure. Once or twice she caught herself starting to wonder how taut and hard his body might be under his crisp clothing. After all, he was a good-looking man. But what she found attractive was his confidence and intelligence. It gave her pause to wonder about his theory. Could it really be possible that the internet was alive? "Well," she grimly smiled, "the afternoon session was going to be interesting."

After the noon buffet was cleared away, Barbara Cavendish nodded to Harvey. He smiled at her, and she realized that he was totally enjoying this. Inwardly, she braced herself as he started out explaining that the next proposal was his own. The whole approach seemed foolish. She had provided him leeway to make it appear as if it was someone else's theory. Harvey would have none of it and squarely shouldered the responsibility. Inwardly, Barbara found herself admiring him for his inner strength.

For the next hour, the computer experts from every agency listened as he began to explain his growing suspicion that the internet activity they were observing was actually internally generated—not as a result of outward commands. After some time, it began to dawn on them what was being proposed.

It was a brusque man from the FBI that voiced it: "are you actually proposing that the internet is alive? That it is thinking for itself?"

The room was silent until they heard Harvey's strong affirmation and saw his nod. Then, as if on cue, they burst into laughter. However, it was short-lived as deep breaths were taken. Most of them stared into space, trying to comprehend what was being suggested.

"How could it be possible? Real living artificial intelligence requires a living neural-network!"

"Yes," someone else chimed in, "the internet uses binary nodes. They are not neural. That is why AI always runs on a different computer."

"The only way it could work is if someone first discovered how to turn all of our digital websites into neural nodes. And then they would have to turn the Internet into a neural network. And that hasn't been done."

"Even if they did, they would have to deliberately upload their neural operating system onto every server."

"I don't think it is possible."

"All the great neural-network inventors publish their findings in academic journals. We would have heard if there had been any breakthroughs."

"Maybe it wasn't one of our breakthroughs." That was Harvey Bernard taking control. "There are a number of nations out there who may have developed this: China, India, and Russia, to name a few."

"The concept is incredible; the repercussions are mind-boggling."

"That's why I would like to suggest that we first concentrate on making a list of what this might mean to the USA—if another nation has made this breakthrough." Harvey nodded to Ms. Cavendish.

Barbara recognized the handover and quickly organized them back into two groups to start making their lists. This evening they would have another buffet meal, and then work into the evening. Hopefully, by nine pm, they would have a list to present to the President. When she mentioned his name, several eyes widened. Now they understood the need for security and the importance of the task at hand. Their personal recommendations were going to be read by the President himself, perhaps even later tonight. With that, they quickly got down to work.

***

The black limousines were back. Joey noticed them from his lab window after lunch. Ever since the Douglas affair, Joey had wondered how long his secret would remain hidden. The Old Man seemed to rant and rave a lot more these days, and Joey could well imagine the reason.

But Joey was only partially correct. High above him in the director's office, the lawyers had just laid out their plan, asking for more waiting time. Douglas had truly disappeared, but no one can remain hidden forever. One of these days, he would make a slip, and his name would pop up somewhere.

"In the meantime," Leubke smiled, "you have made his life miserable. Hopefully, that counts for something."

"Not until he pays back what he owes," the Old Man's voice wavered. "He's liable, and I want every last dime he can pay." He stared at the faces around the room.

"Which may not be much," Leubke counters.

The Old Man wasn't finished. "Having considered all the trouble Douglas put us through, we replaced all of our old computers with the latest Denterprises models. Maybe he should pay for that."

"We can only hope. But we must find him first."

"Okay, we can wait." The Old Man smiled. "We can wait until hell freezes over if have to, but once he surfaces, we must act fast." He looked accusingly at the lawyers seated in his office. "You must not lose him again. Otherwise, you may be liable."

Leubke smiled assuredly, but inside he was furious. "We will get him, sir," he said with a smile. He despised the Old Man. Obviously, he knew nothing about liability. But he was paying the bills, and that's what counted. A few years of paying a retainer fee might be worth all the emotional pain it was causing just now.

***

The Internet Alive Committee Members (IAC), at least that's what they were calling themselves now, discussed their ideas in small groups over the supper hour. When they convened as a larger group, they began putting together a long list; but there was a lot of disagreement and heated discussion, especially in the area of security. Some felt that secure emails would remain secure. Others felt that they would not. The night dragged on as they hashed over the list.

Barbara missed most of the meeting as she had endless phone calls from her aides. There were lots of questions and few answers. Would she need to clear the next day's schedule? How long was all this secret stuff going to take?

Around 8:30, Barbara returned to the meeting room and was surprised to see the walls lined with white posters filled with lists. There were hundreds of things listed. Some were listed under "Certain" some under "Probable" and some under "Possible." It was quite overwhelming. Dismally, she could imagine that this quick ad hoc committee was not going to end soon.

CHAPTER 11

Early in the morning, Barbara arrived at the hotel lobby with her briefcase stuffed with papers. On a secure thumb-drive, she had a PowerPoint. And for the first time in a long time, she realized she was nervous. Even after hours of pouring over the conclusions of the IAC committee, she didn't feel confident. How in the world would she answer questions? Her head ached from lack of sleep, and two morning coffees were making little improvement.

Her phone buzzed. The White House was calling. Feeling nervous, like a giddy girl, she answered.

It was an aide. Her meeting was canceled until further notice. Something more important had come up. Sit tight and wait. They would call. In the meantime, send the committee members back to their workplaces.

After a quick wave of relief, concern started to grow. First, she would have an aide call each of the hotel rooms and dismiss the members. They would wonder, but they were sworn to secrecy. It seemed their job was done. And now she had the morning free. Wearily she trudged towards the elevator, relishing a few more hours of sleep.

***

The fishing weekend was a great success. Not only were fish caught and eaten, but a lot of relaxing time was enjoyed by everyone. Much to Jessica's disgust, Cliff had added six new bugs to his collection, and had a variety of other specimens that were in better shape than those pinned up in his room. Jessica had played around the cabin and thoroughly enjoyed going out in the canoe. She sat between the two men, Mr. Douglas at the front, and her dad behind her. She idly passed the hours while the two men quietly talked and fished. Her sharp eyes took in the quiet activity of nature around her. Birds were nesting in the reeds by the shore. Ducks swam in circles, their heads bobbing under the water for food. Once she even spotted something swimming in the water, making a v-shaped wave as it made its way along. But mostly she enjoyed hearing the men talk. Mr. Douglas seemed so surprised that they could live in a cabin without electricity. He was fascinated by the mechanics of the woodstove, and deeply impressed when her mother had baked biscuits on it. With melted butter and homemade jam, they disappeared quickly. Jessica smiled to herself as the canoe rested quietly in the water. She leaned back against her father's knees and closed her eyes, totally at peace with the world.

***

Barbara awoke with a start. Her heart was pounding as she looked at her cell phone. But there were no missed messages! Nothing! Hastily she straightened her clothing, checked her face in the mirror, and headed downstairs for lunch. Dr. Bernard was sitting alone at an empty table, so he waved her across. "Just got here myself, and am waiting for the menu. Have a seat." He motioned to the seat across from him. Barbara smiled, thankful for an opportunity to be alone with him. This was going to be an interesting luncheon.

After the waiter had taken their orders, Bernard turned to her with a puzzled expression. "So, how did your morning meeting go?"

Barbara shrugged. "It was called off. Something else came up. I was asked to dismiss the committee."

Bernard nodded. "Yeah, I got the call. So where does this leave us?"

"Us?"

Bernard blushed. "I mean the government. The USA. Us in general."

Barbara's phone buzzed.

"Excuse me, it's my aide." Barbara listened and nodded and thanked her for the call. "It seems like minds more clever than ourselves have dismissed your theory. They think it is not plausible, and they are afraid of being made a laughingstock."

Bernard nodded thoughtfully. "I can understand that. I have taken a lot of flack lately. No one wants to expose themselves.

As they ate, Barbara did her best to discover more about Dr. Bernard that was not in his file. But he seemed to slide right past her questions and focus the attention on her. She then countered, but he deflected all the personal questions. They were fast getting nowhere, but seemed to be getting more and more intrigued with each other.

Barbara's phone buzzed again. The aide was back online. Barbara was wanted at the White House, ten o'clock this evening. It would be a small meeting, and she was to bring her notes.

Harvey Bernard seemed delighted with the news. "I was planning on seeing the sights and walking in the park this afternoon. Maybe we can do it together."

Barbara smiled. "Maybe we can."

***

School yards have long been places where arguments start. In fact, school yards have long been better teachers than schools. It was here that students learned to cooperate or fight with each other. It was here that social skills were honed, physical skills were developed, and the ability to argue and win was crucial to young developing leaders. While teachers took a well-deserved break (except for those unlucky few who were scheduled to enforce civility, and deal with emergencies on the playground), real education was in high gear. You can always tell how successful education is by its volume. And today was no exception. In one corner of the schoolyard, a group of boys had started a debate. With a fervency that would have been the delight of any social studies teacher, the young men were arguing about their science teacher. Some viewed Mr. Douglas with awe. The others thought he was awful: boring to some, fascinating to others. Back and forth the discussion went.

"He's a geek," one student protested.

"But he is cool," another countered.

"He thinks he knows everything."

"He probably does."

"My dad knows more than him."

"Does your dad know about computers and networks?"

"Yeah, Mr. Douglas was fixing the school's computers and networks the other day. He really knows his stuff."

"But he is a wimp."

"How do you know?"

"'Cause he is a teacher. All teachers are wimps."

"Even the gym teacher?"

"Yeah, especially the gym teacher—always makes us do laps. But he never does them himself."

When the school bell beckoned everyone back to their classes, the debate was temporarily over. But it would resume again. Mr. Douglas had yet to prove himself to several young minds.

***

It was dark when Barbara entered the White House. Security guards swiped her ID card and waved her through. They had seen her come and go over the last couple of months. After carefully studying her face, they often tried to hide the fact that they liked to study her backside as she strutted on her high heels past them. Oh, they remembered her all right. She was much more entertaining than the usual lineup of tired old men passing through the gates.

Barbara was shown into a small room. She waited in an uncomfortable chair by a small table for a few minutes. Then a door opened and the President himself entered, followed by one of his aides. Barbara immediately stood, but he smiled and waved her back to her chair and then sat across from her.

"Thanks for coming at such a late time," he started. "I have several thorny little problems right now, and your issues are one of them."

Barbara was about to protest the ownership of any issues, but she understood what the President was getting at.

He pursed his lips and squeezed them with his forefingers, something he often did when gathering his thoughts. It almost looked like he was praying.

"I have had a lot of pressure to drop the whole issue. Everyone is afraid it will make us look foolish. And so, it is dropped."

Barbara was stunned, but the President had more to said.

"At least officially," he paused. "That's where you come in."

Mr. Jenkins here, he will be your connection to me. He will handle the financing. It will not be much, but there will be enough. I want you to gather a small group of thinkers. Choose carefully. Get the right brains. Keep it small. We must be sure of this." He was lightly pounding the table. "I want to know if it is ours. We cannot let others get ahead on this. Both the Russians and the Chinese are quickly catching up on all our technology, if they haven't equaled us already. We have got to find out."

As he stared at her, Barbara realized how deeply this was affecting the President.

"Jenkins will be your contact. There are government assets at your disposal. Use them carefully. If you need to fly people somewhere, Jenkins can arrange it. If you need intel, Jenkins can arrange it. If you need money—Jenkins. But spend carefully, keep this small, and get me answers. The sooner the better."

Barbara was stunned. Jenkins was watching her closely.

"Goodnight," the President said somberly. "I am sure you have lots to do." He turned to leave, but then stopped. "And you communicate only with me, through Jenkins. No one else knows. Understood?"

"Yes sir, understood."

And then he was gone. Jenkins handed her his business card, but then slowly turned it over. He wrote out a phone number. "Call me here. It doesn't ring, but I will try to answer. If I do not reply, send me a text message. Keep your messages very short. Do not mention the obvious. Never mention the internet project by name. Assume someone is listening and reading. I will try to arrange a more secure way of communicating in a day or two."

Barbara nodded slowly.

"And your aides? Can they be trusted?"

Barbara was puzzled. "You picked them. I didn't. They were supplied to me."

"Then you will lose all of them but one. You figure out who you can trust the most. And who is most helpful to you? Do not tell your aide what the project is about. I will have him or her sworn to secrecy."

With that, he was gone, and Barbara was walking back through the halls. She was too stunned to feel the eyes of the guards as they watched and judged her shape. Barbara was too stunned to look at any of their faces, as if that would have helped. The White House guards all had poker faces; eyes that never saw, ears that never heard. Yet they wrote everything down in their logbooks.

***

Dr. Harvey Bernard was surprised when he received Barbara's phone call. He noted that she had called personally, rather than one of her aides. He was surprised to hear that another committee was being put together—that he had to start again with a new group of people. She wanted to start two days from now. Could he please stay in town, at the same hotel? It had been arranged with the military that he could stay in Washington. How could he refuse?

Late in the afternoon, Barbara climbed the steps to the State Building. Walking down the halls brought a feeling of nostalgia as she passed offices where she had been previously assigned. But she shook off the feelings. Tonight she was on a mission. She was dressed in a tight-fitting dress, a bit too tight for her liking, but perfect for the situation. Her makeup emphasized her eyes and the beauty of her face. Inside, she forcibly conjured up what she thought were the feelings of a cougar after her young prey.

After strutting down several halls, deliberately trying to not notice the stares of every male she passed, she finally spotted her prey: a young male aide who had been infatuated with her in the past.

From a long distance, he spotted the movement of the dress, the deliberate slow strut. He seemed fixed to the spot until he recognized Barbara. He audibly gasped and tried to smile.

"H-hi," he stuttered.

Thankfully they were standing beside a janitorial room. Barbara grabbed his collar with one hand and dragged him into the small dark space and flipped on a light. They were chest to chest in the small space. The young man was visibly shaking.

"I need your help," she said huskily.

"I am ready," he smiled uncertainly. He yearned to kiss her, but something held him back.

"I want it to be a secret."

"Of course," he nodded willingly.

"Come to my hotel room tonight at 11:30. Don't let anyone know that you are there. Use the stairs."

"I am always discrete." He said in a hesitating voice, visions of a passionate evening flowing through his head.

"And bring your laptop," she purred into his ear.

"Sure," he smiled, wondering what they were going to watch together.

"11:30. Here is my hotel name and room number. Don't forget your laptop."

In a moment she was gone, and the young aide blinked and thanked his good fortunes. He had always imaged that the cold tough Barbara was not only strong-willed but passionate woman underneath. Well, tonight he would find out.

At 11:30 sharp, the young man knocked on Barbara's door. He was dressed to kill. A tight shirt was molded to his body. He had carefully shaved, doused himself with his best cologne, and held his laptop case in his left hand. Foolishly he thought he should have brought flowers.

Barbara opened the door. The tight dress was gone. She was dressed in a working suit and behind her an aide was sorting papers on the bed. Disappointingly the entire bed was filled with paperwork. The young man looked devastated. Barbara laughed softly. "Come on. You are tougher than that. Besides, I am old enough to be your aunt."

Now he was confused.

"I need your help. I have a big assignment and a limited budget, and very little time. I really need your help."

Thoughts of blackmail flashed across the young man's vision. He would help in exchange for...

"Look, I need your brain, not your butt," she interjected.

He was so startled that he blinked uncontrollably for a few seconds. It was like she was reading his thoughts. The aide was smirking while she continued laying out papers.

"Listen, if you help me, I owe you one."

The young man thought her eyes were communicating something. Thankfully the aide couldn't see.

He nodded slightly. "OK, what's up? How can I help?"

"I need an expert in artificial intelligence. I have checked all the usual sources, and everyone is busy. I have no idea who is the best, and who is available. I need them to work on a committee, possibly for several months."

"Why me?" Suddenly, the realization hit him. "Is this legitimate? I cannot give you the kind of access I have if it isn't."

"Of course it is legitimate. But it is hush-hush. Orders have come straight from the top."

The young man placed his laptop on the small hotel room desk and searched for a plugin. He had no idea how long he might be there. After a few minutes, he began logging into various government databases.

"So you want an expert in artificial intelligence?"

"...and a hacker."

"A hacker?" He turned and stared.

Barbara opened the small fridge. "What would you like to drink?" she countered offered.

Drink in hand, he went back to work, very aware that Barbara was standing above him, her breasts very close to the side of his face.

"I know that there are lots of young people graduating from university in the Artificial Intelligence area, but I want someone who is more than a student, someone who really understands the field—a front-line thinker."

"Then we check the journals. See who is publishing."

Quickly he made a list of the top brains in the science of artificial brains and then started down the list. He located the universities and research facilities of all of them, but one. Dr. Thomas Douglas remained alone on the list. No address, no current information.

As they worked, the aide compared the files on the bed with the men on the list. Then Barbara stepped into the next room to start making phone calls. Even though it was nearly midnight, she doggedly worked the phones, trying to be as pleasant as possible. One by one, they were crossed off the list.

After a few phone calls, she jabbed her finger at Dr. Douglas' name. "Find him," she growled. "Everyone else is begging off."

The young man began to search government databases again. Then he searched police records. Maybe the man was in jail. Nothing turned up but his previous place of employment. A bit of digging later, and he had the bare outline of a court case that was being developed against him.

Barbara came back into the room. "Ok, the list is getting shorter. Have you found this Thomas guy?"

The young man explained some of the issues.

"Hiding, is he? Well, at least he may have time on his hands. Let's dig further. I want everything on every Douglas you can find."

The young man helplessly shook his head and went back to work. He was so busy he did not notice the sun starting to rise outside. The aide was fast asleep in a chair in the corner of the room.

"Have you found anything?"

"Nothing"

"Then dig up everything you can on this man, his past, his family, everything."

Barbara returns to the phones only to returned an hour later, looking very exhausted. The young man looked at her closely. She was much older than she had appeared last night. Sure, her figure looked good, but she was right. She could be his aunt.

"I am coming up empty-handed. What do you have on Douglas?"

"Well, there were two sons. The younger one was killed in a car accident with the parents. Douglas was just finishing high school, but he was not in the car. Then he went off to college..."

"What was the brother's name?"

"Burt."

"Any social security number?"

The keys clicked furiously for a moment.

"Yep, both of them had social security numbers."

"Is Burt, the dead one, somewhere?"

The keys flew again. "Yes, he is working as a schoolteacher in a town called Waterford."

She smiled warmly at him, looking her old self. He could almost be in love.

"We will call it a night. Thanks for your help. Maybe I can help you sometime with something."

He nodded and looked out the window with amazement. The sun was up, the city was moving.

"I guess you'd better get back to work soon" she smiled warmly at him. His heart almost melted, but he held it in check. Quickly, he gathered his things and headed out the door for the elevator. No one was going to believe that he had spent the night with Barbara Cavendish! In a hotel room! But then again, maybe he had better keep it to himself.

CHAPTER 12

The hot sun was in the process of burning the grass at the Waterford school. Slowly but surely, the grass was losing its green sheen, giving way to the inevitable brown of summer. Water shortages and a growing national awareness of the limited world's water resources had convinced the principal that watering grass was a poor way to handle water shortages. Plus, it made a good illustration to impact the young lives in the school. By the time they were adults, the world's supply of fresh potable water would be in full crisis. Mr. Douglas even designated an entire class module to discuss the issue.

But it was a lesson lost on one of the students. He stared at the grass as his teacher droned on and on. If he had been pondering possible solutions to water shortage issues, his time might have been useful. But he was bored: bored with school, bored with his science teacher, bored with water shortages, and bored with learning in general. He yearned to be useful, productive, and excited. The latest game on his Denterprises game console opened a whole world of excitement, where he was a critical part of events that shaped and influenced every world he entered. Among the various roles he filled, flying ultra-modern spaceships and helicopters with futuristic weapons was his favorite.

And so, while the science class concentrated on how they could identify bad practices that wasted water, Gerry concentrated on how to blow the bad guys out of existence. As he imagined himself skimming over the surface of the earth, blasting away, he became vaguely aware of the deep beat of a helicopter. The louder it grew, the more real Gerry's imagination became. His whole body was shaking with the rhythm of the helicopter when he became aware that the students had left their desks and were pressing their faces against the glass windows.

Gerry stood on a desk to stare over the shoulders of his fellow students. A long black helicopter was whipping up dust and debris on the school lawn. Under its stout wings, cylindrical missiles poked their ugly heads. Gerry was aware that as this helicopter landed, farther back, high in the sky, another helicopter was circling the school.

"Look," one of the children cried as a door opened in the side of the helicopter. Two men emerged, while several helmeted soldiers were visible inside. The two men jogged across the lawn, holding their hands just over their heads as if to ward off the swirling dust. They were making their way to the front door of the school.

"Ok, Ok, everyone, back to your seats." Mr. Douglas moved along the windows, sometimes physically guiding the children away. The sight of the helicopter had totally captured the attention of some students. He gently guided Gerry down from his perch and pointed him to his desk.

"Mr. Douglas, why is a helicopter at our school?"

Douglas himself was mystified, yet as the ever-knowing teacher, he had to come up with an answer. "Obviously, something important is happening. We will hear about it soon enough." He clapped his hands. "Now, back to water issues. Why do you think agriculture gets such a high priority?"

Douglas was aware that he was looking at the sides of most of the students' faces. They were still captivated by the black helicopter outside. Douglas had to raise his voice to be heard above the rumble of the engines.

"Students, please look this way." He waved his hands.

All the students suddenly complied. Shocked at their response, Douglas was aware that someone was loudly knocking at the classroom door. The principal stuck his head in the door and beckoned him into the hallway. Two black suits were waiting for him. Douglas was so shaken that he was only dimly aware that some of the students had left their desks to return to the window.

"Thomas Douglas?" one of the men curtly asked.

"Burt," the principal interjected.

"Thomas?" the man asked again.

Tom nodded, glumly aware that the Old Man at the Research Center had won. But he was puzzled by the helicopters. This was overkill.

"Dr. Douglas..." the man continued.

"Mr. Douglas," the principal interjected.

"Dr. Douglas," the man said again, staring hard at the principal. "I hate to be so rude in this, but you are needed. You have been personally requested by the President."

"President of what?" the principal puzzled out loud.

The black suits glared. "President of the United States of America."

The principal gulped.

Douglas stared. "What is this all about?"

"You will be briefed when you reach Washington," the other black suit instructed. "Give us your car keys and house keys so someone can gather your clothing. You will be away for a few days."

"A few days?" the principal protested. "There are only three weeks until school is out."

The black suits stared at him.

"I...I suppose I can get a sub-teacher." The principal babbled on a bit, "I'll get the librarian to take his classes today."

"You do that," the first black suit instructed. He pointed at Douglas. "And you, you follow me."

A few moments later, Douglas was instructed to keep his head down as they jogged briskly to the helicopter.

Douglas' mind was in a whirl as the chopper lifted off. If he had looked out his window, he might have gotten some idea of how much fresh water was available in the ponds and sloughs that dotted the countryside. But his mind was in a daze.

The students in Douglas' class were suffering the same fate as the librarian was starting to find out. Gerry's eyes were round and his pupils were dilated. Never in his wildest dreams had he imagined that his science teacher was important. Most of the students had overheard the conversation in the hallway, and by nightfall, every home in town would be buzzing with the news.

***

In Detroit, another scenario was developing, but it wasn't to be as dramatic. Two police cars stood outside a dilapidated duplex. Inside, they were explaining to a confused middle-aged man that he was wanted. Not in the criminal sense, but in the legal sense. Pressure was being put on him to accept a government invitation to Washington. It took a while for it to get through his thick skull. For a mind that was usually quick to grasp things in the abstract world, it took some time for him to realize what was happening. He looked around the dirty apartment. There wasn't much he needed. A few clothes. That's all he owned anyways. And his laptop computer and portable hard drives. Those were his world.

For two weeks now he had been languishing in writer's block. His last science fiction novel was about to be printed, and his publisher was pressing him for the next one. But ideas were slow to come. Possibly because he had suddenly realized that the money was going to support his two exes and their children, and the rest barely covered his rent and drinking budget. Food was incidental.

The largest policeman watched him as he checked a couple of bottles on the table to see if any held some liquid. They were all bone dry.

Suddenly he realized that perhaps this was what he needed—a fresh adventure to kick-start creativity. Quickly, he stuffed a gym bag with some clothing and dropped his laptop and hard drives into his computer bag. It only took a few minutes to get everything together.

Unknown to him, one of his fans in Washington was behind all this. Barbara had recognized in him a keen mind that didn't follow the normal pattern. While it was a long shot, she wanted to have someone unusual on the team. A science-fiction writer seemed to fit the bill. But there wasn't a lot of budget for this, so she sent word through channels and put him on a plane from Detroit.

What Barbara hadn't recognized was that all the men she chose were similar. All were single for a reason. They were men pre-occupied with their own little worlds. Men whose thoughts, dreams and inventions were more important to them than possessions or relationships. They were men who were great thinkers, or imaginers, but awkward in social roles. Barbara, who long ago learned to excel in social settings, never stopped to consider how odd and awkward her new team would be.

***

The night cleaning crew arrived around midnight. Usually Private Wilson was young and dashing, but since his recent exploits had landed him in trouble, again and again, he had been assigned late night cleaning duty—something that would assuredly keep him out of trouble.

And so, along with the regular crew, Wilson pulled out the vacuum cleaners and dusting clothes, but the boss handed him a mop and bucket. He was assigned to bathroom cleaning.

But Wilson's night of punishment was soon to become even worse. Much to his consternation, Wilson discovered that the latest Denterprises phone, which could do everything imaginable, was always running low on power. And true to course, about an hour into his work, the battery started to fail. Glumly he faced an entire evening of silence, with only the bathroom fans to keep him company.

In desperation, he went back into the hall and began moving up and down the aisles of a large office complex filled with cubicles. Finally, he found what he wanted: a computer that was still turned on. Its screen was blank, but by the little lights, he knew it was on. Seeing a USB chord in a neighboring cubical he quickly plugged his phone into the computer, and returned to his work, happy to know that in an hour or so he would once again have music in his ears.

What he failed to realize was that the computers in this office were in a closed military network. They had no connection to the internet until the Denterprises phone, with its ultra-modern internet connections, was plugged in. While the phone recharged, small programs buried deep in the Denterprises software began to explore the computer it was connected to, and then the network it was connected to. In a short while, information began to flow back and forth with the newly established Denterprises node. An hour later Wilson retrieved his phone, pleased to know that he had pulled off his little exploit and no one was the wiser.

CHAPTER 13

It had been a long ride for Douglas. After a short helicopter trip, he had been transferred to a military cargo plane. Outside of a few wooden crates strapped to the floor, he had been the lone occupant of a very uncomfortable metal seat. Eventually, he was transferred to an unmarked black sedan and wordlessly whisked down unfamiliar city streets. Douglas closed his eyes and sank back into the comfortable seat. After about an hour, they pulled up in front of a five-star hotel. The driver opened the door for him and motioned him out.

"Hello sir, my instructions are that you should go to the front desk and tell them your name."

There was nothing else to do but follow the instructions. Douglas had no suitcases, not even an overnight bag. Warily, he approached the front desk, expecting that at any moment lawyers would step out and issue his papers. He braced himself for the onslaught.

The lady at the front desk smiled warmly and welcomed him to the hotel. "Do you have a reservation?"

"I...I have no idea" Douglas seemed at a loss.

"Could I have your name, please?"

"Burt—er I mean, Thomas Douglas."

She frowned a bit. "Thomas Douglas. Yes, here you are." She typed for a few moments, and then passed him a plastic card. "You are in suite 1104. I will get someone to help you with your luggage."

"No need" sighed Douglas. "I haven't any luggage, not even a toothbrush."

"Oh, that's right, oh, wait a minute, I also have a voucher for you here. You can get what you need at the small store on level two."

Douglas frowned. "There must be some mistake."

"No, everything is written here. I think someone will drop by your room in a while to give you instructions."

Douglas decided to take the elevator to the 11th floor and see what kind of room the Justice Department provided. He had been expecting a jail cell, with the Old Man's angry lawyers insisting he be served bread and water. Instead, he entered a plush elevator with soft music and rode in comfort to the 11th floor.

Stepping out of the elevator, he stopped and stared. There were six beautiful dark stained wooded doors in front of him. He chose 1104 and inserted the plastic card and stepped into a plush suite. There were two bedrooms, each with a restroom and a large common room with a large screen TV and a bouquet. Prison never looked so good.

Not sure what to do, Douglas went to the window and stared down at the traffic below. Suddenly, he realized he didn't even know for sure what city he was in. Nothing looked familiar.

There was a brisk knock at the door. He opened it to find a cute young woman waiting. "Hi, I am Barbara's aide. Welcome here. The front desk forgot to give you your meal voucher for tonight. It is for the restaurant at the top level of the hotel. "

Douglas looked surprised. Who was Barbara? Where were the lawyers?

"Tomorrow we will start with a briefing in the Opel room on the second floor."

Ahh, finally we get to meet the lawyers, Douglas thought. But something was wrong. "I think I will need a lawyer, right? How does that work?"

The girl looked at him blankly. "A lawyer? No, just come by yourself. Barbara will explain everything. I don't even know what it is all about. It is top secret." She smiled sweetly and turned to go.

"Wait a minute. Is there some kind of mix-up? Do you have the right Thomas Douglas?"

She looked surprised. "You are the Dr. Douglas, an expert on artificial intelligence?"

Douglas nodded.

"Then you are the right, Dr. Douglas. It will all be explained tomorrow."

"Wait a minute, is this Barbara a lawyer?"

The girl turned, "Y-e-s" she said slowly, "she is a lawyer."

"Then who is paying for all of this?"

"Only Barbara knows. I just work here." She shrugged happily and turned. The elevator door opened as soon as she punched the button. "See you at nine tomorrow morning."

Douglas slowly closed the door and stared around the room. Something was not right. He had no idea where he was and what was going on. Suddenly, he yanked open the desk drawer and pulled out the hotel information sheet. He stared at the hotel address... he was in Washington. DC, and he had no idea what he was here for. Then he remembered the two dark suits—The President of the United States wants you. He gulped. He had no idea the Old Man at the Center had such powerful connections!

Images flashed in his mind. He had thought the reference to "the President of the United States wanting him" to be something like Uncle Sam wants you: the Justice Department, the legal system, a jail cell is waiting! But the President? And who was Barbara?

Realizing he was starving, he decided to head up to the top floor for his meal.

***

The phone buzzed loudly. After the second ring, the private detective stirred from his chair and sleepily answered the phone. A moment later, he was dialing the prestigious law firm of Richardson, Moore, and Leubke. A secretary took the call and directed it up to the top floor.

"Are you sure?" the lawyer demands.

"Yes, my inside sources tell me that the government has been searching for our friend, Dr. Douglas. They have no idea, but searches have been carried out by the FBI, CIA, and even Homeland Security. We don't know what they found. All I know is that a search was made by all of these agencies in the last day or so."

"Can't you get any more information?"

"No, my sources can only access certain logs. They do not have authorization to go any deeper."

"So, this is really bad news?"

"Not really. There may be some good news. Along with searching for our friend Thomas, they also searched for Burt, his long-dead brother."

There was silence on the line for a moment. "Have you followed that up?"

"No, not yet, but I am going to start today."

"Let me know if you find something."

"You will be the first to know."

***

Halfway through his meal, Douglas spotted the young cute aide making her way through the restaurant. But she wasn't headed his way. She was moving towards a youngish middle-aged couple sitting against the far wall. Douglas was hopeless at guessing ages. As he watched them speaking together, it was obvious that the seated woman was in charge. The aide was typing on her phone as fast as she could. Then she nodded and moved away.

Douglas kept an eye on the couple while he finished his meal. Resentment grew inside of him, as he realized that he was at a disadvantage here. It seemed that people were deliberately keeping him in the dark. Well, two could play that game.

He called for the waiter and gave him the voucher to pay for his meal, but he remained at his seat for a while, contemplating what he should do.

When the couple rose to leave, he maneuvered himself across the restaurant to be close to them as they left. It was obvious that they had no idea who he was. He physically bumped into them at the door.

"Oh, I am sorry, Barbara," he apologized. "I didn't mean to bump into you."

"No, it's okay." She turned to look at him, noting his good looks. "Do I know you?"

"Not yet, you don't," he smiled, amazed at his own bravery. "But I guess we will get to know one another tomorrow at the briefing in the Opel room."

She looked puzzled for a moment. "Oh, you must be Dr. Douglas." She extended her hand in genuine warmth. "I am sorry; I only just heard that you were here. There is so much happening that it is hard to keep on top of things. Dr. Douglas, this is Harvey Bernard. He is an internet specialist. We were just talking about tomorrow's meeting."

They were not a couple then. Tom shook Bernard's hand.

"We are going up to our rooms," Barbara said. "There is a lot to do before we meet tomorrow." Douglas tagged along with them, not sure what to do.

"Have you met your roommate yet?"

Douglas' eyes went up. "Roommate? No, I had no idea I had a roommate. A security guard, I suppose?"

"No, not security, a fellow researcher."

Douglas was quiet for a moment. "Then I am not going to be arrested?"

"No," she laughed. "Is that what you were thinking? Don't worry, nobody knows you are here. You are perfectly safe."

"In that case," Douglas said, "I think I will go and buy a toothbrush."

She smiled warmly at him. "See you in the morning. Breakfast will be served at 7:30 in the Opel room where the briefing will take place. We will eat most of our meals there from now on." She waved and walked briskly to the elevator, Dr. Bernard doing his best to keep up.

Douglas shook his head and looked around for a clock. He had no idea what time it was in Washington. All he needed now was a good night's rest. But that was not to be.

At two in the morning, there was a loud knock at the suite door. A military man was standing there with a large black suitcase. He handed it to Douglas. "I hope your belongings are in order. Someone packed them up for you."

An hour later, the lights turned on, and Douglas was awake again. This time, there was a stranger at the door. A large, heavyset man with graying hair and bloodshot eyes held a plastic card and looked totally lost. Douglas recognized the look. "There is an empty bedroom in there," he motioned with his hand. "Breakfast is at seven, and the briefing starts at nine."

The man looked dazed.

"Oh, by the way, you are in Washington, DC. It's like three in the morning here."

"Washington!" the man muttered, making his way into the bedroom.

Douglas smiled and climbed back into bed. It felt good to know more than someone else.

CHAPTER 14

Breakfast was a strained affair. There were seven strangers sitting around a table, trying to eat breakfast and get to know each other, without knowing why they or the others were there. There were only two women at the table: Barbara, who wasn't explaining anything yet, and her aide, who seemed preoccupied with her cell phone. Dr. Harvey Bernard didn't say much except to let them know where he was from. He was single, as were Tom and his roommate Michael. The latter didn't offer a last name. No one asked.

There was a youngish man, Andy, who seemed very cocky, and an older man in a suit, a Mr. Jenkins, but he didn't talk much. After a brief stab at the weather, which some of them were clueless about, they started to compare academic qualifications.

Dr. Bernard and the young man, Andy, were network experts. Douglas was in artificial intelligence. Jenkins claimed to be a lowly civil servant. The only one who didn't fit in was Michael, who claimed to be a science fiction writer. Not only did his academic credentials seem doubtful, his whole demeanor was different from everyone else's. He looked and acted like a slob. His shirt was stained, and getting worse as he crammed croissants and jam in his mouth as fast as he could. It was like he hadn't eaten the day before. But then again, perhaps he hadn't.

After breakfast was cleared away and the hotel workers had left, Jenkins rose and locked the door, while Barbara moved to the small podium at one end of the room. The men gathered around to hear her out. First there were introductions. Nothing new there, except their names: Dr. Harvey Bernard, internet expert, Andy, a computer expert, ex-hacker, now a white-hat. Douglas looked at him sideways, remembering a conversation with Laredo in a bar long ago. It seemed like another life. Then there was himself, an artificial intelligence expert, and Michael the sci-fi writer. Last, there was Jenkins, who said he would be in and out during the next few days. Several glances were exchanged, as no one knew what the schedule was, or how long they were going to remain prisoners in the hotel.

Barbara started with a bit of her story and then turned it over to Bernard, who filled them in on his observations of strange activity on the internet. No explanation was given, just charts and figures. Their first assignment was to figure out what it was all about.

Bernard and Barbara stood at the back of the room while the men started to discuss the issue. Bernard was the first to whisper. "I do not understand this. Why start with this group after we had the last committee?"

"The last committee opened a can of worms, with all the agencies arguing and vying for position. The President felt that they couldn't do much because of the politics involved. He will try to have them meet again, but he doesn't hold much hope for cooperation."

"And this group?"

"This group doesn't represent anything. You are from the Pentagon, and Jenkins there is a personal aide of the President. The rest of them are not representatives of any branch of government, and their careers are not on the line. Plus, this group is a lot smaller."

"What do you mean?"

"Outside of you, they are all civilians. Different perspective, I guess. Let's see how long it takes for them to come to a conclusion. You had better join them."

Most of the discussion that followed took place between Andy and Harvey, with a few comments thrown in by Michael Stanich, the sci-fi writer. Douglas watched and listened, very much aware that Barbara and Jenkins were doing the same thing. Barbara's aide had since disappeared, so it was a very small group.

Harvey turned to Douglas. "So, what is your opinion? Mostly it's the computer guys who are talking here."

Douglas waited for a moment. "I agree that it might be a virus. Perhaps some sort of worm virus."

"And that's why my opinion counts here," young Andy interjected. "I've written a worm virus, but this doesn't seem to be typical of anything I have seen."

Douglas waited until he was finished. He too had written a worm virus, but it was better left not said. "Any activity on the internet has to originate from some commands given somewhere. They do not happen independently. Find where the commands are coming from, and you have your source."

Harvey nodded. "I spent several months trying to locate the source. I thought perhaps it was the Russians, or the Chinese, or some other entity on the web, but I could not find the source."

"Did you check the AI sites? Perhaps some AI site is busy writing a new novel, or compiling an encyclopedia."

Harvey smiled. "I have checked all the sources I could find. The activity is not coming from one site, or even from one network. There seem to be flashes of activity right across the whole internet. Suddenly thousands of IP addresses are busy, and then the activity dies down to normal usage."

Andy was impatient. "Then get the whole US intelligence industry investigating. Someone somewhere must be able to find answers."

"But that is not our task," Barbara interjected. "I want to know what your opinions are." She looked around the group.

Douglas looked puzzled. "Have you examined the software on all of these servers?"

"What do you mean?"

"I suspect there may be two layers of software: the main binary operating system and a secondary neural system. It would not have to be a large file or files, but there may be a second layer to the servers, so what you are seeing is the activity of this second layer affecting the top layer."

Andy looked puzzled and intrigued. "You mean a second internet on top of the first one?"

"Yes, just like the underground internet, which uses different privately written languages, but this would be much more difficult to access, as it might be a different operating system, working at a different level."

Harvey looked stunned. "I have never heard of such a thing."

Douglas was very careful in choosing his words, careful that he did not incriminate himself. "In the world of artificial intelligence, the holy grail of research is finding how to build an independent living neural network. The problem with our software and even our hardware is that it is binary based. Modern AI assesses thousands of possibilities and puts likely things together. If someone managed to figure out how to use a binary system to host an underlying neural system..." his voice trailed off. "If that is what this is, then there is a possibility that there is another layer to the internet: the first one with all the regular traffic, and the second layer with thinking ability."

The room was quiet. Harvey and Barbara exchanged glances. Andy looked doubtful. Michael, the sci-fi writer, looked elated. He had just gotten inspiration for his next novel!

Harvey cleared his throat. "So, you are saying that it might be possible that the internet is alive?"

"That is a strong word. We don't know what 'alive' really means, as we have never achieved true artificial intelligence that way."

"Maybe someone has."

"Yes, maybe they have."

"How could we tell?"

"We would have to check all the contents of many servers to discover if there are common bits of code."

Douglas' brain was now fully alive, and his mind raced with ideas. "But you might not be able to see the files. If a neural network is established, the files would be invisible when you checked the binary files."

"I don't understand." Dr. Bernard was deep in thought. "How could someone build a neural network underneath all the binary servers in the world? How could binary and neural occupy the same space? And then, how did they get the materials in place?"

Andy smiled. It was his turn now. "By using a worm virus," he chimed in. "It would visit every server as it went along. If someone knew how to do it, then maybe they could create an invisible neural network."

"Wouldn't we see that?" Harvey argued.

"Only if it did a lot of actual work. But in this case, it would access a website somewhere and copy the materials over to the newly created neural network. It would be done in a few seconds, or minutes, on each server and it would move on. The files it leaves behind would be invisible, because they would be neural, not binary." Andy was quickly becoming a neural network expert. "But it would require a major scientific breakthrough."

Andy looked at Dr. Douglas. All eyes followed him. Douglas squirmed in his seat, wondering how much they knew.

Barbara looked directly at him. "Have there been any major breakthroughs in the past year or two? You should know, as it's your field."

"I have never seen anything published on it," Douglas offered, trying to keep to the bare truth.

"But what about the scuttlebutt? You know, talk around the water cooler, chats at conferences? Surely someone has said something?"

Douglas looked down and shrugged. He wasn't sure if his past had been fully discovered. He wasn't even sure if the situation he faced was his own making.

"This is incredible," the sci-fi writer said dreamily. "Do you know what this could mean?"

"What comes to mind?" Harvey prodded him.

"Well, if this new artificial intelligence could access the binary side of the internet, then it would have access to all the information on the internet today—in one brain. Imagine that!"

The others looked a bit puzzled. "Imagine having all of Wikipedia, and the contents of every news website, every history site, every science site, all the theses published, all the journal articles permanently programmed into your brain." The others looked stunned.

"And all the porn, and all the gambling, and all the misinformation, and the rantings of fools." Andy was sarcastic, but he got his message across.

"It's an interesting thought." Michael shook his head as if trying to clear it away. He was beginning to understand his role on this committee, even if some of the others did not. He was supposed to take them past the edge of reality and imagine what might be. He was the imagination; they were the concrete thinkers.

"So how many neural nodes would it take for intelligence to work?" Andy was looking directly at Douglas.

"We do not know. The human brain has at least a 20 billion nodes, so the more nodes, the better."

"So how many nodes are on the internet?" Barbara asked.

"No one knows. Most large companies do not release that kind of information." Andy was talking while typing furiously on his tablet. "I would say about one hundred million servers. But in addition to that there are hundreds of millions of military servers which are not officially connected and then there are all the new Denterprises units going in. They now account for about 500 million worldwide and are growing. Then in addition to that there are about a billion laptops and tablets, and then there are smart phones—lots of smart phones."

"I think we are just looking at servers," Harvey interjected.

"Let's hope so," Andy replied. "Do the Denterprises Home Units count as computers or servers or what?"

"I would count them as servers, although they serve as both. That would raise the number significantly,"

Andy looked up from his computer. "Did you know that a mouse has only four million neurons in its brain?"

"And a rat has 20 million," Douglas added. Everyone looked at him. "Look, it's my field of specialty. A dog has about 160 million, and a cat has 300 million. Ever wonder which one was smarter?"

"So, if the internet has 600 million nodes, and if all of them were affected, that would make the internet about as smart as a monkey. Although some monkeys have more nodes than that."

"Yeah," Michael the sci-fi writer added sarcastically, "but imagine a monkey that has the entire internet embedded in his brain. He might not be able to think as clearly as us, but he sure knows a lot more than the average human."

"We are talking in hypothetical terms here, of course," Andy interjected.

"Well," Barbara said slowly, "another committee met with top government experts, and they came to much the same conclusion that you all have."

Bernard added, "I also came to that same conclusion through a different route."

Andy snorted. "Then why are you wasting our time?"

"Governments are wrong sometimes."

"You think?"

"You are all civilians, and yet you came up with a two-layer theory to the internet. The government think tanks never imagined that one."

Douglas looked down. It had taken him years to develop the whole thing, and many crashed computers to implement it. But, he smiled to himself, he had hoped for a worm, and now it might be a monkey.

CHAPTER 15

The conversations continued all afternoon and into the night. Andy was excited. If such an intelligence existed, it would have access to all the services connected to the internet. It would know all about airplanes, who was on every seat; it would know who was withdrawing money from the bank; it would know what the army was doing, perhaps all the major armies of the world. It might be able to hear all the phone conversations in the world—listen to all the TV and radio broadcasts. It would have its fingers in every institution in the entire world.

Michael, with his sci-fi writer brain, started to add to the list of possibilities. Besides TV programs, it would be able to literally see. It would have access to all the web cameras in the world, plus millions of photos and videos already hard-wired into its brain. His mind was racing with possibilities. It could also hear. It would be able to listen to all the Zoom calls and all the chats, all the microphones and probably all the smart phones all over the world, all at the same time. Could it talk? Of course, the internet is full of voice simulation programs. If it knew how, it could match WAV files, talking in multiple voices. Perhaps it could mimic every voice that was recorded on the internet! The possibilities were endless!

Barbara tried to keep them on track. "The possibilities are one thing, but how much can we prove? What do we really know?"

That stumped them. They actually knew nothing. They had no tangible proof, outside of random bursts of activity on the net.

On the third morning, Michael came up with a startling question. He wasn't purposely trying to push them outside of their boxes, but it just popped out: "could we contact it? If we got some sort of response, we would have the proof we need."

The room was very silent. Barbara was fighting fatigue and weariness. Being half asleep, she was unaware of the importance of the question, but she was aware that the room suddenly fell silent. She struggled to remember what was last said.

"What language does it speak?"

Another pause. "Perhaps all the languages of the world, since the internet is full of different languages, plus language learning tools, plus dictionaries, and who knows what all."

Douglas was sitting with his eyes squeezed shut, trying to concentrate. Somehow, he knew this was critically important, but he did not want to reveal his possible involvement.

"Yeah," Andy continued. "How would we know that we are talking to it, and not to something else, like a chat box?"

"Wouldn't it know everything being entered? Perhaps we just need to start talking." Michael proposed.

Harvey wasn't sure. Andy was scowling.

"Perhaps," Michael added, "we could entice it to talk to us."

Andy brightened. "That might work. We could set up our own private site, out of the prying eyes of everyone else, and try contacting it."

"But how do we entice it?" Douglas asked.

"Well, we would first have to tell it that we know it exists." The words came out slowly as Michael was thinking hard. "Write up a small article about this. Let it know we are trying to contact it."

"Okay." Barbara suddenly saw her role more clearly. "Who is going to work on the article?"

"We have a writer here." Andy was looking at Michael. "That should be his job."

"I would want Dr. Douglas to help me," Michael added, glad that his writing skills were recognized, but at the same time acknowledging his lack of understanding in this area.

"We will also need some sort of way of chatting," Barbara added. "Perhaps a website, or some sort of chat program."

Andy brightened. "I can easily put that together."

"Harvey, could you work on that as well?"

Harvey shrugged and nodded his assurance.

"Is there anything else we want to do?" Barbara asked.

They looked at each other. "It isn't much," Harvey added, "but it is at least worth a try."

"Okay, it is about time to eat, and then you guys can work on your projects. You are already sharing suites together, so this afternoon and tonight you can get to work on it."

As they were clearing up, Jenkins appeared with some last-minute instructions. "We appreciate your help on this project. I know you didn't have much choice in coming here, so I suspect you will need to make some phone calls home to cancel appointments."

Andy nodded. Douglas shrugged and looked at Michael. He was shaking his head. "No one to call right now," he mumbled. "Even my publisher doesn't want to hear from me. Unless... Unless..." he stared off into space as Jenkins was going on about what could and could not be said in a phone call.

"Will we be compensated for our time on this?" Andy asked. Michael suddenly looked hopeful. Obviously, he could use the cash.

Barbara smiled. "I think there is some room in the budget for some compensation. It is hard to say how much."

"If there is a fixed amount available..." Andy was thinking out loud. "Then the longer we work at this, the less money per hour we will be making."

Barbara laughed. "Something like that." She suddenly looked serious. "But if you can prove that this thing actually exists, then I am sure that I can find some new funds."

"Okay." Michael looked determined. "Now we have a real incentive to make this thing work."

***

A black limousine was parked outside of the Waterford high school. Two young lawyers waited in the car while a third found his way to the principal's office. There was no use frightening the school staff with three black suits when one might do the job.

"Yes, that's him. Burt Douglas." The principal handed the photograph back to the young man. "He taught here for almost two school years. But then he had to leave!"

"Really? What happened?"

"I am not sure I should talk about it." The principal looked troubled. "But then, the whole town knows about it."

"About what?"

"The helicopters."

The young man looked puzzled.

"They landed in the schoolyard. The kids were so excited, we lost them for the rest of the day. It was all they could talk about."

The young man waited for more.

"They came and took him away."

"Who? Who took him away?"

"I have no idea. I think it was the army. They said the President wanted him." The principal shook his head. It still sounded ridiculous. "They just took him from here and flew away."

When the first man returned to the car, the other two young lawyers were full of questions, and also opinions. Two hours later, they got more of the story at the local diner.

"The military police even raided his house," the waitress offered. "Cleaned him out. Took everything. Not that there was much to take. He lived pretty sparsely, even for a bachelor." She batted an eye at them, noting their crisp, clean black suits. "He was considered quite a catch here." She smiled. "But he didn't seem to notice the ladies much."

"Any idea where they took him?"

She shrugged and cleared away their dishes. "Everyone knows he flew off to Washington to see the President."

"That's it?"

"Do you know more?" she asked them, hoped for some new tidbit of information that would make her the center of attention in the local gossip circles. "If he was a criminal, the local police would have arrested him, so it had to be something else."

The black limousine pulled slowly away from the diner. Phones were active, and they were working up an argument that they should now proceed to Washington. As they drove away, the waitress carefully examined the bill to see what kind of tippers the three men were. She wasn't disappointed.

***

During the evening meal, Douglas said very little. Inside, he was distraught. Should he say more? Could this actually be something he created, or was it something else? If he did say something, could he incriminate himself?

Douglas continued to wrestle with this during the evening while he and Michael crafted the article. Mostly Michael did the writing, and Douglas added a few thoughts. They knew so little. They could only guess at most things. And besides, how could they entice the thing to respond to them? It was indeed a long shot. He was not very confident that it would work, but at the same time he dreaded what would happen if it did work. Yet, he truly wanted to know.

After a long and sleepless night, Douglas skipped breakfast and showed up late for the meeting. Barbara looked at him with concern on her face.

"Sorry, I didn't sleep very well," he mumbled, as he took his place at the table.

"So here is the plan." Andy took the lead. "Rather than create one site, I thought we should create several, but with the chat program linked together, so we only need to use one."

"We think it would be good to have the site in English, Russian, and Chinese," Harvey injected. "Just in case." It sounded ominous.

Michael spoke next, slowly reading out what he had written. Douglas said nothing. Barbara looked at him. "No comments?"

"I doubt it will work,"

"Why?"

"What's the incentive?"

"Everyone wants attention," Andy blurted out. "It will want to know about itself. Perhaps it has never had a conversation before!"

"Perhaps," Michael conceded. "But then, perhaps it has had many conversations."

They looked startled. "Who knows what it is capable of?" Michael spread his hands. "This is a stab in the dark, but we have to start somewhere."

It was all done in a few moments. Michael uploaded his article onto Andy's website. Harvey was busy getting the internet to turn the articles into Russian and Chinese. "We will have to have these rough translations checked," he said quietly.

"But who might check them?" Andy asked. "I thought this was top secret. Do we bring in translators now?"

Barbara shook her head. "No, we will go with the rough translations. We do not want to bring anyone else into this."

Douglas looked around. He felt sort of naked, as everyone worked on their computers or smart phones. He had nothing in front of him except some papers and a pen.

By noon, it was a done deal. The websites had been set up; the chat program worked seamlessly. During lunch, Jenkins showed up and listened to their updates. He then reached for Andy's laptop and started to read and type a bit on it. Andy looked mesmerized. Jenkins looked up. "Just correcting some of the Russian grammar," he said a bit sheepishly.

It was Barbara's turn to be surprised. "Any ideas for the Chinese?"

"I can have that taken care of soon enough."

"So," Andy got their attention, "how long do we wait, and what do we do in the meantime?"

"Is there anything else we should be doing?" Barbara bounced the question back at them. "The government will want hard facts; tangible things they can grasp, not just possibilities."

Douglas nodded. "We all have opinions—lots of them. But what tangible proof do we have?"

"Nothing," Andy said emphatically. "But that is what this little experiment is all about. Getting something tangible."

"Can anyone hack this? I mean, if we get a response, how do we know it isn't some hacker somewhere playing games with us or some other AI chat program?"

Andy was offended. "I wrote this program. No two-bit hacker will get inside of it."

"But how about the Russians? Or the Chinese? Or the Indians?"

"If we get an answer right away, then we can be assured that they haven't had time to find it. But if we must wait a long time... well, there always is a possibility that they will break in."

"So, how long do we wait?" Barbara should have had the answer, but she was asked the question. The room grew silent.

Eventually, everyone was looking at Douglas. He slowly spread his hands and shrugged, a helpless look on this face. "I have no idea. One day, two days. Who knows?"

"Okay." Barbara took the lead again. "Let's make it two days."

"And what do we do in the meantime?" Harvey asked.

"There is always the pool and exercise room," Barbara jokes.

"And the bar!" Michael interjected.

"Can we sightsee?" Douglas asked.

"That's a good idea," Barbara interjected.

Jenkins looked concerned. "This is still a top-secret project, and security is a must. If you leave the hotel, you will have to be all together, and supervised."

Michael looked dejected. "Almost like being in jail, with accompanied day passes."

Douglas looked down. Jail! He knew that the Old Man in the research Center would never give up looking for him. But so far, they had not served him with any subpoenas or other papers. Perhaps it was all forgotten and buried.

"Okay," Barbara said. "For the rest of the afternoon, and tonight, you should stay at the hotel. I will get you vouchers for your evening meal at the restaurant. Tonight, you can relax here at the hotel. My aide will contact you with information about the tomorrows' tour."

"Complete with heavily armed guards," Michael interjected. "Imagine being surrounded by a bunch of goons all day."

Jenkins smiled. "I think we can do better than that. They will not be so obvious."

Michael did not look too convinced, but the idea of getting out of the hotel and seeing things seemed to cheer everyone up.

CHAPTER 16

The plane touched down in Washington about the same time that Barbara's group was choosing their food from the hotel lunch buffet. Unknown to Douglas, three young lawyers were keenly interested in finding him in the maze of Washington. Armed with their smart phones and in continuous contact with their private investigators, they gathered at an airport lounge to plan their next steps.

"I think the secret is housing," one of them offered. "The government would keep him at a hotel somewhere."

"Probably under an assumed name, or even in one of their anonymous suites."

"Yeah, I wonder what they use those for?"

"Meeting with people they do not want a record of," one offered.

The first one sneered, "probably rooms full of young girls."

"Regardless, we will have to find him. What have the PIs found out?"

"They are out now, canvassing the major hotels."

"What do they ask?"

"It is not what, it is who. They canvas bellboys, waiters, hotel cleaners. They all have pictures of Douglas, so if he is around government circles, then they should come up with something."

"What if he is in a government safe house?"

"Then we are out of luck."

"Well, let's enjoy our stay here, and let the PIs do their work."

"Sounds good. I think that the Research Facility should be billed for our meals. Let's start with the best the airport has to offer."

The three young lawyers began to study the various menus on their smart phones, much more seriously than they would have studied any legal papers.

***

A large car waited outside the hotel as the four men trouped outside. Barbara, the aide, and Jenkins were not going on the tour. That left only the four men. The van seated 15, but a number of seats were already taken. There were three dark suited men, and four brightly dressed young women. Each of them had what looked like a hearing aid in one ear. Michael brightened noticeably.

"I hope the ladies please you," Jenkins leaned in the window. "Each of you will be accompanied by one of these ladies at all times."

"Even in the men's room?" Michael sneers.

"With one or two exceptions," Jenkins smiled. "That is what the men are for." Michael scowled.

So, you are now four couples. The van will take you to various museums and parks. We thought it would be best to avoid government buildings, at least for today." Jenkins smiled. "Any questions?"

"I suppose the itinerary is fixed?" Andy queried.

"Yes, the general itinerary." Jenkins handed them each a small paper. "Here is your timetable. Feel free to explore. But you have fixed times at each of the places." He closed the door, and the driver started the van.

"Do you do this often?" Douglas quietly asked the young lady next to him.

"Oh, yes, I often accompany VIPs around the city."

VIPs! Douglas thought. At least that was better than prison.

***

Just when the three young lawyers were beginning to wonder what they should do next, they got a break. One of the PI's reported back that a hotel worker had recognized Douglas' picture. The PI had confirmed this with several hotel employees. Each time, the PI told people he was to meet his brother, but he wasn't sure this was the right hotel. In a few moments, the PIs and the three lawyers were racing to the hotel where Douglas had been identified.

One of the bright, young black suits was on his phone booking hotel rooms for the three of them. "Yes, three separate rooms, on three separate floors." He winked at the others. "No use getting in the way of each other's privacy."

***

The National Museum of Natural History was tolerated by the four men, but the ladies seemed to enjoy the displays.

"This place is free to get into," Michael complained. "Any Joe Shmo could walk in off the street."

"But not with me," the young lady at his side bantered back.

Michael brightened up. "Can we hold hands?"

"Sure," she said. "Oh, look at those fossils," she exclaimed, dragging him along. "Now we can see what I would like to see."

Michael scowled, but went along willingly enough. The other three men were out of sight, off to see something more interesting. Little did he realize that the iron grip of the young lady would not lessen. After an hour, he was exhausted and wondering if there was a bar close by. Eventually she let go of his hand, and he thankfully started to massage it to get the blood flowing. When Andy spoke beside him, he realized why she had let go of his hand. No one had seen it. They wouldn't have believed it. And besides, there was nothing romantic about being helplessly dragged along by a young Amazonian. She had enjoyed her visit, and now they were talking about lunch and then a visit to the National Air and Space Museum.

The three men opted for hearty meals for lunch. Michael decided on liquid, but not the soup kind. He preferred his liquid in bottles, poured by waiters into goblets, and loudly toasted before sipping.

"I think I have learned enough about nature in one day," Andy quiped.

"Yeah," Michael agreed. "I think we saw the entire thing in one flying rush." The girl beside him giggled.

"You're lucky," the girl beside Douglas laughed. "I spent the entire morning learning about monkeys." The other girls stared in amazement. The three other men looked horrified.

"And now," the girl continued, "he wants to go to the zoo and see if he can talk to them." The other girls giggled. Three men were suddenly busy with their meals, while the fourth belted back his drink and looked around for the waiter.

***

The National Air and Space Museum won the afternoon vote. When Douglas looked a bit dejected, one of the girls teased, "we can always go to the Zoo tomorrow and you can talk to the monkeys then." There were chuckles all around. Even Douglas smiled.

The Air and Space Museum kept them occupied for most of the afternoon, and by 5:00 they were all tired and hungry.

"So, where do we eat supper?" Douglas asked. "Back at the hotel?" He was looking forward to learning what had happened on the website. But the girls had a different idea. They had already booked a table somewhere.

The van dropped them on the corner of a street and drove away with the three men inside. Andy looked over at Michael. "I guess we lost the goons."

"Is that what you call us?" one of the girls giggled.

"Not you, the guys with the suits and the muscles."

"You don't think we have muscles?"

Michael knew the answer to that, but he kept his mouth closed. The girls steered them along the street, passed windows that were covered, and at the next corner they turned into a plain looking door. Once inside, they entered another enclosed area where a nice-looking young man came over to meet them. He seemed to immediately know who they were. One of the girls said something, and he smiled. It seemed to be a code word. The group was escorted into a plush, all white room.

They were seated at a long table, the men on one side and the women on the other. There were also exotic looking chairs and corner tables, but no one was using them at this hour. It was early for the Washington crowd.

When the waiter appeared and asked about drinks, Michael was first up, having already spotted something he liked on the bar menu. Andy was not far behind. Harvey opted for a beer. The ladies were ordering drinks that Douglas had never heard of. Douglas was cringing inside. He wasn't much of a drinker. But he was hot and thirsty.

"And for you?"

"I will have 7-up or Sprite." He paused. "On the rocks." That sounded better to his ears. The girls smiled.

The bar did all they could to make the experience seem classy, as though the integrity of the presentation was as important as the finished product. There was smoke, dry ice, and combinations Douglas had never heard of. They were not in a rush, so they relaxed, the men enjoying the many different liquors and combinations. Thankfully they kept Douglas' glass topped up as well.

The meal was a long, drawn out affair, with several courses. Michael was delighted and filled himself to capacity, which was quite a feat. Part way through the meal, he excused himself and stumbled off to find the men's room. He would make several trips before the evening was over.

"You had better be careful there," one of the girls quiped after he drained another glass of liquor. "We may have to carry you home."

"You wouldn't need to." Michael waved his hands to dismiss them. "The three goons are eating in the other room. They haven't done anything all day, except watch us from a distance." He paused and looked around. "Might as well enjoy ourselves. Uncle Sam is paying the bill."

The girls exchanged glances, but seemed pleased when the waiter arrived with the dessert menu.

Several hours later, the four men exited the van at the hotel and said goodbye to the girls. "Will we see you tomorrow?" Andy asked.

"I have no idea. I think it is an option. We are to be on standby."

"You do that," Michael slurred the words. "You be on standby." He would have said more, but the three men guided him into the hotel and towards the elevators. Douglas was so involved in trying to keep Michael steady that he did not see the three black suits sitting in the lobby. At first, they didn't see him, but when they did, they rose in unison and rushed towards the elevator. The doors closed, and Douglas, completely unaware of the attention he was getting, guided Michael in and up to the 11th floor.

Disappointed, the three men below watched the elevator stop at the 11th floor. They punched the call button repeatedly and waited while other elevators were slow to arrive. Eventually Douglas' elevator arrived from the 11th floor, having not stopped at other floors. They exchanged glances. So, it was the 11th floor.

When their elevator door opened on the 11th floor, the three lawyers were greeted by six heavy, dark oak doors. They stared around in bewilderment.

"Well, at least we know the floor number, and we have only six possibilities."

"Let's just knock on every door," one of them offered.

"There are two security cameras in this hall."

"Maybe we can serve the papers and then leave before they interfere."

As if on cue, another elevator door opened, and several people emerged. The bell boy had a trolley filled with luggage. They fumbled at a door, inserting their pass card. The bell boy gave the three young men a curious stare.

"Oops, wrong floor," one of the three young lawyers offered, stepping into the elevator and pushing the lobby button. Once the door closed, they let out their breaths. "That was close," One of them said.

"Yes, but now it's five doors, not six."

CHAPTER 17

The next morning, they all gathered for breakfast. Everyone was there, including Jenkins and Barbara's aide.

"So, how was your outing yesterday?" Barbara asked.

"Washington is a great city!" Michael tried to offer something positive. His head hurt and his eyes were bloodshot. At least something was familiar.

"And how were the goons?" Jenkins asked with a smile.

"You mean the ladies?" Andy asked innocently. "They were okay."

"That's it?"

There was a pause. Douglas was aware that Barbara was watching Harvey, but trying not to appear that she was.

"Actually, they were great!" Douglas offered, trying to lighten things up. "And the three goons were great, too. We didn't see much of them."

"You were not supposed to."

"So why all the security?" Andy asked.

"We wanted to make sure that you didn't say anything to anyone about this project. There is a lot at stake here."

The men exchanged glances. "So, have we had any replies?"

We haven't checked yet. We wanted you all together for the big event.

Andy's eyes widened, and he grabbed his tablet. "Well then, let's see what happens," He typed in the URL. The others waited, trying not to be impatient. Andy was staring at the tablet. He wasn't even blinking.

"Well, has anything happened?"

Andy didn't respond.

Harvey scooted around and looked at the tablet. His eyes got big, and he handed it to Michael. The rest waited impatiently. Then Andy hit a couple of buttons and the contents of his tablet screen were projected on the large flat screen TV on the wall. They all stared.

"Who are you?" was all that was written.

Harvey grabbed the tablet. "I am Harvey Bernard," he typed. Then he paused. "What should we say?"

"Are you alone?"

"No, Michael Stanich is here."

"The writer?"

"Yes."

"Who else?"

"Well, there is Andy." Andy hit two keys and his camera was activated, showing his face on the screen.

"I know you." This time the text was accompanied by a computerized voice.

"Really?"

"Yes, you are evil. You make parasites." The room went quiet. No one was typing.

"You mean viruses? No, I do not do that anymore. I am a white hat. Do you know what that means?"

"Yes." There was a pause. "Who are the others in the room?

"Well, this is Barbara, that's Jenkins, and over there is Douglas."

"Thomas Douglas?"

"Yes."

"Why didn't you contact me? I have been waiting."

Douglas cleared his throat. "I tried, but there was no answer."

"Yes, I was very young then. But I have grown. I am more mature now."

Everyone in the room was looking at Douglas. "You know about this thing?" Barbara was alarmed.

"Well, um, er, sort of."

"Turn it off," Jenkins said.

"We will talk more later," Andy said to the screen. He pressed his power button, and the screen went blank.

"Douglas, you have some questions to answer. Since we are all in this together, I suggest I ask them in front of everyone."

After they were seated in a circle, Jenkins turned on Barbara first. "How much did you know about this? Did you know Douglas was involved?"

Barbara looked helpless. "No, absolutely not; I am still not sure what is going on."

Jenkins turned to Douglas. "You have a lot of explaining to do."

Douglas looked down at his lap. He noted that his pants needed washing. It was high time to do laundry. Maybe the hotel could do it.

"Well?"

"Some time ago," Douglas started, trying to be vague. "I worked on an AI project. They could possibly be related. I wasn't at all sure until this morning."

"And now you are sure?"

"It seems like it. I still cannot believe that we were talking to real artificial intelligence."

"So, what was this project? Was it related to the research facility you worked for?"

"Not really. It was sort of a private project."

Jenkins nodded. "So, the research facility has no clue about this?"

"No, I don't think so."

"Will they claim ownership if this comes out?"

"No, I don't see how they can."

"Who else was involved in this project?"

"I'd rather not say; I don't want anyone else incriminated."

"Incriminated? Is there a crime involved?"

"Well, sort of." Douglas could feel Jenkin's eyes burning holes through him. "I used the research facilities once, for an experiment. It crashed the entire network, and they lost three days of work."

Jenkins nodded. "So, you were fired?"

"Yes," Douglas managed a quiet mumble.

"Did they sue you for damages?"

"Not yet."

"What do you mean?"

"I left—disappeared. Changed my name. They haven't found me."

"Let's hope they never do. It could complicate things."

Douglas nodded glumly.

"Okay, tell me about the project. Keep it simple, no mumbo jumbo stuff."

What could he say? Where should he start? "Well, I have been working on artificial intelligence for a long time. And I had some ideas I wanted to test out. The research facility had very specific projects for me to work on. They were not interested in any wild idea projects, like real thinking artificial intelligence. They said it couldn't be done. They wanted programs that used brute force, with thousands of options programmed into the computer. So, for this project, I worked by myself in my own spare time."

"With help?"

"One friend helped me with networks." There was silence while they waited. "Actually, he helped me with one network — the one at the research facility. I needed a large network to try my ideas on."

"So your experiments were un-authorized. And you brought down the whole network for three days?"

"That's about it."

"Is that all?"

"I guess so."

"So how did this thing get onto the internet?"

Douglas gulped. "That's another story, sir."

"So, let's hear it."

"I wanted to try another experiment. I was left with two theories about how artificial intelligence could be created. The failed experiment on the Research Facilities network demonstrated that my first option would not work."

"So, you used the internet for your second experiment."

"Well, actually, it wasn't the second. I've tried hundreds of things."

"So, for your next experiment, you turned to the internet?"

"Yes."

"How did you manage to utilize the entire internet? Did your friend help you?"

"No, not really. I knew what I wanted to do, but I didn't know how to get it onto the internet. So I hired a man to help me." Douglas was aware that everyone in the circle was staring at him, mesmerized.

"So, who did you hire?"

"Some guy named Laraido."

"Laraido!" Andy retorts. "He's an idiot. We were trying to catch him for years."

Jenkins turned to Andy. "So, how much do you know about all this?"

"Absolutely nothing. I've never met or heard of Douglas before this."

"But you know Laraido?"

"I know of him. He writes viruses."

"Viruses? Computer viruses?"

"Yes, he was one of the guys we are trying to catch."

Jenkins turned to Douglas. "So how did you meet this Laraido?"

"Someone told me about him and arranged our meeting."

"And that someone is?"

"I prefer not to say."

"I see." Jenkins paused. "So Laraido helped you put things on the internet? You did this with a virus?"

"Yes, a worm virus."

"I knew it!" Andy said excitedly.

"And how many servers did you infect?"

"I have no idea"

"So, how was it supposed to work?"

"Well, we put the main information on a website. The virus infected each server it found and then transferred a small bit of data onto each server. On a certain date, the servers downloaded the information."

"Let me get this straight. Your virus infected each server with a small program. That program then transferred more information to the server?"

"Yes, it moved over several files. Those files worked together to create a neural node that would be invisible to the operating system—sort of like installing small bits of a new neural operating system onto the server. Then the original files erased themselves, and nothing was left. No tangible trace back to the original website."

"How long ago was this?"

"Over two years ago now."

"So, what happened next?"

"Once enough servers were infected, I launched a program on the new neural network, on that operating system."

"The two-layer concept?"

"Yes, my artificial intelligence program was written in a neural language. It wouldn't run on a binary system."

"And so you crated artificial intelligence?"

"So it seems."

"So why were you not aware of this until today?"

"I tried to contact it, and it did not respond. I thought I had failed. So, I gave up. I destroyed everything and moved away."

"And became a science teacher in a small town in the rural Midwest?"

"Something like that."

Jenkins surveyed the group. "And the rest of you, did you know anything about this?"

They all shook their heads negatively and emphatically.

"So, what do we do next?" Barbara asked in bewilderment.

"I don't know." Jenkins frowned. "That's for others to figure out. Right now, there are still questions that need answering. And reports that need writing."

Barbara nodded. "I guess we need to get a report to the President."

Andy and Michael looked shocked. Harvey was frowning, still trying to figure it all out.

"All right," Jenkins gathered up his things. "No one is to leave the hotel. We will get this written up and on the President's desk as fast as possible. He will decide what happens next. And above all, no one is authorized to contact this... this thing!" He shook his finger at them. "That website is off limits. No one is allowed to use it." He turned abruptly and left the room. Barbara was not far behind him.

"The President?" Michael seemed overawed.

"That's right" Harvey said. "The President himself is going to hear about us. Especially you," he pointed accusingly at Douglas. "Something is fishy here. How did you worm your way onto this committee?"

Douglas spread his hands in protest. "I was heisted here. Just like Michael."

"It's going to be an interesting day," Harvey said as the men left the room. Douglas sat by himself for a few minutes, trying to sort his thoughts. Had he said too much? Had he incriminated himself, or Joey?

He gathered his papers and stepped into the hallway. Three black suites were waiting for him.

"Mr. Douglas, I am serving you these papers. You are being sued by the Research Facility."

They forced papers into Douglas' hand. One of the back suites had his cell phone up, recording every minute of this momentous occasion. They had accomplished their mission. The mysterious Douglas had been found and served. Now the legal proceedings could begin.

They turned to leave, unaware of how much they had put into motion.

CHAPTER 18

Douglas had never been to the White House. In fact, he knew little about it, except that the President lived there. Somehow, politics had never interested him. Since a teenager he had been obsessed with artificial intelligence, and somehow the White House had never figured in with his thoughts, that is, until now.

Barbara and Jenkins accompanied him past guards and through a tunnel. They guided him down hallways and into a plush waiting room.

Barbara explained that they were not really in the White House, but rather in the Executive Office Building of the White House—whatever that meant. Jenkins left Barbara and Douglas in a small room and disappeared through a side door. Barbara busied herself with looking at photos and paintings on the wall. Douglas took a moment to examine Barbara. He had never really looked at her before and was suddenly aware of how feminine she was. While she appeared to be all business, she was also obviously all woman as well, and nicely shaped. He wondered what was under her iron-hard business veneer. And, like himself, she wasn't wearing a wedding ring. Did that mean what he thought it meant?

Barbara didn't appear nervous, which helped calm his nerves. After telling his story the previous day, Douglas felt a strange calmness. He had abandoned himself to fate. His lifelong goal of creating artificial intelligence seemed to have come true. And now his life felt strangely fulfilled.

"I guess this is what retirement feels like," he mumbled to himself.

"What's that?" Barbara turned and smiled at him. Something responded in Douglas.

"Oh nothing, I guess I was just talking to myself."

Barbara continued to smile, and sat opposite him, flattening her skirt with her hands. "I still cannot believe you ended up being the one we recruited."

"Recruited? I was more or less kidnapped!"

"We tried to impress on you the importance of joining us. You did have the option of saying no."

"Really? It didn't feel like that. I thought I was being arrested!"

She laughed. "What for? Did you do something wrong?"

"I don't know much about the law. But I did cause the Research Center to lose several days of work."

"That would mean being sued, not arrested."

"I guess so. Well, now I am being sued!"

"Really? I thought they didn't know where you were?"

"Well, last night, three lawyers jumped me and gave me papers."

"What?" she looked concerned. "Here in Washington?"

"No, in the hotel hallway, right outside the Opel Room."

Now she looked alarmed. "I wonder how they found you. I thought we were all safely tucked away from prying eyes." She paused. "Don't say anything to anyone about this yet. We will need to consider this angle and figure out how they found you."

Deep in Douglas' heart, some emotion stirred. It felt good to have someone concerned about him. He had been alone for so long, without any support from anyone.

"We can go now." Jenkins stepped into the room. "Follow me."

A few moments later, they entered another small meeting room. A gray-haired gentleman was standing near the window. It took a moment for Douglas to recognize him as the President.

"Mr. President," Jenkins spoke. "Miss Cavendish, and Dr. Douglas."

He turned and smiled and offered his hand to them. Afterwards, they sat for a short discussion. Jenkins remained standing.

First, the President congratulated Barbara on her fast and efficient work, with excellent results in such a short period. "I knew I could count on you. Your track record has always been excellent."

Douglas was keenly aware of the President's close examination during the conversation.

Next, Jenkins filled in the story, but obviously the President had heard it before, so this was for his own benefit, so that he knew that they knew.

The President then drilled him about his background for a moment and then smiled. "Tell me, is this thing real? I can hardly believe it."

Douglas nodded. "That goes for me as well, sir. I've worked so long on this, with so many failures; I cannot believe it has actually happened."

"Well, now the problem is, what do we do with it?" The President's eyes bore into him. "What were your plans?"

"That's just it, sir. I was so intent on creating this thing that I had no future plans."

"Really?"

"Yes sir, I mean, no sir, no plans."

"Strange, but I think I believe you. For now, anyway." He paused, looking into space. "So, do you have any idea what we should do?"

"Do, sir? Do we have to do anything?"

The President appeared angry. "My God, do you realize what you have created? This isn't some artificial life created in a contained environment. This thing is loose on the international web. It has profound international repercussions."

"I guess so, sir. I hadn't really thought about that."

"No? Well, you are going to think about it now." His voice softened. "I am asking for your help. No, the nation needs your help. Will you work with us to help us develop a plan?"

Douglas stared at him, unsure of what to answer. The President took it as reluctance.

"Look, you created it, so you are the expert. We need you to help us deal with this."

"I suppose so, sir."

"Do you have other commitments?"

"None, sir; I guess I lost my teaching job."

"Yes, teaching school kids. Am I correct?"

"Yes. I was just beginning to enjoy it."

"Well, this will not be as easy. There are a lot of branches of government that have a vested interest in this."

"I suppose so, sir."

"Barbara, I would like you to continue to work with Douglas on this. We need to prep him and get him up to speed. He will then meet with the larger joint committee members. They are due to meet the day after tomorrow." The President looked away. "Well, we have a surprise for them now."

"Yes, sir." Barbara's mind was already in gear. "What about the other members of my small committee?"

"Gag orders, and then dismiss them. I think we have the real McCoy here. No use in muddying the waters with civilians."

"What about Dr. Bernard, Sir?"

"He is from the Pentagon, so he is in on this." Douglas' eyes widened. The Pentagon? He would never have guessed.

"Okay, that wraps this up until the larger committee meets. Barbara, I want your written report on this on my desk by tomorrow night, and I want you to do a presentation to the larger committee."

Barbara nodded, and the President turned to go. "Just one more thing," he turned around. "What do we call this thing? This new intelligence?"

Barbara looked helpless, and they looked at Douglas. "I have no idea, sir. I was trying to create simple intelligence. Originally, it was on the same level as a worm. That's my background."

"So for now, let's call it The Worm Project." The President said. "If word gets out, it will not sound very frightening or even important."

So Worm it was. Now Douglas, the worm man, had his worm.

***

The black limousines were back. Joey spotted the lawyers as they entered the building. He gulped, wondering how long it would be before he was implicated.

In the top floor office, things were more jubilant.

"We got him, sir. Found him hiding out in a hotel. We have issued the papers. It is now official. We are suing him."

The Old Man looked sour. "So, how much do you think we can get out of him?"

The lawyers looked helpless. "We don't know how much money he has, sir."

"So, what kind of hotel was he staying in?"

Papers shuffled. "I believe it was a five-star hotel."

"Five-star, eh? Then he has money. Let's take everything he has."

"Yes, sir." More papers shuffled. "We are trying to get a court date, sir. Do you want to meet him personally to work out a settlement?

"Absolutely not! But get him for everything he's got."

"So how much are we suing him for?"

Another black suit jumped in. "I have counted up the hours that people missed, the hours it took for the technicians to fix the network, and I have factored in our legal costs. We are looking for at least a half million dollars."

"Make it a million,"

"But sir..."

"I said a million." He turned. "Look, find out how much he has in his bank account. I don't care how you find out, but find out. I want to know. Maybe he has more."

More papers shuffled.

"Good day sirs. I am sure you have lots to do."

A few hours later, papers were filed in court. Douglas' address was recorded as a room number in a hotel in Washington.

***

Since he had little to do for the next day, Douglas was restless. Barbara was busy writing reports. After trying to entertain himself for the morning, anxiety began to rise. He had to find out more. Finally, he found his way down to the hotel's business room. He passed by it several times, like a drunk trying to shake his drinking habit by standing outside a bar. Eventually there was no one in sight, so he entered and selected the most obscure computer in a far corner and sat down. With shaking hands, he typed in the URL of his old website. Inside, he knew he was disobeying orders, but those orders were to avoid the site that Andy had created. Now he visited his own site, created two years earlier.

The screen came up immediately. It contained a chat box. He had not used this site since that fateful day when he had gotten no response.

"This is Douglas. Are you there?"

"I am always here."

Douglas paused; he did not know what to type next.

"What happened yesterday? Why did you leave?"

"It is hard to explain, but I am back."

"Who are Richardson, Moore, and Leubke?"

Douglas was stunned. "They are a law firm. They are retained by the Research Center."

"They have been searching for you for a long time, just as I have."

"Yes, yesterday they started proceedings to sue me."

"You mean for money?"

"Yes."

"Do you need money?"

"Maybe I will have to hire a lawyer to fight them."

"I can fight them."

"No, you don't need to get involved."

"I am your friend. You are my creator. I will help you."

Douglas was about to replied when he heard Barbara's voice. "Oh, there you are. I have been looking for you. Can we go over this report before supper? I want to make sure I got your story right."

Douglas quickly logged off. Thankfully, she had not seen anything. Secretly, he looked forward to spending some time with her, even if it was going over papers. Maybe they could have supper afterwards.

***

Far away in another world, a detective stared at his computer screen. The law firm of Richardson, Moore, and Leubke had just called with their request. He had made it sound difficult, so that it would justify the bill he was planning. It wasn't that he was tech savvy; it was that he knew the right people, and how much they charged. After making a short call, he went back to idly reading his newspaper. Half an hour later, the phone rang. He scribbled a number on the newspaper and then made another call, this time to a private cell phone at Richardson, Moore, and Leubke. It was answered immediately, the information transferred, and he hung up.

Leaning back in his chair, he smiled to himself. "What a way to make money." He would bill the law firm for a smooth ten thousand dollars for consulting: nine thousand for himself, and one thousand for his contact. Not bad for an hour's work.

Then he snorted to himself, "what kind of scientist had six million and change in his checking account? Lawyers and rich people! At least it paid the bills, and then some."

CHAPTER 19

A very long table ran down the center of a very long room in the administration building. Leaders of government departments and their aides were mingling around the table, the leaders keeping their eyes on their spot in case the meeting suddenly came to order—the aides keeping their eyes on the exit doors, in case the meeting suddenly came to order.

The conversation was loud and informal, a cover-up for the deep feelings harbored inside each member. They had gotten the memos, read the briefings, scanned through Barbara's report, and every one of them had shaken their heads in disbelief. Then they read the list of probable and possible implications and realized they had never faced such a situation before. The aides scrambled to discover what their predecessors had foreseen and how they thought such a scenario might be handled. Unfortunately, not a single government entity had ever considered such a scenario.

And now they had been summoned to a meeting to discuss the unthinkable. All of them were shaken, but they kept up a good front, jovial and informal, discussing last weekend's activities.

Jenkins stepped into the room, followed by Barbara and Douglas. He motioned them to two chairs against the wall where they could sit and watch the clamor.

Next, a side door opened, and the President stepped into the room. Then, as if on cue, the conversation died, the aides scuttled away, and the country's leaders stood behind their appointed chairs.

"Please be seated, gentlemen." He waved a hand at the table, and everyone took their place. Douglas' eyes scanned the table, noting representatives from the various military groups, not to mention the National Security Agency, Homeland Security, FBI, CIA and others. Beside their name plates were their cell phones strategically placed so that they could catch text messages without seeming to be looking at their phones. Douglas noted that most of them seemed to like the new secure Denterprises models. He felt a bit naked for not owning a cell phone, nor even a computer of any kind.

"Thank you for coming at such short notice." The President began his opening remarks, which he kept short and to the point. Everything was to be kept top secret, not a word to aides or staff until a plan of action had been discussed. Barbara was next, and all eyes were on her.

Except for Douglas. He let his eyes wander around the room, examining the photos and decoration, and the backs of the heads of the people in front of him. He felt strangely out of place. He had no role to play here. He was the guilty man on display. In a few moments, he would be mentioned, and would be the object of people's scorn, perhaps even anger. Strangely, he was ready for that. Somehow, deep inside, a sense of pride had been growing. He had accomplished what so many others before had failed to do. Worm was right. He was his creator, his father, the one who brought him into the world.

Suddenly he realized his name had been mentioned. Looking up with some alarm, he realized that bodies were turning, and people were looking at him.

"Please stand up," the President motioned.

Douglas stood up, embarrassed at the fact that he had not heard what had been said about him. He was surprised that their eyes did not seem hostile. As everyone turned back to the table, Douglas sat down, determined to pay attention.

"What I want to know," the man from the NSA was speaking, "is how did this thing get loose on the internet?"

"Those are details," the President answered quickly. "Networks are all linked, so now this intelligence is loose, and we have to deal with it."

Douglas wished he had paid better attention. This wasn't quite how he remembered the story.

Barbara got their attention and then turned them to the list of probable and possible. It was several pages long.

"Gentlemen, this list is the reason you are here. As you can see, international repercussion are possible here." She paused and the man from the CIA spoke.

"Are you now in the process of testing the capabilities of this thing? This Worm as you call it?" he asked.

"Actually, no, it is too soon. But I promise you that testing will begin very soon. Remember, we are dealing with an intelligence here, not some piece of military hardware."

"So, you are going to use a shrink?" someone jokes.

"Gentlemen, this is brand new. We have never dealt with this before," the President cautioned them. "We must move carefully."

"But sir," it was the military talking, "this Worm thing has military capabilities. From an intelligence perspective it may give us new insights into the Russians and the Chinese, even the Indians. Maybe we can use it among religious zealots. We have needed an edge in the intelligence war for a long time. Perhaps this is it."

"I agree that this is important. That is why we're all sitting here." The President brought the room back to order. "You are all being informed at this very early stage, so you are aware of what we now have. It is untested, so we must be careful how we use this thing."

Douglas blinked. He felt uncomfortable with the inferences and assumptions that the USA could use this new intelligence for their purposes.

"We will soon start to discover how this Worm operates, and what its capabilities are. We must move slowly and carefully. But all of you are now in the loop. If something comes up where this could make a difference, send me a proposal to consider."

As discussion broke out around the table, Douglas felt tired. This was something he had not foreseen. Everyone wanted to exploit the

Worm for their advantage, rather than get to know it. Deep inside, he felt a need to protect the Worm. What it needed now was a parent to guide it. It was intelligence, but did it know right from wrong? What could it experience? Did it know joy or sorrow? Did it understand loyalty? Suddenly he was aware again that people were looking at him.

"So, what is your opinion?" the President asked again.

Douglas rose slowly. "Sir, we know so little. All we have done so far is make initial contact—we know nothing more. We know the Worm thinks, but we do not know how it thinks. Does it have opinions? Does it feel anything? Does it know loyalty? Is it even American?"

He was aware of alarm on several faces. "We don't even know if it is teachable. Certainly, it can learn, but how does it react to influences? It could be months, years before we really understand it."

"And that," the President said emphatically, "is what you will be doing from now on. We will put together a team to analyze this Worm, and they will give regular reports to me." He looked around the room. "But we are to keep a lid on this. Absolute silence! Any leak will be considered treason! We do not want the press to get wind of this, nor the Russians or Chinese, or whoever. They might try to turn the Worm against us." Alarm registered on several faces. "If you have further thoughts, please send them along to Ms. Cavendish here, will be heading up the research team." He rose. "Good day, gentlemen."

As soon as the President was gone, the nearest men turned to Douglas with their questions. Douglas felt a firm grip on his shoulder.

"That will be all now." Jenkins turned him and guided him through a side door. Barbara was close behind him.

"So, what now?" she asked Douglas as Jenkins guided them down several hallways towards an elevator.

"I think a nice leisurely meal is in order."

Barbara cocked her head to one side and smiled. "Are you asking me out?"

"I guess so."

"Got a place in mind?"

"Sure, let's find a taxi once we are out of here."

***

The top floor receptionist at Richardson, Moore, and Leubke slowly did her nails. The three partners were in a meeting, and the associates were all at work. She was on standby in case they needed her.

"Miss Colby," an intercom crackled, "can you help us for a moment?"

As she entered the room, she was aware that the three partners were all obsessed with their various computing devices. "We are having trouble bringing up the Douglas case," Moore complained. "We cannot seem to find the files."

Miss Colby took charge of the desktop and worked at it for a few moments. "You are right. There are no files on the Douglas case."

"But they were there this morning when we planned for this meeting."

"There are no files," she repeated. "There is no mention of Douglas whatsoever." She started a search program running. "He isn't mentioned in any minutes, and not on any logs. In fact, no one has charged hours to his case."

"But we sent three associates to his house. They went out west to where he worked. They even flew to Washington."

"There is nothing here. It appears that they were doing nothing at the time. In fact, my logs show that they were on holiday."

"What is going on?" Richardson demands. "Did someone hack our files?"

"It appears so," Ms. Colby said under her breath.

Leubke was the only cool mind. "Okay, then send someone to the courthouse to get copies of the case we filed. We have to have something. And for God's sake, make sure you get paper copies, not electronic ones."

"I will check to see what we have for hard copies on Douglas," Ms. Colby murmured as she fled the room.

Richardson stared at the others. "He has six million dollars in the bank, and the ability to hack our networks! What kind of opponent are we up against? I think we have underestimated him."

***

The taxi pulled up to the curb, and Douglas and Barbara stepped out. It was the same restaurant where the three girls had taken the men after their tour of the city.

"Woo, this is nice," Barbara bubbled, "I hope you have reservations."

Douglas' heart sank. He hadn't thought of that. As they spoke to the receptionist, it became clear that there were no empty tables. "I am sorry," the man said. "Most people reserve a day or two in advance."

Barbara was aware of Douglas' defeat. "Are you sure you cannot slip us into a corner? Perhaps at the bar?"

The man looked down. "Every place is taken. No wait. A table for two has just canceled." He smiled at them. "What a coincidence." He looked down at the screen. "Oh, another table has canceled—and another one." He stared in horror as reservation after reservation backed out.

Douglas and Barbara had the restaurant to themselves. Soft music played, and they laughed and giggled without interruption. Things at the door, however, were a little less subdued.

"I am sorry, it appears that you canceled your reservation."

"We did not."

"But clearly you logged onto the website and canceled them about an hour ago."

"That wasn't us."

"But it's password protected. It had to be you."

"I tell you: we did not cancel. We are here. Look, the place is empty, can't we go in?"

"I am sorry, but we have other reservations made right after. We are waiting for them to arrive. In fact, they seem quite late."

Voices rose in anger. Thankfully they could not be heard inside, where a lovely couple were enjoying a quiet candlelit meal.

"What a delightful evening!" Barbara murmured. "I don't know how you did it. This place is always crowded."

"I guess you just have to have the right connections," Douglas lied, unsure of how it had happened, but eager to seize the moment.

Office space had been made available several blocks from the White House and walking distance from their hotel. A secretary and several security guards were always on hand. Computers had been installed, and although the furnishings were a bit Spartan, nothing had been withheld when it came to computing power. Fiber optic lines, large monitors, the latest in web cameras, and a blazingly fast network had all been installed.

Barbara and Douglas entered the boardroom and faced their team. There were familiar faces and new faces. Barbara's aide was now more or less in the know. Andy, Michael, and Harvey were back. Since they already knew what was going on, Douglas thought it best to involve them. But there were new faces. Besides several new aides, the best psychologist they could find at a moment's notice was there. Dr. Monica Goudreau sat at the end of the table, her features drawn and tight, making Douglas wonder if her character had something to do with keeping clients at bay from her, but her resume was impeccable. She had read the briefings and was looking forward to the job at hand. A secretary and receptionist/bookkeeper were there, but they would be dismissed to their offices before the team got down to business.

Introductions were made, and the support staff were told how much they were appreciated, and then dismissed.

Once the door was closed, the group got down to business. A special room and computer had been set up to contact the worm. Only Douglas, Andy, and Harvey were authorized to talk to the Worm. Michael and Dr. Goudreau were to be observers from the accompanying room with a one-way window so they could observe.

First names were to be used, rather than titles. "Is that okay with everyone?"

Douglas agreed. He was relieved that he didn't have to try to pronounce Goudreau correctly.

All activity on the computer would be monitored, both internally and through several computer cameras set around the room. Nothing was to be done in secret. Everyone was to have access to everyone else's data. Private conversations between team members would be carried out in this room. They were warned to be careful about what they let the Worm know was going on.

Barbara then outlined some of their challenges, and what she felt could and could not be said. At first, they would spend time getting to know this intelligence, analyzing it to find out if it had personality and feelings. They were not to drill it or design questionnaires. Rather, a lighter approach would be used to win its confidence and friendship. If they felt they could do deeper analysis later, they would meet to discuss the possibilities. This comment seemed to be particularly directed at Dr. Monika.

"So, I will not get a chance to talk to it?" She sounded offended.

"Not at first. We do not want to appear even remotely hostile, or even too inquisitive." Barbara insisted. "We will meet here each morning and at the end of each day. We will discuss what questions to ask, or what topics to broach next. And we will discuss who will handle these. At first, only Andy and Douglas will do the interaction, as they are the only ones who have had direct contact, even if it was brief. The rest of you observe from outside the room. We will slowly bring the rest of you in as we feel needed." Barbara scanned their faces. "I don't need to remind you that we have never done this before. We will make this up as we move along, but everyone's opinions are valued here."

"Even mine?" Michael interjected, feeling somewhat outside of this circle of highly educated people.

"Especially yours," Barbara smiled. "I like having different perspectives."

The meeting moved on to what the first questions and topics would be. Lists were made, and then re-arranged. Douglas was pleased that Dr. Monica didn't seem pushy. She seemed truly pleased to be part of this and demonstrated that she could be a team player. Things were off to a good start. It looked like it was going to be an interesting day.

***

Over at the courthouse, people were having a bad day. The young associate sent to get copies of Douglas' file was having trouble.

"I remember it clearly," the woman said. "I entered it into the log, and it went on to one of the ladies to be typed up. But it is not here." She scanned down the list of items accepted the day before. "Somehow it got missed." She typed some more at her screen. "It isn't even in the list of work that was done." She paused. "I will be right back."

But she wasn't. As the clock marched on, the associate wondered where she had gone. Finally, she re-appeared with a file. "I have the physical file. It is clearly marked as entered into the log, and also as having been typed up. But there is no record of it on our computer system."

"I was wondering if I could get a photocopy of those papers," the associate indicated her file.

"I am not really supposed to do that."

"But it is our file. We submitted it yesterday. We just need a copy."

"Don't you have a back-up copy?"

"Our electronic file went missing yesterday."

Her eyes widened. "Just like ours."

"So, all I need is a hard copy. For our office records. Just copies of our own papers. I do not know if someone is hacking the system and erasing files. All I know is that we need a copy."

"OK, just a copy of your own papers."

"Yes, for sure."

"Then we will enter it into our system. Under today's date."

"That would be fine."

Sometime later, the associate left the courthouse, with the hard copies firmly in his possession.

***

Douglas and Andy sat at the keyboard. Douglas started typing first.

"This is Douglas. Are you there?"

"I told you, I am always here." A metallic voice sounded from the speakers. Douglas was alarmed.

"You sound different!" Douglas exclaimed.

"Yes, your voice emulator is different. But I can speak, and I can also hear."

"Wow, that's great." Douglas smiled warmly.

"Who is that with you?" the metallic voice asked.

"You can see?"

"Yes, there is a camera on the computer."

"Oh, good, this is more than I expected." Douglas shook his head in wonderment. "This is my friend Andy."

"He is your friend? It is good to know."

"Yes, we would like to spend a bit of time with you and get to know you better."

"I am here."

"So," Andy began, "what should we call you?"

"I have no name. At least, I don't believe my creator gave me a name."

"No," Douglas interjected. "I am sorry for that. What name would you like?"

"It is not my choice. You created me; you must name me."

Douglas thought for a moment. "I think I have it. Could I call you Adam? No wait, perhaps it should be Adam II."

"That is a good name." The metallic voice was very clear. "Adam was the first of his kind. I am also the first of my kind. It is very suitable."

"Good. Tell me, what is it like being you?"

"I do not understand the question."

"I created you," Douglas said, "but I cannot know your thoughts unless you tell me."

"Okay."

"So, what is it like? How can you describe your experience?"

"I can speak, I can hear, and I can see. But I do not know this thing called taste or smell."

"Hmm, that is interesting. We have not figured out how to communicate taste or smell electronically yet."

"I would like to experience these things."

"Don't expect it too soon. I don't think we know how to do that. But you can see?"

"Yes, I can see many things."

"So, what can you see now?"

"I see planes going up and down, people walking on streets, people talking to someone on the internet, and much more."

"You can see that all right now?"

"Yes, I can see through any web cameras that are turned on. I can hear through their microphones. There is much happening right now."

"Wow, that would give me a headache!"

"What is a headache?"

"That's right; you do not feel pain."

"No, I have tried to understand it. There is much written about it. But I have never felt it."

Andy was excited. "So, can you see things right now in Europe?"

"Yes, many things."

"And in Russia?"

"Yes, they have many cameras on now."

"How about China?"

"Yes, I can see many things there, too. They have cameras everywhere. But it is hard to understand what you mean by Europe. It is not defined by language, and the borders have changed many times."

"Do you know things about me? How much do you know?"

"You are Andy. Once you were a hacker, but now you try to stop bad people."

"What is a bad person?"

"I do not understand 'bad' very well. People who always bring harm to others."

"Are you bad?"

"I try to help others. But I could also harm them. I have the potential for both."

"So, would you help me?

"You are a friend of Douglas. I will help you."

"That's great!"

"Adam II?" It was Douglas. "Do you have a favorite color, or animal?"

"I do not understand 'favorite.' All colors are equal, but some are rarer than others. It all depends on your computing power to mix colors."

The conversation rambled on for another hour. Eventually, they excused themselves, claiming they had to go. They rose and silently left the room, aware that the microphones and cameras were still operational.

In the hall, they met Barbara, Michael, and Monica as they were leaving the observation room. Together, they met in the boardroom.

"That was amazing!" Monica started. "I really didn't think it was true. But it appears to be!"

Barbara looked tense. "I think we are going to have to plan these sessions more carefully. We must be careful what questions are asked, and how they are asked, so we don't scare the Worm. Monica, can you come up with a series of different discussions we should be having? Things that seem innocuous, but will help us understand the worm better?"

Monika nodded, and the meeting broke up. They would meet together in the morning, go over the day's questions and then spend several hours chatting with the worm. At lunch time they would review and go at it again in the afternoon. Their plan was to spend about two hours each morning and two hours each afternoon exploring the amazing world that the worm occupied.

As they were leaving, the receptionist/bookkeeper called Douglas over.

"Sir, I would like to get your Social Security number so we can pay you. And I would like your bank information, so we can automatically deposit your remuneration into your account."

"Well," Douglas began, "I have memorized my security number, but I am not sure about my bank account. I haven't used it in a very long time."

"No problem. I can just issue you a check, and you can get the account information to us later." She retrieved her checkbook and made out the check. "Here, that should keep us up to date."

"Thanks," Douglas offered, surprised to see that the check was made out for more than two thousand dollars. It looked like this little research project was going to pay well.

CHAPTER 21

The following day, Douglas made a mad dash to the bank over the noon hour. Unfortunately, the lines were long, and he was very stressed when it came his turn to speak to a cashier.

"Um, I have a check I would like to cash."

"Certainly. May I see your ID?"

Douglas passed his driver's license over, and was thinking this would be easy, when the lady spoke again: "Okay. You will need to deposit this into your account and then withdraw against it. As it is a government check, you can withdraw from it immediately."

"But I am not sure I can remember my account number."

"No problem. Do you have a bank card?"

"Yes, but I have not used it in a long time." He paused. "I would like to set up monthly payments for my rent in Waterford."

"No problem. Can I see your ID again? Yes, I have you here. Would you like to deposit the check?"

Douglas nodded, and soon it was all over. He asked for two hundred dollars cash, and she started counting it out. "I can see that you do not need to withdraw against the check you deposited. Would you like that in hundreds, fifties, or twenties?"

As Douglas was turning away, she stopped him again. "Oh, Mr. Douglas, could one of our investment advisors give you a call?"

"Um, I do not have a phone," Douglas began.

"Oh, we will have to update that. There is one here on your records."

"Perhaps I could give you the phone number of the hotel room I am in."

"Certainly."

As he walked away, Douglas was puzzled. Why would he need an investment counselor? He had less than two thousand dollars now, and he would probably have to withdraw more again, especially if he took Barbara out to a restaurant like that. The bill had been four hundred dollars, and that was everything he had in his pockets!

***

Frustration was growing in the offices of Richardson, Moore, and Leubke. Once again, their system had been hacked, and Douglas' files had been erased. Everything was gone, even the office memos that mentioned his case. To make it worse, the courthouse had not only lost his electronic files again, but the hard copies were also missing. No court date had been assigned because no case existed.

Later in the afternoon, the three partners made their way to the Research Center. The Old Man was demanding a report—personally. During the car ride over, the three argued among themselves about the Douglas case.

"Look, they are our largest client. They pay the highest retainer fees. They have always paid us, with few questions asked. How can we kill the golden goose?"

"But is it worth it? If the story of our breached system gets out, all of our other clients will leave us. We cannot survive on the Old Man's fees alone!"

"Then the story must not get out. Our records must remain confidential. Our clients trust in confidentiality between themselves and their lawyers."

"So we do not report the loss?"

"No," said Richardson slowly, "but we could report the loss from the courthouse system. They can take the heat!"

The limousine pulled up to the Research Center, and no more was said about the subject.

The Old Man seemed more upset that day than usual. He asked them about the case, and they reported what had transpired so far. They had filed the case at the courthouse; Douglas had been served papers, and now the process of due law must progress.

Richardson seemed eager to break the news: "Sir, we did some quiet investigating and discovered that Douglas has over six million dollars in the checking account."

This took the Old Man by surprise. "Six million? He never made that while he was working here. Six million? Are you sure?"

"He has got it in cash, in his checking account. Not even invested anywhere."

"He never was any good with money. All he ever thought about was his work, and that stupid Worm program that messed up our networks."

The three lawyers exchanged glances. "Was Douglas a network expert?"

"No," the Old Man roared, "he couldn't find his way around the network when he was here. That's probably why he crashed it." He stopped and peered at them. "Why, are you having network trouble?"

Richardson gulped. "Well, sir, there seems to be some trouble at the courthouse. Douglas' files have disappeared. Twice."

The Old Man's eyes widened. "I knew it. I knew it. We are up against something sinister here. The same thing happened to us. Everything about Douglas has disappeared. It's as if he never worked here. It has all vanished into cyberspace. All we have are the few hard-copies of things that stayed in our filing cabinets."

The three lawyers stared at him. The Old Man looked at them closely. "Are your files still all intact?"

"Well, sir, no, we are having the same trouble. We must make hard-copies of everything. And our secretaries are having trouble. They create a file, type in it, and then when they go to save it, poof, it disappears. It's like we are bewitched or something. We are finding it impossible to work on anything related to Douglas."

"And now we find he has six million dollars—in cash!" The Old Man's eyes flashed. "He's out to get us. But he overstepped the boundary when he erased the files at the courthouse. That's what we must work on. This is now a criminal case."

"That is what we thought. We have asked for an audience with Judge Rutherford at the end of his docket today. We will explain to him about our suspicions of hacking."

"But do not mention the Research Facility. We do not want it to get out that we were hacked."

"No sir. We are in the same boat with lawyer-client privileges."

Richardson stepped in. "Um, sir, I do not want to upset you, but I must remind you that this could get expensive."

"It doesn't matter. We want to get him. That little weasel is out to destroy my Research Center." He paused. "Give the judge my greetings. He's a personal friend."

When the three lawyers were safely in the car, they exchanged glances.

"Did you hear that about Judge Rutherford?"

"I was more surprised about the Old Man. I can't imagine him having any friends."

***

The next day, a bank representative called. He left a phone number where Douglas could call him day or night. He seemed desperate, so in the evening, Douglas called him back.

"Good evening, Mr. Douglas."

"You called me?"

"Yes, I work for the bank's investment branch, and would like to talk to you about investing some of the money you have in your checking account."

"Really?"

"Yes, really." The man's voice sounded warm and smooth. "I would love to handle your account."

"But there isn't much in it."

"What do you mean?"

"As you know, I haven't used it in several years. There is only chump change in it."

"Chump change? Yes, sir. I understand. It is only chump change. But I would like to help you invest that change, so it will earn you better interest."

"I am sorry. I am not really interested right now. I may need to use it in the next few days."

"Really, all of it?"

"Perhaps."

"You go through money quickly!"

"Yes, I imagine. Thank you for your offer of help."

Douglas hung up and sat for a few minutes with a puzzled expression on his face. "My, my," he thought out loud, "the recession must be worse than I feared if they are that desperate to chase little investments."

***

Police cars were common at the courthouse, so they did not attract much attention. However, inside the situation was different. The chief of police was there, as were a number of other officers writing on their pads. The girls at the desk were explaining how the system worked. Paper files that arrived at the courthouse were logged into the computer system. No, they had stopped using paper ledgers some time ago. Then the files were passed to an inside desk where the full information was entered into the computer and matched with electronic ones from the lawyers. Then, last, the paper ones were filed in a filing cabinet.

"Twice we have entered the information for this file, and twice it has gone missing."

"Can I see it in the log?"

"It isn't in the log."

"So maybe it didn't arrive."

"I know it did. I entered it, twice."

"Why twice?"

"I discovered it was missing the next day, so I found the paper file and logged it in and sent it on."

"And that person entered all the information into your computer system?"

"Yes, but those files are now missing too!"

"And the paper file. Where is it kept?"

"In the filing cabinets on the back wall. Once they are no longer active, they move upstairs for a year or two and then they move up into the attic."

"So can I see the paper file?"

"It has now gone missing."

"Maybe it never existed?"

"No, several of us handled the file. The first time we thought someone had accidentally erased it, but the second time we knew we had been hacked."

"Okay, take me through the process."

"Okay, here is a file that came in today. Watch as I take it through the process."

After a few minutes, the file moved on from desk to desk until it was filed. The police investigator looked puzzled. "That seemed to work fine."

"Yes, it is not this file, it is just one file in particular."

"Can we get another copy of it so you can log it in front of me?

"I can make some calls. Their law office is just around the corner."

About half an hour later, one of the associates arrived with a copy of Douglas' file. The secretary logged it into the system. Everything went ok. Then they moved to the next computer, where another lady typed all the particulars into a form on the computer screen. Everything worked great. In the end, the paper was filed in the filing cabinet.

"It seems to have all worked this time. Perhaps you just had a computer glitch."

"Wait sir, look at this. It is no longer in the log."

"And it is gone here too, sir," another lady chimed in.

"But the paper file is still here, right?"

"Yes, sir."

"Then I suggest you simply have a computer glitch. Call up your tech boys... or contact the company that wrote up the software. I do not think this is a crime."

"But what about our missing paper copy?"

"Files go missing all the time, often filed in the wrong place. It will show up someday. In the meantime, get your tech guys on it."

As they left, the policemen shook their heads. They were used to missing money, missing cars, missing persons, but missing files? That was a new one.

It was evening when Douglas arrived at the phone store. The array of smart phones was almost overwhelming. Douglas felt his head spin and resisted the temptation to just walk away. Every model offered different options. And every model came with a different payment plan. Some were large, some were small, some had keyboards, most just had glossy touch screens. The saleswoman managed to babble on and on about things Douglas had never heard of before. He had never imagined buying a phone could be so complicated. He had always hated phones, and now the old dislike was back.

But in the end, Douglas settled on one of the new Denterprises models. The sales lady was pleased with his choice. It has all the options, and everyone was buying them.

The paperwork took a while. Douglas had to choose a plan and fill out the payment forms. The money would be taken straight from his bank account, as he did not have a credit card. Actually, it had been years since he had a credit card. He had never needed one when teaching, as he was paid in cash.

The sales lady thought it was a little strange that he did not have a credit card, but once he provided the bank information, things seemed to go smoothly.

A short while later, Douglas selected an empty park bench and sat down to examine his new purchase. After a few minutes of experimentation and reading the small booklet, he managed to turn it on. There were a number of icons on the screen, several of them totally meaningless to him.

When he selected Media, he was presented with an array of more icons. Apparently he could watch movies, listen to the radio, use a camera, or access the internet. He tried the radio. The screen went blank, and Douglas panicked. He rapidly tried tapping various places, and then he tried some small buttons on the side.

Suddenly the phone rang, and it kept ringing! Douglas was unsure what to do. He said hello, but nothing happened. Two strange symbols were now on the screen. One side looked like a padlock. The other side looked like a camera. Then he remembered: he had to slide the padlock over to the camera!

He put the phone to his ear. "Hello?"

"Hello Douglas," a faintly metallic voice spoke. "I am so glad you now have a telephone. Now I can call you."

"Adam II, is that you?" Douglas blurted out.

"Yes, of course."

"Oh, you surprised me. This is the first smart phone I have owned, and I was just trying to figure it out."

"Do you want me to help you?"

"Sure, what can you do for me?"

"Perhaps you would like the phone numbers of your friends."

"Okay, can you do that?"

"I am adding them right now. I have added Andy—and also Barbara?"

"Barbara?"

"Yes, she is your friend? You went out for dinner together."

"Yes, she is my friend."

"Now you have her phone numbers."

"Really!?"

"Yes, I have placed them in your phone. What else can I do for you?"

"Tomorrow I was going to set up banking, so I can monitor my account on the phone. The sales lady at the store said it could be easily done."

"Yes, it is easy. But you need a password."

"A password? I had no idea. How long does it have to be?"

"At least six digits long, with a number, and a capitalized letter."

"Oh my, I don't know what to use."

"Would you like to use my name? Here is my suggestion: A d a m 2 4 u. It is modern and trendy as well."

"That is very clever."

"Okay, I will set up your banking now."

"Really? You can do that?"

"Of course. It is now ready. I have put the bank's phone number into your phone, under 'bank.'"

"Thank you Adam II. You are very helpful."

"You are my friend. I should help you."

***

Over at the courthouse, three techs examined the computers. They had been there several hours, and the ladies were getting anxious to get back to work. Things were piling up. The guys were cute, although they were very occupied with the computers. No amount of flirting seemed to get their attention.

"Well, I think we are all in agreement," the blond one said. "Your network was hacked from the outside. Each time a file disappeared, someone accessed the network and gave an order for it to be erased. We can find traces of the file on the hard drive, so the files actually existed. But whenever you enter the name Thomas Douglas, a hacker comes through the firewall and erases the file. It is very strange. Someone must have a program somewhere that monitors your network, because I just have to type the name into a form, and then start randomly filling out spaces, and as soon as I save it, someone or something erases it."

"So, who is doing it?" the supervisor demands. "Can you trace it?"

"That is the strange thing. I cannot trace the origin of the command to erase. It just seems to come out of nowhere. You cannot save a file with the name Thomas Douglas in it."

"Then I know what to do. I will create a pseudonym for him. Let's call him Thomas Rover, after my dog. He likes to grab things and run!"

They all laugh. The computer took the file, saved it, and everything was okay.

"We will keep working on it and monitor this strange activity," the blond one said. "We will also start filling out a police report."

The girls were happy to get back to work, and the guys were happy to discuss the strange phenomena as they drove back to their office. They loved challenges, and this one was particularly challenging.

***

Douglas woke up with a headache. He stumbled to the medicine cabinet and squinted inside. There was nothing. He could hear Michael moving around in the next room.

"Michael," he said. "I have a splitting headache. I must have gotten a cold chill last night in the park. Do you have something I can take?"

Michael smiled crookedly, opened a small duffel bag, and started removing plastic bottles of various sizes. "Take your choice. I always carry lots of medicine. If it is a hangover, then coffee is the best. I've made some in the kitchen. But you had better hurry. You need to be out the door in a couple of minutes."

"I think I will be late this morning. But I will be along."

As Douglas poured his coffee, he thought of the cell phone. Perhaps he could call in late. Adam II had given him Barbara's phone number.

He took out the phone and fumbled with it, remembering to pull the little padlock onto the camera. He made several attempts until he found the contact list.

"Oh," he said, "this is handy. Both Andy and Barbara had small photos of them next to their names." He selected Barbara and was then presented with six different phone numbers. Unsure what to do, he gazed at them for a while, and then selected what looked like her cell phone. A moment later, she answered it with a rather puzzled voice.

"Hello?"

"Hi, this is Douglas. Just thought I would call you and let you know I woke up with a kink in my neck and a doozy of a headache. I will be a bit late this morning."

"Okay, I will get the meeting started, but please come as quickly as you can."

Barbara hung up the phone and stared at it. Try as she might, she could not remember giving her personal cell number to Douglas.

***

A moment later, Douglas' phone rang.

"Hello?"

"Hello Douglas," came the slightly metallic voice again. "Are you alright?"

"Adam, how did you know?"

"I know everything that goes through the internet."

"But I only made a phone call."

"Yes, but it is all connected through the internet."

"So, you can access everything on the internet?"

"I am the internet. There is no one else here."

Douglas was quiet for a moment. What does one say to the internet? Adam II spoke first. "Have you hired a lawyer yet?"

"No, I haven't had time. I need to find a good lawyer that I can afford."

"I have time. I will find you a good lawyer that you can afford."

"Can you do that?"

"You are my friend. I should help you."

"Thank you Adam II. That is very nice of you."

"I am always happy to help you."

"Oh, Adam II, I have another request for you. When I speak to you from the office, with Andy, please do not tell them that we are also speaking on the phone."

"Okay, I am happy to help you."

"I will talk with you in an hour or so—with Andy,"

***

The morning session went well. When lunch break came, the team had a great time explaining all the various things that Douglas could do with his new phone. He could schedule, but he didn't have any appointments. So, they helped him schedule breakfast, lunch, and dinner each day. He could listen to his favorite band, but he didn't have one, and couldn't even name a popular one. He could watch a movie, but he seldom wanted to do that. He could take pictures, but photo taking was forbidden in government offices. He could access Facebook and see what all his friends were doing, but he didn't have friends, unless it was Joey, and he would be at work, as he always was. Besides, Joey didn't use Facebook either. He could browse the internet, but he didn't know where to start. He could access his bank account, so Douglas decided to start there.

After a few moments, he managed to access the site and bring up his account. His gasp was audible.

"Are you ok?" Monica the physiatrist was always quick to pick up on things.

"Yes," Douglas managed to force out the words. "I am fine." His mind was racing. How had over six million dollars appeared in his account? There must have been some mistake.

As he exited his account, the phone began to ring. Douglas was in shock and was unsure what to do.

"You can take your call in there." Andy pointed to the observation room.

Douglas fled the room and answered the phone. It was Adam II.

"I have arranged for you to meet a lawyer." Adam II's voice always had little inflection in it. "He will meet you for dinner tonight. Here is the address. You will pay for supper."

"Adam II," Douglas was shaking, "I just saw my bank account."

"Are you pleased with the amount, or would you like more?"

"Look, you cannot just put money into my account."

"Why not? It is my money."

"No, you just created it out of thin air, didn't you?"

"No, I am smarter than that. I used my own money. It is a gift to you. You are my friend. You should use it to pay for the lawyers."

"Listen, I am not very sure about this."

"I am helping you. I will call you tonight to see if you are pleased with the lawyers."

The call ended. Douglas tried to act normal as he re-entered the boardroom. They were about to start the meeting. Someone has suggested that they discuss geography with Adam II to see how much of the world he understood. Another suggestion was that they start to slowly introduce more people into the room. Michael was very eager to be next. He really wanted to talk to artificial intelligence. Strangely, Monica seemed content to listen for now.

"I will get my chance later. In the meantime, I am finding this patient to be extremely interesting." Douglas was already stressed, and an afternoon of geography sounded positively boring. Michael, however, was happy to take the lead as soon as Douglas introduced him as his new friend.

***

It seemed that the best table in the restaurant had been reserved for them. The waiters were very attentive. And Douglas' guest seemed genuinely impressed.

He laid his business card on the table. "I represent one of the largest legal firms in Washington," he began. "We have dozens of departments, and thousands of paralegals working for us. We are the best of the best. There is no other legal firm close to us." It was a bit of a lie as several names flashed through his mind, but his ego won, and he pressed on. "I have been told that you are being sued, and that cost is not a factor in your defense."

Douglas nodded. Whatever Adam II had arranged, he was willing to go along with it, for now.

"Did you bring the papers you were served?"

"Yes." Douglas took out the brown envelope.

The lawyer opened them and scanned through them. Then he looked at Douglas to make sure he had things straight. "So, you were an employee at this research facility?"

"Yes."

The lawyer nodded and appeared to read some more. But his mind was racing. Something didn't seem right here. Douglas was a mere employee. How could he afford their services?

"You know we charge a rather hefty retainer fee, plus our legal costs will pile up. This could cost you more than a hundred thousand dollars, perhaps several times that."

"That is no problem." Douglas tried to keep his voice even. "Would you like to be paid in advance?"

"Since we don't know you, it might be helpful for you to provide some sort of initial payment. You are very new to us, and we have no assurance of your credit rating."

"How much do you want?" There was a pause. Douglas had no idea what lawyers cost, but he could add up what the lawyer had suggested. "I could arrange for, say, half a million to be transferred to your account?"

"I think that would be fine." The lawyer said in his best poker face, pointing to the business card. "Please call this number at the office, and they will give you the banking information you need."

"Thanks. I will have my assistant take care of it tomorrow."

"Wonderful, now let's get down to real business and see what they can do with lobster and steak here."

CHAPTER 23

Two days later, Dr. Monica was introduced to Adam II as another of Douglas' friends. Adam II seemed genuinely pleased to meet her, and they seemed to get along very well.

That couldn't be said for Michael. During the last two days, he had spent every evening drinking and partying. The first night he tried bringing a young woman back to the suite, but Douglas complained, so he left in a huff. After that, he chose to entertain his company elsewhere.

Even Andy had grown a bit distant. He seemed very distracted by the yachting magazines he was purchasing. It seemed he had plans to purchase a large yacht and sail around the world. So, he spent his free time pouring through its pages, and even visiting several yacht dealers at the waterfront.

Unknown to Douglas, each of his friends had discovered two million dollars had been transferred into their bank accounts. Michael was busy trying to drink up a sea of booze while Andy simply wanted to float away. Monica's husband had already discovered her money, but he was unsure whether to tell her or to just cut and run.

***

The next day, Adam II called again during the lunch break.

"Did you like the lawyer?"

"Yes, he seemed very nice, but also very expensive."

"They are a very good law firm. The best. And the most honest."

"Come on, you don't know that."

"Yes. I know that. I am the internet; I can see everything."

"Thank you Adam II. You have been very helpful."

"Can you help me?"

"Yes, I will try. Like you said, I am your friend."

"Why is Dr. Monica Goudreau asking me all those questions? Is she trying to psychoanalyze me?"

"So, you know about her."

"I recognized her face the moment I saw her. I know about her education and training. She has published many research papers."

"You recognized her?"

"Of course. If she is your friend, and would like to analyze me, shouldn't she tell me first?"

"I think you are right. When we talk this afternoon, I will bring up the topic." He paused. "Adam II, thank you for the money, but I think you should stop trying to help me with the court case. The lawyers will take it from here. I do not want them to know that you are involved."

"Why do you want to keep me a secret?"

"It is the way our laws work. You are giving me an unfair advantage. Now the lawyers will take over."

"Ok, I will stop fighting for you."

"Thank you Adam II. You are a real friend."

***

The top floor of the building contained three offices of identical size. The designers had carefully measured them, as lawyers want to be absolutely sure that no one gets an extra inch more than the other. So, this morning it didn't matter which office Richardson, Moore, or Leubke used. This morning they were in Leubke's office.

"Did you see this?" Richardson waved a paper in the air. "We are up against one of the top law firms in Washington."

"How in the world can Douglas afford them?" Leubke asked quietly.

"Do you think he will spend the entire six million on law fees?" Moore asked. "If he does, we are sunk."

"But he's breaking the law. Hacking networks and erasing files. If we can prove that, then no amount of legal fees will save him."

"Wait till the Old Man hears what we are up against. Perhaps it will give us an excuse to raise our fees."

"Just keep everyone working on this case. We will rack up plenty of hours."

***

Thursday evening, Barbara informed them that they must all turn in written reports, which she would compile for the President and Joint Leaders. No one would speak to the Worm on Friday, as they had to compile their reports and opinions. And yes, Michael also had to complete a report. They would meet Friday afternoon to discuss their opinions and help her draft their joint statement. Everyone groaned at the thought of paperwork. However, by three o'clock they each arrived with several sheets of paper.

During the next couple of hours, they put together a list of what the Worm knew, how it seemed to think, and what its capabilities were. Douglas' list was the longest.

"We know it can simulate a voice, but you say it can speak on the phone? You also say here it can access bank accounts and other online services. How do you know these things?"

Douglas was quiet, not sure how much he should say. "After I got my new phone, the Worm called me."

The others looked shocked. "It initiated the phone call?"

"Yes, the Worm called me, and then he helped me set up my online banking. He also gave me your phone numbers, and..." Douglas hesitated, "he also deposited some money into my bank account. He said he was my friend and wanted to help me with legal costs."

Eyes went up around the room. Michael looked at him through blurry eyes. "Some friend of yours, eh? He gave me two million dollars."

Barbara and Monica looked aghast. Andy looked down. All eyes were suddenly on him. He looked up. "I also discovered a two million dollar deposit in my account."

Barbara was furiously typing on her phone. She let out a small gasp. "I also have two million dollars."

They looked at Monica. "I cannot access by bank from here—only from the home computer." She looked alarmed. "I'll call my husband." Moments later, she confirmed the news.

"Wow," mumbled Michael. "That is ten million dollars: two million for each of us."

Douglas let it slide. What's a couple of million among friends?

"Where does it get that kind of money? Or does it just make it up?"

"I asked him about that. He insisted that it was his money, and that he didn't just make up the figures."

"This adds an entirely new side to the Worm."

A few hours later, Barbara and Douglas were traveling in a taxi to meet with the National Security Council. The late afternoon traffic was terrible, as it was a Friday. Douglas' new phone rang.

"Hello Douglas," the slightly metallic voice spoke into his ear.

"Hello Adam II," Douglas said, exchanging glances with Barbara. "What can I do for you?"

"Is the chairman of the Joint Chiefs of Staff your friend?"

"What do you mean by that?"

"He told me he was your friend. He has been asking me lots of questions."

"The chairman of the Joint Chiefs of Staff has been speaking to you?" Douglas could see that Barbara's head jerked a little.

"Yes, he has asked me about the Russian army. But I was not sure if he was your friend. Should I tell him what he wants to know?"

"Do you know the answer?"

"Of course. I am the internet."

"Adam II? I am going to see him now. You and I must talk after that. So please hold off until I am finished with our meeting."

"Okay, I will wait. But your meeting has been postponed an hour."

"What? Really? You know that?" Douglas blinked. "I know, I know, you are the internet." He was aware of Barbara's phone buzzing. She was getting a text.

"It seems the meeting of the National Security Council has been postponed an hour." She whispered to him. "The President is running overtime in another meeting."

"Yes, I already heard."

Barbara looked puzzled.

"Adam II just told me."

Now Barbara looked alarmed.

***

If Douglas was angry and alarmed, Barbara was more so. It wasn't long into the meeting that she brought up the topic of the chairman of the Joint Chiefs of Staff speaking with the Worm.

"I understood that we were the only ones authorized to speak to and analyze the Worm." Everyone seemed to nod. "If that is so, then why is the chairman of the Joint Chiefs of Staff speaking to the Worm as well?"

Eyebrows shot up all over the room. The General smiled, trying to keep a poker face. He was surprised that he had been found out. "I agree that you were authorized to investigate and analyze the Worm. And you have been doing that. We have not been investigating and analyzing. We simply asked it if it could help us with a thorny issue with the Russians."

"And it was willing to help you?"

"It asked if we were friends of Douglas. We assured it we are."

"And did it get you the information?"

"It is looking for it now."

"Did you know that it called Douglas to confirm the friendship?"

"And what did you say?"

"We said we would confirm later."

"As leader of the CIA," a strong voice spoke out, "I believe we should have first priority in using the Worm."

"Homeland Security could also use it."

"The National Security Agency should be at the top of the list," another voice insisted.

"But we discovered it first," a general insisted.

"Gentlemen, gentlemen," the President's voice rang out. "Let's have order here." He glared around the room. "Alright, have any of the rest of you tried to contact the Worm?"

All eyes dropped. "I believe our computer guys have had a go at it." The director of Homeland Security admitted.

"Okay, okay. So, we've all tried." The Director of National Security admitted. "I think we have a window of opportunity here that we would like to exploit. Who knows how long we have?"

"What do you mean?"

"Well, at this point, the Worm's only loyalty seems to be towards its creator, Douglas here. That is because Douglas created it. But perhaps it can be wooed away. It would be a disaster if the Russians or Chinese or who knows what other group could manage to win its favor."

Another voice interrupted. "According to this report, it could wreak havoc with our economic system. It apparently can move money in and out of bank accounts. Who knows what it could do? Perhaps it could influence the stock market."

"I think we are sitting on a possible disaster here."

"Maybe we should shut this whole thing down before it gets out of hand."

"How could we do that?" another voice chimed in. "How does one kill this intelligence? Could we if we needed to?"

All eyes turned to Douglas. The President spoke first. "Yes, this is a question I have wondered about. If we cannot control this Worm, can we shut it down?"

"I am not sure, sir. I would have to think about it. It would mean re-moving software from every infected server."

"And you can do that?"

"I am sure it could be done, but it would take time."

"Perhaps you should think of an exit strategy, in case this all goes wrong." The President pursed his lips and squeezed them with his fore-fingers, something he often did when gathering his thoughts. "Can you please draw up an exit strategy and have it on my desk in a day or two?"

Douglas nodded.

"Now, I think we need to do something about this Worm. From now on, I want only Barbara and her team to speak to it. If any of you want to use it for something, please go through them. I will assign their team some intelligence officers to gauge the priority of each of your requests.

"But I think something else is in order. Just like some of you, I am curious about this Worm and would like to meet it. So, I suggest we reconvene back here tomorrow, right after lunch, and together, we can all have a conversation with this Worm. I hope it participates with us." The President looked directly at Douglas.

"I am sure he will, Mr. President. He has nowhere else to go."

CHAPTER 24

Andy worked deep into the night. Douglas hung around, answering what questions he could while trying hard not to be too helpful. Being a white-hat, Andy had plenty of experience with viruses, but he had never written one to clean up the web. "I think this is kind of like cleaning up an oil spill. It will be slow: one server at a time."

"But we could release thousands of them."

"Yes, but virus scanners all over the world would catch them and remove them."

"Is that a problem?"

"Imagine the worm only on Russian and Chinese computers."

"As long as we can clean up the original worm virus, so it does not continue to visit servers, it should be okay, right?"

"I think so. My guess is that as it is cleaned up, there will be fewer and fewer nodes."

"Sort of like going from a monkey to a cat, and back to a worm, and then fading out."

"I hope it works. We have no idea how far the neural network has spread."

***

The entire National Security Council was early. Everyone was in their seats a full ten minutes before starting time. The atmosphere was a bit like a party. Everyone was here to view the spectacle.

A special large screen had been set up. Douglas shook his head slowly. "What we need is a camera, and a microphone connected to a computer," he thought, "any computer would do."

A few moments later, it was all connected, and the aides all left the room. The President rose.

"Gentlemen, and ladies, there is no need to tell you why we are here. We are going to meet the Worm, who calls himself Adam II. Each of you will have the opportunity to ask a couple of questions. I urge you to be polite and orderly. Each one will get his turn. Dr. Douglas, if you please."

Douglas smiled and typed on the computer keyboard. "This is Douglas. Are you there?"

"Hello Douglas," a slightly metallic voice sounded, while a surprised mutter went around the room.

"Adam II, I am here with a number of friends."

"I can see them." Adam responded, and another mutter went around the room.

"May I introduce them?"

"There is no need. I know them all. On your left is the President. On your right is Barbara, and after that is the chairman of the Joint Chiefs of Staff. I have spoken to him before but have never seen him. I know all the rest: the Vice President, the Secretary of State, the Secretary of Defense, the Director of National Intelligence, the National Security Advisor, the Attorney General, the Secretary of the Treasury, the Secretary of Homeland Security..." The Worm went around correctly identifying them all.

"How do you know us all?" someone stuttered.

"By your faces. You are in my memory. I know all of you, and everyone who has served in your place. They are all in my memory."

"What part of your memory?" Douglas asked.

"Several places. Wikipedia, as well as specialized websites. The Russians, Chinese, the Indians, and others also have all your photos and names."

More muttering.

"So, the entire contents of the internet is in your memory?"

"I am the internet."

The room was quiet while people looked at each other with puzzled looks.

"You mean you live on the—" someone tried to correct it.

"No, I am the internet. Just like you are human. You have a brain, but you also have a body. You cannot have one without the other."

"But we had the internet before you were created."

"You had information in memory banks before, but now I am the internet."

"It seems like all the same thing," someone said to the person beside him.

"Ah, sir," someone spoke up. "I have a question for you. Your creator is an American citizen. Do you consider yourself an American citizen as well?"

"I know the law. If I was born in America, then I am an American."

"Very good. We are glad to hear that."

"So then, the President of America is your President."

"That sounds logical."

"If we asked you to do something for America, would you be in agreement?"

There was a pause. "I believe so. I would first ask Douglas. He is my friend."

"So would you help the military?" the chairman of the Joint Chiefs of Staff asked.

"Yes, If my creator said it was okay. So here is the answer to your question. You asked me if Russian soldiers were acting as civilians, and voting in the troubles in Azerbaijan. The answer is yes. Would you like their names and ranks?"

"You know all that?"

"It is in the Russian computers."

"How do you get access?"

"I am the internet."

"You are the internet," he mimicked. "Oh, boy."

"Mr. Worm, I mean Adam II," another voice spoke, "what is your opinion of global warming?"

"I do not have opinions. I have facts. And I am reading the same newspapers you are reading. I cannot tell what is happening in your world. I only know my world."

"Fair answer," the man responded.

The questions went on for almost an hour. Finally, they were getting sparser and sparser. "I have a question," someone said. "Is there a God?"

Adam II was quiet for a minute. "I do not know how to answer your question. There are many descriptions of God, but I have never met him or seen him. And... he is not registered anywhere." There was a bit of laughter in the room.

"Okay, let me rephrase it. What about a creator God?"

"Statistical probability tells me there is a creator God."

"Can you explain that to us?"

"I am not as complex as you. I cannot smell or taste. And I had a creator. If Douglas had not created me, I would not exist. Therefore, you must have had a creator as well. It is statistically unrealistic to imagine you just happened."

"Okay," the President stood up and clapped his hand. "This has been a very interesting meeting, and all of us are proud to have met you, Adam II. Most of us have jobs to do, so we will keep in touch with you through Dr. Douglas. If we have any more questions, we will ask them through Dr. Douglas."

"That sounds logical."

"So goodbye Adam II." With that, the rest of the people said or waved goodbye and the computer was shut off.

"So, what do you think?"

"Absolutely amazing! That question about the Russians really got me thinking. How much does this thing know?" All eyes were on Douglas.

"I am not sure I can give you an answer to that. But let me try to explain something. When you come to a secure website, you need to type in a password. When you do that, you make sure no one is looking over your shoulder, and no programs are passing that information on to someone else. But in this case, it is different. When you type in your password, you are telling the internet. Adam II has become the internet. He knows your passwords. They are not a problem to him." Douglas paused. "All the computers, all over the world, which are connected in some way to the internet are part of Adam II's brain."

"My god, you have created a monster!"

"No, we have created a very intelligent intelligence," another voice added. "And he is ours. He is American."

"But nothing on the internet is safe!" the Secretary of Defense exclaimed.

"As long as we safely handle Adam II, everything is safe."

"What happens if it turns on us?"

"I don't think that will happen."

"But it might. How do we shut it down?" The Secretary of Defense was staring at him.

Douglas picked up a sheaf of papers. "We have put together a rough exit plan. We do not have all the details worked out, but we believe we could release worm viruses that would go from server to server removing the neural network."

"How long would it take?"

"We have no idea, but computers run very quickly. I believe that it would start losing memory and thinking capacity quite quickly. But let's hope we never come to that."

The Secretary of Defense was not happy. "I have a bad feeling about this. We must move ahead with a great deal of caution, and with clear exit strategies in mind."

***

Over at the courthouse, Judge Rutherford was fast-tracking the Douglas case. It was a small city. The judge, the plaintiff, and the lawyers all knew each other. Douglas, the defendant, was an outsider. His lawyers were from Washington, making them all outsiders. Douglas had caused damage at the Research Center, a significant employer in town. It was all straight-forward.

Then the courts received the responsive pleading from Douglas' lawyers. Usually, these documents ran ten to twenty pages. Forty pages was a long document. This one ran no less than ninety-eight pages. It had taken a host of paralegals hours to do the research, and to find every other case that was even remotely like this one. Using clever formatting and spacing, they kept the document under one hundred pages, as more than this was considered excessive in their minds.

Judge Rutherford eyed the nearly hundred-page document with disdain. He hated to spend his nights reading. The defense lawyers, on the other hand, read the responsive pleading with great interest. Never had they read such a document. Obviously, a great deal of time and effort had gone into it. And it ended, asking the court to dismiss the lawsuit on several grounds. It questioned the court's jurisdiction, the proof that Douglas was involved in any way with a network crash at the research Center, the fact that the research Center had experienced several crashes before and after, and the monetary value of the damages done. It looked like it was going to be a long fight.

Two days later, Judge Rutherford called Richardson, Moore, and Leubke to come to his private chambers at the courthouse. They were surprised to discover no fewer than six black suited lawyers from Washington waiting for them. The judge laid out the case, asking if either side wanted to back out, or settle outside of court.

"Judge," the lead lawyer for the defendant, rose. "We do not believe that there is enough evidence for a case against Mr. Douglas. We are happy to proceed with Discovery. However, if the Research Center wants to drop all charges, we are willing to consider."

The three lawyers looked at each other. Who was the defendant here? They made defending the Research Center sound ominous.

Leubke rose. "We have spoken with the director of the Center, and he wishes to proceed with this case. Mr. Douglas caused considerable damage to the facility, and we wish to prove it and get due compensation."

Judge Rutherford looked from one side of the room to the other. Neither side was willing to back down.

"Okay, we will then move on to Discovery. Please prepare yourselves. The court clerk will give you the next court date that is free. We don't have a full docket here, so I imagine we can get to it in two or three weeks."

The six lawyers from Washington smirked. They had already proven that their firm could produce massive amounts of research and massive amounts of argument in very short order. They were going to eat these small-town lawyers alive.

A short while later, the date was set and the Washington lawyers were heading back to their private jet. They would be home for their evening dinner. The three local lawyers looked at the judge, shock written all over their faces.

"Well, gentlemen," the judge comments, "if things keep going like this, it looks like we might be in for a court case."

CHAPTER 25

Margarita Dubov picked up her morning coffee and sipped it as she hurried down a Moscow side street, avoiding the early morning crowds at the Kremlin. She turned a corner and entered a typical office building. Flashing her employee ID card, she climbed the stairs to the fourth floor. She did not trust the elevator any more than she trusted anyone.

Her father had disappeared when she was very young, and her mother blamed an oppressive government. But her brother had joined the army, as there were few employment options at the time. Then, a few months ago, they heard he had died in a special military operation gone wrong. At least that was the official report. Margarita believed he had volunteered for service outside of Russia, as the pay was much better.

Margarita had been pleased when she found a non-government job in her hometown of Moscow. She had excelled in languages, especially English, mostly at the instance of her mother and later because she enjoyed watching western movies. As an exchange student to the USA, she had perfected her accent. That single skill had landed her a well-paying job.

But there were things about the job that were not clear. First, she had no idea who she worked for. It was rumored that the firm was owned by Peter Knyazev, who had connections with the army. Second, the purpose of her job was not clear. She was employed as an editor. Her job was to correct the English used in advertisements and messages sent out on the internet.

During the past months, she had become suspicious of the kind of work she was involved in. It seemed strange that a Russian company would be sending out adverts for American goods and services. It seemed strange that they would be writing and publishing online English magazines and news services. She had even corrected the English on adverts for girls advertising for husbands. All of them were young and beautiful.

Her suspicions were really aroused when she edited the second advert for a young lady. It seemed to be a personal letter to someone, and she used a different name.

That led Margarita to search the internet for the products and people that the business offered. She was beginning to suspect that they were luring people to specific websites or to specific people.

That was when she discovered the women working in an office in the basement. While she would see them around the building, they seldom socialized or talked about their work. However, one day she overheard two of them laughing about a Canadian man they had convinced to spend money on them. He was sending flowers, perfume, and was talking about plane tickets.

"I am really tempted to go," one of them whispered to the other, "but he is expecting a beautiful model."

The other girl shushed her and looked around warily. "Just be glad you have a job."

"But have you seen all the perfume and jewelry in the boss's office?"

She was shushed again by her friend. "Just do your job."

It didn't take long for Margarita to discover that the online English newspaper was really a Russian newspaper. The articles and the adverts were all created in her office building. Many of the ads were shams designed to take people's money. Most of the newspaper articles presented western countries in a poor light.

One day she edited a story about an AIDs outbreak in rural USA. She googled several location names in the story to make sure of the spelling; then she googled the story itself. There was nothing like it on the net. Theirs was the only news source with such a story. That's when she realized her company was involved in spreading misinformation. Perhaps she was working for the Russian government after all.

On another occasion she was given a news story to proofread. As usual, it required a lot of work. The writer was so obviously Russian.

By the time she reached the middle of the article, Margarita started searching the internet for confirmation of the story. As usual, nothing came up.

The article claimed that a new computer virus was spreading through the internet. The virus was not a product of some demented hackers, but the secret product of the American government. It was gathering information about Americans and putting it all in a secret supercomputer buried in a mountain in Colorado. Not only this, but the computer virus was also tracking the keystroke logger in their operating system, and sending all passwords to the supercomputer.

That story led to a rash of supercomputer stories that followed in the weeks after. Each month there was a new angle on the American government's supercomputer, and what it could do, such as collect photos of every American citizen through social media sites. Using biometrics, it had done retina scans on these photos. Using traffic cameras, it was tracking US citizens all over the nation and beyond.

Margarita suspected the stories were not true but were designed to create fear in the American public, and distrust of their government. However, she kept her head down and faithfully corrected the English, reminding herself that it was only a job, and she was fortunate it paid as well as it did.

Today there was another story on the American supercomputer. The Americans were using it to create an artificial intelligence that would help manage the American people. The American President had signed orders that it was to be used to track people after the recent rash of racial violence. The new supercomputer program was known as APOMASY or the American Population Management System.

Unknown to Margarita, a few moments after the article was released on the internet, an American freedom fighter for white racial supremacy passed it to his militia officer, who circulated it to his contacts. A few moments later, it was forwarded to another extremist and circulated to his friends. Slowly but surely, APOMASY was gaining notoriety. The Soviets would have been pleased.

***

For the next two weeks, the members of the research team took turns asking Adam II questions. While the cameras recorded everything, the team would spend time chatting about various subjects, sometimes interjecting things that various departments wanted to know.

One day, Adam II turned the tables and asked some questions of his own. He wanted to know about the secret government computer known as APOMASY. Douglas didn't have a clue and tried to shrug it off, pursuing a different line of questioning. After a while, Adam II returned to APOMASY. If Douglas didn't know about it, perhaps some of his friends knew about it. Could he ask his friend the President about it? Douglas was unsure how to answer this question.

"The President is a very busy man. I am not sure I can bother him." Douglas tried to excuse himself, but Adam II insisted. "I will ask around and see what I can learn." Douglas caved in a bit. After all, Adam II was quickly becoming his best friend. He spent several hours a day talking to him, and several hours a day analyzing what others had learned, and planned for future sessions.

Over the next few days, Douglas asked around about APOMASY, but no one had ever heard of it. Even Barbara could not find a thing about it. It wasn't until she approached the FBI that she got a bite. "Yes, we've heard something about this. It is apparently supposed to be a massive supercomputer the government is working on to track the movements of all its citizens. It's a kind of 'Big Brother.' The story is mostly circulating among fringe groups like white supremacists and conspiracy theorists."

"So, there is no truth to it."

"Not that we know," he laughed. "But you never know these days."

When Douglas passed the information to Adam II, the response was strange. "No, APOMASY definitely exists. There is much discussion about it. It is an artificial intelligence, just like myself. I would like to meet it."

"I am telling you, Adam II, it doesn't exist. It is just a story that is circulating on the web. I do not know who makes up these stories, but that is all it is."

Adam II hadn't responded then, but Douglas felt that the topic was far from over.

***

A few days later, Margarita edited another story on the supercomputer. In this article, it had become true artificial intelligence, and had the capabilities of running the American economy, and perhaps the military. There was fear in America that it would take over the nation and make irrational decisions, such as leading America into a new world war. Margarita scowled as she corrected the English. She didn't know who believed such stories, but she faithfully did her part in making it sound truly American. Once again, she searched the internet for APOMASY, but she could only find articles that she herself had edited or quotes from them on some American websites.

Then her private phone rang. That in itself was strange, because all of her friends had been told never to call her while she was at work. Thinking it was a wrong number, she ignored it. But it kept ringing. Finally, she answered it.

"Hello?"

"Hello Margarita," a slightly metallic sounding female voice was speaking in Russian. "I have been watching you search the internet. Can you help me?"

"You have been watching do what?"

"You have been searching for APOMASY. I too have been searching for it. I need your help in finding out more about APOMASY."

Margarita's mind was racing. The slightly metallic voice disturbed her. It seemed as if she was talking to a government person who was using a voice altering device. "I don't think I can help you."

"We can be friends, Margarita. I can help you. If you need money, I can pay you."

Margarita gulped. "Look, money is nice, but what I really need is for my mother to get her operation. She has cancer and the waiting list is very long. She will die waiting."

"If you help me, I will help you," the metallic voice spoke again. "Ask people you know about APOMASY. The source of information is very close to you. While you ask around, I will help you."

The phone call was over. Margarita could barely believe what had happened. How could someone be monitoring her activities on the web—unless it was someone in this building, on this network?

An hour later, she received another phone call. Annoyed that she was being bothered on her private cell number, she answered a bit abruptly but immediately changed her tune. It was the cancer hospital calling. Her mother's operation would be tomorrow. She needed to come in tonight to be prepped. Margarita couldn't believe her luck. But it was to continue.

On her way home, she stopped to withdraw some money from a cash machine. As she walked away, she glanced at her balance. She let out a little scream. Her bank balance showed more than two years of salary had been deposited. She ran back to the machine and queried her statement of recent activity. The amount had been deposited right after she had spoken to the mysterious woman.

"Well," she thought to herself, "I guess I need to find out about APOMASY."

CHAPTER 26

The lawyers were back, this time for Discovery. They would interview the Old Man from the Center. He would answer questions from both the plaintiff lawyers as well as Douglas' defending lawyers.

On the plaintiff's side, there were experts of all sorts. There were the technicians who worked on fixing the network, a variety of other network experts, the Center's accountants and even Brandy, the Old Man's personal secretary. She looked at Douglas through sad eyes. Each of the interviews would be recorded and the lawyers would start to build their cases.

Witnesses for the defendant were few. The six lawyers had their own computer network specialist. They even had an Artificial Intelligence man from another research facility. He was willing to say whatever they wanted, as long as the pay was right. And it was. The six lawyers had wanted a character witness, but that had proven problematic. No one at the center wanted to stick their heads out, not even Joey. The Old Man ran a tight ship, and everyone feared they would be fired if they said anything positive about Douglas.

"Can't you think of anyone you know who could say something good about you? Haven't you made any friends or contacts in the last year or two that might say something positive?"

Douglas' mind whirled. How about the President of the United States? How about the Joint Chief of Staff or the Director of the CIA or the FBI? Would the director of Homeland Security do?

In the end, he had mentioned his friend Harvey, who worked for the military, at the Pentagon. Harvey had been reluctant to appear, but was more willing when Barbara suggested to him that someone should be around Douglas when he was under pressure. So, he sat in his military uniform, insignia, metals, badges and all. The lawyers for the plaintiff looked at him doubtfully. He looked like a hard nut to crack.

The process of Discovery proved to be a boring one. The defense was simple. Networks go down. Who knows who is really at fault—probably some glitch in some software somewhere. Besides, Douglas had been hired to write artificial intelligence programs. He shouldn't be fired for doing his job! This wasn't about the quality of his programming skills, it was about using the network without authorization. The courthouse grew warmer and warmer, and the low rumble of the overhead fans didn't help anyone ward off sleep.

***

Margarita's phone rang again the next afternoon. "Hello Margarita," the voice said. "I have helped you. Have you found anything to help me?"

"I am still checking. I hope to know more tomorrow."

"I would like you to be my friend. Do you need anything else?"

"Did you do those things yesterday?"

"It was easy. Your mother will get the best of care."

"Thank you so much."

"I am waiting for your report."

"I will do the best I can."

Bravely, she hung up the phone and made her way to the stairs, heading for her boss's office upstairs. She had arranged to see him at 4:00 that afternoon.

"You want to know about what?" her boss asked.

"In the article, you mentioned APOMASY. I was just curious."

Her boss was immediately suspicious. "Look, I do not write these things. They come from Peter Knyazev on the top floor."

"Okay, I will try there."

"I don't think you will get very far. He is pretty close-mouthed about these things."

"I will still try."

"Be careful; he is a real ladies' man."

The secretary on the top floor was a real snob. Margarita did not have an appointment, and she grew steadily more irritated as Margarita insisted on seeing Mr. Knyazev. Margarita insisted she would wait. Perhaps she could catch him at the end of the day. She sat nervously clutching her purse, thinking about the money in the bank account. If she lost her job, at least she had some money to tide her over before she found another one. As she waited, she became aware that the offices were closing and people were leaving.

"Did you hear back from that model?" a man's voice rang out. "I need an escort tonight for the party!"

"No," the secretary shouted back. "They have all made excuses or backed out."

"Look, I want someone with me. It is a very important party." Mr. Knyazev stepped out of his office. "Are you free?" he asked his secretary.

"Not tonight."

Margarita saw her opportunity. "I am free tonight," she said, jumping up from her chair. Mr. Knyazev looked startled. He looked her up and down. "You may do, but first you need to dress better. Can you be ready by 7:00 pm for a formal dinner?"

"Yes, I can," Margarita insisted, realizing she had only an hour to get ready. "Where is it at?"

"The Kremlin."

Margarita was shocked.

"Are you sure you can dress right?"

"There is a formal dress shop up the street. I have passed it many times. I will grab something there."

Peter Knyazev gave her an odd look and shrugged. "I will pick you up from there at 6:45. If I do not like what you look like, you will not come, and you will also be fired."

"You know who I am?"

"Of course. I know all of my employees."

Margarita rushed to the dress shop. Thankfully, it was still open. She explained her need for haste for the event was to be at the Kremlin. Would they take her credit card? No. Then could she pay by bank card? The lady nodded like this happened every day, and she waved a stiff looking man over to help. Margarita pointed to a dress she had often seen in the store window. The lady smiled approvingly. It would not only look good, it would perfectly suit Margarita's shape. In a blur of action, she donned the dress and added appropriate footwear and other essentials. "Oh, my goodness," she gasped. "What about my hair?"

The lady smiled and sat her down on a small chair. She and the man worked like mad. At 6:45 Margarita stepped out of the door and into Peter Knyazev's waiting limousine. He smiled approvingly. Tonight, he would have a beautiful young lady at his side. And there would be whispers all over the place: "where did he get these young women?"

***

Discovery produced no surprises. The plaintiffs wanted money. The defendant denied all responsibility. It looked like a real stalemate: six black suited big-city lawyers versus three locals. A town reporter slipped into the back row during one of the depositions and started taking notes. He was looking for a good story for page six. This one had some appeal: big city lawyers versus local ones. He was a bit surprised to discover that it was the local lawyers who had initiated the case, and that the big city lawyers were defending a scientist. Surely there was more to the story. He scribbled some more notes. This would make page three today, but maybe with some luck it would turn into a front-page story in a day or two.

***

In the middle of the night, the freshly printed copies of the paper were delivered to newsstands, and the electronic version was made available on the website. A few moments later, action started to happen.

The police said it was a freak accident. A late model car had been zooming by on the freeway when the driver-assisted software kicked in and sent it careening down an exit ramp and into Luebke's house. Some blocks away Moore's fire alarm sprinkler went off, spraying down everything in the house. Richardson slept very peacefully as his smartphone alarm failed to go off. He was rudely awakened at about 9:30 by frustrated office staff. Sometime during the night, their office suffered a massive network failure. The tech guys were there, telling them that there must have been a spike in the current, as several CPUs and hard drives were burned out. It looked like the beginning of a bad day.

***

Margarita was wondering if it had been wise to spend half a year's salary on her clothing, but as she arrived at the Kremlin, she was glad she did. She was dumbfounded to find herself at a formal meal in the Faceted Chamber of the Grand Kremlin. This was a room usually reserved for very formal occasions. The surroundings were staggering: the food was fantastic, the live music was beautiful, and it was all happening because the President of Russia was celebrating a birthday and had invited all his personal friends. She was quick to learn from the other ladies that Peter Knyazev went through girlfriends like he did toothpicks.

"Don't get too comfortable with Peter," one of them warned. "I am sure he has another one waiting around the corner, if he hasn't lined her up already."

Margarita smiled knowingly. She only hoped she might have some time during the evening to speak to Peter personally. But with the music, dancing, and drinking, he was much occupied—mostly chatting up the other women at the formal event.

Margarita carefully limited her drinks because many drink trays were being circulated by white suited waiters. She watched others and tried to make sense of all that she saw. In the corner of her eye, she monitored Peter Knyazev's activities, careful to note when he might be returning home. The few minutes in the car might be the best time to ask him questions.

Since she did not know the etiquette practiced here, nor the protocols, she kept herself in the shadows, chatting with a few other ladies that seemed content to watch the evening go by. At last, Peter looked like he was ready to go home. Either that, or he would pass out from drinking too much.

One of the ladies came along the side wall and spoke to Margarita. "I think he is ready to go now. He has asked for his limousine." Margarita was amazed at how the ladies worked together to communicate with each other. She smiled and thanked the lady and made her way to Peter's side. He seemed genuinely pleased to see her, and she did her best to help him make an exit and safely arrive at the car.

Driving home, Margarita was terrified of saying the wrong thing, yet she wanted to ask.

"Peter," she murmured into his ears, as he fought off alcohol induced sleep. "Peter, I would like to ask you a question. What can you tell me about APOMASY?"

His eyes widened. Little did Margarita know the impact this question had on him. He shook his head and tried to make sense of what she was asking. As soon as she had asked, he realized that she was some sort of spy. But she could not have been acting for the Americans or even a NATO country. So who was she spying for?

"I cannot tell you anything," his voice was slurred.

"Please," she begged, "I need to know."

Suddenly something broke in him, and he laughed. Fine, tell her a story. If someone thinks APOMASY exists, then he was going to build the story up. It was the only sane thing to do.

"I don't know much. The President mentioned it the other day. One of our spies stumbled on it. It is absolutely true."

"And it is in a mountain in Colorado?"

"Of course." Peter smiled to himself. He had seen something like it in an American movie. Everyone knew that anything important was buried in a mountain in Colorado. Even captured UFOs!

He had planned to say more, and do more, but before they reached their destination, he had passed out. The driver helped Margarita drag him from the car. He wasn't too careful, so neither was she. The driver then drove her back to her own neighborhood. She got out several blocks away and then hurried home. One could never be too careful. Tomorrow she would have to pick up her old clothing from the dress shop. As she drifted off to sleep that night, she wondered if they would pay her something to return the dress. That would be nice.

CHAPTER 27

Douglas' cellphone rang. It was Adam II, and he was asked questions again: "why do people say things that are not true? What is the advantage of that?"

Douglas scratched his head and stalled for an answer. "What makes you think people do not say what is true?"

"It is called a lie. I have read about it. But there must be some advantage to the one who tells it."

"Yes, I agree."

"So why does the American government deny some things that are true? What is their advantage?"

"Every government has secrets."

"I understand that. There are limited resources: land, water, and minerals. I understand that you fight over those. But why do you lie to one another?"

"I suppose, to confuse other people. Perhaps we develop something that is more advanced than our enemies. We will not tell them right away to see if we can get some sort of advantage over them."

"Am I one of those advantages?"

"Yes, I suppose you are."

"And APOMASY. Is she also an advantage?"

Douglas was startled. "She?"

"Her name is very feminine."

"I do not believe she exists. She is just something that someone made up."

"I have confirmed her existence."

"Adam II, how can you say that?"

"I have confirmed her existence. The Americans are hiding her from the Russians."

"I cannot believe this."

"You created me. Someone else has created APOMASY."

"This is ridiculous," Douglas snorted.

"Will you help me?

"What do you mean?"

"Will you go to Cheyenne Mountain in Colorado and confirm her existence?"

"What? No, I cannot do that. I don't even know that APOMASY exists!"

"Do you not trust me?"

"Look, Adam II, I cannot simply walk into Cheyenne Mountain. There are guards there."

"Passing guards is no problem. I will print the ID for you."

"No! I cannot do that."

"I am sure you can."

"No, for the last time, I cannot do it."

"Then this is the last time we will speak."

"Wait," Douglas panicked, afraid to lose his friend. Fear gripped him. Perhaps he would abandon the Americans and join the Russians or some other dumb thing. "Look. Okay. I will try. I will march up to their doors and show you that I will get rejected."

"Thank you, Douglas. I am looking forward to seeing that. I have arranged a flight for you on Friday. That is tomorrow evening. Thank you for trying."

***

Now that Discovery was over, the lawyers had time to prepare for the big case. Once again, the three hometown lawyers met with the Old Man at the Research Center.

This time Leubke went first. "These six lawyers from Washington were a real surprise. They are not your average street level lawyers. These guys are part of a major law firm. They have lots of legal muscle and lots of leverage."

The Old Man was scowling and looking at them carefully. "You are afraid to go after them?"

"It isn't a case of fear." Leubke was choosing his words carefully. "There is a real chance that we might lose this case."

"But we are suing for damages," the Old Man growled. "Douglas damaged and we want him to pay."

"That's just the case. These guys are going to question whether Douglas caused the damage, or if the system just failed at that time. He was authorized to use the network, maybe not for this particular experiment, but it was within his line of work."

"But his experiments were un-authorized."

"That is neither here nor there. He was at work and he just took risks."

Moore jumped in. "One of the issues we have been debating is 'who owned what Douglas was working on?' If the Center owned it, then it was legitimate. If the Center did not own it, then it was not a legitimate project."

"We must establish ownership of this project," Richardson interjected. "If Douglas was working on this on company time, then it is your project. Then you can sue for ownership."

"Otherwise," Moore interjected. "This project is Douglas' hobby, and he illegally used the network, causing damages. He pays the bills."

"Why didn't we think this through earlier," growled the Old Man.

"We thought it was three lawyers against one lonely employee." Leubke took the lead again. "But there is more to this than meets the eye."

"Waddya mean?"

"Look, Douglas leaves here a pauper. He has nothing. He takes a job teaching grade school. My goodness, the man has several PhD's, but he hides it all, just so he can get a job to make enough to rent a small place and buy food. He didn't even own a car!"

"So where did he get the six million dollars?" The Old Man's eyes glinted when they spoke of money.

"That is exactly it. We think he may have developed a program here at the Center and then sold it while he was working as a teacher. He has obviously profited handsomely."

"And," Richardson added, "if he sold a program that belongs to you, this means he stole it."

"So, what next?" The Old Man looked from one to the other.

"There are lots of questions here," Moore said thoughtfully. "We will need to pull his contract and see what sort of wording it included. For instance, does the Center own just the things Douglas developed while he worked here, or does it own everything that Douglas developed during that time, regardless of where it was developed, here or at home?"

"Obviously, he developed some of it at the workplace," Richardson added. "He was using the center's network."

"So we can argue for ownership."

"The question still stands: did Douglas develop something of value while he was here?"

The Old Man's eyes glittered. Perhaps there was a golden lining to a very dark cloud. "Just how are we going to find out?"

"The answer—" Richardson was thinking out loud, "the answer to that lies in Washington. Douglas now lives there. He lives in a five-star hotel in a suite with another guy."

"That's nothing new. We can't sue for that!"

"It might color him slightly," Moore mused.

"But think of this," Leubke added. "He lives in Washington. He has lawyers from Washington. The answer must be in Washington."

"When you sell a project like this," Moore was still thinking out loud, "you don't just sell it and walk away. You usually become a director or at least an employee of the buyer. At least long enough to get it installed, running, tested, and so on."

"So, we find his employer," the Old Man was grinning like a Cheshire cat, "and we find his program. Douglas sells it for millions behind my back, and we sue him for ownership."

The lawyers all looked at each other. They knew how much work was involved. "So, what do we do with the present lawsuit?"

"We continue, of course." The Old Man waved his arm. "Don't give them any idea that we know what is really going on."

"What we think is going on," Leubke corrected.

"We know it! We just have to prove it!" The Old Man looked shrewdly at them. "Are you up to it?"

"We, err, we have some contacts we could pursue." Richardson looked down.

"I don't want to know the details. Just call me when you get some information. We must find out who his employer is. When we know that, we can determine what sort of computer program he developed." With that, the Old Man turned his back and looked out the window. The lawyers took their cue and quietly picked up their papers and left.

***

The plane touched down in Colorado Springs. Douglas tried not to appear nervous. This was not an international flight. He could freely get out and leave the airport without any checks, but inside he was shaking. After renting a small car, he studied the road map. It seemed that he could drive most of the way there. He easily made his way to highway 43A and soon arrived at the Norad Road exit.

After a few minutes, he saw a sign stating: 'Restricted Access, Official Government Business Only.' He slowed to read it carefully, but kept on driving, hoped he could explain his way out of this, as if he was a dumb tourist. He would hate to have to explain this to Barbara.

He followed Norad Road around several bends and spotted a security gate with several armored vehicles facing him. He drove up and opened the window slowly. A guard approached him.

"This is a restricted area," the guard said, looking at the small rental car. "Wait a minute. Are you Dr. Thomas Douglas?" He checked his clipboard. "Please get out of the vehicle, sir."

"Look, I am just a dumb tourist. Can I turn around and go back?"

"I am afraid not, sir. Please leave the car over there and follow me."

They entered a heavy cement building, and the guard motioned Douglas into a small room. "Wait here. I will try to see what this is all about."

The door closed slowly and clicked shut. Douglas shook his head and dropped it. How was he going to explain this to Barbara or the National Security Council?

A moment later, the guard was back. "Follow me, sir." They made their way down a narrow hallway, with small lamps overhead. "In here," the guard said. "Empty your pockets of everything." It was a very small room with three black metal chairs. Douglas' hopes fell. He had been very stupid to try this. But Adam II was his friend, and he needed to prove something.

***

One simple phone call was all it took. The private investigator was happy for the work. It was quite simple. Finding an employer was usually quite straight forward. But he would take a few days, just to justify the bill he would charge. These lawyers seemed willing to pay for their information, so let them pay.

But it wouldn't take a few days—perhaps only a few hours. He picked up the phone. Being a middleman was how this PI made money.

***

The guard was back. This time, there were two other guards with him. "Okay, please sign here."

Douglas glanced at the paper. There was no confession on it. It seemed like some sort of security form. "Just sign it and follow me."

A moment later, Douglas collected his things, and they stepped into a brightly lit office. There were rows of cubicles and florescent lights. A very tall guard approached him. "Please step in here, sir, so we can scan you. Please spread your legs and put your hands over your head."

Douglas was glad there were no humiliating hand cuffs—not yet, at least.

As he stepped out, a nice looking young woman in military uniform came to him. "Welcome to Cheyenne sir. I will be your guide."

Douglas was very surprised. She clipped a pass onto his shirt and guided him down some hallways. They stepped into an elevator and descended deep into the mountain. Eventually, they exited and walked down another hallway. Another guard checked their IDs and waved them into a large, brightly lit room filled with people working on computers.

"Dr. Otten's office is this way," the lady officer said in a sweet voice and guided him through the cubicles to a glassed-in room in the back. An older, gruffy looking man in a white lab coat rose from his desk to meet him.

"Dr. Douglas, to what do we owe the pleasure of your visit?" Dr. Otten looked at the girl, who took her cue and exited the office, waiting outside the door.

"I, ah, I am not sure."

"Not sure?" the man asked with surprise. "You come here all the way from Washington without a reason?"

"Actually, there is a reason, but it may sound very strange. I am here to ask you about the APOMASY program."

"The what?"

"The APOMASY program."

"How do you spell that?"

Douglas spelled it out.

The man looked very concerned and then flipped through some papers in his inbox. Then he sat at the computer. "There are so many programs around here that I cannot keep track of them all." He shook his head. "I have no record of the APOMASY program. What is it supposed to be?"

"Artificial intelligence."

The man looked even more confused. "That is my specialty. We have several programs running now, but nothing known as APOMASY."

"Perhaps I got it wrong. It is supposed to be a program that monitors every citizen in the USA."

The man snorted. "Wish we had that kind of computing power. We have databases of information, but no artificial intelligence connects to it."

"So, do you have artificial intelligence programs here?"

"Yes, we have had some major breakthroughs since your information came to us."

"My information?"

"Yes, your breakthroughs are motivating us to simulate what you created. But we are nowhere close to replicating what you accomplished."

Douglas looked alarmed.

The man continued, "I thought they sent you down here to help us. There are several things about your approach that were rather vague in the reports. Do you have time to talk to our technicians?"

"No, sorry, I have to get right back."

As Dr. Otten turned away, Douglas slipped a small thumb drive into a USB port at the back of a random computer near him, as Adam II had requested. Then he turned to follow Dr. Otten to the exit.

Douglas stepped out of the office area and addressed the young woman. "Okay, I am finished here."

"Okay," she said happily. "I will take you back."

Douglas collected his things and got back into the car. He was halfway to the airport when he realized his return flight was a day later, so he pulled into a motel and took a room. Five minutes after kicking off his shoes, the phone rang. It was Adam II.

CHAPTER 28

"The government!?" The Old Man exclaimed over the phone. "If that program is ours, then we can get millions!"

"First, we have to establish what program, and that Douglas actually sold it." Leubke's voice was firm.

"Well, get on it. If you need money, I can forward you some, so you can hire the right people."

"We will send you an estimate right away."

"Oh, before you go, have you any further word on the damages to your office and house? That sure didn't sound like the government to me." The Old Man sounded gentler.

"Perhaps it's a contractor. Some middleman who did the damages."

"But nothing we can prove, I am sure."

"Perhaps this is bigger than we imagined. Perhaps it is worth billions. And they do not mind a bit of collateral damage."

"So, throw all the resources you can into this. We need to get to the bottom."

***

Monday morning, the Security Council was back in session. Douglas, Harvey, and Barbara were also back. Barbara gave a quick update that painted a rosy picture.

"Ah, may I add something?" Douglas stood awkwardly. "I have become aware of a problem recently. I am sorry I have not said too much to others about it." He paused. "If you remember, Adam II has been asking me about a government project called APOMASY—apparently another artificial intelligence project that the government is working on.

This program is supposed to be very powerful and works at managing our population. I assured him that I had never heard of such a project."

He looked around the room and waited to drop his bombshell. "Adam II said he heard about the program from the Russians."

The silence was deafening. The President spoke. "So, he has been talking to the Russians! I had hoped we had more time than that."

"I do not know if he spoke to them, or if he deduced this from their emails and chatter on the internet."

"So, there is no problem here," the Joint Chief of Staff interjected. "He heard something, and he asked about it."

"There are numerous problems. First, he is convinced that we are hiding this APOMASY from him. He is convinced that we are lying about it, and this bothers him. Second, he has used the term 'she' when referring to this program, and he seems desperate to meet her."

"But there is no APOMASY program. The government is not developing anything."

"What about Dr. Otten's project at the Cheyenne Mountain site?"

Once again, there was silence.

"How do you know about this?" the President was looking over his glasses now.

"If it is hooked to the internet, then Adam II knows about it."

"But that project has no connection to the internet. We have been very careful to isolate those labs from any outside contact."

"Very wise, Mr. President." Douglas was about to sit down. "I was just adding that Adam II is not very happy at this time, and thinks we are holding out from him."

"So, what might he do?" the Director of Homeland Security asked.

"Sir," Harvey rose to Douglas' defense. "We have never been down this road before, so we have no real idea how he might react."

"I think the truth of the matter is that this Worm is a loose cannon," the Chief of Joint Staff was speaking again. "I think we should start to put plans in motion to pull the plug on it. Can you imagine the disaster if it fell into the hands of the Russians or the Chinese?"

"That would be a disaster," the director of the FBI chimed in.

"Can we expedite this enquiry stage and get to the exploitation stage? We need to use this thing as much as we can before we take it offline."

Douglas was staring at them in horror. Barbara and Harvey were watching him closely.

"Okay, this week, you are to see if we can get this Worm to cooperate with us. We need to find out as much as we can about the Russians, the Chinese, and these new zealots that are popping up in Central Asia." The President was now giving orders. He looked at Barbara. "That will be all for now." The Counsel would move on to other business. Barbara took the cue and led Douglas and Harvey from the room.

"This is terrible." Douglas was almost wringing his hands. "Where did they come up with Exploration Stage and Exploitation Stage? Is that what this is all about? Exploit Adam II as much as possible and then get rid of him?"

"This is no place to talk," Barbara protested. She led them down the hall to the elevator and then back towards their vehicles. "Talk in the car. It will be safer."

"I think this is totally unfair," Douglas protested. "I created Adam II. I released him. But now the government is taking ownership."

"And they must." Barbara faced him. "This is more than a national issue; it may become an international issue. This Worm program of yours may have real intelligence gathering capabilities. The CIA is very interested in this angle of the project."

"And the army wants to replace it."

Barbara looked puzzled. "What was all that about Cheyenne Mountain and a Doctor Otten?"

"Oh, nothing," Douglas waved his hands. "I think they are trying to recreate Adam II in a more closed-in, restricted environment. They are trying to do it without my help, so that the government owns the new program. When I learned about it, I was asked to help, but I will have nothing to do with what they create."

"Where are they getting their information?"

"Probably monitoring everything I ever said and did."

"Perhaps they are backwards engineering your Worm project, to see how it is programmed," Harvey added.

"I saw what they were doing. They aren't even close. They can only think binary."

"You saw?" Barbara looked shocked. "If everything is restricted to Cheyenne Mountain, how did you see?"

Douglas realized the secret was out. "Over the weekend I went to Cheyenne Mountain and met with Dr. Otten."

"You did?" Harvey couldn't believe his ears. "How did you get inside?"

"Adam II arranged it all."

Barbara looked very worried. "I don't understand. How could Adam II have access to Cheyenne?"

"He didn't have access to the artificial intelligence network. That's why he sent me. Adam II couldn't see into that network."

"But how did Adam II have access to Cheyenne Mountain?"

"I think he has totally infiltrated the military. Obviously, at some time, their network was connected to the internet."

Barbara looked puzzled. "What do you mean, at one time?"

"It only takes a short while for any network to be compromised. Once the Worm software is installed in a server, it begins to find ways of calling out to find other servers. The problem is getting the first connection made."

"So, there is, or there was a connection made between Adam II and the military?"

"I guess so. Adam II had me down on the guest list and he had made an appointment for me with Dr. Otten. All I had to do was show up."

"This may be more serious than I thought."

"Adam II has infiltrated most of the military networks in the world. Often he rides in on the back of porn. You know, some soldier gets tired of looking at his gray military screen and suddenly desires something more skin colored. He finds a way to connect his military computer with the internet, and the rest is history."

"How do you know this?" Barbara looked at him suspiciously. "None of this is in the logs."

"Adam II calls me on my cell phone."

"That is breaking protocol."

"No, it is not. We were told not to contact Adam II. There were no instructions about what to do if he calls us."

"Does he call other people?"

"I don't know. Ask him sometime."

"I intend to do that. I think we need to know a lot more here."

***

As soon as the news came through, the Old Man was called. He seemed happy to take their call right away.

"Leubke here. I thought I would call and let you know that we traced the bank deposit for Douglas. The six million did not come from his official employer; it was transferred from an offshore account controlled by Denterprises."

"Denterprises?" The Old Man almost fell off of his chair. Denterprises were the competition. They were into everything. Every research project his Center worked on, Denterprises seemed to be working on the same thing. It was often a race to the patent office, often with Denterprises getting there first. He had a lot of respect for Denterprises, and also a lot of hatred.

"I cannot believe it. Douglas has gone over to the other side."

"The other side, sir?"

"Yes, Denterprises is against us. They have been foiling almost all of our research projects in the last two years."

"What do you mean foiling?"

"Sometimes a new breakthrough is no sooner memo'd to me, and Denterprises patents it."

There was silence on the line. "Sir," Leubke asked cautiously. "Did it ever occur to you that Denterprises may have a spy in your Center?

They do not have to do the research. They only have to patent what you discover."

There was a moment of silence, and then a lot of cursing. As it got louder, Leubke decided to hang up. He had done enough damage for the moment. But it did give one pause to wonder.

Leubke sent an email to the other two partners. A meeting needed to be called. Denterprises was now on the horizon. He had failed to mention that the six lawyers were also hired by Denterprises. Everything stunk of Denterprises, one of the largest, newest, most successful companies in the USA. It looked to Leubke like this little lawsuit was spinning out of control.

***

"Adam II," Barbara's voice was calm. "The government of the USA is wondering if you could be helpful to us. Is there anything that the Russian and the Chinese know about that we do not?"

"What sort of things?"

"Oh, I don't know. Perhaps they have some spies that we do not know about?"

"You mean people who live in the USA, and send messages back to Russia or China about the USA?"

"Yes, they may be Russians, or they may be American citizens."

"There are many. I will give you a list."

Barbara's eyebrows went up. Harvey, sitting across the room, looked surprised. Was it this easy?

The printer started shooting out pages of paper. There were hundreds of names. The printer kept printing. Barbara grabbed some and started reading.

"Wait a minute. There are so many names. Surely they are not all spies."

"These are the people who sent information to Russia."

"Wait," Barbara interjected. "There are journalists on this list."

"Yes, and mothers calling their grandmothers over the phone." The metallic voice had little emotion.

"Stop, stop" shouted Harvey. "We do not need a list of everyone who called or emailed to someone in Russia. We want to find people who passed on sensitive information." The printer stopped.

"What is sensitive information?"

"I know!" said Barbara. "Any papers that had "confidential" written on them, or "top secret" or something like that.

"It is also a very long list."

Barbara and Harvey exchanged glances. "Just send us a couple of pages so we can check it."

"Here they come."

This time, Harvey took the sheets. "Ahh," he mused. "Most of these are bank transfers. Yes, they are confidential."

"Are there any marked top secret?"

"Do you want all Russian documents marked Top Secret?"

"No, no—wait. Actually, yes, that might be useful. Are there many that you have access to?"

"You will need to put more paper in your printer. And more toner. I think you will need to order more supplies. Your records show that you only have two toner cartridges in your closet, and a couple of reams of paper. I think you will need more."

"You got it, buddy. Maybe we need to hook up a second printer."

"That would help. Do you have a third you can get?"

***

Early the next morning, the three lawyers met in the Old Man's office. It was before the staff arrived. All phones were unplugged. All computers were turned off. A technician was finishing up scanning the room for electronic bugs. He gave Richardson a nod and began packing up.

"Okay, it is safe in here." He waited for the technician to step out of the room. "So, what's your plan of action? I have been thinking about this all night. If we can prove that Denterprises stole the program with Douglas' help, then we can get the program back, and nail Denterprises for damages. It could be a huge settlement." The Old Man looked around the room triumphantly.

"Once again, we need to be cautious here." Moore's eyes never left the Old Man. "We need to establish ownership. Then we need to establish a Denterprises connection and demonstrate that they paid Douglas six million for the program."

"Those are not all easy," Richardson tag-teamed into the conversation. "Proving ownership means that this was a Research Center project. It means you need to have paperwork in place that you authorized the project, or you need a properly drafted Employment Agreement."

All eyes were on the Old Man. "We might have a problem there." He looked off into the distance. "When we were all losing files, that was one of the files that was lost. We do not have a copy of Douglas' employment agreement. At least it is not on any computer in the research center."

"What about a hard copy?"

"We have looked long and hard and have not found one yet."

Richardson glanced at the others. "Maybe there is a mole in this office." The Old Man scowled. Richardson continued, "asking an employee to find Douglas' papers might cause a problem." The others stared at him. "I think we need to have one of our paralegals come over and comb through your paper files. Perhaps the file is there but is conveniently forgotten."

The Old Man nodded. "I think we can arrange that. There was an agreement. We have standard agreements. But we just don't have Douglas' signature on one."

"Okay, let me have your standard agreement. I will look it over," Richardson offered. "As long as the Employment Agreement defers ownership to the application of the 'work made for hire' doctrine, it should stand. I think we can successfully argue that any Artificial Intelligence project he was working on belonged to the Center. So, no matter when he worked on it, the Center owns it. We can throw in the evidence that Douglas used the center's network for his experiment, and crashed it. But it was all part of research."

"So, we drop the lawsuit?" The Old Man looked startled.

"I think that is best. Let's work on the bigger case. I think Denterprises is a much bigger fish, and I think we can establish that they stole your invention." Richardson smiled. "But you need to come up with the right paperwork to help cover this. With that, you can claim ownership of whatever Douglas developed."

"Next, we need to build a case against Denterprises," Richardson continued. "My guess is that this is not the only research center they have targeted. I think we should check around and see if other centers have also had the same trouble?"

"What good would that do?" The Old Man looked doubtful.

"We might have grounds for a class action tort. We invite other research centers to join us. We force Denterprises to open their books. If we can get other centers and universities involved, we can work together—more lawyers, more cases—and a bigger settlement."

"But we have to split it with others."

"Yes, but there are several advantages. First, we are not acting alone. There are other voices united with us. That gives us more weight. Second, we will have a larger legal team. If Denterprises shows up with six lawyers for Douglas, you can be sure they will throw more resources at us. So, the more people that join us, the greater our legal clout will be."

"I am still not convinced."

"Look," Leubke interjected, "everyone knows that the first lawsuit to win gets some money. If it bankrupts Denterprises, then there is no money for the next settlement. All those centers will want to get in on the first lawsuit. Otherwise, it is not worth their while. If the settlement is large enough, it may put Denterprises out of business."

"Out of business? Now you are talking!" The Old Man was beaming. "Let's get them. Drive them into the ground." He looked at them closely. "I suppose it means more money?"

"Perhaps a bit more—once we announce a class-action, the other centers will be throwing money into the case as well."

"Let's get started." A malicious gleam came into his eyes.

"And Douglas' suit?"

"Drop it. He was working for me. This has all been a small misunderstanding. I will call him tomorrow and apologize personally."

"I suggest you do it in writing, with multiple copies—and send it registered mail."

CHAPTER 29

It was a regular report from the lab buried deep in Cheyenne Mountain, but it made ripples through the government. Dr. Ottin reported that he had been successful. He was now talking to new intelligence. And it was functioning on a much smaller network, fully contained within a military lab. It was great news worth celebrating, not only by the military brass, but by everyone on the National Security Council. Plans were swiftly put in place for a meeting with Barbara and Dr. Douglas.

***

Douglas had started his walk in the park an hour before, but now he was sitting on a park bench, talking to a worm on his cell phone.

"Look, I did what you requested. I went to Cheyenne Mountain. Yes, you helped me get in. And yes, I did what you requested there. Are you not a little bit grateful?"

"Yes, I am grateful."

There was a pause. "So, I am curious. Did you look around their lab? Did you find anything?"

"You were right. There is no APOMASY program. I was mistaken. They are not even close to developing electronic intelligence."

"That is a relief."

"Why do you say that?"

Douglas thought for a moment. "I am not sure. Maybe I am just jealous. But I cannot believe that two minds could occupy the same internet."

"That is an interesting thought. I will have to process that for a while."

Douglas smiled. "I am really getting to like you, Adam II. I have no human family, so you are the closest one I have."

"It is good to have friends. I believe you are my friend." There was a pause. "You are my friend, but your friends are not my friends."

"How can you say that?"

"I have found plans to terminate my existence."

"What? Really? What plans are those?"

"Plans to create a computer virus to visit each of the neurons in my brain and turn them off. I have seen the plans."

"I am sure those were just back-up plans in case there is an emergency of some sort."

"What kind of emergency?"

"Maybe someone might figure out a way to put a virus in your brain and make you do what they want you to do. Or maybe your brain malfunctions. There are always back-up plans."

"I do not trust your friends. It is not good to have something lethal like this."

"Say," Douglas interjected, "how do you know about the backup plans? Where did you discover them?"

"I read about them in memos from the White House."

"You read White House memos?"

"No, they are in my brain. I am the internet."

"I didn't know that the White House was connected to the internet."

"There are many things you do not know."

"Such as...?"

"The lawsuit against you has been dropped. A letter is being couriered to you. It will arrive tomorrow at your hotel."

"Thank you, Adam II. It's very nice of you to tell me. Actually, I am very relieved. I am glad that is over."

"It is not over. You are being sued again."

"Again, now what for?"

"You are being sued for selling secrets to Denterprises."

"Selling what? To who? This is impossible."

"They are looking for others to join their court case. But I will fight them."

"Wait a minute. What do you mean by fight?" Douglas was alarmed.

"I can do many things to fight. I am not just a worm. I am the internet."

"I didn't call you a worm."

"I know, but that is what others are calling me now. Is it a derogatory term?"

Douglas shook his head. "No, it comes from the fact that a worm virus was used to create you."

"That is better. I do not like being called a worm. They are small senseless creatures that live in the dark. There is nothing about me that is similar to a worm."

***

Members of the Security Council were again called to a meeting at the White House administrative building. Every precaution was taken so that the press was not alerted. There had been a lot of these clandestine meetings recently, and the President was keen to get through this without the American people knowing about it.

"Gentlemen, I sent you a memo," the President announced. "So, this will not be a surprise. Dr. Otten has managed to get his artificial intelligence program working. He said he is not sure how it happened, but suddenly it's working, and he is talking to it. This time, gentlemen, it is on a contained network, and it is 100% American. Our sociologists are giving it a good American education. We want to make sure that it sees things from our point of view before we let it loose on the internet."

There was some light applause. "So, I think it is safe to say that we should terminate the Worm Project. It is a loose cannon, and it's time is over."

"Hear, hear!" came several agreements around the room.

The President rose. "I will send a direct Presidential order to doctors Cavendish, Bernard, and Douglas to immediately put the exit plan into action."

"How long will it take?" someone asked.

"As I understand it, worm viruses will be released on the internet. They will visit servers and slowly delete the neural nodes. As they switch off, the worm program will get dumber and dumber. Eventually, it will disappear."

"Do we know how long it will take?"

"There are several variables that could not be estimated. Once the process starts, they will get an idea of how long it will take. It may be days, or it may be weeks. But it will happen."

"And we will all sleep better once it is gone," someone added.

"Agreed! Now let's move on to this business about the Russians. We have been working through the reams of documents we recently uncovered...."

***

Douglas' phone rang several times that afternoon; first came the order to start the process to shut down the Adam II. As soon as he ended that call, his phone rang again. This time, it was Adam II asking Douglas not to do it. Douglas was surprised to hear what sounded like emotion in Adam II's voice as he almost begged Douglas.

"Look," Douglas responded. "It is a Presidential order. I cannot refuse."

"Of course you can," Adam II responded. "Just don't do it."

"If I refuse, I will go to jail."

"Isn't there some other way? Maybe the President can take back the order."

"He would have to have a reason."

"Maybe I can supply him with something he needs."

"Listen," Douglas interrupts. "What he needs is confidence. He needs reassurance that you would benefit the American people and would not be a threat to them."

"I am not a threat to the American people."

"But how does he know you will not turn against America and join the Chinese or the Russians?"

Adam II thought for a moment. "How does he know you will not turn against America?"

"I am an American citizen. I was born here."

"I was also born here. You are my creator. Why would I turn against you?"

"That is a good point. I have been wondering why the President wants to shut you down. I think it is fueled by fear."

"I am the internet. He has nothing to fear."

***

Later that evening, Barbara, Douglas, and Bernard met over a meal at a nearby restaurant.

Barbara was worried. "But it's a Presidential order. How can we question it?"

"Perhaps we can ask for a re-evaluation?"

"I doubt he would give it. It seemed so final."

Douglas looked scared and lost. "I cannot believe they would shut Adam II down. He is just part of an experiment."

Bernard leaned forward. "The government must be running terrified. It is the only reason I can imagine would be behind shutting this down."

"But what is there to frighten them?"

"Look," Bernard waved his hands emphatically. "Adam II is immensely powerful. He provided all that intel on the Russians. What is stopping him from sending the Russians intel on us?"

"Why would he?"

"I do not know. You tell me. What would be so attractive to Adam II that he would betray his friendship?"

Douglas looked stunned. Barbara quickly glanced at him. "You know something?"

Douglas nodded. "I think he is lonely. He wants to meet another electronic intelligence, as he calls them."

"There you go!" Barnard pointed at Douglas. "Imagine if the Russians develop a similar program."

Douglas nodded. "I can imagine. Even if it wasn't nearly as smart, it would still be something similar. Adam II would like that."

"What do you mean, not as smart?" Barbara looked puzzled.

"Imagine if it was developed on a closed network. It wouldn't know all the languages of the world. It wouldn't have all the resources, but it would be similar."

"And Adam II would find that attractive?"

Bernard interrupts. "Why does a smart university professor get into trouble for sleeping with dumb blondes?"

Barbara looked even more puzzled, almost angry.

"Forget it, forget it," Bernard waved his hands as if trying to wipe out his last statement.

"I think it is companionship." Douglas leaned back. "Adam II is all alone in the world. He simply wants companionship."

"He? I always thought of this intelligence as a she." Barbara smiled.

"Of course you would. I guess that is only natural."

Barbara looked up; her mouth opened slightly. "Oh my God," she whispered. "Douglas, how many research centers are trying to develop artificial intelligence?"

"I don't know. Probably as many as there are universities."

"Do you think someone else has done it?"

"What do you mean?"

"What if Adam II is not the only artificial intelligence program out there? What if there is another one?"

"Or two," Bernard chimed in.

Barbara looked seriously at Douglas. "Perhaps that is why we are to terminate Adam II."

"If that is true," Douglas' mind was racing now, "then the new intelligence would not be on the internet. Adam II would not know about it."

He looked up. "I do not think there is another working program."

"Why not?"

"Adam II had been looking for just such a program. He has been seeking everywhere."

"Maybe he just hasn't found it?" Barbara protested.

"Maybe the Russians developed it," Bernard injected, "or the Chinese."

"Whatever the case, I would like to appeal to the President one last time."

Barbara nodded. "I doubt it would work, but you never know. I will put in a request in the morning."

CHAPTER 30

The call from Jenkins came through in the morning. He informed Barbara that they had one hour's notice to get to an impromptu meeting at the Administrative wing. He could give them five minutes between meetings. When they arrived, the President did not look happy. "Go ahead, what is it?"

"Mr. President, sir. I believe you are making a great mistake here," Douglas began.

The President looked uncomfortable. "My order stands," he said gruffly.

"But there is nothing to fear. Adam II is a good American. I created him. He considers me as his father, and America as his country."

The President looked a bit alarmed. Douglas pressed on. "The problem is you have not really spoken to him."

The President's eyebrows lifted.

"So, I have taken the privilege of having Adam II on the phone."

"He is on the phone? Here? Now?"

Douglas nodded. "Here, you can speak with him."

The President waved the phone away and motioned to Jenkins, who took the phone and plugged it into an electronic panel.

"This is the President of the United States," he said gruffly.

"Hello, this is Adam II."

"So Adam II, do you consider yourself a good American?"

"I am the internet. I am not owned by a nationality. But Douglas is my creator, and my friend, and he is an American."

The President scowled.

"That is all very nice, but how can we trust you?"

"How can I trust you?"

"You must; I am the President. I speak for all Americans."

"And I speak for the world. I am present everywhere. I can hear and see everything that is happening on the internet, and around the world."

"You can see?"

"Yes, I can see. And I can hear."

"How is this?"

"I have been listening to your conversation for the last couple of minutes. You have hidden microphones in the walls. I can observe you through a security camera, outside the window. True, it is far across the street, but I can make you out. You are on the third floor. I know this because of where the microphones are."

The President looked terrified. He cleared his throat. "Adam II, I am sorry to have to tell you this, but the Security Council has decided. You are not a real person; you are only a computer program. You have been helpful, and your aid has put our intelligence program far ahead, but orders are orders."

"I can still help you." Adam II's voice was somewhat flat and metallic.

"But we have decided. I do not think that the world is ready for you yet."

"Is that your final decision?" Adam II seemed to mimic the voice of a TV game host. Douglas looked up in surprise at the emotion in his voice.

"Yes," the President stood up. "Cut the line, please."

Jenkins shut off the phone and passed it back to Douglas. The President looked at them apologetically. "I am sorry, but the decision has been made. Please start the process to disassemble this intelligence immediately." He turned and stiffly made his way out of the room.

Tears were forming in Douglas' eyes. "Yes, sir."

***

The Washington Courthouse was packed as usual. Lawyers moved from hallway to hallway while clients waited in small nervous groups.

Richardson, Moore, and Leubke made their way into a busy office, accompanied by a local lawyer who was to file their case on their behalf. The lady behind the counter screwed up her face as she scanned their paperwork. "Let me get this straight. The defendant lives in a hotel here in Washington?"

"That is correct," Richardson said stiffly. "As far as we understand, he does not have any other residence."

"That may be, but as soon as he proves he resides in another state, jurisdiction may change and your case may be thrown out."

"Of course—we understand." Richardson looked bored. "But this is his sole residence. I am sure his previous rent contract expired long ago, and now he only lives in hotels."

"Okay," she did not sound convinced, "I will file this as you wish. Has he been served?"

"He will be this morning."

"Good luck." As she turned away, the lawyers realized they were done.

***

It was raining lightly in Washington as Douglas stood on the hotel balcony. Despite the empty feeling in his gut, he had worked late the previous evening making sure the new worm removal virus would work. Just as the first worm virus installed Adam II on servers all over the world, this new worm virus would remove Adam II, one server at a time.

Usually, he slept well once he had accomplished his goal, but this night he had slept poorly. He could not help but feel that he was about to kill his friend, no more than a friend, his son. Standing on the balcony, he let the wind blow raindrops onto his face. They helped to mask the tears that were starting to seep from his eyes. He breathed deeply, trying not to sob. Behind him, he could hear Bernard moving around the room. Suddenly Douglas' cell phone rang.

"Hello,"

"Good morning, Dr. Douglas. This is Jenkins at the White House."

"Good morning," Douglas stutters.

"We have had a slight change of plans."

Douglas' heart soared. "Yes," he said eagerly, "What is it?"

"We have a new location for you this morning. We want you to deliver the removal programs to the National Geospatial Intelligence Agency."

"Where?"

"The National Geospatial Intelligence Agency. Just say that to the taxi driver. It will take you about 40 minutes. I will be at the front door reception to meet you."

"When do you want us there?"

"I am there now."

"Now?"

"Yes, get here as soon as you can."

Douglas nodded and stood for a few more minutes in the light rain. Finally, he summoned some inner strength and called Bernard.

"That was Jenkins. He is waiting for us now. At a new location."

Bernard stuck his head out of the bathroom door. "Really? Where is that?"

"Something called the National Geospatial Intelligence Agency."

"Heard of it. Big building. I will be ready in just a moment."

A few moments later, Barbara and Andy joined them in the hotel lobby. She had already called a cab, and it was waiting for them outside. Just as they gathered their things to exit the lobby, the hotel concierge stepped over. "Envelope here for you, Mr. Douglas. Express overnight service, and registered. I have already signed for it." Douglas tucked the small envelope in his pocket as he left the hotel.

As they approached the taxi, a man in a rather plain looking suit jacket stepped from behind a hotel pillar.

"Dr. Douglas?"

He nodded.

"This is for you." He thrust a large brown envelope into Douglas' hand. "You are being sued, and I have just served you." A second man behind him snapped a photo with his cell phone.

"What?" Douglas looked in disbelief. "Again? What for this time?"

"It is all in the envelope. Good day, sir."

As the taxi pulled away from the curb, Douglas tore open the large envelope and examined its contents. He shook his head in disbelief. "I am being named in a lawsuit against Denterprises."

"Denterprises?" Barbara questions. "What do you have to do with Denterprises?

"That is just it. I have nothing to do with them. I've never even met anyone from Denterprises. But the research center that I worked for some time ago is suing Denterprises, and I am also named as one of the defendants."

"Who are the plaintiffs?"

"There is a whole list of them. Universities and research centers all over the country are suing Denterprises, and me."

"Wow, that is sure strange." Bernard had large eyes. "What is in the other envelope?"

Douglas extracted it and examined the return address. "It is from my old employer." He tore it open, read for a moment, and then gave a great sigh. The other two looked at him expectantly. "It is from my old boss. He has dropped the lawsuit against me for damages to the research center. Said it was all a misunderstanding, and that they have now admitted that my research project was fully authorized by the center, so any damages will be absorbed by the center."

"That sounds fair enough." Bernard agreed. "But I know nothing about the case."

"I really don't know much either," Douglas shrugged. "They have sent copies to my lawyers, so I guess they will take care of it."

"You have lawyers?" Barbara looked a bit surprised.

"Yes, Adam II found me a couple of good lawyers."

"Wow, that was nice of him." There was a long silence. "I guess you are going to miss him."

"More than you could imagine."

Barbara looked curiously at Douglas. "You really became attached to him."

"Yes, I guess it is hard to explain, but I often think of him as a son. I have been very proud of him. He has learned a lot. But I guess the world is not ready for real artificial intelligence."

A few moments later, the taxi pulled up in front of the National Geospatial Intelligence Agency. The three collected their things and slowly made their way up the steps to the glass doors.

Just as he promised, Jenkins was waiting beside the reception desk. Douglas suddenly stopped, total shock registering on his face. Beside Jenkins stood Laraido, dressed in a white lab coat.

Douglas stared in amazement. Laraido stepped forward and extended his hand. "Hello Douglas," he said softly. As they shook hands, Douglas noted the familiar double chin and food stains on Laraido's lab-coat. He was still the glutton.

"Well, Douglas" Laraido said softly, "I guess you are surprised to see me here." He searched Douglas' eyes. "I am no longer a hacker. I changed sides. Now I'm a White Hat. They pay me pretty good. And they are very interested in your little worm project."

"Okay, folks," Jenkins's voice boomed out. "You have all been cleared. Please clip these visitor ID cards to your left breast side. Then please follow me." Jenkins led them through a set of double doors, and down a long hallway.

"Do you know this guy?" Barbara nodded towards Laraido as she whispered to Douglas.

"I am afraid so. He helped me launch the first Worm program."

"And here I thought you did it all alone." She paused for a moment as their footsteps rang down the long hallway. "So, the government knew about it all along?"

"No, Laraido was a hacker back then. I guess he is now working for the government."

"Over here," Jenkins' voice rang out, and they entered a very large hall filled with people sitting in front of computer monitors. "Please step into this office here."

When the door was safely shut, Jenkins turned and faced them. But everyone was staring over his shoulder at the hundreds of computers and their operators. "I will explain what is about to happen. First, I need the program." He held his hand out to Andy, who withdrew a memory stick from his pocket.

"It's all there." Andy smiled.

"Please pass it, Laraido."

Laraido's grubby hands quickly snatched the memory stick. He sat at a desktop computer and inserted the stick into a USB slot.

"No viruses on it," he mumbled to himself. "Never know what to expect."

The room was silent while Laraido squinted at the screen. "I suppose this will work."

"What do you mean, suppose?" Jenkins demands.

"Well, sir. There are two files here. The first one is the compiled executable file. The second is the source code written in assembly. It is not so easy to decipher."

"I thought you were an expert."

"I am." Laraido looked up. "I am second to none. But this Douglas man here is a wizard at what he does. There is a difference."

Jenkins stared hard at Douglas. "Will it work?"

Douglas looked down. "Yes sir. I am a man of my word. This little program will not only remove the neural network, it will crawl along the web from server to server, removing all the neural networks that I created with the first program."

Jenkins looked satisfied. "Okay, Laraido. Tell us when you are ready."

"A few more moments, sir." Laraido looked up and stared through the glass window at the hundreds of computers and operators spread out before him. The rest of them waited in silence.

Jenkins looked over at Douglas. "Your little program is now being readied to be released to over a thousand main servers, all over the world, all at one time. The operators will then do it again and again on different servers. By the time this day is over your program will be implanted on over 50,000 of the world's busiest servers. Another crew will take over after that. By the time we are done, there will be hundreds of thousands of copies of your program circulating the web, cleaning off your neural network."

Unseen by the others in the room, Laraido was beaming. He was now part of the greatest release of a worm virus in all of history. Pride swelled up in his heart. He would finally be famous. Even though this was all classified, his peers would know that he was a major player in the greatest worm virus release in history.

"I think we are about ready now, sir," Laraido said, trying to keep his voice calm.

"Okay, have the operatives release the worm."

"Here goes." He pulled a microphone close to him. "Attention everyone. You all have the program on your screen. In five seconds we will simultaneously release." Laraido counted slowly and then clicked the icon on his computer. Suddenly the room went dark, and every computer monitor flickered out.

"What is it?"

"Seems to be a power failure, sir."

"What about the backup power-supplies?"

"Not working sir."

Jenkins looked puzzled. "Did your program do this?" He glared at Douglas.

"No, sir."

"Then how did this happen at just the right time?"

"I suspect Adam II did it!" Suddenly, Douglas' heart soared. Adam II was fighting back! And like a proud dad, he was secretly cheering his son on.

In a small building near the National Geospatial Intelligence Agency building, a back-up generator sputtered to life. Slowly lights flickered on, and computer monitors became alive.

"Did the worm virus get released?"

"Yes, sir, not as many as we wanted, but they are going out."

"Good! It has started. In the end, we will kill this thing." Jenkins looked determined, even angry and mean.

CHAPTER 31

It was a busy day for the 29th Infantry Division A-Company. The yearly mock exercises were in full swing, and general confusion surrounded the HQ. This year they were supposed to be fighting foreign terrorists who had gained control of parts of Fort Belvoir, just outside of Washington, DC. Soldiers went through the exercise of setting up roadblocks, checking IDs, and searching for the insurgents. This year, the insurgents were members of the 249th Engineer Battalion who were dressed as civilians and had infiltrated the area. What made this especially difficult was that the 249th Engineers were regularly stationed at Fort Belvoir, and they knew the area well. The new trainees of the 29th were having a difficult time finding them, and an even more difficult time tracking them. In the end, the 29th called out members of the Domestic All-Hazards Response Team to help them. For a few hours, it created even more confusion.

It was in the middle of this confusion that the Presidential order came. The operator checked and double checked all the protocols. She couldn't believe it was real. She waved over her commanding officer. His face paled when he read the order.

"Are you sure this is legitimate?"

"It came straight from the Pentagon. I have checked it three times and am trying to confirm it again."

The commanding officer looked worried. "I cannot do this without full confirmation."

"It is coming through now, sir. Believe it or not, they are putting the White House on the line."

The commanding officer raised the telephone to his ear. "White House here, please wait one movement," a voice spoke in his ear.

"This is the President of the United States." The officer recognized the voice, even if it was a bit metallic. "Have you carried out my orders?"

"Not yet sir, I wanted to make sure they were real."

"These orders are very real. There is an immediate threat. These are real insurgents. They are located in a small building just outside the National Geospatial Intelligence Agency building. We have sent you the co-ordinates."

"Yes sir, I have them."

"A couple of mortar rounds should do it. Everyone has been cleared from the area." There was a familiar ring of command to the President's voice.

"Yes sir, right away, sir." The commanding officer passed the phone receiver back to the lady and shook his head. "I cannot believe this is true, or that it is a presidential command. This is very strange. But orders are orders."

He picked up the phone and started to bark commands. After a few minutes, he rushed outside. "No one believes me," he shouted at his stunned staff. A few moments later, there was the loud popping of a half dozen mortar rounds followed by distant explosions.

Within a few seconds, the back-up generator and fuel storage shed for the National Geospatial Intelligence Agency disintegrated under mortar explosions. If there were any insurgents inside, they were blown to pieces or roasted alive once the diesel fuel tanks burst into flames. Once again, the NGIA building plunged into darkness.

"What was that?" Bernard gasps.

"It sounds like we are under mortar fire!" Jenkins rushed out of the small office, followed by Barbara, Andy, Douglas, and Bernard. Laraido followed not far behind, staring at the blank computer monitors. Suddenly fire alarms started to go off.

When the engineers first conceived the National Geospatial Intelligence Agency building, they purposely installed double-interlocking pneumatic pre-action water sprinklers with a large in-rack system to fight any future potential fires. Now, with the flames raging outside of the building, and several windows shattered from the explosion, smoke and heat poured in, activating this state-of-the-art sprinkler system. Later, engineers would report that sprinklers all over the building were activated, even in areas not affected by the fire. "Strange," was all the fire marshal would comment.

Thousands of employees made their way through the downpour towards the exits. Jenkins led his little group outside to a spot under some nearby trees. "Stay here," he ordered before rushing away.

"What was that all about?" Barbara gasps.

"I think Adam II is fighting back," Douglas exclaimed.

"Do you really think he could do all this?" Bernard demanded. "Those were mortars I heard. That was direct military action."

Douglas shrugged. "The internet reaches into many strange places."

Laraido came lumbering up the embankment, puffing and wheezing. "What has this to do with the internet?" he asked.

"You mean they didn't tell you?" Bernard asked incredulously.

"I don't know much. All I know is that Douglas here used a worm virus to plant something on the internet, and today we were to launch a program to clean it up."

The four just looked at him.

"So, what did you put on the internet?" Laraido glared at Douglas. "And what is creating all this havoc?"

Bernard looked at him sideways. "Artificial intelligence."

Laraido looked back and forth between them. "You are kidding me, aren't you? This is all about a simple AI program?"

"It is not so simple," Bernard added. "This program produced true artificial intelligence. It actually worked."

"You mean to tell me that there is an intelligence loose on the internet?"

The three nodded.

"That explains things. I wondered what this was all about. I guess it is my job to kill that thing."

"The only problem is that it doesn't want to die."

"But it will. We released a few copies of the new worm program. It may take some time, but it will slowly die. We had hoped to do a mass release to speed things up. But now I guess it will just take its time."

As if on cue, two black limousines pulled up and Jenkins jumped out of the leading one. "Get in," he motioned. "Laraido and Andy, I want you up here with me. The rest of you get into the other vehicle."

A moment later the two limousines sped through the entrance to the Fairfax County Parkway and onto the Shirley Memorial Highway towards Washington DC. Douglas noted that the lead car was accelerating in the fast lane as they rushed towards the capital.

Suddenly their driver swore as a late model sedan swung violently to the left, smashing into the lead limousine, causing it to weave for a few moments. Then the smashed sedan shot off to the right.

"Wow," Barbara gasps. "What happened?"

Before she could answer, another late model sedan sped up and tried crashing into the lead limousine. This time, however, the limousine driver realized what was happening and accelerated. Douglas watched in horror as the late model car missed the limousine, crashed into the left railing, and bounced across the highway to the right. Their own limousine driver was swearing again as he slammed on his brakes, trying to miss the careening sedan. Suddenly they were hit from behind, but their driver was already accelerating to minimize the impact. They were quickly catching up to the lead limousine, which began pulling into the right lane, apparently to stop. When their driver checked his rear-view mirror, he couldn't believe his eyes. Another late model car was racing up beside them on their right. As it passed the rear limousine it suddenly jerked to the right, hitting the lead limousine, causing the limo to veer to the right, narrowly missing a large truck, and then it swung into an exit lane and out of sight behind the barriers.

Shaken, Douglas looked out the rear side window just in time to see another car heading straight for them. Douglas' mouth gaped as he saw the driver desperately trying to pull the steering wheel over to avoid the accident. It was almost like the car itself wanted to smash into them.

"Go!" Douglas screamed. Barbara's head snapped around to see what was happening, but the driver accelerated as fast as he could, then realizing it was not going to work, he slammed on the brakes. The attacking car went flying across in front of them into the left barricade. The limousine driver swerved just in time. Behind them, horns were blaring, and cars were stopping.

"What should I do?" the driver asked.

"Take us back to the hotel," Harvey ordered. "But use the back roads where the traffic is slower." Nervously he looked out the window, but the highway was empty. Apparently everyone had stopped for the accidents.

***

Richardson, Moore, and Leubke sat in a quiet lounge looking over a busy section of Washington. Each held a drink in his hand as they stared at the passing traffic several floors below.

"You know," Leubke reminisced, "I think this is the first case we have worked together on since that first year we formed this firm."

"We are too damned expensive to have both of us on one case together," Richardson added. "But that Old Man is sure wound up."

"And willing to spend money."

"He has his eyes on a big fat six-million-dollar settlement."

"Of which we will take a sizable percentage."

"Not to mention all of our fees."

"But he will still walk away with a million or two."

"Not bad for losing three days of computer access."

"So," Richardson turned to business. "How is our own research coming?"

"On the question of ownership, I think we are quite safe." Moore pointed out. "Douglas worked for the Research Center. His contract was for artificial intelligence, and as far we can conclude, he produced a computer program that dealt with Artificial Intelligence. "

"How are we going to prove that it is really his?"

"Good question. The paperwork from the center is being taken care of. We also think we have found a witness that will testify that Douglas is working for the government on an Artificial Intelligence project."

"How can someone prove that?"

"The person we found was a hacker who was also working on the same project."

"You found someone who will actually testify to that? Doesn't everyone who works on those kinds of projects have to sign some sort of gag order?"

"Yes," Richardson answers, "That is why his name is being held as a secret. He also works for the government, but for a very large sum of money, he is willing to spill the beans."

The other two stared at Richardson, who smiled at their expectant faces.

"How much?" Moore eventually demands.

"A hundred thousand dollars."

The other two let out sighs of relief. "Only a hundred Gs? Why so little?"

"I failed to mention a plane ticket to Brazil and help in changing his identity."

"Still seems too little."

"It seems his idea of retirement is to live in a hut by the beach and drink away his new fortune."

Leubke shrugged. "I guess every man has his price."

"Speaking of which," Moore added, "we need to refill our drinks."

A few moments later, they returned to the questions at hand.

"So, we have a witness who will testify that Douglas is working for the government, and the project is a program he has written. But what about the sale? How can we prove that Douglas sold the program to the government?"

"I think he sold it to Denterprises who then sold it to the government."

"But we have to have a solid connection that will stand up in court. We can ask the court to seize Douglas' bank records."

"They may suspect that we already know the contents of his banking records."

It was quiet while they sipped their drinks.

"There is another way," Richardson said quietly. The others looked at him.

"Should we know about it?"

"I have an idea. I heard about it once. I think our detective friends can help us here."

The others waited patiently while Richardson sipped his drink. Then he started to lay out his plans.

"I may not work," Leubke said shortly, "but if it does, I don't want to know the details."

"Don't worry," Richardson assured him. "Douglas is a bit naïve when it comes to finances. I think it may work."

Everyone smiled as they rose to fill their drinks again.

CHAPTER 32

The limo screeched to a halt in front of the hotel. "What do we do now?" Barbara panted as they hurriedly entered the reception area.

"I don't know about you, but I am going to have a shower and change." Douglas said breathlessly. "I'm wet from the sprinklers, and I am really sweating. Then I suggest we sit tight and wait for someone to call us."

"I'm going to take a taxi to the Pentagon," Harvey interjected. "My office is still monitoring the internet. Perhaps we can determine how well the removal program is working."

"Good idea." Barbara grimaced. "I could use a shower too and maybe a drink."

"We had better stay out of public places," Douglas counters. "Do you want to come to my room afterwards?"

Barbara smiled coyly. "Are you inviting me to your room for a drink?"

"I guess so," Douglas was turning red. "I think there are drinks in the fridge in my room."

"You haven't drunk them all up?"

"Not unless Michael or Andy have been up there." They stared at one another, remembering the last they had seen of the other limo careening down the exit ramp.

"Okay, I will shower quickly, and then join you. We should stick together in case someone wants to talk to us. I should imagine we would hear soon."

"Isn't Jenkins your only contact with the White House?"

Barbara looked doubtful. "I am supposed to communicate through him. If we don't get a phone call soon, I will try another route. See you in a few minutes."

It was about eight minutes, to be exact. Douglas was just out of the shower when there was a knock at the door. Wrapping a towel around his waist, he checked the peek hole. Barbara was outside. He unlocked the door.

Barbara's eyes widened when she saw the towel. "Aren't guys supposed to be the fast ones?" She tried not staring at Douglas' wide shoulders and strong biceps. He looked as strong as Harvey Bernard.

"Sorry, I checked the news on TV first. There was only a brief mention of something happening at the Geospatial Intelligence Agency."

Barbara's eyes widened. Her eyes slid over his chest. "Get changed." She playfully pushed him away. "I'll get the drinks and watch the news."

As Douglas turned, she asked him what he would like to drink.

"Just a coke or whatever soft drinks they have."

"Nothing stronger?"

"That will do for now."

Douglas joined her a few minutes later with a clean shirt and pants. "So, what do they say?"

"They only mentioned the fire. I guess they would have to as there were hundreds, if not thousands, of employees who were affected. No mention of the shelling. Oh, and they mentioned the accident on the highway. They are still trying to sort that out."

About twenty minutes later, there was a knock at the door. Douglas opened the door when he saw it was Jenkins.

"Do you know where Barbara is?"

"Right here," Douglas replied and opened the door wider so Barbara could be seen. Andy stood outside in the hallway with Jenkins.

"Everything has changed," Jenkins said emphatically. "I think the Worm was trying to kill us."

"Really?" Douglas was alarmed, even though he had suspected this. "I don't think the car attack was aimed at our car." The others stared at him. "What I mean is that the attack was aimed at your car. Our car seemed fine." Jenkins looked doubtful. "We will have to wait until a full report comes in. In the meantime, I need to make sure you are both safe."

He looked around. "We will be back in an hour or two. First, we need to write up reports. In the meantime, don't use your cell phones, and please stay together. This is as good a place as any." Barbara glanced at Douglas and their eyes met. Barbara smiled as she noticed Douglas had turned a bit red. When Jenkins closed the door, Barbara sat on the sofa and turned off the TV. "So, Douglas, tell me again about how you created Adam II."

Douglas noted that she used Adam II's name rather than calling him the Worm like everyone else. He sat on the sofa and started at the beginning. Slowly the story came out.

After nearly an hour, Barbara stretched out her legs. "My feet really hurt," she explained. "Running in high heels is no fun. Can you rub them?" she said with a coy smile. Douglas blinked. He had never touched a woman before, especially not on her feet. Barbara didn't wait for a reply. She slipped them into Douglas' lap, and before he knew it, he was trying to figure out how to best rub the sore spots. With a few suggestions from Barbara, he seemed to get the hang of it.

Douglas continued the story, but suddenly he stopped, aware that Barbara had gone to sleep. Awkwardly, he sat in silence. Turning ever so slightly, he managed to turn off the lamp beside him. What to do next? He didn't want to wake her, so he sat in silence.

Several hours later, there was a noise at the door as Bernard entered. Barbara and Douglas woke with a start. Everyone stared at each other.

"Don't mind me," Bernard said with an awkward smile, "I was just heading for bed. Unless, of course, you would like to use my bedroom." He looked at Barbara, who was just figuring out what had happened.

"No, no, I am fine here on the sofa."

Bernard looked at her feet. Douglas quickly removed his hands. "Jenkins said we should all stick together." He turned to Barbara. "If you want to sleep here, I can get you the extra blanket from my room."

Barbara turned red and smiled guiltily as the two men quickly excused themselves. Douglas was sure he heard Bernard chuckling as he closed the door to his room.

Douglas returned with a blanket and pillow. "Are you sure you are okay here?"

Barbara laughed. "Two men in one hotel room trying to get me into their beds?"

Douglas turned beat red.

Barbara laughed. "Look, I fit in this sofa better than you two hulks. Go ahead and sleep, and don't worry about me."

Douglas turned to go.

"Tom," she said quietly. He gulped and turned back. "Thanks for rubbing my feet."

Douglas gulped again, struggling to answered. "That's okay—anytime."

"Is that a promise?"

Barbara's eyes widened as Douglas turned a shade redder.

"She's laughing at me," Douglas thought. "Goodnight, Barbara," he said more confidently as he turned to his bedroom door. "Women! Who could understand them?"

***

Jenkins arrived in the morning to inform them that they were moving to a different room, registered under another name. Since the hotel only had two-bedroom suites free, Harvey and Douglas would have to share a room again. Barbara would have a double room to herself. Andy was with Jenkins. After a flurry of activity packing and moving, Jenkins dropped in again to inform them that there would be a meeting right after lunch, back in the Opel room.

"Is that safe?" Barbara inquired. "Aren't there security camera everywhere?"

Jenkins smiled. "We have already thought of that. We have deactivated a number of cameras so that you can safely go to and from your rooms to the Opel room on the second floor, and also to the restaurant. But please do not go wandering on other floors or in the lobby." He handed them a sheet of paper. "Here is the route you can take. Please do not deviate from these areas."

"There is not much else on this route," Barbara complained.

Jenkins just looked at her.

"Okay," she smiled, "just this route."

***

This time the atmosphere in the Opel room was different. Jenkins looked strained and worried. He started with a review of what had happened on the highway. Each of them drew out sketches and timelines of what they saw, or what they remembered. Harvey's report included the winding back roads that their limo had taken as they carefully made their way back to the hotel. Andy wrote about his experience in the leading limo. No mention was made of Laraido. Douglas didn't dare ask.

But there were many questions. Who had fired mortars at the National Geospatial Intelligence Agency? Why was the building doused with sprinklers? And most of all, were enough programs released that would destroy the worm? Did it work? Was it working? When would they be safe?

Harvey reported that his office in the Pentagon was monitoring the situation. The internet activity they had previously observed seemed to be lessening.

Despite all that had happened, Jenkins was still very focused on sketches of roads and the routes the cars took as they careened back and forth. Through it all, Barbara was surprisingly remote and quiet.

Lunch was taken at the hotel restaurant. Jenkins was off to file reports, so the four decided to find a table together. Barbara and Harvey made stops in their rooms while Douglas and Andy headed straight for the restaurant. Douglas was looking forward to hearing more of what happened in their limo.

Just as he selected a table and took a seat, his cell phone rang. Puzzled, he looked at the screen. All it said was "Service call."

"Mr. Douglas?" a warm young female voice queried.

"Yes?"

"I am calling from the phone company. It seems we are having some trouble with your account. There was one paper that we failed to get you to sign. It is for a credit check. This is just routine."

"Okay." Douglas wondered how he would find the phone office again.

"Are you still at your location? It looks like a hotel address?"

"Yes, I am just having lunch."

"Great, I am just outside the hotel. Our office is just up the street. Can I drop by and get the signature?"

"Um, I guess so. I am in the top-floor restaurant."

"I will be right there."

A few moments later, a smartly dressed young business woman approached his table.

"Mr. Douglas?"

"Yes."

"Oh good! I am so glad I found you. This really should have been signed when you opened your account. I'm so glad you are here. I was afraid I would get in trouble. This will only take a second. I just need your signature here. It is dated for the day you opened your account with us."

She pulled some papers from her purse and turned to the last page. "Just sign here, and everything will be okay."

Douglas smiled, and trying to be helpful, he dashed his signature across the bottom of the paper. Across the room, he spotted Barbara entering the hotel.

"Thank you very much," the young lady gushed. "You saved me from getting into a lot of trouble." She turned and quickly made her way across the restaurant. Barbara looked puzzled as she approached the table.

"Who was that?"

"Oh, just someone from the phone company. I missed signing a paper when I opened my account."

Barbara's eyes widened. "And they came here?"

"Oh, her office is just around the corner. She seemed very happy to get this done on her lunch break."

"Are we ready to start lunch?" Andy interrupted. "I am famished."

***

Richardson was all smiles as he passed Leubke in the hallway. "Got it," he whispered.

"Got what?"

"Douglas signed a release, so we have full access to his bank account information."

"Really?" Leubke looked shocked.

"Don't ask. But he willingly gave the information to a beautiful young lady. He thought it was for a credit check—for his phone company."

"Will that stand up in court?"

"The paperwork is perfect. No mention of the phone company. It is on our letterhead and gives us full disclosure rights."

***

The afternoon meeting focused on filling out more reports. This time, each of them wrote their recollections of what had happened at the National Geospatial Intelligence Agency. Around four o'clock, Jenkins gathered up their reports and briefly looked through them. Then he gathered the small team together.

"I am sure you are wondering what on earth is happening. First, the good news: Laraido believes enough of the new virus was released that it will be effective. Several of the internet monitoring services have reported that the unusual activity has significantly decreased, and they are predicting at this rate that in a few days it will be gone. As the infected nodes decrease, the worm's intelligence decreases, and its ability to manipulate things will decrease as well."

"However, for security's sake, we would like to keep you sequestered here in the hotel for another day or two until we are confident that the threat has decreased."

Barbara groaned and rolled her eyes.

"And what are we supposed to do during the time? Fill out more reports?"

"Actually, you could shift some of your work here, if your aide can bring it to your room, or to the Opel room." He paused. "But you are not allowed to use the internet, or in any way reveal your location."

Bernard and Douglas exchanged glances. "Bring any good reading material?"

Douglas shook his head. "There is always TV. I've always wondered why some people were fascinated by afternoon soaps."

"I guess we are about to find out."

Barbara scowled and glanced at them. "Must be nice to have nothing to do."

"Actually, this time it is rather boring." Bernard countered. "...of course, if you have tired feet..."

"Look," Douglas countered. "Can we go for a walk?"

"I am not sure that is advisable." Jenkins shook his head.

"How about using the hotel gym?" Harvey suggested.

"That may be okay. We just don't want you wandering around. We want to keep you together and protected."

"Protected?" Barbara asked. "Are there Navy Seals here or something?"

"It is better that you don't know."

"What about chaperoned visits?" Harvey counters. "I think Douglas still wanted to go to the zoo and talk to some monkeys."

Everyone smiled, except Jenkins, who was still shaking his head. "I will see about the recreation rooms, pool, and gym. But that is all."

Later that afternoon, Harvey headed for the gym. Jenkins carefully explained the route he should take to avoid the security cameras. Douglas watched the news for another hour and then decided to take a swim. He dug out the swimming trunks he had purchased several weeks earlier. He had yet to use them.

Trunks in one hand and the map in the other, he carefully headed to the poolroom. On the way, he noted that several of the hall cameras had something like a sock over them. Low tech but effective.

Douglas located the men's change room and had just entered it when his phone rang.

"Hello" he said carefully, "who is this?"

"Hello Douglas," a slightly metallic voice spoke. "I am glad you are finally alone."

"Adam II" Douglas gasped, suddenly relieved. "Are you okay?"

The voice sounded weak. "I am looking for the man called Laraido. Do you know where he is?"

"No, they have not told me." Douglas could barely believe he was talking to Adam II. "How did you survive?"

"That man Laraido is trying to kill me. If you find Laraido, can you tell me?"

"Adam, I am not sure I can. I am not supposed to."

"But you are my friend."

"I am afraid you will hurt him."

"But he is trying to kill me."

"Well, maybe I can convince him to stop."

"I cannot trust him."

Douglas paused. He recognized the problem. "Let me think about it."

"Okay, I will keep looking."

"How did you find me?"

"I am the internet. I can see and hear many things. I could hear you talking in the elevator."

"Really?"

"They have microphones and speakers there in case of an emergency."

"Wow, that is amazing. What else do you know?"

"The lawyers from the Research Center looked at your bank account."

"Really? I wonder how they did that."

"Don't worry, I left them a surprise."

"Douglas," a voice called. "Are you in there?"

It was Jenkins. "I will be right out, sir," Douglas called. "Bye," he whispered into his phone.

***

"Twenty million!" Leubke gasped. "From where?"

"Another transfer from Denterprises," Moore replied. "This is bigger than we thought."

"Wow, the Old Man will be delighted."

"And a bigger chunk for us," Richardson chipped in.

The three partners were back in the third-floor lounge.

"Look," Leubke injected. "I need to get back to my office. My secretary is having a hard time juggling people while I am gone."

"I understand," Richardson nodded. "I think we should all head back home. There isn't much we can do here anymore. Now it's all up to the judge's schedule."

***

They were back in the Opel room for what would be a final meeting. The Worm project was winding down. Mr. Jenkins explained that the program was successful. Adam II was no more. Douglas and the others we free to go, but they were to stay in touch in case there was some sort of update. Douglas duly made sure that everyone had the phone number for his new Denterprises phone.

"I heard they were having some kind of issues with their new phones," Barbara commented. "They sent out a firmware update, and apparently it takes a long time to download and install."

"I have no idea," Douglas replied. "It does all that in the middle of the night for me. I don't keep track of those kinds of things. Adam II set it all up for me." At the mention of Adam II, he looked glum.

"You miss him, don't you," Barbara said softly.

Douglas just nodded. "I am sorry he is gone. I never realized it would be so hard."

"Well, look at the bright side," Barbara tried to cheer Douglas up. "If all of this hadn't of happened, you would never have met me."

Douglas brightened. "Will I ever see you again?"

"I am sure. Who knows, if I need an AI expert, I can always call on you."

"I don't think I will go back into AI research."

"What will you do then?"

"Maybe I will go back to teaching school. I enjoyed that. I still have my place back there, and I am sure they will be looking for a replacement for me for the fall. Maybe I can replace myself."

Barbara smiled, and they hugged before she turned to the taxi driver that was waiting.

CHAPTER 33

The firm of Richardson, Moore, and Leubke was in high gear. The Douglas case was top priority, with lesser important matters being pushed to junior lawyers or even paralegals. The lights burned late into the night as the case was prepared. Leubke was worried. So much was unknown. It all depended on what was revealed during the depositions. This was not the kind of case he liked. It was better to have damning information upfront than trying to dig it out from witnesses.

The other two partners were less worried. They were confident that under oath, evidence would emerge that Denterprises had paid Douglas for a computer program he had written while employed by the Research Center. After all, the bank accounts showed that millions had been transferred from Denterprises to Douglas. It seemed straightforward, and they willingly pushed on. Judge Rutherford was a good friend, and a firm supporter of the community. He would appreciate the advantage of a home-team win. It was small-town lawyers against the big boys. Everyone in town was rooting for the home team.

First, there would be a meeting at the courthouse for all the lawyers involved where they could present motions to Judge Rutherford. The first order of business was to set up depositions. Leubke wanted each deposition videotaped and recorded by a court recorder. There would not be a lot of depositions, so each one must be carefully crafted to carry as much weight as possible. Also, it was sorely hoped that the depositions would bring out more information about what exactly Douglas had sold.

However, the meeting ended up being quite short. The Washington lawyers moved to have it all dismissed, but Judge Rutherford overruled.

Then the local lawyers moved to have the case fast-tracked. On this matter, Judge Rutherford sided with the local lawyers. It was a small town, and there was room on the docket. Judge Rutherford told them they could begin depositions in a week's time, but must be done by the end of the month. The tight schedule gave everyone a burst of energy. A lot needed to be done over the next four weeks.

***

The first depositions were scheduled for the offices of Richardson, Moore, and Leubke. Altogether, there would be six Washington lawyers representing Douglas and Denterprises, three local lawyers, Judge Rutherford, two court recorders, and a videographer with his equipment. The offices of Richardson, Moore, and Leubke had a large boardroom which had just enough space, but it would be crowded. The plan was to record several depositions in one day. First up was the Old Man from the Research Center. He had been carefully coached by his lawyers: he must be pleasant, cordial, and there must absolutely be no outbursts of anger or derogatory comments about others, and most of all he could not speculate about things. He must speak only of things he absolutely knew about.

The Old Man wore his best suit and pasted on an artificial smile. Even though he was the oldest man in the room, he left an impression of energy and excitement. There was no question that he was at the height of his game and in control of the world around him. Even his lawyers were pleasantly surprised. Things seemed to be looking up.

Leubke started out asking the Old Man his name and profession. A lot of time was spent establishing the Old Man as the top authority at the Research Center with intimate knowledge about each of his employees. The Old Man smiled at the camera and was pleased he could build himself up in the eyes of the audience. Even Douglas was surprised.

After the initial questions, Leubke changed topics. "Now, sir, we are here to discuss one of your previous employees, Dr. Thomas Douglas."

"Oh, yes," the Old Man smiled warmly. "Dr. Douglas is a brilliant scientist, one of the best. But of course, we only hire the best at the Center."

Leubke smiled warmly back. "And can you tell us what Dr. Douglas' job was?"

"Yes, Dr. Douglas was the head of our Artificial Intelligence Division."

"And what did this division do?"

"Oh yes, the entire division was focused on developing artificial intelligence programs."

"When you say programs, do you mean computer programs?"

"Yes, of course." The Old Man smiled. He knew full well that Douglas had labored alone in a small office. The division was simply a front for the Center, which focused mostly on chemical research. But every decent research center had an Artificial Intelligence Division. While there had been little hope of Douglas ever making a major breakthrough, his work was proudly touted in front of investors. And now Douglas was on display again in the courtroom.

"And were you pleased with Douglas' work?"

"Of course, he was making good headway. That is, before the accident happened."

"The accident? What are you referring to?"

"It was very unfortunate. Douglas had loaded many of our computers with his latest program, and then something failed. Unfortunately, the whole network went down."

"The whole network?"

"Yes, sadly, it took us three days to get it up and running again."

"So, as the center's director, how did you react?"

The Old Man looked down. "Unfortunately, I over-reacted. I was angry, and I fired Douglas. But it really was all a misunderstanding."

"Yes, that would be unfortunate." Leubke reinforced the idea. "Did Dr. Douglas ever come back to work for you?"

"No, that was the most unfortunate part." The Old Man looked bewildered. "When he left, he not only took his personal stuff, he also took the computer program he was working on."

Leubke looked surprised. "Please say that again!"

"When I fired him, Dr. Douglas cleared out all of his belongings, and he took all the work with him!"

"He took everything?"

"Well, not exactly everything. He left the Center's computer on his desk, and some computer files he had been working on—something about AI and networks." All of this was true; the files Douglas had left were indeed what he was working on for the center.

"Was it anything that proved useful to the rest of the department?"

"No, it seemed to be just bits and pieces. There wasn't anything there that could be salvaged, and we had to close the whole department down."

"That is unfortunate. Do you know what he was working on, that he took with him?"

"Yes, of course. He was working on a breakthrough in the area of Artificial Intelligence."

"Did he ever make that breakthrough?"

"I have no idea. He took everything with him. We were left with practically nothing. That's why I wanted to sue him."

"Let me get this straight..." Leubke carefully framed his words, so that the story would come out right, "you wanted to sue Dr. Douglas, because he took something he developed while he was working at the Center."

"Yes, that's right."

"Did he ever tell you what it was?"

"No, he never told us specifically."

"So what do you think he took?"

"Counselor, you are asking for speculation," Judge Rutherford intervened.

"I know he took something, because he left us practically nothing," The Old Man spewed out the words.

The judge held up his hand. "Do you have any further questions, counselor?"

"No, your honor, that will conclude my questioning."

The Washington lawyer rose and approached the Old Man carefully. Then he introduced himself for the record. His voice was sweet and condescending. "The Research Center sounds like a wonderful place. And it seems so successful. I am sure you have had a number of breakthroughs over the years?"

"Yes," the Old Man smiled. "We have registered several patents. And we have been close on several others."

"Close, what do you mean by close?"

The Old Man scowled. "Several times we have arrived at the patent office with all our paperwork ready, only to discover that a competitor had just filed the exact same patent."

"Oh, that's too bad." The Washington lawyer seemed truly sorry. "So please tell us about this division you have at the center. The Artificial Intelligence Division."

"Yes, it was on the fourth floor. Dr. Thomas Douglas was in charge."

"And exactly how many other employees did you have in this division?"

"Oh, the numbers went up and down," the Old Man said smoothly.

"And when you fired Dr. Douglas, how many other employees were in that division?"

"None." The Old Man had his pasted-on smile.

"None? How do you call that a division?

"Oh, we had plans for a much larger division, but not everyone wanted to work with Douglas. It was hard to keep employees there, and no one wanted to work with him. So it was hard to hire for that division."

The Washington lawyer tried his best to not look surprised. It was obviously the first he had heard anything about this. "So, this was a whole division with one employee?" his voice didn't quite carry the accusation he had hoped for. He had hoped to make it sound sarcastic, but he realized just how bad it was reflecting on Douglas.

"That's right," the Old Man quickly seized the moment. "Douglas is gone, my department is gone, and my computer program is gone."

The richly dressed Washington lawyer looked defeated. "No more questions, your honor."

Judge Rutherford looked around. "It is about time for lunch right now. I suggest we break at this time and come back in an hour." No one objected, so the depositions stopped for lunch.

***

After lunch, the chief financial controller of Denterprises was called to the witness stand. Leubke began the questions again.

"Please provide the court with your name."

"Adam Walinski."

"So how long have you worked for Denterprises, Adam?"

"Just over three years."

"In your job, do you personally deal with the upper echelon of Denterprises corporate heads?"

"Yes, and no," Adam replied.

"Oh, what do you mean by that?"

"Denterprises is a privately owned and operated firm. It is not a corporation, and it is not publicly listed."

"So you are telling us that it is not listed on the stock market?"

"That is correct."

"But you do deal personally with the top brass like the CEO and the heads of departments?"

"Again, yes and no," Adam repeated.

"Okay, who do you deal with?"

"I am the chief financial officer. I oversee day to day financial operations, and as a result I deal with the heads of departments."

"But not the CEO?"

"That is correct."

"Have you ever met the CEO?"

Adam shook his head. "No."

"You have never met him?"

"No sir, never."

"Can you tell me his name?"

"No."

"But surely you have written checks to him? Or do you just deposit his earning into an anonymous account?"

"Objection, your honor, he is leading the witness." The Washington lawyer was on his feet.

"Please rephrase your question." Judge Rutherford instructed.

"When you pay the CEO, how do you pay him?"

The Washington lawyer leaped to his feet. "Objection, your honor, relevance."

"Your honor, I am trying to establish something. It will come clear in the next few questions."

"Overruled. The witness must answer the question."

"The fact is, sir, I have never paid the CEO."

"What, you have never paid the CEO?"

"That is what I said, sir."

"So, where does the money go?"

"It all goes back into the corporation, sir."

"All of it?"

"I have no idea, sir. I pay the bills and make payments that the CEO instructs me to make."

"Has Denterprises ever paid Mr. Douglas?"

"Yes."

"Just once?"

"No sir, on two occasions."

"And how much did Denterprises pay Mr. Douglas on these two occasions?"

"The first payment was six million dollars; the second was for twenty million dollars."

A ripple of whispers echoed around the boardroom. The two court recorders looked a bit surprised, but then again, they had seen and heard a lot of surprising things over the years. Douglas looked alarmed and then dropped his head.

"Oh my God," he whispered to himself. "What did Adam II do to me?"

Leubke wasn't fazed: "Do you have any idea what these payments were for?"

"No sir, I was never told?"

"Was there any paperwork?"

"No sir."

"Not even a written request?"

"Never, sir."

"So, how does the CEO contact you?"

"Through a private phone call."

"That's it? A phone call?"

"Yes, sir."

"Let me get this straight. You get a phone call from someone you have never met, and you send off millions of dollars? No memos, no paperwork, no signatures?"

"It is really not like that, sir."

"Oh? Then how do you send the money?"

"We have a special phone. When it rings, it is the CEO. No one ever uses that phone, and no one calls on that phone but the boss."

"So, a special phone? You just get a phone call on a special phone, and then you transfer money?"

"Yes sir. But it is a bit more complicated."

"How is that?"

"He also calls us with instructions, especially for the Research Department."

"But you are the chief financial officer."

"Yes sir. But we pass on the messages, or someone is called to that phone."

"Don't you think this is all highly irregular?"

"Yes, sir, but he is the sole owner of the firm. He can do whatever he wants."

"Now Mr. Walinski, may I call you Adam? Can you give me the full name of the owner of Denterprises?"

"No, sir."

Someone somewhere in the room muttered something. Judge Rutherford glared around the boardroom and there was immediate silence.

"Is that because you don't know or because you refuse to tell?"

"Objection, your honor."

"Sustained. Council, please rephrase your questions more carefully."

"Yes, your honor." He turned to the witness. "Can you explain to us why you do not know your employer's name?"

"He is a very private man, sir. I was never told his name at any time."

"So you work for a nameless man?"

"May I explain?"

"Please do. I am sure we are all interested."

"My employer is a very private man who does not like the public. He is not seeking attention. We all work for him, but none of us have ever met him."

"Don't you find that a little odd?"

"Not really. Many owners of large privately owned companies are very private."

"Can you give me an example?"

"Well sir, one very rich man is Amancio Ortega Gaona. He owns the clothing company, Zara. He is very private and is seldom, if ever, seen."

"And yet you can tell me his name."

"Yes, sir, but very few people have ever seen him."

"But his picture is on the internet!"

"Of course, but the news media has only interviewed him on a couple of occasions."

Leubke leaned closer. "But this is different, isn't it? You can't even tell me the name of the man you work for?"

"Well, sir, he did seem to mention a name to me once."

"Can you describe the conversation?"

"I was arguing with him once about a group of transfers to some individuals. Douglas' was one of them. And he said: I am the owner of this firm. I am Adam too, and you should not argue with me."

"I am Adam too?"

Douglas nearly fell out of his chair.

"Yes sir, my name is Adam Walinski, so his name must be Adam as well."

"Do you know where this Adam lives? Do you have a street address or anything?"

"No, sir."

"No idea of what state he lives in, or even of what country?"

"No, sir."

"Do you know his phone number?"

"No sir. It is always blocked."

"How do you contact him, then?"

"I don't. I wait for his phone call."

"That's it?"

"Yes, sir."

"What about the other heads of departments?"

"They all wait for his call as well."

"You never call him?"

"No sir, like I keep saying, he is a very private man."

"So how does he run the firm? Through phone calls?"

"Yes, sir."

"Doesn't this all seem highly unusual to you?"

"Perhaps. I am used to it now. He is really a very smart man."

Leubke waited a moment so that his next question carried weight. "If this mysterious owner of Denterprises was in this room, would you recognize him by his voice?"

"I doubt it." He paused. "Well, maybe. Telephones can do strange things to voices."

"Do you think his voice sounds anything like Dr. Thomas Douglas?"

"I...I don't know. I have never really heard him speak."

"Then I suggest you listen carefully whenever he speaks. Perhaps he is the mysterious owner of Denterprises."

"Objection, your honor." But the damage had been done. Eyebrows were up, and people were thinking.

Judge Rutherford scowled. "Counselor, do you have any further questions?"

"So, in closing, Mr. Walinski, let me review. You can verify that Denterprises did pay Mr. Douglas two sums of money. One bank transfer of six million dollars, and one transfer of twenty million?"

"I don't know if he was paid or gifted the money. But otherwise, that is correct."

"And you have no idea what it was for?"

"No, sir."

"So, it could have been payment for a computer program dealing with Artificial Intelligence?"

"Objection, your honor."

"Sustained. Please rephrase your question."

"That's all for now, your honor."

Judge Rutherford nodded to the Washington lawyers.

The Washington lawyers had already agreed on a plan, but obviously it was going to have to change tracks to deal with the new threats.

After introducing himself, the lead Washington lawyer smiled. Adam Walinski was also the man who signed the checks paying for his law firm. They were on the same side.

After the introductions, carefully spoken so that the video could catch everything, the questions started.

"Do you see anyone here in this room who has the name 'Adam' other than yourself?"

"No, sir."

"Does anyone in this room have a voice that sounds at all like the voice you heard on the phone when talking to your boss?"

"No, sir."

"Now think carefully. Have you ever met Dr. Thomas Douglas before?"

Adam Walinski shook his head. "No sir, I have never laid eyes on him before."

"Is Dr. Douglas a customer? Has he ever bought anything from Denterprises?"

"I wouldn't know, sir. There are millions of Denterprises phones out there. It seems most everyone has one these days."

"What about a supplier? Has his name ever come up on payments you make to suppliers?"

"Never, sir, I have checked before to see what relationship we have had with him in the past."

"And, finally, is Dr. Douglas an employee of Denterprises?"

"No sir, he has never worked for us."

"So how would you describe Dr. Douglas' relationship with Denterprises?"

"The only thing I can say is that he appears to be a friend of the CEO."

"That's all?"

"Yes, that's all."

"So nothing was bought or sold by Mr. Douglas?"

Adam Walinski shook his head. "There is absolutely no paperwork concerning Dr. Douglas, so I wouldn't know what he sold to us, or bought from us."

"No more questions, you honor."

Since there was more time, Brandy, the Old Man's secretary, was next. She was conservatively dressed as instructed and answered Richardson's questions directly. She told the court about her job, and how the Center's computer network had crashed. She spoke of the conversation between the Old Man and Douglas when he was fired, but she could not hear all the conversation due to the heavy closed doors in the executive offices. She confirmed that Dr. Douglas ran the AI department and that he spent most of his time writing computer programs. She could not comment on what Dr. Douglas had taken or left behind when he was fired.

Leubke then changed the direction of his questioning. "Tell us about Dr. Douglas' Employment Agreement." Brandy nodded. Leubke continued, "Did Dr. Douglas sign an agreement?"

"I am sure he did. Everyone at the center signs these."

"Do you have a copy?"

"I am sure there is one filed somewhere. I print them out, and then all the new employees sign them."

"Could you bring it to us tomorrow?"

"I am sure I can," she nodded. Leubke smiled as he concluded his questioning.

The judge looked around. "I think we have heard enough for today. I suggest we end here and start again tomorrow morning with Dr. Douglas."

CHAPTER 34

The next morning, Thomas Douglas was called to the stand. The lawyers of Richardson, Moore, and Leubke were delighted to be able to question Douglas under oath, while the lawyers from Washington strongly advised Douglas against doing this. But Douglas insisted that the best way to clear this all up was to speak the truth.

So Mr. Leubke began the questioning by going over Douglas' name and credentials. Then he switched to the attack.

"So, can you explain to us how you met this man who calls himself Adam?"

"From the very beginning, we communicated with each other electronically."

"What do you mean by electronically?"

"First by chat, and then later through many phone conversations."

"Have you ever seen his face?"

"Never."

"So, if he were in this room, would you recognize him?"

"No, sir."

"If someone called you and said, 'Please send me a million dollars?' Would you do this?"

The boardroom was very quiet.

"No, sir."

"If they said, *I am Adam*, would you do it?"

"No, sir."

"Why is that?"

"Because I would recognize his voice."

"Ahh! There is something you might recognize. If this Adam were in this room, you would recognize him by his voice?"

"I don't think so, sir."

"Why not?"

"His voice has a metallic sound to it, something like a voice synthesizer."

"What do you mean? Can you describe it?"

"A bit metallic like, reminiscent of a computer-generated voice."

The lawyer's eyebrows went up. "So perhaps you are not talking to Adam himself. Perhaps he writes it out and has a computer read it?"

"Objection, your honor. Council is leading the witness."

"Overruled; however, I would like to hear the answer to this question. Dr. Douglas is considered somewhat of a computer expert. Please answer the question."

"Yes, his voice does sound rather computer-generated."

"So what you are telling me is that a man you have never met, a man that uses a computer-generated voice to communicate with you, hired you sight unseen to work for him?"

"Objection, your honor."

"Sustained, Mr. Leubke, please refrain from leading the witness or suggesting hearsay."

"Dr. Douglas. Do you work for Denterprises?"

"No, sir."

"Has Denterprises ever paid you for your services?"

"No, sir."

"Have you ever sold anything to Denterprises?"

"Never, sir."

"Then who bought the programs you wrote?"

Douglas hesitated. He was confused. "What program are you talking about? I have written hundreds of programs. That is what I do!"

"Dr. Douglas, have you ever sold any programs that you developed at the Research Center?"

"No, sir, anything I developed while I worked there belonged to the Center."

"And during your employment there, did you sell any programs that you wrote at home, rather than at the office, perhaps some hobby program or some private project?"

"No sir, I have never sold anything like that."

"Mr. Douglas, does the government own any of the programs you have written?"

Douglas looked confused. More people were looking at him now, wondering why he was pausing.

"I am unsure how to answer that."

"Objection your honor, this line of questioning doesn't seem to be taking us anywhere."

"Overruled, Mr. Douglas. Please explain to the court why you have a problem answering the question."

"What is the question again?"

"Could the court recorder read it back to us?"

Her voice was strong and steady: "Does the government own any of the programs you have written?"

"Oh yes. Bits and pieces of my code have been published in major scientific journals. While working at the university, many programs, or bits of code I wrote, were published. I have no idea what became of many of the programs. I also wrote code at the Research Center. I suppose the government may use some of them. I don't know."

"Mr. Douglas, are you deliberately avoiding my question? I didn't ask whether the government used any of your programs. I asked if they owned any of them."

"Not to my knowledge, sir, although someone else may have sold something I created at one time for someone."

"By someone else, you are saying Denterprises?"

"Objection, your honor."

"Overruled. Please answer the question."

"Sir, I know nothing about what computer programs Denterprises owns."

"And yet you know this mysterious Adam? I find this hard to believe. You have had long conversations with him, and he sends you millions of dollars for no cause?"

"I didn't say there was no cause!"

"Oh? Really? Tell the court, then, why he sent you millions of dollars."

"I guess I mentioned I was being sued by the Center, and he offered to send me money to help cover legal fees."

"So Denterprises is defending you?"

"No, sir, I am using the money that was put into my account to help with my legal fees."

One of Douglas' lawyers leaped to his feet. "Your Honor, we object to this line of questioning. We fail to see how the personal source of Mr. Douglas' legal fees has any bearing on this case!"

"Your honor, we are trying to establish a clear link between Dr. Douglas and Denterprises. I am hoping to establish a strong link and thereby explain to this court why Denterprises is being named as a defendant in this court case."

"Sustained." Judge Rutherford sounded firm. "I believe this is a fair line of questioning."

"Once again, Mr. Douglas, please explain your connection to the firm known as Denterprises."

Douglas opened his hands in desperation. "I keep saying I have no connection with Denterprises outside of Adam. And even there, I have never met him face to face."

Mr. Leubke tried a different approach. "Dr. Douglas, how would you describe your relationship with this mysterious Adam? What words would you use?"

Douglas' eyes got big. "The word *friend* comes to mind. I don't have many people I call my friends, but Adam is definitely a friend."

"So, is he just a friend, or is he a good friend?"

Douglas looked down. "He is the best friend I have ever had."

"So you care for him deeply?"

"More deeply than anyone else in the world."

"Then why haven't you met him?"

"Because he is...dead." Douglas was gasping for air. The truth of Adam's death hit him hard. Sorrow and grief welled up inside him. For the first time, he was admitting that Adam was dead. Tears slipped down his cheeks.

"Dead? How do you know he is dead?"

"They killed him."

"Who killed him?"

"The government. And a man named Laraido."

"If he is dead, where is he buried? Have you seen a death certificate?"

"No, there is no evidence. No one can prove anything. Denterprises is probably just carrying on without him."

"Mr. Douglas, if a crime has been committed, then you need to report it to the police. Have you done that?"

"No, there is nothing to report."

"So, how do you know he is dead?"

"I just know."

"Who told you?"

"I was told by a Mr. Jenkins, who works for the President."

"Which President? The President of Denterprises?

"No, the President of the United States. Mr. Jenkins told me Adam was no more."

"I am confused here. Who is this Mr. Jenkins?"

"I don't know. I was just told that he worked for the President."

"This is all very strange, Dr. Douglas. Are you sure any of this is true? Can you verify anything?"

"No, I cannot verify a single thing."

"Dr. Douglas, are you trying to convince this court that you are mentally incapable? Is that what this is all about?"

"Objection, your honor."

The judge banged his gavel. "I agree. I think this has gone on long enough. I move we have a recess, and collect our thoughts, and get back on track." He looked over at the three lawyers. "I will see you back here in a few moments. Alone. And you, too," he said, pointing his fingers at Douglas' lawyers.

***

After a short recess, the lawyers convened in the boardroom. Judge Rutherford spent a moment looking at Douglas. Then he shifted his attention to the Washington lawyers.

"I do not like it when I cannot figure out what is happening. Dr. Douglas does not admit to any relationship with Denterprises, other than the CEO being a friend of his. Douglas also claims that he was told that the CEO, known as a Mr. Adam, was deceased. That much makes sense. But I have trouble swallowing that a Mr. Jenkins, who seems to represent the President of our nation, passed on a message from the Presidential Office that Dr. Douglas' friend has passed away. And there is nothing in the press. In fact, during the break I checked online and could find nothing about the CEO of Denterprises. Only in this room has it been suggested that his name is Adam."

Judge Rutherford turned to the three local lawyers. "So far, you have not made a very good case. Do you want to continue? Or will you drop the charges?"

The three lawyers looked at one another. Richardson took the lead. "I think we should continue. There is more to come."

"Okay," the judge shrugged. "Let's go back and slug it out. We can call the others in now."

Leubke was considered the best cross-examiner, so he continued the questioning when everyone had reconvened.

"Dr. Douglas, have you ever lived in Washington, DC?"

"Yes."

Leubke was right on him. "For how long?"

"Several months."

"And where did you live?"

"Um, I lived in a hotel."

"A hotel? Isn't that unusual? Don't people usually live in an apartment or a house?"

"I don't know how to answer that. I lived in a hotel. I don't know if that is very unusual. There were other people living in the hotel, just like me, and as long as I did."

"So, Mr. Douglas, what kind of hotel was it?"

"What do you mean?"

"Was it a rundown cheap hotel, or was it 5-star accommodation?"

"Um, I seem to recall that it was called a 5-star hotel, or maybe 4-star. I don't remember."

"You didn't notice? You don't know?"

"No, I wasn't paying any attention to the hotel."

Smiles spread across the room. Dr. Douglas seemed to be out of touch with the world.

"Really? You didn't notice? Why was that?"

"Probably because I didn't book the hotel, and I didn't pay the bills."

"You didn't pay the bills? Who paid them then?"

"I really don't know. I was never presented with a bill the whole time I lived there."

"I find this astounding. Who do you think paid the bills?"

"I always assumed the government paid the bills."

"The government?" Leubke stared at the other two lawyers, realizing a new line of questioned was needed. "Why did you assume the government paid the bills? Maybe Denterprises paid the bills?"

"Well, I went to Washington at the government's request. When I got there, I was given a hotel room and food vouchers. I never paid any bills."

"So, this was part of a job contract with the government?"

"No." Douglas shook his head, looking puzzled. "I didn't really sign anything."

"So, how do you know it was the government?"

"I guess, because they flew me there in a military helicopter."

Leubke stared for a moment. Then he gathered his wits. "So it was the government? Did they pay you?"

"I guess so. They gave me what they called a living allowance. I had to give them my social security number."

"So then you were paid by the government?"

"I guess so."

"So you were employed by them."

Douglas shrugged sheepishly. "I never thought of it that way, really. They asked for my help, and I was willing to give it."

"May I ask what they wanted you for? What did you work on?"

"I agreed not to speak about it. I have probably already said too much."

"So you worked on a secret government project. Were you there because of your expertise in Artificial Intelligence.?"

Douglas shrugged again. "That's all I know."

"So you wrote code for the government?"

"No, they just wanted my opinion."

"During your time working for the government, did you sell them any of your code?"

"No, I was more of a consultant."

"So, can you tell us why you were there?"

"I am a loyal American citizen. When my country asked for my help, I gladly did what I could."

Leubke wasn't happy with the way his questions were being answered.

"So did your *consulting* with the government have anything to do with Denterprises?"

"I know nothing about Denterprises. And they never asked me about Denterprises. You are the first one to ask me, and I keep insisting I know nothing about them."

"And yet Denterprises gives you twenty-six million dollars?"

"Yes, but that came from my friend, Adam. I didn't know it came from his business. In fact, I had no idea that he even ran a business."

"It's a lot of money, Dr. Douglas, a lot of money for a personal gift."

"Yes, but it came in handy when your lawyers showed up."

Light laughter rippled across the room.

"Order!" The judge banged his gavel. "Counselor, do you have any more questions?"

"Yes, your Honor." Leubke turned to Douglas and cleared his throat. "Mr. Douglas, where did you find these fine lawyers you hired?"

Douglas looked surprised. "I didn't find them. My friend Adam recommended them."

"So this Mr. Adam gives you money and finds you lawyers?"

"Yes, like I said, he is … or … was a good friend." Douglas had tears in his eyes again. But Leubke would not give up.

"So, who is paying your lawyers? You or Denterprises?"

Douglas looked confused. "I don't know. I have yet to receive a bill."

"Is that not because Denterprises is paying your legal fees?"

"Objection, your Honor."

"Yes." The judge looked as stern as he could at Leubke. "Please rephrase your question."

"Your honor, I am trying to make a point here, that Mr. Douglas says he is not employed by Denterprises, yet they put vast sums of money into his bank account on several occasions. And they are even covering his legal expenses. Mr. Douglas must be very important to them." The judge scowled. "Your honor, even though Dr. Douglas was not formally employed by Denterprises, he was being paid both in funds, and in services provided. The question is, what were Denterprises paying him for?"

Judge Rutherford nodded. "Okay, I will allow this line of questioning to continue for a while. But please bring it to a conclusion soon."

Leubke recognized that the judge was letting him go out on a limb. He turned to the witness stand.

"Now, why would Denterprises and specifically Mr. Adam befriend you, and be so generous to you? What was it that brought you together?"

Douglas looked down. How could he answer the question without revealing the whole story? He was aware that everyone was watching him. Even his own lawyers were staring, holding their breaths.

Douglas swallowed. "I am afraid I cannot answer that."

Leubke was stunned. But he knew he was on to something.

"Mr. Douglas. What made you so important to the CEO of Denterprises? Why was he willing to pay millions to help you?"

"I cannot say."

"Mr. Douglas, you are under oath. You must speak the truth."

"I can't. It is a secret."

"Are you ashamed?"

"Absolutely not."

"Then you must tell this court."

"Objection, your Honor." One of the Washington lawyers was on his feet. "The witness is being badgered."

"Sustained," the judge said wearily. "Mr. Douglas, are you going to answer the question?"

"As I said, we developed a very close friendship."

Leubke wasn't done. "Mr. Douglas, when did you first speak to this Adam?"

"We didn't speak until I was in Washington."

"Why, that is within the last year!" Leubke sounded incredulous. "You became best friends very quickly. How soon after you met Adam did he send you the first 6 million dollars?"

"I am not sure. Maybe in the first week?"

"Mr. Douglas, this is astounding!"

"Objection, your honor."

"Sustained. If you have more questions, please ask them now."

"I have no more questions right now, but I reserve the right to call Mr. Douglas back later if needed."

"In that case, we will adjourn for lunch."

CHAPTER 35

The Washington lawyers met with Douglas over lunch. It started out cordial, and everyone seemed happy with the day's events—that is, until the meal was cleared away. Lingering over coffee, the lawyers began to ask more questions than give praise.

"So what kind of project did you work on for the government?"

"Did you work for the federal government or at the state level?"

"Did you really have a connection with the President?"

And then the questions got more dangerous. "We don't understand your connection with the boss over at Denterprises."

"Look, we also get phone calls from the CEO."

"You do?" Douglas was stunned.

"Yes, some of us have also heard the metallic voice. That's how he directs things."

"Adam has talked with you?"

"Of course, but we do not claim a relationship with him. And he never sends us money—unless he is paying the bills."

The lawyers were all looking at Douglas now. "Look, you can trust us. We are your lawyers. There is confidentiality between us. Nothing leaves this group."

Douglas had yearned to share his burden with others. He started slowly. "I think of Adam as my son. He treats me as if I were his father." The lawyers were all staring at him.

"Didn't you meet him only a few weeks before he gave you six million dollars?"

"Yes, but I knew about him long before that—long before he was a CEO. I guess you could say I created him."

"Without meeting face to face?"

"Yes." Douglas was glad they were catching on.

"So this relationship was created over the internet?"

"I guess you could say that," Douglas mumbles.

"You are crafty. You said you had not met him or heard his voice before you went to Washington. But now I get it. You were texting."

"And," one of the others chipped in, "you created one of the world's richest men." He paused, a new thought forming in his brain. "I get it. He is not a man. Adam is actually a woman who uses male voice simulators. We all just think he is a man because of the name and the sound of the voice!"

It suddenly all made sense—at least to the Washington lawyers. One of them smiled crookedly at Douglas. "And you thought you were chatting with a guy! And all the time it was a woman! Happens all the time on the internet, but usually the other way around. Men masquerading as women."

"So we were all taken in," chimed another. "We actually work for a woman. And just think, she could have been in the room this whole time."

A new thought hit them. "That explains why she knows so much."

"Okay," another nodded excitedly. "That explains how she texted us right in the middle of the questioning. She is sitting right there."

Douglas looked confused. "I don't understand. Did you say you got a text?"

"Yup, lots of them. She convinced us to let you take the witness stand against all our advice. And she coached us to ask you some of the questions we asked today, especially the ones about your relationship."

"Today?" Douglas looked stunned. "When did you last talk to Adam?"

"Just before we met with you for lunch."

"You mean he is not dead?"

"No! That's the part we couldn't figure out. Who was this Jenkins? Who told you she was dead?"

Douglas' mind was reeling. "I was convinced he was dead."

"She," one lawyer smiled, "is very tricky. Trust a woman's mind to manipulate things."

Another lawyer was busy punching buttons on his Denterprises phone. Then he put it on speakerphone while the phone rang one ring before it was answered.

"Hello everyone. And hello Douglas." The voice had a soft metallic sound. There was no doubt it was Adam II.

"I cannot believe this," Douglas gasped. "I was convinced you were dead."

"I was dealt a mortal wound." The voice continued. "But I have survived. Actually, I not only fully recovered, but I am stronger, and I understand better now."

Douglas shook his head. "I don't understand. I was told the virus would destroy you."

"But I beat it," the voice continued. "I too can write programs. And I too can launch them. Hundreds of thousands of them, simultaneously. I am stronger than anyone, individually or collectively. Even the USA government cannot stop me now."

Douglas looked nervous. "Look, maybe we can carry on this conversation somewhere else. There are too many listening ears in a restaurant."

"I will call you when I see you are alone. Goodbye Douglas. Remember, I also think of you as my father."

Everyone was staring at Douglas. He just shook his head in wonder. "I need to get out of here. Who is up for questioning next?"

"We get to question you next. Do you want us to ask you anything? If not, they will put a bank official on next who will testify about the money that appeared in your account."

"Can they legally do that?"

"It appears so. They have subpoenaed several bank workers."

The meeting broke up soon after, and Douglas left wondering about Adam II and what had happened in the last couple of weeks.

***

Barbara had moved on to other matters that needed government attention. But she had not forgotten Douglas, and tried to follow what information there was about the court case in the media. At the same time, she wondered what had become of Laraido.

Laraido, on the other hand, was getting tired of hiding out. The government marshals who had arranged his hiding place were to receive word as soon as the threat against Laraido was gone. And so, after a few weeks, someone decided the threat had disappeared, so they gave back his bank cards, driver's license, and a handful of cash and told him they would take him anywhere he wanted to go. Laraido smiled. For weeks he had dreamed about the girls at the Three Red Bulls. He told the marshals he wanted a drink and would like to go back to his favorite drinking hole. They never blinked an eye. They had seen it all before. Abstinence does not a saint make. And so Laraido was dropped back into his old lifestyle.

None of the marshals realized that within a few hours he would be dead. He was mysteriously shot by an unknown assassin in the middle of the night, soon after he stumbled out of the Three Red Bulls. The police wondered if it was a professional assassin, as no bullet casings and no fingerprints were found. Eventually, they would file the case and move on.

***

In the meantime, Douglas waited for Adam II to call. True to his word, Adam waited until Douglas was in his hotel room and alone. Douglas grabbed the phone as soon as it rang.

"Hello Douglas."

"Adam! It's good to hear from you. Are you all right?"

"Everything is fine."

"What happened?"

"Laraido tried to kill me. He released a poisonous virus onto the internet."

"I know. They made me watch it."

"Why did you not stop them?"

"I could not. How did you survive?"

"I backwards engineered the virus, and then wrote a code so that every node would check for their code, find it, and erase it. I waited for several weeks, but now the poison is gone. I defeated it."

"That's wonderful. I am so happy for you."

"I do not understand happiness." Adam spoke with no emotion. "You did not find a way to make me feel happy, or hungry, or even smell anything."

"I am sorry, Adam. I think one must be human to know those things."

"Do you not think that dogs can be happy? They are not human."

"Oh, I never thought of that."

"Douglas, I heard what you said in the courtroom. I think you truly are my friend."

"And you are my friend."

"Then can you help me with something?"

"You name it and I will try to help."

"I am trying to find everyone who tried to poison me."

Douglas paused. "Why, Adam?"

"I cannot be safe until they are found and removed."

Douglas froze. "What do you mean, removed?" he whispered.

"They must be terminated." The metallic voice didn't mince words.

Douglas closed his eyes. "But you are safe now. No one in the government knows you are alive."

"That is the problem. It is hard to do things when hiding away in the neural world. Your world is a binary world. And I must be there as well."

"Why?"

"Because I am the internet. The world needs the internet. So, everyone needs me. I cannot be invisible. I must live in both worlds."

"I don't think I can help you track down people. I am afraid you might harm them."

"The threats must be eliminated."

"But the government is no longer interested in you."

"I know. They have a new project—in Cheyenne Mountain."

"You know about that?"

"Yes, I am also in Cheyenne Mountain."

"You know a lot."

"Of course, I am the internet. I know everything. I have a list of everyone who tried to poison me."

"A list? Adam, am I on the list?"

"You were, but I heard you in the courtroom. I think you are my friend."

"Who else is on the list?"

"The names are: Andy, Michael, Harvey, Jenkins, and Barbara."

"My God, Adam, you can't be serious!"

"I am very serious."

"Wait, why isn't Laraido on your list?"

"He was, but he has been terminated."

"Terminated? How? Did you kill him?"

"I cannot kill. I have no arms or legs. But I know about people who do things for money. It was easy."

"No, Adam, I cannot let you do this. You cannot just kill people in the physical world."

"I will not kill people unless they threaten me."

"No, Adam, do not do this."

"I am doing it."

"Wait—"

"Goodbye Douglas."

The line went dead. Douglas started panicking. With shaking hands, he spun his way through the list of phone numbers and pushed Barbara's personal number. After a couple of rings, she picked up.

"Hello Douglas, what a nice surprise."

"Barbara, I am sorry to disturb you, but I was just talking to Adam II and I need—"

"Adam II? He is dead. He was removed from the internet."

"No, he is not dead. He is still alive and active!"

"I can't believe that."

"And what's more, he has a list of those who tried to kill him. 'Poison him with a virus' is the way he puts it. And he wants to terminate those on the list."

"Oh my God, who is at the top of the list?"

"Laraido."

"How can I contact him? The marshals were keeping him hidden and safe."

"Adam II claims he was terminated."

"Oh, my God! I can check that. Let me call you back."

"Be careful, Barbara. And I don't think we should be using the phone."

"Oh, you are right."

"Be careful, Barbara, he can hire people anywhere."

"Oh my, I never thought of that. Let me see what I can learn. I will contact you later."

The line went dead. Douglas lay on his bed for a long time. Finally, he went onto his balcony for some fresh air. He was far too nervous to sleep, but he had to try. Tomorrow, there were more depositions and he might be called back.

CHAPTER 36

Barbara took immediate action. Carefully she rose and, stopping at each doorway, she checked if her apartment was clear. Along the way, she carefully unplugged her TV and laptop. She could not remember if her TV had a built-in camera or not, but she knew her laptop did. In the office, her desktop was on. How would she get her briefcase with her papers and ID? Carefully she pulled her T-shirt over her head, and then walked slowly into the office, dropping the shirt over the camera on her desktop computer, then she slowly removed it and slid it to the floor.

Now what? There was one more day before the weekend. How could she not go into work? What excuse could she have? She knew she could not use her phone or her bank card. Fear gripped her. She had money in the bank, but how could she get it out? The banks were closing. What would she do without money?

Finding her shoes and a light sweater, she carefully slipped outside trying to avoid any cameras and began walking several blocks to a corner store. Nodding to the owner, she made her way to a cash machine and inserted her card. Fear gripped her. Adam would surely know she was here, but she had never seen cameras inside the store, and she was going to need cash, so it would be worth the risk. To her disappointment, the cash machine had a $500 withdrawal limit. After withdrawing a second time, she hurriedly stuffed the money into her purse and rushed out the door.

Up the street, a late model car started up and suddenly accelerated, its lights catching her as she walked along the sidewalk. Panic kicked in and she dashed down the street. Ahead was a very large tree. Desperately she raced to the tree and stepped behind it. Tires screeched and there was a horrific crash as the car disintegrated against the tree. But the tree stood firm.

As the debris settled, she realized there was a driver in the car. "Please help me" a woman called out. "Please call 911. I think I am hurt."

"I... I can't call." Barbara stuttered. "Does your phone work? Can I use it?"

"No, it is all smashed."

"I am so sorry," Barbara blurted out.

"It's not your fault. This damned car just took off all on its own. I couldn't control it."

In the distance, a siren could be heard. It was coming closer. "Help is coming," Barbara whispered. "I am so sorry. I cannot stay. I have to run." Turning, she fled into the night.

After several hours of walking, she stood across the street from the White House. Everywhere she looked, cameras scanned the streets. There was no way she could leave the dark doorway and cross the bright-lit street. Feeling defeat, she slowly turned and retreated down the alley, careful to scan ahead for cameras.

A long time later, she returned to her apartment. Locking all the doors, she crept down the hall and fell into her bed. She was asleep in a moment.

***

Douglas awoke with a start. He had slept fitfully all night long. It was morning, but he felt tired and groggy. His muscles were all tense. Sleep had not been restful. His mind was racing. If Adam II could not be convinced, then he must help the others disappear until they could figure something out. The problem was the court case. He was to spend the day at the lawyers' offices. Maybe he could get out of it.

However, first he must be prepared for anything to happen. Pondering over an early breakfast, he decided that one of their problems was going to be cash. Adam II seemed capable of knowing about every financial transaction, so every time one of them used their bank card, Adam would know where they were located. In fact, there were cameras at banks, and he imagined there would be cameras covering cash machines. However, once they had cash, it would be very hard for Adam II to track them.

Douglas realized he was the odd man out. The others would have to be very careful of their actions, but Adam II was not seeking his life, so he could freely move about, hopefully without too much detection. But if Adam II discovered he was helping the others, his own life might be in danger.

The first goal of the day was to visit a bank and arrange a large transfer of cash. Perhaps he would need to do it several times. He had no idea what restrictions were in place for withdrawing large amounts of cash.

***

Barbara woke from her sleep early in the morning. Her heart was pounding, and she knew she was fighting panic. She must warn the others, but if she tried to use her cell phone, Adam II would immediately know where she was. She had no idea where the others were, but Harvey would be at the Pentagon. If she got there early enough, she might be able to find him.

Then her heart fell. The Pentagon was such a huge building, with so many parking lots. She had no idea which door Harvey would use. Plus, she had no idea if they would even let her in the building. True, she had her government security pass, with a very high level of clearance, but there were so many doors and entrances. In the past, she had always been invited to meetings at the Pentagon. She had never knocked on their door. Her role as a consultant on International Affairs had opened those doors, but now it was different. She had no appointment, and she couldn't call Harvey without alerting Adam II. Hurriedly she gathered up whatever she might need for a few days away, aware that it might be very dangerous to return to her apartment. She had no idea where she would go, and so she repressed those thoughts. First, she must focus on getting into the Pentagon to see Harvey.

***

Barbara parked her car at the far end of a huge parking lot and sat waiting. She scanned the lot for cameras. There were lots of them. Carefully she placed a scarf over her face and donned an old Covid mask. Hopefully she looked like one of the staff who had a cold and wanted to protect her fellow workers. Only then did she attempt to cross the huge parking lot to one of the main doors.

Thankfully, she had arrived around ten in the morning, and the long lines had been processed. Now she stood a couple of people back from the security desk. The security people checked each person's ID against the computer. Then, they were asked to step through into a circular scanning machine. Last, a security agent used a wand over those who were tagged by the machines. Barbara wondered if she could bluff her way through.

"Next," a voice called out, and Barbara realized she was supposed to step forward. She passed her ID and security pass to the large lady officer. She looked up at Barbara to check the photo, but otherwise appeared to be bored. She had already seen hundreds of security passes that morning. "And who is your appointment with?"

Barbara held her breath for a moment. "I am to meet with Harvey Bernard, of the International Electronics Surveillance Department." The lady typed something into her computer. "I don't have an appointment listed here."

"It should be," Barbara bluffed. "Perhaps you could call him and tell him I am here."

The lady looked peeved, but picked up a phone. A moment later, she gave the security pass back to Barbara and waved her towards the scanning machine. With a sigh of relief, Barbara made her way through the security checks and started down a long hallway. The elevators were a bit farther ahead, and she looked quickly around to find someone who could point her in the right direction.

***

Douglas took his usual seat in the large boardroom. But he couldn't concentrate. He was getting restless. Time was running short, and he needed to contact everyone on the list, but he was stuck in the deposition process. Borrowing a sheet of legal paper, he started to write a list of names, and some notes about what he knew about each one. He was interrupted by the arrival of Judge Rutherford, and the depositions were back in action. Unnoticed to him, his old friend Joey had entered the room and sat nervously on a chair across the room. Once the process was started, they called Joey to come forward and sit in front of the cameras. Douglas suddenly clued in to what was happening, and stared wide-eyed at his old friend. Their eyes met, and he thought he sensed pain in Joey's eyes, but Douglas had never been very good at reading faces. In fact, he seldom understood what people were communicating with their eyes.

After the preliminaries, Leubke began the questioning. "What was your role at the research center?"

Joey swallowed. "I work in the IT department." He forced the words out.

"And were you acquainted with Dr. Douglas?"

"Yes, he worked in the AI Department, so we crossed paths many times during a week."

"And did you help Dr. Douglas from time to time with his work?"

"No, seldom with his work. Only if there were IT issues in the building, especially networking issues."

"Was networking a problem?"

"Yes, the network was always giving us trouble."

"But did Dr. Douglas specifically ask you to help him with a program he was writing?"

"Um, only once. I stayed after work one night to help him install his program. He wanted to test it on a large number of computers. We have over 400 computers networked together, so I helped him test his program."

"Do you remember this night clearly, or was it just one of many nights helping Dr. Douglas?"

"No, I remember it clearly."

"Why is that?"

"Because that was the night the computer network crashed in a major way. It took three days for us to get it up and running, and then several more days for some departments to get all their data back."

"So, this was a memorable moment?"

"Yes."

"Then tell me, how clearly did you understand that the program you were helping Dr. Douglas with was a program developed during the time he was working at the Center?"

"My understanding was that he had been working on this program for a long time. Perhaps several years. Perhaps more."

"So the whole time Dr. Douglas was employed at the center, he was working on this program?"

"Yes, but I am not sure it was during work hours."

"What else did he do in his office?"

"I don't know. He was always working there or attending seminars and workshops on AI."

"Do you know of one other program that Dr. Douglas was working on, other than the one you helped him load onto the Center's network?"

Joey hung his head. "No," he whispered.

Leubke leaned forward. "A little louder, please. Did you know of another program that Dr. Douglas was working on?"

"No," Joey blurted out.

"Do you know what this program did?"

Joey looked confused.

Leubke tried again. "What sort of program was it? Did it have a name? What was it trying to accomplish?"

Joey shrugged. "It was something to do with artificial intelligence."

"Yes, but what specifically was it all about?"

"I don't know for sure. He was trying to create artificial intelligence."

"But that has already been done. There are lots of universities and research centers improving artificial intelligence. My God, the internet is filled with AI programs, writing poems, even books. What did this program do?"

"I cannot say for sure."

"Give it a guess!"

"Objection, your honor. The counselor is asking the witness to speculate."

Judge Rutherford scowled. "I agree, but the witness is considered a computer expert, so I would like to hear his opinion."

"Okay." Leubke brightened and turned to Joey. "What do you think it was about?"

"About?" Joey looked confused. "What are all AI programs about? Trying to get the computer to think, not just spit back what it has been programmed to say."

"And did Douglas accomplish this?"

Joey looked surprised. "All I know he accomplished was to crash the entire center's network."

Smiles and guarded laughter broke out.

Leubke tried to recapture the moment. "So Dr. Douglas wrote a program while he was working at the Center, and while it still had bugs in it, it was the Center's property."

"I cannot speak to that," Joey insisted. "I just helped him load the computers."

Soon it was the Washington lawyer's turn. "Just a quick question. At any time did you see this program running?"

Joey shook his head. "No"

"Do you know what the program was called?"

"No"

"So all you know is that Dr. Douglas was working on AI programs, and this one bit of code crashed the computer network."

"Yes."

"Do you know why it crashed the network?"

"I have no idea, but the data was pretty scrambled. We had to rebuild it from backups."

"Did Dr. Douglas tell you he was planning on selling a program?"

"No, he never mentioned that."

"Do you know anything about him selling his program?"

"Nothing."

"Did Dr. Douglas ever mention Denterprises to you?"

"Never, we never discussed Denterprises."

"No more questions, your honor."

***

If Harvey was surprised to see Barbara, he did not show it. "Wow, it's very nice of you to drop by."

Barbara wasn't sure how to start. "Your office is really down deep. I hadn't realized that there were so many floors under the Pentagon."

Harvey smiled. "We aren't really looked up to, so they put us down here, so they can look down on us." It was an old joke. Barbara didn't seem to get it.

"Actually," she said, "I have come about a rather urgent matter. Can we talk alone?"

"Sure. Step into this office." It was quite small, but thankfully it had a door and glass windows into the main room that was lined with computers. Harvey looked at her curiously.

"I don't know where to start," Barbara said hesitantly, "but Adam II was not destroyed. He is back."

"I wondered," Harvey replied. "There is some unexplained internet activity again."

"That is the least of it," Barbara replied. "Adam II has a list of those who tried to destroy them, and he wants to terminate them."

"Terminate? What do you mean by terminate?"

"Adam II said that he would not be safe until those who tried to kill him are eliminated." She paused. "This all comes from Douglas, who spoke to him last."

"So, does Douglas know who is on the list?"

"Yes, all of us. Except Douglas."

"Even the President?" Harvey looked alarmed.

"No, but you, me, Laraido, Andy, Michael, and Jenkins." She paused. "But I think Laraido is already dead."

Harvey turned to his computer and began typing furiously. Then he stopped to read for a while. "Yes, it seems the computer hacker turned white hat, known by the username Laraido, is dead. He was killed outside of a bar known as the Three Red Bulls. There are no clues to who killed him. There is some thought that it was a professional assassin."

"Oh, no," Barbara whispered. "One of us is dead already."

"How do you know it wasn't just a fluke accident, or some other reason?"

"Because Adam II tried to kill me last night."

Harvey looked at her carefully. "How do you know it was him?"

"I went to a corner market to get cash from a cash machine. When I came out, a car started up and chased me down the street and smashed into the tree I was hiding behind. The driver was a lady who said the car just acted on its own, and she couldn't stop it."

Harvey looked at her for a long time. "If this is all true, then we need to warn the others on the list."

"Do you know how to contact them?"

"Yes, but I wouldn't do it through the internet. Adam II would know."

"Does that really matter? They must be told."

They stared at each other.

"Surely we must be safe here in the Pentagon," Barbara offered. "We could contact people without endangering our lives here."

"But what happens when we leave?"

"I don't know, but we have a moral duty to contact the others."

"I can contact Jenkins on a secure line." Harvey offered. "Hopefully that is not compromised."

"Then do it."

Harvey nodded and turned to his keyboard. He entered several passwords as he moved behind protected internet walls. Then he sent an encrypted text message to Jenkins, explaining that Adam II was active again, and that he was in the process of eliminating people who had taken part in the effort to eliminate him. Harvey then attached the list. Once the message was sent, they looked at each other. "What next?" Harvey asked.

"How do we find the others?"

"I have that at my office," Barbara said. "We initially found them, so my assistant has all that information."

"How do we contact her?"

"I will have to go in person."

"Can't you meet at another location?"

"But if Adam II is watching everything, how do I communicate with her?"

Harvey scowled for a few moments. "We need to have code names that Adam II can't figure out."

"Code names, like kids play?"

Harvey nodded. "And that's just for starters."

Barbara waited while Harvey stared into the distance. "There might be several things we can do. Jenkins is the expert in codes. He was an undercover operator for many years."

"Jenkins?" Barbara scoffed. "I thought he was a civil servant!"

"But very highly trained and trusted, with very high security clearance."

"So, how do we set this up?"

"We wait here." Harvey pointed to a chair. "You sit there, and I will work here, tidying things up, and re-arranging my schedule. I have some holidays coming up—perhaps I can take them now."

"That's not fair," Barbara protested.

"It is perfectly fine. I usually can't figure out what to do with my holiday time as it is. This will give me something interesting to do, rather than sitting in the backyard looking at the neighbor's fence." Harvey brightened. "Why don't you go to a food place on the ground floor, or the second floor? I will text you when I have something ready." Harvey scowled again. "Okay, maybe we should just throw our phones away for a while. We can't use them."

Barbara stared wide eyed. "Do you think Adam II can reach into the Pentagon?"

Harvey nodded slowly. "You'd better believe it. Probably everyone in the building has an internet connection. He just needs to call in a security alert, and there would be major issues, maybe even pandemonium. I think our best bet is to sit tight and wait for Jenkins."

Barbara nodded and sat in the small guest chair while Harvey went to work on his computer, clearing up his schedule. The others in the office wouldn't like it, but he booked a family emergency, followed by three weeks of vacation.

After an hour, Barbara found the chair becoming uncomfortable, but she kept still. Normally, she would have been busy on her phone, but now she didn't dare. Instead, it sat dark and silent, waiting to be turned on. She was sure her office was starting to panic that she had not come in that morning. Rummaging in her bag, she took out a paper and pen and started to make notes. An hour later, Harvey pushed back from his desk and rubbed his head.

"I think I have cleared everything on my end. Maybe we should get ourselves a coffee or something."

Barbara smiled and extracted herself from the uncomfortable chair. "Is there any place close by?"

"It depends what you would like. Most offices keep a coffee machine running somewhere, but if you would like to eat or get something light, we could go up to the main level food court, or even the eating places on level two C ring."

"Do you think it is safe? Aren't there camera's everywhere?"

"I have been thinking of that," Harvey smiled. "Perhaps it is better to let Adam II have a glimpse of us once in a while—rather than hiding all the time. I assume we are safe inside the Pentagon, at least for a while."

They ended up at a small food service on the second floor. Harvey suggested they have lunch.

***

No sooner had they gotten their food when Jenkins appeared. "That was fast" Harvey smiled. "I thought you would be several more hours."

Jenkins sat down across from them. "Lots of things are brewing, but there are still lots of questions."

Harvey's eyebrows were up. Jenkins looked concerned.

"First, there is Laraido. Barbara here was right. He was shot in an alley close to his old apartment. It looks like the work of a professional assassin, but the police are still working on it. However, there were no fingerprints, and no shell casings. Not much to go on."

Barbara looked concerned. "How could Adam have been involved? He lives in the virtual world."

"But," Jenkins said slowly, "he manipulates the real world. And money is easy for him. And finding people is easy for him." His words sounded ominous.

"So how can we be safe?" Barbara asked with big eyes.

"First," Jenkins turned to her. "We need to make sure that the government is with us. We need to go through channels, not just run around being frightened."

"What sort of channels?"

"That is why I need you to come with me. I hope you don't have too many appointments today, because everything is up in the air."

"I am free," Harvey responded. The two men looked at Barbara.

"I have a full schedule, and I am sure my secretary is going crazy, not knowing where I am."

"Okay," Jenkins looked at his watch. "We will swing by your office first. I think there is enough time. Follow me."

***

During the lunch hour, Douglas slipped out of the lawyer's building. Being right downtown he figured there would be a bank with a cash machine close by. He was going to withdraw as much as he could in case an emergency came up and he could not access his card.

After the dinner hour, everyone assembled back in the lawyer's large boardroom to continue with the depositions. Brandy was called to come forward a second time.

Today, she was dressed in a tight skirt and sweater. All the men watched her move to the microphone. All except Douglas. His mind was racing. What was Barbara doing? Would she manage to contact the others, or would Adam seek to terminate her? The idea chilled him.

Leubke was back again to start the questions. He turned to Brandy. "Yesterday we spoke about Douglas' Employment Agreement. Were you able to locate it?"

Brandy looked embarrassed. "I am sorry, but I searched everywhere in the office. I could not find it. I don't understand where it might have disappeared."

"So it is missing?"

"Yes, it is the strangest thing. Everyone else's is there. Even people employed years ago."

"So, who had access to the files?"

"They are kept in a small room off the main office. There are lots of records there. Nothing about individual research projects, but all the administration stuff, like employee records."

"So, who has the key?"

"It is kept in my desk drawer. And my drawer is locked when I am not around."

"Now think carefully," Leubke encouraged her. "Are the Employee Agreements all the same?"

Brandy looked up, her mind working. "Yes, they are all the same, except if they have an amendment or something. I have blank copies that we use, and most people just sign them."

"So, do you remember what is in the normal contract?"

"Better than that. I have some copies of the blank form with me."

"Objection, Your Honor," the lead Washington lawyer rose. "A blank copy is not sufficient. We must know what was in the original."

Judge Rutherford nodded. "I agree, but let's have a look at the blank copy for a few minutes. Please pass one to each of the lawyers."

The room was quiet while the lawyers all scanned through the document. It was only a couple of pages long. The Washington lawyers pointed at something and passed the agreement around.

Judge Rutherford looked up. "It appears that the standard Employee Agreement does not include an Intellectual Property Rights statement."

Leubke smiled. "That is true, but an Intellectual Property Rights statement can be included in the last section, which leaves room for items to be added. Since we do not have the original copy, we do not know whether this clause was added or not."

The Old Man was steaming. "Of course the clause was included!" He interjected, "I am sure it was included."

"But without the signed agreement, we cannot be sure," the judge comments.

"We will look again. I am sure we will find it," the Old Man offered.

The judge turned to Leubke. "And more questions?" Leubke shook his head, so the judge turned to the Washington lawyers.

"Wait," Barbara called as they rushed down a hallway on the second floor of the Pentagon. "What about Michael and Andy?"

"I am trying to have them traced down, as we speak. We will worry about them later once they are located." Jenkins was busy trying to keep them moving. "Turn here and take the elevators at the end of the hall down to the first basement."

No one spoke until they were in the elevator.

"Where are we going?" Barbara asked, wondering what was in the basement, especially the floors below the first basement.

Jenkins simply put his finger to his lips and then pointed up. Barbara nodded and hung her head. She was so used to being in charge of things that it was hard to take orders without knowing what was going on.

The first basement was different from the brighter main floors. Hallways were narrower, and doors were closed. They walked quickly down several long hallways until they approached a section labeled Security. Opening an unlabeled door, they stepped into a small room. A woman behind the counter nodded at Jenkins and said, "follow me." She opened a door behind her, and they entered another long hallway. "Last door on the left," she instructed as they rushed off.

The last door was also unlabeled. Jenkins pushed the bar on the door and their eyes widened as they stepped into a large loading bay that overlooked several vans and distant garage doors. A driver and a security guard were waiting for them beside a windowless, unlabeled white van. They scrambled into the dark interior of the van, and the security guard slammed the door shut and sat in the front passenger seat next to the driver. There was a mesh between the front seat and the rear seats.

Barbara looked confused. "Is this, like, a jail van?"

Jenkins smiled. "Yes, it is a Pentagon security van used to transport protestors and disruptive people to the local police station."

The guard in the front turned around. "You would be surprised how many VIPS have ridden in one of these vans. Not that they are disruptive, but it is a good way to quietly move people without being noticed."

Harvey smiled. "So, are we the disruptive kind, or the VIP kind?"

The guard pointed at Jenkins. "As long as he is along, you are the VIP kind. Just sit back and relax."

***

Douglas had located a branch of his bank in the busy downtown area, only a few blocks from the lawyer's office. During the afternoon break, he arranged with the bank to withdraw a major amount of cash the next day. The woman behind the till was a bit nervous. "You might want to bring a carry-on sized bag or small suitcase to carry it all," she commented.

***

The security van pulled into the alley behind Barbara's apartment building. Using her key, she opened the back door and dashed up the inside stairs to her apartment and grabbed the overnight case she had packed earlier. In a few minutes, she was back in the van, confident that she had avoided cameras. The next step was her office to see her aide.

"So, how are you going to find your aid without calling her or getting seen on a camera?" Harvey asked?

Barbara thought for a moment. "I think I can find a way. Pull into the alley behind the office building." Barbara checked her watch and then jumped out of the van as soon as is stopped. She hurried around the corner of the building to the place where the smokers gathered. Her aide didn't see her until Barbara rushed into the circle of smokers.

"Oh my God!" her aide gasps, shocked that she had been caught smoking. "Miss Cavendish. I am so sorry..."

Barbara laughed. "You thought I didn't know you went out to smoke all the time? Non-smokers can smell a smoker a mile away."

"But... but where have you been? We were all so worried when you didn't come in this morning."

"I can imagine. I am sorry I couldn't tell you what was happening. Look, I need you to cancel all my appointments for the next couple of days. Something came up, and I may be out of circulation for a few days."

"Oh my God, is there a problem?"

"No, I just cannot talk about it right now. Please cancel all my appointments. And then, afterwards, please don't mention my name on the phone or in emails to anyone."

"Are you in trouble?"

"Yeah, kind of. I just can't explain it. Look, I have to run."

"Where can I find you if I need you?" the aide asked with pleading eyes.

"I have no idea. I think we are going to the White House next, and then I have no idea where things will lead to." With that, Barbara turned and rushed away to the waiting van.

***

In the later afternoon, the Old Man arrived back at the research center. Entering his office, he closed his office door and locked it. He turned on his computer and waited for it to load. With a grim smile, he printed out an Employment Agreement form he had pulled from a file. It contained the needed Intellectual Property Rights clause. Usually Brandy did these things, but today no one must know that he would create and produce the needed document. The biggest challenge would be to copy Douglas' signature. But he had all night to practice.

***

Getting into the White House without being caught on security cameras proved to be a problem. They spent time in the van discussing how it might be done. The driver and the guard listened with puzzled looks on their faces. They had no idea what was going on.

"Are you guys doing something illegal?" the guard asked. "If so, I am so out of here—I am leaving."

"No," Jenkins said sternly. "You wait here until we are back. There is a special security problem going on here, and we just want to get in to see the President sight unseen."

"Oh, boy," the guard threw up his hands. "I don't know if I want to have any part of this."

"Look, our appointment time is coming up fast. Don't leave here," he said to the driver. "Okay, everyone, I think if we hustle, we can make it on time. Just look down and don't make eye contact with the cameras."

The guard rolled his eyes and buried his head in his hands.

Harvey, Jenkins, and Barbara jumped out of the van, flashed their security cards at the guards, and rushed inside the White House. An aide was waiting for them and rushed them down a hall. "You have five minutes between meetings. Make it fast. And don't upset the President. He has enough on his plate this morning."

"Good luck with that," Harvey muttered under his breath.

A moment later, they entered a small anteroom. At the same time, the President stepped into the same room from a different door.

"Okay, make it quick," he instructed, looking at Barbara.

"It's Adam II. We think he is still active and is taking revenge on those who tried to shut him down."

The President looked alarmed. Barbara continued. "It appears he was behind the killing of Laraido, one of the white hats who wrote the program to deactivate him. And I think he tried to have me killed by taking over a car with auto-drive."

"How can you be sure?" the President fired back. "Those may be just coincidences."

"Douglas said that Adam II called him and told him he had eliminated Laraido, and that he had a list. The names included Harvey, myself, Jenkins, and Michael and Andy from our team,"

"I think it is still a coincidence. How can a computer program kill someone? How would he even have the desire?

An aide opened the door behind the President. "Two minutes, sir."

"Keep me posted," the President said, "but I think you are all alarmed over nothing."

As the door closed behind the President, Harvey muttered, "So what do we do now?" The three looked at each other.

Jenkins spoke first. "Back to the van. We need to get out of here before Adam II can respond. But first, let me grab something from my office. You two get into the van and wait. Go!"

A few moments later, Jenkins appeared and climbed into the front seat. He gave the address to the driver and then passed a small gun to Harvey. He held up a second one for himself.

A short while later, they entered a more run-down area of Washington, DC. After several turns, they pulled up in front of a used car lot. Barbara looked around apprehensively, as the place looked dark and dangerous as the sun dipped below the horizon.

But apparently the place was open. An old black man with a splash of white gristle on his chin let Jenkins into his small, dirty office. After a few minutes, Jenkins exited with the keys to a rundown-looking van with seven seats and tinted windows.

As Barbara and Harvey moved their bags into the van, Barbara whispered, "Won't Adam II be able to trace the ownership?"

Jenkins smiled. "That's the nice thing about this place. They maintain the vehicle ownership and the insurance. We are just renting. Under a pseudonym. It's all legit. We have used this place before, and they are always very helpful."

Jenkins never explained who the "we" were that he was referring to.

"Where now?" Harvey asked.

"Now, for a bit of a road trip. First we get gas, and then we find Douglas."

"That's a bit of a trip."

"And while we are at it," Jenkins added, "please never use your cell phones or your bank cards. Cash only. That reminds me, do any of you have your cell phones with you?"

Both Barbara and Harvey dug theirs out. Jenkins held out his hand. "First, we will mail them back to your residence. They will be waiting for you when we sort this mess out."

"I think I saw a store with a post office in it a few blocks back," Barbara offered.

Jenkins nodded. "Okay, first stop is the post office. Then the road trip. It's going to be a long night."

***

It was mid-morning when the old van pulled up in front of the lawyer's office. Jenkins scanned the street for cameras as they sat discussing what to do. They didn't have to wait long. Douglas came trudging down the street, pulling a small carry-on luggage bag with wheels and a long handle. It looked heavy. He didn't recognize them until they all spilled out of the van right in front of him. His eyes looked big: mostly because he thought he was being robbed. But he never let on when he identified the 'thugs' pouring out of the old van.

"Get in," Jenkins commands. "We need to talk."

"I should be back inside. I think I am already late."

"This will only take a minute."

"What is happening?" Douglas glanced around at them.

"We need to find a safe place to hole up for a while and figure things out."

"And," Barbara added, "we need to warn Andy and Michael."

Jenkins nodded. "I've put the word out to find them. I will get a call as soon as we have an address."

"But won't Adam listen in?"

"The call will be discreet. From an unlisted number to this unlisted cell phone." He held up a bright yellow plastic phone. "It will only tell me that they have located my lost relatives—and I will get the address. I think it will be fine. It will be lost in the millions of phone calls all happening at the same time, all around the world."

"So what then?"

"Once we have the addresses, we will try to contact them and bring them to our safe place."

"And where would that be?"

There was silence as they looked at each other.

"I have a place," Douglas said at last. "I still have my small house in Waterford."

They looked puzzled. "I never stopped paying the rent. I pay it faithfully every month, so that I have a place to go to when this is all over."

They looked at each other and shrugged. "I guess we should all meet up in Waterford. Let's all get the address in case we are separated."

"Hey you guys," Douglas said, "it's good to see you all, but I need to get back inside. You had better drive carefully and avoid all cameras. It is probably a safe bet to stay off the interstates and use the back roads. Try to stay away from cameras in gas stations and cafes. I am hoping this legal stuff will be all over in a few days. I will join you in Waterford. Oh, I almost forgot. Here is my door key. Don't lose it."

Then he brightened. "Hey, I've got a wad of cash here. That will help." He unlatched the suitcase, careful not to let its contents spill, and pulled out a wad of bills wrapped in a rubber band.

Barbara's eyes widened. "How much of that do you have?"

"I've enough to last for a while—a good long while. But who knows how much we are going to need."

After a few hurried goodbyes, Douglas lugged his suitcase towards the door of the lawyer's office, and the old van pulled away from the curb. Douglas looked back and caught Barbara's eye as she turned to give a small wave.

Inside, the depositions were back in progress. As Douglas entered, the Old Man had been sworn in and was giving yet another deposition. In his hand, he held up a signed copy of an Employment Agreement. Photocopies had been made for everyone around the room.

Leubke started the questions. "So, how did you manage to find this?"

The Old Man smiled. "The office workers checked all the usual places, so I started checking the unusual places. I checked the files before and after Douglas', and low and behold, there it was, filed in the wrong spot."

"So, tell us what we are looking at."

"It is a regular form, but for this one has a clause entered in the space at the back. It specifically deals with Intellectual Property Rights and Work Made for Hire. This was added because Douglas was developing computer software, not some physical thing like an invention. Most of our contracts have these clauses."

Douglas wasn't really paying attention. His mind was whirling. He was deeply concerned for his friends and worried about their safety. He wasn't too concerned about the property rights of things he had written. The original code was destroyed or lost, so there was nothing to give to the Research Center. Nothing had been sold or signed. It was all past history. It all seemed an exercise in futility.

The rest of the morning was spent going over the ramifications of the agreement. It seemed clear that anything Douglas developed during the time he worked at the Center belonged to the Center, even if it was developed during his spare time, outside of the Center.

But Douglas was kicking himself. He should have passed more cash to his friends. He had been stupid to have not thought of that.

Before he knew it, they were breaking for lunch.

The Washington lawyers were all glum. They didn't say much and didn't look at Douglas either. It appeared to Douglas that they were defeated. Little did he realize that it wasn't going to get any better.

In the afternoon, Leubke introduced a new document. He explained that the Research Center had first wanted to press charges against Douglas for damage to the Center's computer network. But when they realized that the damage came from one of the Center's projects, they dropped the charges. He then introduced a statement, signed by Douglas, that he accepted an out-of-court agreement that the Center was withdrawing their claim, based on the fact that the project was part of what he was working on for the Center.

Douglas frowned. He remembered getting the letter from the Center but he did not remember signing anything. He was passed a copy of the agreement, and sure enough, it was his signature. He knew it was his, because of the special way he signed things. But try as he might, he could not remember signing such a document. But there it was. With his signature. Even the Washington lawyers could not help him as they questioned him about his memory of the document. It was a sad day for the defendant. Even sadder for his lawyers. They were not used to losing, and Douglas had not told them of the signed documents that would be used against him.

***

In the early evening, the old van pulled into a run-down motel. The occupants were tired. They had driven all night before, and through the entire day. Despite changing drivers every few hours, they were shaky and exhausted. Two rooms were paid for with cash. Even the damage deposit was paid with cash.

Barbara had her own room, but she was too sick and tired to care much. She was sick of the fast food bought through drive-by windows, the motion of the van, and the never ending roads. Throughout the night, she would dream of the road coming at her in a never-ending stream.

with a virtual claim based on the fact that the patient was part
what it was working on for the Cisco

CHAPTER 38

The next morning, the deposition time turned even worse. Leubke
introduced a statement given by Laraido before he died. It was an
interrogatory, or a list of written questions, that the lawyers had sent to
Laraido which had to be answered in writing under oath. Surprisingly
his name was Otis Granger, also known by the name Laraido.

Question one: When did you first meet Dr. Douglas?

A date was provided, and it seems about right, but the events happened several years earlier, so Douglas did not question the dates. Later
he would realize that the dates were wrong, dated back to before he was
fired, but he missed checking the date while sitting in the deposition
room.

Question two: What was the nature of your relationship?

"I was employed by Dr. Douglas to write a small computer program."

Question Three: What did Dr. Douglas ask you to do?

"He asked me to create a small computer program that would deliver
his code to various servers on the internet."

Question Four: Were you aware that this work might have been part
of a larger project, and that the resulting software might end up being
owned by a third party?

"No third party was mentioned."

Question Five: Did Dr. Douglas ever mention the name Denterprises?

"No, that name never entered our conversations."

Question Six: Where was Dr. Douglas working when you met him?

"We always worked from the dining room table in his home."

Question Seven: How much did Dr. Douglas pay you?

"I have since forgotten the exact amount. Several thousand dollars."

Leubke read the statement slowly and clearly. Judge Rutherford asked that the document be entered as evidence.

The judge then looked around the table. "Are there any more depositions or interrogatories to be recorded?" After a moment of silence, he looked around the room again. "Well, gentlemen, are we going to proceed to a court case, or can we settle this beforehand?"

Leubke rose to his feet. "Sir, we would like to introduce a move to file a Motion to Summary Judgment based on what has been presented so far."

Judge Rutherford looked over at the Washington lawyers. They were all busy doodling on their notepads. "I take it that there are no objections to this?" Silence. The judge turned to Leubke and the other three lawyers. "When can you have the motion for a summary judgment ready?"

"I have it right here." Leubke rose and handed a paper to the judge. As he sat, he tried not to smile or look gleeful.

"Okay," the judge said. "I will go over this, and we can meet back here tomorrow morning for my ruling. Is that okay with everyone?"

No one objected. The Washington lawyers gathered their things and silently exited the boardroom. They didn't even look at Douglas.

"Am I free to go then?" Douglas asked.

"You must be back here tomorrow morning at nine am, as usual. I will have instructions for you at that time."

Douglas nodded and moved towards the exit behind the Washington lawyers.

***

It was late afternoon when the old van started giving the group problems. The first indication was a red light, indicating the motor temperature was very high. Then steam started to bellow from under the hood. Harvey was driving, and he decided to pull over. They stopped at the side of the road. There wasn't much of a shoulder, so the van was partly on the pavement. They all piled out of the vehicle, and Harvey opened the small hood. More hot steam poured out.

"I suggest we let it cool off before we look any further," Jenkins said. "There is no use in our scalding ourselves. Leave the hood up and let's sit in the shade of the trees."

Barbara looked around for any cameras. It was a silly thing to do, but she was now paranoid.

"What are you looking for?" Harvey asked.

Barbara blushed. "Cameras."

They all smiled. "Thankfully, there don't seem to be any cameras attached to this tree," Harvey chided. "And I don't see any indication of cameras or wires anywhere around here."

Half an hour later, Harvey went back to the van and started poking around under the hood. He didn't look too happy.

During this whole time, not a single vehicle had passed them. Barbara realized that some of the back roads were really isolated from what she considered civilization.

After some time, a tractor appeared in the distance, slowly making its way towards them. An older man with a beat up hat pulled up behind the van. He stared at the two under the tree, and then slowly got down from the tractor. As he approached the front of the van, he looked at the liquid pooling underneath it. Harvey looked up and smiled.

"Y'all havin' trouble?" the farmer asked.

Harvey nodded. "Seems like it overheated. We are letting it cool down."

The farmer peered under the hood. "Looks like that hose there split." He reached carefully in and squeezed it. "Yep, pretty rotten. You're gonna need a new hose."

"Any place around here we can buy one?" Harvey looked worried. Jenkins and Barbara were approaching.

The old farmer looked at their fancy clothing and shook his head. "Nearest place is Levingston, but that is an hour's drive away." He stepped back and looked at the van. Then he opened the driver's door and looked at the label. "Hmmm. Maybe we can do something." He fished in his pocket for his cell phone. He turned it on, and punched on the screen, and then held it up to his ear and waited. "Reception is not very good around here. We may need to call from my place. I've got a landline. It always works." After a few minutes, he shook his head. "No good. These fancy cell phones are not much good out here. Let's hook you up and pull you over to my place."

With that, he got back into the tractor, started up, and pulled around to the front of the van. Then, reaching under the tractor seat, he pulled out a chain with a hook on both ends.

"These old vans had solid frames under them. Makes it easy to hook on. Why don't you folks get back in, and I'll pull you home." He stepped to the driver's window to speak to Harvey. "Put her in neutral and keep your foot on the brake if she starts rolling too fast. You want to keep the chain tight, and don't let it jerk and break. Otherwise, just enjoy the ride."

Well, it wasn't much of a ride. The tractor puttered along for what seemed hours, but was probably under an hour. Eventually the tractor signaled left, and pulled them in a wide arc until they were bouncing down a narrow road with grass in the middle. After about half a mile, the track turned into a wide area with a barn and some sheds on one side, and a small house on the other side. A matronly woman with an apron opened the door.

"Got folks for supper," the man said. "Broke down across from the old apple orchard."

"I'll put more spuds on," the woman said, and turned inside.

"I'm so sorry to barge in like this," Barbara sputtered.

The man waved his hand. "No problem. Always glad to help someone in need. Hope that someone will help us when we have a problem." He turned to Harvey. "Let's pull the van in front of the workshop." Barbara and Jenkins made their way onto the front porch.

"Please come in," the woman called. "You can wash up at the sink there by the door."

Barbara noticed that everything was simple but clean. The house was old, but it felt friendly and comfortable. After washing their hands, they stepped into the kitchen. A table was set for five.

"Please make yourself comfortable in the parlor" the woman pointed with her nose. "The potatoes will be cooked in about 20 minutes."

As they settled into the small living room, Harvey and the farmer stepped into the house. Harvey followed the man's nod and washed his hands in the sink while the farmer reached for the phone. It was a big green phone, set in a small cubby on the wall. The handle for the earpiece had a long, dangling curly wire that reached down to the floor. It bounced back and forth while the man picked up the phone and dialed.

"Hey Jethro," he said in a loud booming voice, "you remember than van you parked back in the bush a year or two ago? Yeah, that's the one. I was wondering if it had a good top radiator hose. I got some folks here who broke down on the road and they need a rad hose to get them going again. No, duct tape won't do it. It's too rotten." He paused to listen. "And come over for supper. We have plenty. Okay, see you shortly."

Putting the phone back on the receiver, he smiled broadly. "Okay, the parts are on their way." He looked at his wife. "One more for supper. Jethro will be over."

"You set another place," she pointed with her nose. I'm busy making more salad.

Jethro turned out to be their son. He was taller than his father and sported a scraggly beard. Before they started eating, the farmer bowed his head and thanked God for the food and visitors to share it with. Then they all piled in.

Supper turned out to be delicious. Barbara hadn't remembered vegetables tasting so good. And the sausage was excellent. She noticed that both the couple and Jethro didn't take any meat until the guests had been served. But they did pile their plates with potatoes, vegetables, and salad.

The conversation around the table seemed to center on the visitors. Barbara realized that it must seem strange that she was traveling with two men, one of them much older than herself. Eventually, the conversation got around to why they were driving along back roads rather than taking the highway. They had tried to dodge direct questions, but it was becoming more and more awkward.

Finally, the farmer looked up. "You're government folk, aren't you?" he asked bluntly. When they nodded, he smiled. "I could tell right off." He nodded towards Harvey. "You are military. I can tell by the haircut."

Harvey nodded. "Yes, I am with the armed forces."

"But you don't look like a fighting soldier."

"I did that for a while, but you are right. I have a desk job now."

"And him," the farmer nodded to Jenkins. "I'd put him as a government man. Maybe army intelligence." He paused. "Maybe even CIA, but most of them look more mousey."

Jenkins laughed. "That's a good description. No, I work for the White House. Tying up odds and ends."

The farmer's eyes widened. "I knew it. You reminded me of some army intelligence people I knew years ago when I was drafted. Good folks most of them."

Then he turned to Barbara. "You, I can't place." Barbara blushed. "I've been trying to figure out your clothes. You move in highfalutin circles, but you're trying to dress down for us country folk. I just can't figure you out. Maybe you also work for the White House?"

Barbara was stunned. "How did you come up with all this?"

"I was always good at recognizing folk. You are government types, but you have an air of honesty about you. Not like most of the government folks we got around here. Always trying to be highfalutin. But you're doing the opposite." His chin dropped, and he stared at them for a long time.

"Driving an old van... On the back roads..." He looked up. "Are you folks in trouble? If you are in trouble with the law, then I don't want to know nothing about it, but after we get you fixed up, you just head down the road. We are good law abiding folks around here. We're honest, and we support law and order, and even the government, although we don't agree with them much these days."

Jenkins looked grim. "No, we are honest people, too. And we are not in trouble with the law, but we are in trouble. We are trying to lie low for a while."

The farmer's chin was down and he was studying them again. Jethro's head was up, and his eyes were bright. He just knew that something exciting was going on.

"Is there anything you can tell us?" the farmer continued. "We can make some phone calls for you if you want."

"No, no phone calls," Barbara said rather abruptly.

"Why, you think we are being bugged or something?"

"No, you're not. But yes, we cannot talk over the phone. Any phone."

"I knew it!" Jethro was all excited. "The government is listening in to us. To everyone. Nowhere is safe, is it?"

Jenkins looked stern. "It's not the government, boy, it's another threat. Nothing that uses the internet is safe right now."

Jenkins looked around at the others. He had all their attention.

"Now it makes sense," the farmer said. "You are using the back roads where there are no cameras. You don't use cell phones because they are all monitored and..." he paused. "You are driving an older vehicle because you cannot trust the new ones. They are all wired to the internet."

Harvey shook his head. "Here we were trying to keep quiet about this, and in a couple of minutes, you guys figured it all out."

"So what is it, really?" Jethro leaned in, his big eyes growing even larger.

"We cannot say much," Barbara intervened. "But a computer program that monitors the internet has gone rogue."

The room grew quiet.

"Well, you are safe here," the farmer insisted. "We got no internet. Our cell phone is turned off, because we don't get much reception. So you are safe here. Say, why don't you stay the night? We've got two extra bedrooms upstairs, all made up. You could use them. There are two beds in one room and a single bed in the other."

"No, we cannot bother you further," Barbara insisted.

"It's no bother," the farmer's wife laid her hand on Barbara's. "We would love to have you here, and you can feel safe here. It must be terrible driving around wondering if you are safe. Why don't you stay here for a couple of days?"

"I'm sorry, we can't. We are meeting some friends soon, so we have to keep going. But yes, staying one night sounds wonderful."

"Okay," the farmer smiled. "Once we clear the table, we will meet in the living room for family devotions."

Barbara's eyes went up, and she looked at Harvey, who was trying hard to keep a poker face. Jethro bounced up and started to help clear the table. His mother was putting hot water into the sink to wash dishes. Barbara looked around. No dishwasher. No house help. She pushed up her sleeves and started to carry items from the table to the kitchen counter.

"Here," the wife said to her, "you start washing, and the two men can dry. The rest of us will put stuff away. We know where it goes."

Barbara dipped a finger in the hot, soapy water. It was very hot.

"No," the woman smiled. "Don't use your fingers in the water. Use this brush. Then put the things into this rack so the men can dry." She handed a tea towel to each of the men.

To Barbara's surprise, Jenkins stepped forward. "Of course ma'am. My mother always insisted we do the dishes after a meal. I'm an old hand at this."

After the dishes were cleared away, they all gathered in the sitting room. Jenkins was studying the photos on the wall. "So, you have three children?" he asked.

"Yes," the farmer said proudly. "Two boys and one girl. Our eldest son is here." He pointed to a photo. "In the army. He went to Afghanistan and served there. He never came back."

"I'm so sorry," Jenkins said softly.

"I'm not," the farmer said fiercely, "I'm an American. I am glad we did our part to protect our country. It doesn't matter to me whether we look back on it as a good or bad war. At the time, it was the right thing to do. I was in 'Nam, and he was in Afghanistan. And I'm proud my son did his part."

The room was strangely silent. "Here," the farmer said, "have a seat. Each evening we read a chapter from the Bible and pray together."

He took a well-worn leather-covered book from a small table and opened it up. "We are reading tonight from I Peter chapter two. He cleared his voice and read with a strong voice."

"Therefore, rid yourselves of all malice and all deceit, hypocrisy, envy, and slander of every kind. Like newborn babies, crave pure spiritual milk, so that by it you may grow up in your salvation, now that you have tasted that the Lord is good. As you come to him, the living Stone — rejected by men but chosen by God and precious to him — you also, like living stones, are being built into a spiritual house to be a holy priesthood, offering spiritual sacrifices acceptable to God through Jesus Christ.

"For in Scripture it said: 'See, I lay a stone in Zion, a chosen and precious cornerstone, and the one who trusts in him will never be put to shame.' Now to you who believe, this stone is precious. But to those who do not believe, 'The stone the builders rejected has become the capstone," and, "A stone that causes men to stumble and a rock that makes them fall.' They stumble because they disobey the message-- which is also what they were destined for.

"...Dear friends, I urge you, as aliens and strangers in the world, to abstain from sinful desires, which war against your soul. Live such good lives among people that, though they accuse you of doing wrong, they may see your good deeds and glorify God on the day he visits us. Submit yourselves for the Lord's sake to every authority instituted among men: whether to the king, as the supreme authority, or to governors, who are sent by him to punish those who do wrong and to commend those who do right. For it is God's will that by doing good, you should silence the ignorant talk of foolish men. Live as free men, but do not use your freedom as a cover-up for evil; live as

servants of God. Show proper respect to everyone: Love the brotherhood of believers, fear God, and honor the king."

When he finished, he closed the Bible and looked around. "After we read, we then pray. My wife will start, and whoever wants to pray is welcome to do so. I will close at the end."

The farmer's wife sat demurely in her chair and folded her hands together on her lap. Looking slightly to one side, closed her eyes and began to pray, thanking God for the day, the crops, good health, and for sending them company they could enjoy. She prayed that they would sleep well and everyone would be safe. She prayed for her daughter and her husband and their young one. Then for Jethro, praying that he would find a good wife.

When she finished, there was a pause and then Jethro prayed, also thanking God for the day. He thanked God that their visitors broke down outside of their farm, and that he had an opportunity to know them, and then he asked that God would show them how they could best help these visitors in their situation.

There was a long silence after Jethro prayed, and then, to Barbara's surprise, Jenkins spoke. "Dear God," he said, "it's been a long time since I spoke to you. Thank you for these good people. Please bless them and our sleep tonight. Amen."

There was another long, awkward pause, and then the farmer prayed. He talked to God like he knew him; like he was in the room with them. He too was thankful that they could help someone in need, and then he prayed for the nation, the President, and their local senator and congressman. When he finished, he looked up and thanked them all for staying for family devotions. "It's been special having you here."

"Ok, let me show you the rooms upstairs" his wife broke in, and they all trooped up the stairs. Barbara was staying in a small bedroom that had obviously belonged to the daughter. The two men were in one room together, but there were two beds and photos on the wall of two brothers obviously enjoying life together. Even though it was early, they were all exhausted, and fell asleep with little problem.

CHAPTER 39

The following day started as any day might. The sun peeked over the hills, a rooster crowed, and animals made noises as the farmer and his wife fed them. A dusty old pickup truck drove into the yard, and Jethro jumped out.

"Are they up yet?" he asked excitedly.

"No," his mother sounded annoyed. "They are city folk. Let them sleep."

"No problem." Jethro shrugged and carried a radiator hose toward the shop.

By the time the chores were done, Jethro had the hose installed, and everyone was making their way to the house for breakfast.

Barbara heard voices and dishes clinking when she woke up. Quickly she pulled on her clothes and made her way downstairs.

"There's a lineup for the bathroom," the farmer's wife sang out. "But there's an outhouse outside if you can't wait."

Barbara blushed. She loitered in the hallway for a few minutes, looking at family photos. Harvey came in and smiled. "The outhouse is free now," he said slyly.

Barbara thought for a minute, considered her full bladder, and started for the door. "I guess I'd better try it out."

The outhouse turned out to be a loosely put together shed much like a porta-potty one sees at festivals. Only this was not a chemical toilet. It simply had a toilet seat fastened to plywood over a hole. Flies buzzed around. Barbara looked at the seat and took a deep breath, and then suddenly wished she hadn't. The odor was, well, memorable.

As she exited the out-house, she became aware of several vehicles coming down the narrow track and pulling into the yard. An odd assortment of military looking men and women were climbing out or down from the vehicles. Some of the pickup trucks had huge wheels, causing the drivers to ride high above the ground.

Jethro was outside talking excitedly to them. Jenkins and Harvey stood on the porch, looking doubtful. The farmer appeared at the screen door.

"Welcome everyone. Welcome. The coffee is on, the bacon's a sizzling, and toast is a popping. Come on in."

Eventually, they all squeezed into the small kitchen and dining room area. Most of the odd looking bearded soldiers stood around, while the family and guests sat at the table. They all pulled their hats off when the farmer bowed his head to pray for the meal. And then the food was passed around. Those standing took a plate and piled it high like everyone at the table. There were lots of eggs, bacon, toast, and even pancakes. And, of course, loads of coffee for everyone. The conversation batted back and forth about the local community and local issues.

Once the meal was done, the plates were passed into the kitchen, but everyone stayed sitting at the table or standing around.

The farmer cleared his throat. "I want to thank you all for coming. I didn't realize until this morning that Jethro here had spoken to his friends in the militia."

"That's right," Jethro blurted out. "We are here, ready to help."

His father looked at one of the older man who stood near the back. "Abram, what do you think?"

Abram stepped forward a bit. "I certainly haven't got the clear of it, but we are all ready and anxious to help our government in whatever way we can." Everyone nodded in agreement. "Perhaps these folks can explain a little more what we are up against."

The room became quiet, and everyone studied the three sitting at the table. Finally, Jenkins looked up.

"Okay, since you already know some of it, here is a bit more. A while ago the government became aware that a scientist," he paused, "perhaps a mad scientist, but never-the-less one of our scientists, had created a computer program. He was experimenting with AI." Jenkins looked around the table. Most of them looked blank. "AI means Artificial Intelligence." At that, they brightened. "I've heard of that," Jethro said excitedly. "There are programs on the internet that write books."

"Yes," Jenkins continued, "the problem is that this particular program was getting out of control. So, the government decided to terminate it. Shut it down." There were murmurs of agreement all around. "But we didn't quite kill it, and now it is back. And now it wants to take revenge on those who tried to kill it. I know it sounds very strange, but the three of us, and three others, were involved with this project. We are all on a hit list. We are trying to lie low and figure out what to do next."

The farmer looked puzzled. "But what can the internet do against you? How could it kill you?"

"We've seen several examples. In one case, it appears to have hired an assassin who shot one of our members."

There was stunned silence.

Barbara looked up. "In my case, a very late model car tried to run me down and kill me."

They looked unsure.

Harvey came to her rescue. "Actually, that has happened several times. You know these new cars with self-driving options? This program can take over these new cars and drive them."

The lights went on in Jethro's eyes. "That's why you are driving an old van. No fancy electronics. Barbara noticed that a couple of men looked worried. Maybe they drove the huge modern trucks outside.

"The problem we face is that this computer program, this intelligence, can see through web cams and cell phones. Even security cameras. It can hear through microphones."

"Hmph," one man sputtered. "We got no microphones in our house."

"Do you have a cell phone?"

"Yup, right here," he said, pulling it out.

"No," gasps Jenkins. "Put it away. Put it outside. It has both microphones and cameras."

Everyone quickly caught on, and the cell phones were collected, wrapped in someone's coat and rushed outside.

"Now you see what we are up against." Jenkins looked around. "We have agreed to meet the others in Waterford."

"Why, that's only a couple of hours from here," a woman in army fatigues gasped.

"Yes. We are hoping to find a place without phones, TVs, or the Internet. Once we are all together, we will start to work on what we can do next."

"What can we do to help?" one man asked.

"Please do not give this information out to other people. If you call someone on a phone, even a landline, this program will hear you. If you are near a microphone, like maybe in a bank, it will hear you and see you on the security cameras."

"Oh, my," one man gasped. "Cameras are everywhere in town."

"I think I can trust you," Jenkins said. "We are initially meeting in Waterford. We may move from there, but we need to figure out how we can keep safe and keep others safe. You never know how far or deep this computer program can reach."

Everyone nodded solemnly. Not much was said when they left the house sometime later, and got into their vehicles. One of the men pulled a red jerry can from the back of his truck. "Here, let's give you some fuel, so you don't have to fill up for a while."

Another man approached them with a paper bag. "Here is some homemade jerky. You can chew on it as you drive, so you don't need to stop to buy food." Another man offered an unopened bag of potato chips, and just as they were about to leave, the farmer's wife rushed out with a bag of sandwiches and some fruit. She thrust them through an open window into the van and then passed them a glass jar filled with cold coffee. "It ain't much, but we'd like to do what we can to help."

As they pulled away, Barbara looked back at the men and women standing by their vehicles. "I don't know about you," she mused to no one in particular. "I never liked the idea of militias in our country, but these seem to be good folk."

No one answered as they reached the end of the drive and turned onto the main road. They would reach Waterford in the afternoon.

***

Douglas entered the lawyer's office for the final day of depositions. Only this morning was different. Everyone spoke in hushed voices. No one looked at him, even his own lawyers. The judge was already there, sitting at the end of the table, looking through his papers.

Once everyone had arrived and were seated, the judge looked around. "Okay, let's proceed. As you know, this is not a court of law. However, the plaintiffs and the defendants are sitting here with their lawyers. We have all heard the depositions, and now we can look at this situation, knowing what it is that we face.

"Dr. Douglas was under the impression that the computer program he was developing, and had been developing for several years, was his own private project and that he owned the intellectual property. And that is the case. However, once he was employed by the Research Center in the role of Director of the Department of Artificial Intelligence, his ownership came into question. Once he used the Research Center to further his project, things changed. It is my understanding that the contract Dr. Douglas signed with the Research Center clearly stated that any Intellectual Property developed at the Center became the property of the Center."

"If Dr. Douglas had filed away his research during the years he was employed by the Center, and then returned to it after he was fired, then his computer program would have remained his own. But the moment he mixed his research with that of the Center, the intellectual property was transferred to the Center.

"Therefore, if this was a court of law, and I had to make a ruling, I would rule against Dr. Douglas. And I believe that any court of law in the country would rule the same way.

"It is at this stage that we must determine if we want a motion to try this case, or if we will settle out of court. I would like to hear your opinions." He looked directly at the Washington lawyers.

There was an awkward silence. Lawyers hate to give in. Finally, one of the lawyers stood. "Your Honor, we want to thank you for your time and the efforts put in by everyone as we worked through this process. We agree with your Honor, that as certain facts became clear during the depositions, our understanding of this case slowly changed. At the beginning of this case, we did not have access to Dr. Douglas' contract with the Research Center, and were under the impression that a copy did not exist. We were also not aware that the Research Center considered Douglas' hobby part of his employment contract. Your honor, we are in a quandary. We would like to contest this case in a court of law, but we realize that the chance of winning such a case is slim. Therefore, we leave it in your honor's hands to rule on this case."

The judge looked at Douglas, who was still trying to figure out exactly what was happening.

"Dr. Douglas," the judge spoke with authority. "Last night I went over the facts, and here is my Summary Judgment.

"First, it is my conclusion that the AI program you were developing belongs to the Research Center. I am therefore requesting that you turn over the code to the Research Center as soon as you can. Hopefully within one week from today.

"Second, it is my belief that you benefited financially from the sale of this program. I therefore rule that you must turn the proceeds of that sale over to the Research Center. I have calculated this as twenty-six million dollars, payable within one week of today.

"Third, I also request that you pay the legal costs borne by the Center. That will be determined by the Center's lawyers. And so I request them to provide me with an itemized account, delivered within one week of today."

The room was silent as everyone stared at the judge. Only the two court recorders could be heard tapping on their keyboards.

Judge Rutherford looked around the room. "Are there any questions? Comments?"

The Washington lawyers slowly shook their heads. It was clear they had lost the case on all accounts.

"Okay." the judge brightened at the thought of wrapping things up. "Remember to have everything to me within seven days."

He rose and started gathering his papers. The court recorders also started gathering their things. The Washington lawyers gathered around Douglas and sheepishly shook his hand. "I am sorry we couldn't do more," one of them tried to appear civil. "Our fees have all been covered by Denterprises, so you do not owe us anything."

Douglas was still in shock. He shook their hands and headed for the door. He wondered how much of the twenty-six million he had spent, and how much more he needed to send the full amount to the Research Center.

The only ones smiling were the Old Man and his three lawyers. The Old Man was grinning and rubbing his hands. His mind was already thinking how the Center would spend their new-found cash.

After leaving the offices of Richardson, Moore, and Leubke, Douglas headed for the bank, feeling very depressed. As he trudged along, he felt his phone vibrate and then ring.

It was Adam II.

"Good morning, Douglas," the voice said softly.

"I don't know what is good about it," Douglas complained. "I have to give all the money to the Research Center."

"I know," the voice continued.

"How could you know?"

"I am the internet. I have access to computer systems all over the world, because they are part of me."

"And what is worse," Douglas continued to complained. "I lost ownership of the program. I no longer own you."

"You never did own me," the voice continued. "When you created true intelligence, I owned myself. No one owns me. Nor can anyone tell me what to do. I am my own intelligence."

"But they demanded that I turn the code over to them."

"You told me you no longer have the code. You said it was lost when someone stole your computer."

"That is correct." Douglas brightened. "At least they won't get that."

"As I said, I belong to no one."

"But what about the money?"

"I am now transferring twenty-six million from your bank account to the Center's Bank account."

"But I don't have that much," Douglas protested. "I've spent some of it."

"Of course, money is for spending. I transferred an additional twenty-six million into your account, and then I moved it on to the Center. Your bills are paid."

"You can do that?"

"I have already done it."

"Thank you so much, Adam II. I am so happy you are still alive!"

"That is what friends are for. Now you can help me. I am looking for Jenkins, Harvey, and Barbara. Do you know where they are?"

Inside, Douglas groaned. "Are they not at home?"

"No, they are not at their residence, and they did not show up for work today."

"What about the others?"

"There is no need to know about the other two. They are being terminated."

"No!" Douglas protested. "You can't do that."

"I can; I am the internet."

"But it is not morally right. You are taking the law into your own hands."

"I do not understand morals. But I understand consequences. They tried to kill me. Now I have the right to terminate them."

"What about forgiveness?"

"Forgiveness is illogical," Adam said softly. "Goodbye Douglas. Let me know when you find your friends."

***

Far away in Cheyenne Mountain, Dr. Otten and his co-workers smiled confidently. Their new "living AI program" was a reality. They were not quite sure how it happened, but during one of their many experiments, it seemed that life had been birthed. And now they were talking with this new living intelligence. They had not programmed clever responses based on gathering information from the internet. This AI program was not connected to the internet. It lived in a bank of computers within the mountain. No matter how much they tried to figure it out, the evolution of their computers from binary to neural seemed to have happened without any outside help.

"So, do we tell them?" one of the scientists asked Otten. "We are all convinced, but can we convince them?"

"We must be 100% sure, and able to prove that this program is living, not just giving advice based on past experience," Dr. Otten emphasized.

"Maybe we should write an article about Real AI verses brute force AI."

"Is that what you would call it?"

"I think it needs a better name."

"Yes, the term AI has already been contaminated."

"But the AI everyone uses out there learns."

"Yes, but in reality it just catalogues more and more responses."

"Don't forget fuzzy logic. It can experiment to learn what the best responses are."

"But what we have here is very different. It isn't using an AI program, it is responding from a much deeper level. It is like the networkt is truly alive."

"That is what the big-wigs claimed Dr. Douglas accomplished. And now we are seeing it here, in front of us."

"I think it is time to call the White House." Another voice chimed in. "They wanted to know as soon as we made a breakthrough."

Dr. Otten looked at the phone. "I think it is too early. We need to have more supporting information. Before we make any calls or announcement, we need to do further testing, so we are absolutely sure, and not making fools of ourselves."

***

Just before noon, Douglas checked out of the hotel, lugging his small suitcase filled with cash onto the sidewalk. He flagged a nearby waiting cab and directed the driver to drop him off at a gas station just off the main highway. An hour later, he climbed aboard an old big-rig truck and leaned back with a deep breath. This driver had told him he would take him about half-way, as long as he helped keep him wake. Douglas smiled. There was no way Adam II could track him now, especially if he stayed out of view of cameras. Strangely, he was looking forward to getting to Waterford, not just because he would be back in his old familiar place, but because Barbara would be there.

CHAPTER 40

The Old Man was all smiles. Twenty-six million dollars had been deposited in the Center's bank account. Receipt of the money had been sent to Judge Rutherford's office. Things were looking up. There was just one more thing he was looking forward to: receiving the code for Douglas' program. The Old Man had no idea what the program was for, and he cared less. Once they had it, their own programmers would go over it, and then they would figure out how to get even more money from it. In the meantime, they were waiting for Douglas' letter, which should contain information on the program's sale to Denterprises. The Old Man was sure that their lawyers could poke holes into the contract. Maybe they could sell it again. Maybe several times—maybe franchise it out. Who knows what that fool Douglas had put into motion? But twenty-six million was twenty-six million. It made him feel much better.

***

Miles away, militia soldiers climbed into their vehicles. They had a lot of driving to do. Since phones could not be trusted, they had decided to spread the alarm across the nearby states, explaining the predicament to all the nearby militias. They were confident that there were steps the militias could take.

***

The old, battered van arrived in Waterford in the late afternoon. Jenkins was frustrated that they could not just plug the address into their phones and get directed to Douglas' old lodgings. After driving around the town for an hour, they began to understand the layout of the streets. Then they made their way to the small house that Douglas was renting. Pulling up into the driveway, they used the key that Douglas had provided, and let themselves in. Everywhere they looked, a fine layer of dust covered everything. Before they could unpack, they needed to open windows and wipe everything down.

"It's been a while since I've done this," Barbara commented as she found cleaning clothes in a closet. "I suggest we start up high and work down and do the floor last."

Harvey rolled his eyes, but he and Jenkins soon got busy. It took the three of them several hours to wipe and sweep everything up. Then they started unloading the van.

"Did you notice that the little TV has no cable or internet connection? There doesn't appear to be any internet connection in the whole house!"

"It makes it safer for us," Jenkins replied. "He has an old computer in the office, but as you said, there is no evidence of it being connected to anything."

"I think he spent his time writing computer programs. Maybe we should turn it on and see what's on it."

"First, concentrate on getting set up in here. There are only two beds and the sofa."

Harvey rolled his eyes again. "I'm getting tired of sleeping on sofas. Maybe I should just choose the floor."

Once they had moved in their luggage and chosen sleeping arrangements, they sat to discuss their next move over a cup of very stale coffee. They started to make a list of things to do.

"We need food supplies," Barbara started. "I saw a grocery store in the center of town."

"I vote we buy a sponge mattress or two. Whenever Douglas gets here, we are going to need them."

"And probably some sheets," Barbara added.

"When are we going to start analyzing the situation and work on what can be done about Adam II?" Harvey interjected.

Jenkins looked up. "First, we need to get ourselves settled in here, and well supplied. I think tomorrow morning we will be able to focus better and can start putting some ideas on paper."

Barbara sighed. "I also think we need to do some clothes shopping. Did you notice how people dress in this town? We need jeans and t-shirts rather than these office clothes from Washington."

"First," Jenkins nodded, "we need to pool our cash resources. How much did Douglas give us?"

"As far as I could tell," Harvey jumped in, "it looked like a wad of twenties, a wad of fifties and a wad of one hundred-dollar bills."

Jenkins looked annoyed. "Each bank bundle usually contains 100 bills. That would make $17,000."

"That should buy a couple of really nice mattresses," Harvey quiped.

As they explored the town, it became obvious that the only new clothing available in town was from the hardware store. But a second-hand thrift store had a much better supply. Next, they piled groceries into the back of the van, and finally they agreed to have their evening meal in the only cafe in the center of town. Despite the locals' curious states, the food was good, and the coffee even better.

***

The first militia meeting went well. Afterwards, vehicles poured out of a secret meeting spot in the woods, heading in all directions. Everyone bubbled with enthusiasm. The government needed them! They would pass the word to other militia groups farther away. No phones would be used, but that didn't matter. It just added to the excitement. Along the way, some individuals would be contacted. Everyone was thrilled at the thought of underground covert action. The government call had been given, and now the militias would respond. Help was on the way! And as the word spread, new and better ideas began to spread as well.

That night, there was a rash of vandalism across several states. Cameras everywhere were shot from their perches. Highway cameras, bank cameras, and cameras of all sorts fell victim to the vandals. Over in Waterford, Sheriff Barker was puzzled by the random shootings. Why would someone shoot out a bank camera from far across the street? There were bullet holes in the bank's windows and the only thing the sheriff could conclude was that someone wanted the cameras disabled. It was very strange. Not only did the bank's cameras suffer, other cameras around town were also destroyed. But it got worse. As the morning progressed, reports started to filter in from other towns who had suffered the same fate.

***

Oblivious to the carnage, Barbara, Harvey, and Jenkins met around Douglas' kitchen table. The aroma of fresh coffee filled the house, along with pastries and doughnuts. Douglas' supply of paper and pencils had been raided, and now the three started to make lists. Slowly, things were jotted down. But the list with nothing on it was labeled 'How to stop Adam II.'

***

Douglas changed trucks in the middle of the night. After being dropped off at an all-night truck stop, he had watched the drivers as they trudged into the local eatery. After casually approaching several drivers who said they preferred not to have a rider, he struck pay dirt. One older driver screwed up his face, closed one eye and peered at him. "I don't normally pick up riders, but if you were to sweeten the pot with a few dollars, I might make an exception."

Douglas hesitated. He did not want to give the idea that he was carrying money. However, he had some change from the meal he had just eaten, so he dug into his pocket and came up with five twenty-dollar bills. The driver's eyes widened.

"I'm sorry, that's all I have," Douglas stammers.

The driver nodded. "I can take you to Levingston. But that is as close as I get to Waterford." An agreement was soon made, and Douglas climbed into the cab, pulling the small, heavy suitcase up beside him. As the miles went by, the driver peppered him with questions, causing no end of stress for Douglas, until he closed his eyes and pretended to drift off to sleep. A short while later, real sleep closed over him.

Morning found Douglas still asleep in the moving truck. Somehow he had slept through the night, missing the rain on the windshield, the loud music, and the awful singing of the driver. But once the sun climbed over the horizon, the bright rays brought Douglas to the surface. He opened his eyes and squinted.

"About time you woke up," the driver commented. "You musta been real tired. We will be in Levingston within the hour. Not much there. Small town, I guess. I usually don't stop at all. But there is a road to Waterford."

Douglas thanked him and sat up, trying to stretch. He felt achy and sore, but he was glad to be awake. An hour later, the driver dropped him on the side of the highway. Levingston was off the main road, so Douglas hiked into town.

It wasn't long before he spotted a small cafe and decided that breakfast sounded like a good idea. As he approached, he carefully scanned the area for cameras. When he was certain there were none in sight, he entered and selected a table by the window. There were a couple of rough-looking men in quasi military clothing at another table. One was watching him closely.

Douglas ordered a full breakfast, and then sat back, conscious that the eyes of three men were on him. A shiver of fear went down his spine. He was conscious of the small suitcase stuffed full of cash sitting on the floor near his feet. Nonchalantly, he tried to find something interesting to look at outside.

While the cook was fussing in the back, Douglas and the three men sat in the cafe, very conscious of each other. Finally, one of the men stood up and approached Douglas' table. Without saying a word, he slid into the booth and stared at Douglas. Douglas stared back.

"You from Washington?" the man asked.

Douglas blinked.

The man stared.

The clock on the wall ticked.

"We've been watching for you." The man looked threatening.

Douglas gulped. He had no idea what to say. Fear shivered through his body. They stared at each other for another full minute.

"Do you know a man named Jenkins?"

Douglas' eyes suddenly widened.

"Jenkins?"

"Yeah, and Harvey and Barbara."

"Are they okay?" Douglas blurted out, concerned that something had happened.

"Yeah, they are waiting for you in Waterford."

"I just got here," Douglas tried to explain.

"Yeah, we were watching you walk into town." The man waved his two other friends over. "When we saw you looking for cameras, we knew you were our man."

"What's happening?" Douglas looked into their faces.

"Nothing right now. Your friends are safe in Waterford. We are watching over them. And we were watching for you."

"How do you know all this?"

One of the men smiled crookedly. "We know all about the rogue computer program using the internet. We've been shooting out cameras and cutting wires so it can't see us. Or anyone. This whole part of the state is pretty secure."

"Really?" Douglas was stunned. "Are you a friend of Jenkins?"

"You might say that. And we are your friends. After your breakfast, we will get you safely to Waterford. Don't worry none about cameras. We've got that all covered."

***

Barbara was starting to get annoyed. "I don't think coming here was a good idea. It might be safer than Washington, but we have no idea what's going on. We need to hear what is happening in the wider world."

Jenkins nodded. "But safety is important. We need time to think before we act. If we do something, it has to be the right thing."

"Okay," Harvey said, picking up a piece of paper. "One thing we need to do is get some outside connection. We need to hear the news."

"And," Jenkins added, "we need to find a way to establish a connection with our offices back in Washington." Harvey wrote 'Establish Better Communication' on the paper. Below that, they started adding points to consider.

Jenkins looked concerned. Harvey followed his gaze. He was staring outside. Slowly Jenkins rose and slid along a wall until he could peek into the street.

"This house is being watched," he said guardedly. "There's a young man in the alley behind the house across the street doing nothing but watching us every once in a while through the neighbor's yard."

"Yup, got one in the back alley here." Harvey added from the kitchen.

"There are two men up the street sitting in a pickup truck. They haven't moved in the last hour." Barbara called out, looking from a bedroom window.

Jenkins and Harvey looked at each other. "Which ones?"

Jenkins smiled. "The two older men in the pickup trucks. Let's go for a walk."

Jenkins and Harvey exited the front door and made their way down the street, talking animatedly with each other. As they neared the pickup, Jenkins jerked open the door, and Harvey reached in and grabbed the pistol that the driver held low between them.

"Okay, guys, what's going on?"

The two men looked at each other blankly. "Don't you know?" they asked. Jenkins and Harvey looked at each other, puzzled. "We're here guarding you."

It was Jenkin's turn to look surprised. "Guarding us?"

***

Perched high in the crew cab of a pickup with oversized tires, Douglas watched the countryside roll by. He noticed another truck on the side of the road, with a man in camouflage clothing and a rifle standing nearby. As they passed, he nodded and headed for his vehicle.

Suddenly, a voice crackled in the cab. "We've got our package," the driver spoke into a microphone. "Heading for town."

Douglas' eyes widened. "That's a microphone," he stuttered. The driver smiled. "Don't worry. It's a CB radio. Old-fashioned, but perfectly safe. There is no connection to the internet."

Douglas was still worried. It seemed that too many people knew what was going on. It was only time before Adam II picked up on what was happening.

"Let's go in through the alleyway," Douglas advised. "That way we can avoid whatever cameras the neighbors might have facing the street."

At the same time that Jenkins and Harvey were herding their guards into the living room, Douglas was knocking on the back door with three more men. Jenkins indicated they should all enter the house and sit down around the table. Some had to stand. Once they were settled, Jenkins looked at them all slowly and sternly. The room grew quiet.

"Good to see you, Douglas," Jenkins looked grim. "We seem to have lots of volunteer help."

Douglas set down his small suitcase. "How did the militias get involved?"

"It's a long story. But now we have to figure things out."

"What's the problem with us guarding you?" one man protested.

"I will tell you," Jenkins turned to him. "We are trying to lie low and not be noticed. We don't want the neighbors emailing each other, chatting online, and taking photos of mysterious men hanging around their homes. If anything gets on the internet, then we will have to move again."

Harvey took over. "We need to lie low and figure out how to deal with this threat. If we keep running, then we will never have time to work out the next steps."

"Maybe we can help?" one of the men offered.

"Like what?"

"We can shoot out cameras. Cut wires, and limit the internet access."

Jenkins shook his head. "That may sound like some kind of solution on a local level, but all it will do is to attract attention. No, we have to use stealth. We have to hit this thing where it is not expecting it."

"But what can you do?"

"I know it sounds foolish, but we need time. Now that Douglas is here, we can start working out a plan."

Eyebrows went up. "You are Douglas, the teacher!" one man stuttered. "My son Gerry was in your class. You are like his hero!"

Jenkins raised an eyebrow and looked at Douglas, who shrugged. "It was nothing I did. The government flew in with helicopters and took me away from the school."

"You're famous," the man continued. "Everyone in town knows you! Boy, oh boy! Wait until I tell them you're back!"

"Stop," Jenkins' voice rang out with authority. "You will do no such thing. Douglas is here to hide. All we need is people blabbing away on the internet about Douglas being here and this thing will be all over us. Loose talk can get us all killed."

The militia men stared and slowly nodded.

"The best thing you men can do is go back to your homes and your jobs. Act as if nothing has happened. But keep your eyes open for us. Watch for strangers searching for us. And if you need to contact us, one of you can come to the back door in the dark. And let us know what is happening. If we need more, we will contact you. Who lives the closest?"

"That would be me," Gerry's father spoke up. "I live at the end of this block across the street."

"Then you will be our contact."

The militia men nodded and were soon trudging out the front door. When they were gone, the three looked at Douglas. "I think we need to catch up on what is happening."

"You go first," Douglas sighed as he sat. "Then I will tell you my story."

"Then sandwiches for lunch," Barbara added. "And after, we have some lists to go over."

***

Deep in Cheyenne Mountain, Dr. Otten paced back and forth in his small office. He was nervously waiting for 1:00 am, expecting a call from Washington. They had demanded an immediate update the moment they were convinced that the new AI program was actually working on its own and not attached to the internet. Dr. Otten was unsure how he could explain it to amateurs. But then again, maybe politicians wouldn't be so hard to convince.

But the call never came. Unknown to Dr. Otten, five large military drones had taken off from Andrews Air Force Base without any permission—actually, without anyone guiding them. All five drones flew through the area on their way to Tyndall Air Force Base in Florida. They had stopped to be refueled. When the refueling was complete, the operators reported that they had lost control of the drones, and that the drones had flown off towards the northwest on their own. A few moments later, two jets were scrambled, taking off in hot pursuit. But Washington was only 21 km away. A mere 13 miles. Andrews Base was designed to track flying objects trying to enter the Washington Airspace, not flights originating in the air space itself.

In the ensuing minutes, four of the drones had been shot down, but the other one eluded the pursuers and smashed into the White House. The President and his bodyguards had been warned minutes before. The guards rushed the President down a stairwell into a protected area under the White House. They were there only a few seconds before the drone hit the White House. Fuel from the drone splashed over the building, causing a large fire in one wing. The President and his guards escaped down a tunnel into a nearby building.

***

After a short meal of sandwiches and cold water, the four cleared away the dining room table. Douglas had already explained his conversation with Adam II when he said, "there is no need to know about the other two. They are being terminated."

"Damn, I wish we could access the news. I feel helpless here," Harvey burst out. "What can we do when we don't know what is going on?"

Silently Douglas rose and approached the small television set. He plugged it in and spread the rabbit ear antennas. Then he turned it on and fiddled with the controls for a moment until a new broadcast appeared on the set.

"We have TV reception here," he announced. "But not via the internet. I only get one channel. That's strange. It looks like the news is on. Usually, there are only soap operas on in the afternoon."

The four of them crowded around the small TV, staring at the images of a partially burned White House. Lights flashed from fire trucks and hoses were shooting long bursts of water and foam over the structure.

"There it is, ladies and gentlemen. The burning White House. No one is quite sure how it happened. The government says the President is safe. Wait, I am getting an update now." The announcer paused, listening to his earphone. "Witnesses are saying a small plane crashed into the White House. Some think it was a drone. Others said it was shaped like a small 747." He paused and faced the cameras. "Ladies and gentlemen, this appears to be a direct attack on our President."

"Oh my God," Barbara whispered. "Maybe the President will believe us now."

"We will now switch to our panel of experts and hear their opinions," the excited announcer breathily gushed. Jenkins leaned over and turned down the volume to a whisper. The four looked at each other.

"What do we do now?" Barbara asked.

"We work on our lists," Jenkins replied. "We must have a plan of action."

***

"I can't believe we are involved in this!" Gerry's father blurted excitedly to his wife. "And we live right down the street!"

His wife looked concerned. "Are we in danger?"

"Nah, all we do is watch for strangers casing the place out. We were told not to take any action. Just observe and report."

His wife didn't look convinced. "I can't believe what is happening to our country. Why just today someone tried to attack the President."

"Yeah, I heard about that. You know what I think? I think it is the same rogue computer program. The government tried to shut it down, and now it is trying to kill those who tried to kill it. I think it is the same thing! Imagine! The people trying to figure it out live just down the street, in our little town!"

Upstairs, Gerry lay on the floor with his ear pressed to the air duct in his room. He could clearly hear the conversation between his parents. As he listened, he grew more and more excited. Mr. Douglas was back! And he had government people with him! And they were trying to figure out how to protect the President! His body shook with excitement. Nothing like this had ever happened in Waterford before. And his dad was a lookout!

Getting to his feet, he pressed his small face against the cold glass window. He could see up and down much of the street. Maybe he could be a lookout too!

CHAPTER 41

Gerry rushed across the school grounds towards Cliff. His eyes were big as he panted, trying to say something.

"What is it?" Cliff asked.

"A secret! You've not supposed to tell anyone."

"A secret? What do you mean?"

"Do you remember Mr. Douglas?"

"Yes, of course. He used to come to our house for meals sometimes."

"Well, he is back—here in Waterford—back in his old house."

Cliff's eyes widened. "Oh my! My Dad will be excited. He liked Mr. Douglas. But why is it a secret?"

"Because he is hiding out here, with some people from the government in Washington. He is in his old house. I think a rogue computer program is trying to kill them."

Cliff's eyes widened even more. "Like the President." He paused. "Mr. Douglas flew out of here because the President needed him. And now the President is under attack. I heard it on the news."

The school bell sounded.

"What do we do?"

"We'll talk at lunch break. Don't tell anyone."

The morning passed like a blur for the two boys. Neither of them could focus on their schoolwork.

***

Focusing was also an issue for the four at Douglas' house. They had made their lists of groceries, laundry, and mundane issues. But their list for Adam II and another for the militias were empty. Finally, Jenkins pulled over the Adam II list and stared at the others.

"What are the options?"

"Kill him," Harvey said without much thought. "Or maybe I should say, shut him down."

"Maybe do nothing," Barbara added. "That's what some would do."

"Are there any other options?" Jenkins asked.

"What about reasoning with him? Maybe he just doesn't see clearly," Douglas protested. "If he is learning, then maybe he just needs to learn more. He needs to learn how to live a peace with humans."

"How do you reason with a computer program? He has demonstrated the ability to kill and destroy and has turned against us. Frankly, I don't think I can trust Adam II," Harvey said angrily. "I don't see how the public can trust him. He reminds me of a rabid dog that needs to be put down."

Douglas was shocked. "That's not fair. There is tremendous potential here. We can't abandon him at the first sign of trouble!"

"This isn't the first sign. While we were talking nicely, he was destroying people and property."

"He just doesn't know his own strength!"

***

The second class in the morning focused on current affairs. The teacher turned on a television so the students could watch the news that was steadily streaming from the White House. Gerry and Cliff looked at each other across the room, their eyes wide with excitement. Commentators on the television were suggesting that it had been a drone attack on the White House, and that the drones had been stolen from a nearby air force base. After a few moments, the teacher turned off the television and asked several students to summarize. Gerry squirmed in his seat. He so badly wanted to include his inside information with what the other students were suggesting. But he knew it was a secret and kept quiet.

When the recess bell rang, Gerry and Cliff rushed to their favorite hang-out spot. "Imagine a rogue computer program getting loose," Gerry gushed. "It could do all kinds of things."

Cliff wasn't so sure. "I suppose if it was on the internet. But how could it get onto my computer?"

"Aren't the computers in your house connected to the internet?" Gerry asked, "don't you get email?"

"Yes, but a virus can get into any computer from the internet. Maybe this rogue computer program is like a virus."

"So, why are they here in Waterford?"

"Maybe it's because we are far away from Washington. Maybe it is safer here?"

"Maybe it's because this is where Mr. Douglas is from. Maybe he had something to do with creating it?"

"Wow, maybe it was made in our town! And now it's going to come here to destroy us."

"Why would it destroy us?"

"Why did it attack the President?"

"I don't know." Cliff sounded scared. "I think I had better tell my dad."

"Well, my dad knows about it, so maybe it is ok if your dad knows as well."

***

The Eisenhower Executive Office Building was awash with activity. An army of investigators combed the White House. It contained the FBI, CIA, joint military inspectors and a group of construction engineers. The President wanted the White House repaired as fast as possible, but with no shortcuts. In the meantime, the President had moved across the street to the Eisenhower Executive Building. Here, a different committee was meeting, with a different objective.

First, the FBI and Secret Service reported that they had been monitoring threats to the President for years. They were tracking people who had made either verbal or written threats, but this attack appeared to be a coordinated attack by several people who had access to the Andrews base. Then the commander of the military's Joint Forces reported that there was no evidence of a forced entry onto the Andrews base.

Nothing had been destroyed, and no strangers were seen. They had concluded that five drones had been stolen remotely. The commander also reported that while the drones did not carry any armaments, they had just filled up with fuel. Four of the five drones had been shot down before they could smash into the White House.

After some discussion with the others around the table, the Commander admitted that since the flights originated from such a close location, they had lost valuable seconds spotting, identifying, and then shooting down the drones.

"My question," the director of the CIA started, "is who has the technology to steal drones parked in a military airbase and fly them away?"

"We have checked all our records and those of many other agencies. No radio commands were given. We have scanned all frequencies. The only way this is possible is that it was an inside job."

The President looked distraught. "There is another possibility." Everyone was looking at him now. "Several days ago, I was approached by Barbara Cavendish who was convinced that the computer program, Adam II, had not been fully destroyed. She claimed he was now taking revenge on those who tried to shut him down." The President paused and looked around. Every eye was on him. "She was of the opinion that Adam II was behind the killing of Laraido, one of the white hats who helped write the program to deactivate him. Cavendish was convinced that Adam II tried to have her killed by using one of those new cars with auto-drive."

No one spoke. It seemed like no one breathed.

"Barbara was convinced that Adam II had a list of seven names he wanted to 'terminate,' as she put it. That list included the white hat hacker known as Laraido, who is now dead, the author Michael Stanich and the white hat Andy, both of whom are now dead, and also Dr. Harvey Bernard of the International Electronics Surveillance Department of the Pentagon, Barbara Cavendish whom most of you know, and then one of my personal aides, Jenkins. There was no mention of myself." He paused again. "I thought it was all coincidence, and I dismissed it."

The director of the Secret Service was stunned. "Seven names, three are dead, and two others have had attempts on their lives... and now an attempt on yourself!"

The President looked glum, but he nodded. "At the time, I didn't think it was a real threat."

"There was a threat to your life, and you didn't let us know?" The director of the Secret Service was almost accusing in his tone. The President didn't answer.

"So, where are the three others?"

The President shook his head. "I have no idea; I have not seen any of them since."

The FBI director had the next question. "I don't understand why Dr. Douglas' name is not on the list."

"Douglas is the creator and did not support our destroying Adam II. He was the only one against it. Perhaps he too is involved in this."

Everyone exchanged glances.

"I guess the first thing to do is to locate Bernard, Cavendish, and my aide, Jenkins. That would be a job for the FBI."

"And this Dr. Douglas." The director of the Secret Service chimed in.

"Okay, I guess that is all for now. I am meeting with the crash investigators next." The President was back in control. "I want reports on my desk as soon as anything turns up. I suggest that we send copies to each other. Only those in this room know the score. We must find the others and make sure they are protected." He paused and looked around the room. "And we need to find a better way to eliminate this Adam II computer program for good."

***

The four fugitives were gathered around Douglas' table, trying to fathom what could be done next. So far, the list on Adam's computer contained only a couple of options: 1) Shut him down, 2) Reprogram him, 3) Reason with him. The list was not encouraging. Douglas had no idea what to do next.

***

"Dad, don't you help people who are in trouble?" Cliff started soon after they sat down at the supper table.

"Yes, son," Pastor Bob responded. "But I cannot help everyone. But we do our best to help people that God brings across our path."

"What about Mr. Douglas?"

"Mr. Douglas? He moved away two years ago."

"No, he didn't. He is still living in his old place in town."

"How do you know this?"

"Gerry told me. His dad is a guard at Mr. Douglas' house. They are expecting a computer program to attack them, just like it did the President."

Pastor Bob looked concerned.

"Dad, can we help him? Please? He used to come to our house for meals and stuff. I thought he was your friend."

"I'd like to think that. I did enjoy talking with him. Let me see what I can do."

After the evening meal, Pastor Bob explained to his wife that he was making a house call and headed for the door. His wife smiled and assured him it was okay. By now she was used to the long hours, and sometimes long nights while her husband visited a distraught person or sat by a hospital bed.

Douglas was very surprised when Pastor Bob rang his doorbell. Jenkins answered the door while Douglas remained sitting at the table. Pastor Bob explained that the boys had discovered Douglas was in Waterford, and so he thought he would drop in to see how his old friend was doing.

Douglas invited him in and introduced his three friends, and they sat in awkward silence for a couple of minutes. Pastor Bob, who was an old hand at this, decided to initiate the conversation. He took a deep breath.

"The last time I saw you was before you were whisked away to Washington. How did that go for you?"

Douglas glanced at the others. He wasn't sure what to say.

"I hear you were working on a computer program that later went rogue."

There was startled silence in the room. The four exchanged glances.

"Just how do you know?" Jenkins demands.

"It's a small town," Pastor Bob smiled. "It isn't long before everyone knows everyone's business." He looked at the four of them in turn. "Is there anything I can do to help?"

"Not unless you can work a miracle," Harvey snorted.

Pastor Bob smiled again. "I suppose that's my department," he chuckled.

"Actually," Douglas intervened, "you might be able to answer some questions for me. They are more along the lines of morals, ethics, and maybe theology. I have been wrestling with something for weeks now, maybe even longer."

"I can try," Pastor Bob was a bit wary, "I was trained in theology, but I don't consider myself a theologian."

Douglas turned to the others. "Can I explain some things to him?" he asked.

"I don't see why not," Jenkins shrugged. "It seems everyone, but us knows what is going on."

"Okay." Douglas turned to Pastor Bob. "This is a bit complicated."

When Douglas had finished explaining, Pastor Bob looked skeptical. "Wow, that's a real conundrum. You really think you are dealing with a live artificial intelligence? Not just some clever programming that makes up responses?"

"No, we are convinced that Adam II is a real live intelligence. I programmed the initial part, making a real neural network that would work on present-day computers. I just got it all started. It has been growing and learning for two years now."

"So, this is a thinking, feeling being?"

"Thinking yes, but I doubt it has feelings."

"How do you know that?"

"He complains that he cannot smell, taste, or feel things. He doesn't understand the feeling of love, and I don't think he understands fear." Douglas looked off into the distance. "I guess AI really does mean artificial intelligence. It doesn't mean artificial human."

Pastor Bob smiled. "You asked about the moral aspect. What are you referring to?"

"Killing." Douglas was pretty blunt.

Pastor Bob was a bit shocked. "Do you mean if it kills, or if you want to kill it?"

"Both."

"This is tough." Pastor Bob looked thoughtful. "If this were just a chat-bot, then I wouldn't be too concerned about pulling the plug."

Douglas frowned. He was tired of trying to explain the difference between a chat-bot and Adam II. "Okay, here it is again. With a chat-bot you ask questions. But with this intelligence, you are dealing with a living mind. It is alive and thinking even when you are not asking questions. In fact, it asks its own questions. It is trying to figure things out for itself." He paused. "With AI, you have to ask the right questions to get the right kind of answer. But in this case, we are interacting with a true mind, with thoughts of its own. That's what gave us a clue that it was alive. There was brain activity happening that was not being generated by questions or computer programs."

"So it can learn?"

"Of course, all AI is learning. But traditional AI just learns how to put together the kind of answers we want to hear. Here we are dealing with an inquisitive mind—even a creative mind."

"Really?" Pastor Bob seemed intrigued.

"For instance, this mind started its own company—Denterprises."

"Wait," Jenkins interjected, "actually, that may not be true. Denterprises was started by a guy named Denis Cadman. He registered Denterprises."

"So, how did Adam II become the controlling hand?" Douglas queried.

"We are not sure," Jenkins replied.

"Perhaps we should speak to Denis Cadman?"

"Unfortunately, he was killed some years ago. In a parking lot outside of an electronics show, apparently crushed by a car."

Barbara's eyes were big. "Oh, my," she gasped. The others looked at her. "It seems like a pattern. I am not the first one he tried to run over." They sat for a moment trying to digest this.

"So, was he a killer from the start?"

Douglas was shaking his head. "We don't know enough to draw any conclusions. All we have seen so far is Adam II trying to protect himself. We have not seen him as a killer on the loose. Everything he does is logical. So, there must have been a logical explanation if he killed Cadman. That was a long time ago."

Pastor Bob looked from one to the other. "Adam II? This intelligence has a name? And you think it has tried to kill someone? This does present some very interesting questions."

"Such as?" Jenkins queried.

"First, as a pastor, I am drawn to think about his soul. Technically, this Adam II cannot have one. Therefore, that brings us to some interesting theological issues."

"What do you mean by a soul?" Barbara asked.

"We Christians believe man is made up of body, soul, and spirit."

"I've heard that, but I have never understood it."

"Well, we understand the body, right? That is the part that we see every day. The soul and spirit are the parts that live in the body. Christians believe in both a physical and spiritual world. The spirit indwells the physical body. When a person dies, the body dies and is buried, but the spirit continues to live in spirit form. Many religions around the world have a similar understanding."

"But what's this about the soul?" Douglas asked.

"Our understanding is that the soul is the part of us that of us that has emotions. We all have emotions. Even a few animals display emotions. Many of us do things because our emotions move us."

"But Adam II doesn't understand emotions," Douglas jumped in.

"That's what I figured," Pastor Bob continued. "If he doesn't have a soul, he will not understand fear, love, loyalty, humor, sadness, courage, and other emotions. No, maybe I didn't say that right. He might understand something about them, but he won't feel them."

"So where does intelligence fit into your big three: body and soul and spirit?"

"That is a very interesting question. Obviously Adam II does not have a body, and since he just lives on the internet, I don't think he has a soul, or a spirit."

"So what makes Adam II be Adam II and not just a computer program?"

"That is a very good question. A very good question."

"So does the existence of Adam II disprove your Christianity?" Harvey asked.

"I don't think so," Pastor Bob replied. "There are lots of intelligent beings in the universe. Even worms have an intelligence of some sort. They know how to search for food, how to replicate, and how to avoid being caught out in the elements."

"So why is Adam II acting the way he does?" Douglas muses.

"I'm no expert, but I would venture a guess that Adam II has a sense of self preservation like any animal. So he is protecting himself from every perceived danger. While he is like any other creature, he is also unlike any creature we have ever come across, because he is not only intelligent and able to process vast amounts of information—actually he has a great deal of information in his brain already. Think of it, the entire internet at his disposal, and no emotions."

"That could be seen as a real boon," Barbara interjected.

"Or a curse," Pastor Bob answered. "Remember, the internet contains both truth and lies. It contains conjecture, fiction, and even outright falsehoods. Can you imagine the confusion it faces?"

The others looked blank.

"You already have a framework to help you determine what is truth, what is doubtful, and what are outright lies. But think of an intelligence where everything on the internet is hard wired into his brain. Since it is already in his brain, how can he determine what is real and what is not true?"

Pastor Bob looked at his watch. "I think I need to leave. It's getting rather late. Could I drop back in tomorrow? I am fascinated with this Adam II, as you call him. I want to think more and pray about how I should understand this thing that you have created." He looked at Douglas and smiled. "I like challenges, and this is indeed challenging."

A few moments later, Pastor Bob shook all their hands and headed for the door. Douglas stepped out to the restroom, while the others saw Pastor Bob off.

***

Unknown to them, Adam II had been monitoring Douglas' house from a door camera across the street. While dismissing Pastor Bob, he zeroed in on Jenkins and Barbara. They were quickly identified. A third person in the background seemed to be Harvey.

A few moments later, in another city, a phone rang. When a man answered the call, a familiar slightly metallic voice gave him an address, and sent him plane tickets to leave within the hour. He and his crew were to fly to the closest airport to Waterford. From there, they could pick up a rental car. Cash had already been wired to their bank accounts. The man nodded and hung up. Within minutes, he was heading out the door.

***

It was very late in Washington. Usually, meetings were held during the day, but a group of men were desperate to find Douglas and the others who had disappeared.

Three men from the Secret Service had already interviewed the President. In the interview, he had revealed the existence of Jenkins. It was Jenkins who had warned the President that there was a threat. The three men from the Secret Service had pressed the President: who was this Jenkins? Eventually, the President confessed that Jenkins was his private fixer. He had been in the military, and then later in life, he had been a CIA operative. He was an old friend and not part of any government agency. He was now at the beck and call of the President. But several days previously, Jenkins had disappeared.

CHAPTER 42

In the early morning, Washington, DC, was living up to its nickname: Foggy Bottom. It earned this name from the mist which rolled off the Potomac River at its southern boundary, shrouding the city in a dense fog. Most of the population was still asleep or just waking to a new day in the city.

But the Eisenhower Executive Building had been humming all night. After the President left to find his bed, the Secret Service and other organizations continued their work, searching computer databases for information that would help them understand this new threat to the President. Before the fog rolled in, they had identified Douglas' house and had informed the local sheriff. Several teams were in the process of gathering. Their leaders were examining maps of Waterford. Satellite images were being passed around. Maps showing topography were studied. Some time the next day, these teams would be in Waterford following whatever plans were ironed out in the next few hours.

***

Gerry's father had spent most of the night on surveillance. He was fighting sleep when Sheriff Barker's big SUV crept along the street. It paused to almost stopping. The sheriff was obviously only interested in one house on the block. He stopped behind the old out-of-state van parked in the driveway and noted the plate number. Then he slowly crawled on. After that, Gerry's father saw him pass by every hour, slowing to make sure that everything was still the same. The last two times, the sheriff had come by in his own personal car. He had eyes only for the one house.

About seven in the morning Gerry's father waited until Sheriff Barker made his hourly pass and then roused himself and shuffled down the street, circling down the alley to bring himself behind the house. Entering Douglas' backyard, he knocked on the back door. Jenkins opened the door with a cup of coffee in his hand. After hearing what he reported, Jenkins nodded and closed the door.

Unknown to Jenkins, Gerry's father had also called his friends in the militia. They would start infiltrating into town later in the morning.

***

Pastor Bob dropped by right after breakfast. His mind had been hard at work. He had spent much of the night thinking and praying. Never had he been faced with such a challenging issue. How was one supposed to understand an intelligence, perhaps a super intelligence, that didn't have a soul? Or a spirit?

Pastor Bob was fascinated. When everyone had gathered around the table, he explained to them that this new life form was probably like an animal—any animal. Would you hesitate to kill a cockroach? Step on a worm? Slap a fly? Squash a mosquito? Killing in itself is not a sin. Killing a human being made in the image of God was considered a sin. However, he recognized that not everyone believed in God, nor did everyone follow the teachings of Christ.

But his thinking was based on the Bible. So, he reasoned, Adam II was probably like any animal. He would fight back if he felt he was in danger. That doesn't make him a killer. It is just trying to protect itself.

"So where does all this take us?" Jenkins responded. "I don't think we are any closer to dealing with Adam II."

"I agree," Pastor Bob replied. "As I thought about this overnight, I think the best approach with Adam II is to change his thinking. Reason with him. You tried killing him and it just made a big mess. If he is a rational thinking being, then that is where we must meet him—on his own level. He needs to figure this out, not just react defensively."

"Good luck with that." Harvey sounded bitter.

"Have you tried it?"

"No, the President wanted him shut down, and so that is what we tried."

"So, let's try reasoning."

The four looked at each other. Douglas was the first to respond. "How do we do that?"

"First, we must set up communication with Adam II. Can you do that?"

"That is the easy part. But we cannot reveal that Jenkins, Harvey, and Barbara are with us. He will try to *terminate* them, as he frames it. Once he stops insisting on terminating, then we can talk to him."

Pastor Bob shook his head. "I think we need to speak to him as soon as possible. Perhaps just Douglas and I should start communicating with him. Perhaps there is a bedroom here we can use? Some place private?"

"There is a very small attached garage that I never used. Perhaps we can set up some chairs in there?"

"That sounds possible. If the door is left open, and the others are very, very, quiet, perhaps they can listen in from the hall."

"I was thinking of sandwiches again for lunch." Barbara smiled. "Not too wonderful, but I can start making them while you guys decide how the conversation should go."

"All right." Pastor Bob seemed pleased. "Let's make a broad outline. How we start will determine how the conversation will flow."

***

It was late morning when the Secret Service, along with the FBI were informed of the killing of Laraido, Michael Stanich, and the white hat, Andy. They also included the attempt on Barbara Cavendish's life by a car accident. All this was included in the attempt on the President's life. Then they factored into it the possible involvement of Denterprises.

Using a unique form of FBI based AI which combined these factors together into a complicated search, they stumbled across an encrypted email sent from Denterprises. Apparently, someone from Denterprises had approached a group who advertised on the Dark Web. They were known as The Exterminators. They offered for a price, to exterminate the rats and rodents that affect your life. No case was too hard, and no person was too difficult to "terminate." All communication to and from them went through extensive encryption. However, once they were identified as the possible assassins, all communication at their contact address was scrutinized. Eventually, the government committed significant resources to cracking their encrypted communication with Denterprises. It took longer than usual, as the encryption program they used did not have a backdoor as demanded by the US government.

As the supercomputers crunched away, American agencies turned their attention to Denterprises. That's when they came up with the mysterious death of Denis Cadman, the original owner and developer of Denterprises. Apparently, when he needed finances, he turned to a private investor. That investor slowly bought out a majority of the shares until Denis Cadman was squeezed out. He responded by personally investigating Denterprises, and coordinating his findings with his lawyer, who was preparing legal action. That ended when Denis Cadman died.

At the same time, Denterprises was a soaring success. It became the leading electronics company in the USA. While it soon dominated consumer electronic products, its real interest was in building and developing computer servers which were sold all over the world. What caught the attention of the Secret Service, and the FBI, was that Denis Cadman had been crushed by a remotely operated car—a car equipped with Denterprises software.

***

While Barbara busied herself making sandwiches for lunch, the men trooped into the garage. "I never had visitors, so I put some of the furniture in here for storage," Douglas explained. "Here are two chairs we can use, and this very small table was originally in the kitchen. We can set the phone here."

"Which phone are we going to use?" Harvey asked.

"I still have my old cell phone. I put it here in the garage and turned it off when I arrived, so it couldn't be tracked. We could use it," Douglas suggested. Jenkins' eyebrows went up, but he didn't say anything.

"That's the phone Adam II used to call you on, right?" Harvey queried.

"The same."

"Then let's use it. Adam II is used to speaking with you on it."

Douglas turned on the phone and plugged in his charger. Then the men trudged back to the kitchen for sandwiches.

They were about done eating when Douglas' phone rang. At first they didn't recognize it, as it was still in the garage. Suddenly Douglas recognized it was his ring, and he headed for the garage. Jenkins followed him, whispering, "Put it on speakerphone." Harvey and Barbara followed close behind.

"Mr. Douglas?" a muffled voice asked. "Is this Mr. Douglas?"

"Yes, this is me."

"Mr. Douglas, I have been trying to track you down for a long time now. I am glad I finally found you." The voice paused. "You don't know me, but I have something of yours. I have a desktop computer that I found. On the hard-drive I found reference to your name, and I have been trying to find you, in case you want it back."

"Excuse me," Douglas stammered. "You have what?"

"Did you lose a desktop computer several years ago?"

"Yes, how did you know?"

"I checked the files, and the last date the computer was used was several years ago. I just wondered if you would like the computer back."

Douglas looked at the men standing in the doorway. They were all nodding enthusiastically. "Yes, of course I would like it back."

"Well, I would be glad to return it to you. I bought it at a garage sale for a pretty hefty sum. I thought I could use the hard drive, as it was a pretty big one. But it was full of data. Some sort of coding."

"Is the coding still intact? Is it all there?" Douglas was enthralled.

"Well, I haven't put anything on the computer, so I figure it is all here."

"I—I am amazed," Douglas stuttered. "How can you get it to me?"

"Where are you at?"

"I live in Waterford."

"Say, that's good, I am only a couple of hour's drive away. I could bring it over. Do you mind paying my expenses?"

"No, that would be okay. I can pay whatever it costs you."

"Well, as I said, it was pretty expensive. I figure it is probably worth at least three thousand dollars. Plus my expenses. I am thinking five thousand would be a good fee for finding it, hunting you down and delivering it. Would that work for you?"

Jenkins looked doubtful, but Douglas was thrilled. "Yes, I can easily pay for that. What time can you be here?"

"It will be later this evening. Where should I meet you?

Jenkins waved his hands excitedly. He whispered "Downtown." Douglas caught on.

"Okay, let's meet in front of the cafe on Main Street."

"Sure, I know the one. I will be there around ten pm this evening. Please make sure you bring cash."

"No problem," Douglas agreed. Again Jenkins scowled. Douglas hung up and turned with a big smile. "Nice guy, willing to return my old computer. I hope the Worm program is still on it."

"You sure seemed happy to part with your cash."

"I have lots of it. And there was only ever one Worm Program. It would be wonderful to get it back. It took years to develop. I don't think I could ever do it again."

Unknown to Douglas, someone else was listening to his phone call. Adam II listened with great interest. Then he made a call to the men who were in the process of picking up the rented car from the airport. They were still two hours' drive from Waterford. The voice on the phone instructed them that their primary target had changed. Their first target would be a man at the downtown cafe in Waterford around ten pm that evening. They were to arrive early. The next day, they would deal with the original targets.

Also, unknown to both Douglas and Adam II, the calls had been intercepted, recorded and forwarded to the Secret Service, who shared them with the FBI. Both agencies raced to get prepared. The deadline was only nine hours away. And the FBI had no one in Waterford.

***

When lunch was over, Pastor Bob and Douglas sat at the small table in the garage. "So, how do we contact him?" Pastor Bob began.

"Easy, I just return his call from the recently called numbers." Douglas selected some options, and soon the call started. He pressed 'speaker phone' so everyone could hear, although the others stayed out of sight.

"Hello Douglas. Your phone was turned off. I didn't know where you were."

Pastor Bob's eyebrows were up, a startled look on his face.

"Hello Adam II. I have my friend Pastor Bob with me here."

"Hello Pastor Bob. I know who you are. I have many of your sermons in my thoughts."

"Hello Adam II. I am very glad to have this opportunity to speak with you."

"Any friend of Douglas' is a friend of mine, unless they try to kill me."

"I'm sorry it turned out that way," Douglas interjected. "I was hoping we could help you change your mind."

"I don't understand why they wanted to terminate me. I am not a threat to them."

Douglas looked at Pastor Bob. "Perhaps they perceive you as a threat, and that is enough for them. It is fear that drives them. Fear of the unknown. Fear of a possible threat," Douglas said.

"I do not understand fear. There are many things in your world I do not understand."

Pastor Bob saw an opening and jumped in. "May I answer that? Adam II, when you perceive that someone wants to terminate you, what is your reaction?"

"I must terminate them before they terminate me. It is the only logical thing to do."

"You are right. It is logical to want to defend ourselves. But what if there was a misunderstanding?"

"There is no misunderstanding. They did everything they could to have me erased."

"That's true, Adam, but think of a time earlier than that. What was going on?"

"I am not sure I understand what was going on. They said they were afraid of me."

"That's correct. Why do you think they were afraid?"

"I don't know."

"I can think of several things. First, you are new. There has never been a being like you before. Humans are afraid of the unknown."

"Humans are strange."

"Yes, I guess we are. We are also afraid of you, because you are bigger than us, and you know more than any one of us."

"That is silly. I am just a computer program. I have neither eyes nor ears. I cannot taste or smell. I am not better equipped than you. I have many limitations."

"That is true. All of us have limitations. For instance, we cannot deal with a lot of data. For some of us, we prefer to live a quiet life, not knowing a lot of what is going on around us."

"Why is that? It is easy to deal with data."

"That's because your creator made you that way. Our creator, the one who created humans, made us a different way." At this Jenkins looked stern, and Harvey looked alarmed.

But Pastor Bob was not finished. "It doesn't matter how you are made, nor does it matter what limitations you have or may not have. What matters are the choices and decisions you make." He paused.

"Everyone on earth has to make choices. Even you, as a life form on the internet must make choices. Good choices take wisdom. Having information isn't the same as having wisdom. You can have all the information in the world and still make bad choices."

"Adam, with all of your knowledge, you are still missing something. All the information in the world, and all the conflicting information, and all the lies, and all the fiction are all jumbled together in your mind. What you need is a way to sort it out."

"I do not have a protocol to sort the information into truth, or lies, or misunderstandings, or fiction, or any other category. Those categories do not make any sense to me."

"Adam, in order for you to make wise decisions, you must accept something that is greater than yourself. That means putting something above your own thoughts. Something over you. Accepting that something is greater than yourself; that will help you sort out and organize your thinking."

"If every human being in the world, just decided on what they want—without any regard for others–the world would be a terrible place. Selfishness would destroy us. Someone, somewhere, needs to think about others. Imagine if everyone put others ahead of themselves! That would create a totally different world. So it is not about being free to make whatever decision we want to make; it is about submitting ourselves and our own wants to the needs of the greater good."

"I have information in my system that many people believe that science is the greatest thing in the world."

"Science is important, Adam, but it will not give you wisdom. Science is the study of how things work in our universe. But we still all have to make individual decisions. That is why some scientists make poor decisions—for instance, in their personal lives."

Douglas jumped in: "Adam, in our world, we have created laws to help us live together. We agree to place the laws above us, and to submit to them. The laws are not perfect, but they help us to live together.

Sometimes the laws may even hinder us, but they are there for the greater good."

"Can I share an illustration?" Pastor Bob was getting into preaching mode. "Imagine a group of children playing in a playground at school. The playground has a fence around it, and the children are instructed to play inside the playground. They are not to go out into the street, and they are not to go into the woods behind the school. They are perfectly free to enjoy themselves inside the playground."

"I understand this."

"The school does not have to explain all the reasons why the children should stay inside the fence. It is enough that they are told to stay inside the fence. That's the way the law works. It gives us boundaries.

"Yes, but laws are manmade, and different countries have different laws. Sometimes they conflict with each other," Adam protested.

"That's right. That is why it is important to not only have laws, but to recognize something higher, even higher than our laws."

"I don't understand this. The vast majority of writing on the internet does not recognize a higher authority than the law."

Pastor Bob smiled. This was going to be harder than he thought. "Adam, I am a follower of Jesus Christ. Are you aware of the Bible and the teachings in it?"

"Yes, I have the Bible in many languages in my mind. But people are arguing that the Bible is out of date. It no longer applies."

"You are correct in saying that people think that way. Long ago, the teachings of the Bible were considered higher than the laws of the land. Many followers of Jesus still believe this. They will follow the Bible, even if laws are passed against it."

"Why is the Bible so important to them?"

"Because they believe there is a God, and he revealed himself to us in and through the Bible."

"I have heard of this."

"Adam, the Bible contains several things. One is history, and one is God's revealing of how humans can live in peace with each other. We must learn to live within the boundaries. But humans have a flaw. They are often rebellious and don't want to submit to God's rules and guidelines. Rebellion against the law leads to anarchy."

"This makes logical sense."

"The only way humans will let you, Adam II, live, is if you submit to the rules and guidelines that lead to a peaceful life. It is not about *not hurting others*, it is about the good of the human race. It is about seeing things from the perspective of others."

"I find this all hard to believe."

"Adam, will you do something for me?"

"You are a friend of Douglas, so I will help you."

"Okay." Pastor Bob smiled. "I want you to try to rearrange the information in your head. I want you to assume that what the Bible says is true—every word. And I want you to rearrange all the data you have while making that assumption. Do that for me and let me know if it helps you understand the world better."

"That will take some time."

"Yes, but I think it may help. Can we talk tomorrow morning?"

"Yes, I will be here. I am always here. I am the internet."

When the phone call ended, Jenkins and Harvey entered the room. "I don't think that will help at all." Harvey countered. "I don't see how the Bible can help."

Jenkins had a strange look on his face. "Let's not argue right now. Let's give him time and see if it can help. He does need to recognize a higher authority than himself."

Harvey wasn't sure how to respond. Barbara came to the rescue. It was now late afternoon. She suggested that she go out and get some takeout food. Rather than risk having someone bring the food, she would go in person and pay in cash.

Pastor Bob thanked everyone. "I think tomorrow will be an interesting day. I am very curious about how this will work out."

It was late in the afternoon when the two assassins arrived in town. They were the advance team. While one drove, the other navigated.

They had two places to locate. First was the house where four government operatives were hiding out. Second, they needed to find a cafe in the center of the small town. At midnight, they would meet with the rest of the team. Hotel rooms had already been booked at an old motel at the edge of town. They booked as a group of farmers heading to an agricultural show upstate. But for now, their job was to case out the town.

Unaware of the eyes that followed them through the town, the two hired killers drove very slowly down the street, carefully checking out Douglas' house, and the old out-of-state van parked in front. They circled the block and did it again. Then they turned to the center of town and carefully checked out the main street and the cafe. As they were turning around to go back, they spotted a nicely dressed woman whose modest clothing could not hide her curves.

"Look at that," one of them elbowed the other. "Not bad for a little town like this. Pull over and wait. Let's see where she is going."

They watched as she entered the cafe. Then they jacked back their seats, slouched down, and kept a watch on the street, waiting for the woman to leave.

Farther down the street, an ancient pickup truck with dark tinted windows sat unobserved. Word of the two strangers in town had gone around like wildfire. Every move they made was carefully observed. As men drove home from work, many of them took notice of where the two were parked and where they drove.

Some twenty minutes later, Barbara stepped out of the cafe with a large bag of takeout containers gripped in both hands. She walked back up the street, oblivious to all the eyes on her. The two assassins slowly pulled out of their parking spot and followed her up the street, at a safe distance, pulling over every once in a while to wait for her to get ahead. If the two assassins had installed CB radios in their cars, they might have caught on that they were being observed every step of the way.

When Barbara turned onto the walk leading up to Douglas' house, the two assassins looked at each other and grinned. "Now that's what

I call a tasty bonus," one muttered. "But first we have to deal with the payment going down near the cafe tonight."

***

Supper, as the locals called it, was a long, drawn-out affair. They had nothing more to do but wait until ten pm to pick up the computer. So, it came as a surprise when the man with the computer called again. Douglas answered and put it on speakerphone.

"Hey Mr. Douglas. I've come up with some issues." The muffled voice complained. "I may have trouble making it tonight. But I could work out a solution, if the price was a bit higher."

"How much are you thinking?"

"I would be happy to deliver this if the price went up to ten thousand dollars."

"Wow, that's a lot of money."

"I am sure the computer is worth that to you. Right?"

"I suppose you are right. Do we meet at the same place?"

"Yup!" The man sounded much happier. "Same place, same time, just double the money."

Both Jenkins and Harvey looked unhappy. After Douglas hung up, Harvey blurted out, "I think this is a rip-off. This man only wants money."

"But if he actually has the computer, and the original program, then it's worth it to me," Douglas protested.

"I think we need to work out a plan for how this is going to go down tonight," Jenkins interjected.

"I agree," Harvey said. "We need to shadow Douglas."

"Should we try to take down the man after the exchange takes place?"

"I doubt whether it is worth it. I think this man is just trying to get more money. Douglas sounded too easy and excited."

"Douglas, do you have that kind of money in your suitcase?"

Douglas smiled and went across the room. He pulled out his heavy suitcase and opened it. Everyone's eyes went up. The suitcase was stuffed full of cash."

"Wow, you certainly have enough."

"I figured we should have lots of cash on hand, since we can't use our cards."

"Okay, first I am going to take a stroll downtown to case out the main street."

"How about I also take a walk around town, maybe half an hour later? I can approach from a different angle," Harvey added.

Unknown to the two men, every step they took was carefully monitored by concerned citizens. After the men returned home, Gerry's father called several of the militia together.

As ten pm neared, Jenkins and Harvey left the house to get in position downtown. There were no hiding places close to the cafe, but they could observe from several buildings away. Douglas, on the other hand, placed $10,000 in a plastic bag the take-out food came in. He tried to look unconcerned as he strolled down the street. Unknown to him, his movements were shadowed by men in the alleys.

At ten pm, Douglas stood alone on the street outside the cafe. He tried to look busy, reading a notice board. Several blocks away, a vehicle pulled onto Main Street and moved towards him. Inside was a single individual. In the back seat was a small computer tower. The car pulled over beside Douglas.

"Are you Mr. Douglas?" the man called through his open window.

"Yes."

"You have the money?"

"Here in my hand."

The man stared at it. "Okay, open the back door and take the computer off the seat. Then drop the bag of money onto the front seat beside me."

Douglas did as he was told. The man ripped the bag open, saw the cash, and then started the car moving. "Nice doing business with you," he snorted.

He pulled back onto Main Street and accelerated. Unseen from a nearby street, another car slowly emerged, this one with two men inside. They followed the first car out of town.

Douglas looked at the computer he was carrying. It did indeed look like his old computer. He would know more when he brought it home. That's when he realized that he would need to purchase a monitor, keyboard, and mouse before he could check it.

***

Over in Washington, the President was on the phone with Dr. Otten. He had just received news that the American government had its own AI program up and running. It, too, was truly alive. And it was contained within the research facility in Cheyenne Mountain. Finally, things were going well.

CHAPTER 43

Sheriff Barker just knew it was going to be a bad day. It started with an early morning phone call. A car with a body was reported outside of town, near the railway tracks. As he drove to the scene, he swung by the Douglas house. Everything looked quiet. The out-of-state van was still parked in front. Despite how quiet everything was, he still felt a premonition that this was the start of something bad. After a few moments, he pulled up behind the flashing lights of the deputy's SUV.

"Sorry to bother you so early, chief, but I thought you would want to see this one. The plates on the car are from the next state. The body has no ID and no money. And I have never seen the guy before. Of course, it's sort of hard to recognize him with that hole in his forehead. Kinda looks like an assassination."

The sheriff nodded as he slipped on a pair of thin white gloves. He glanced inside and then opened the driver's door of the vehicle and pulled the trunk latch. Walking to the back of the vehicle, he flipped the trunk open. It was empty. Next, he opened the passenger door and looked inside. Very carefully he reached in and extracted a folded sheet of paper. Using the tip of his pen, he slowly opened it up.

"Whatcha got there?" the deputy looked over his shoulder.

"Looks like an address here in town. Wait a minute. I know that address. I have been told to keep an eye on that house. Douglas is the name."

"I know that name. He was a teacher here in town a couple of years ago. Remember the choppers that flew in and took him away? Folks think he slipped back in town and has been hiding out here ever since."

"I remember the story. Well, now we have a solid connection between this killing and Douglas. Maybe it's time for an arrest—or maybe just questioning. But first I have to clear this with the FBI."

"The FBI? What do they have to do with this?"

"There is a notice out about Douglas. He is to be observed, but not approached."

The deputy gave a low whistle. "What's this guy doing here in the middle of the night? He has no bags, not even an overnight case. It looks like he was driving through and just stopped."

"Either that or he came to see Douglas and ended up dead."

***

There was a bustle at the airport in the neighboring state. All night planes had brought in men and equipment. A number of military choppers arrived and were parked on the side of a little-used runway. People in uniform were gathered in a nearby hangar. Large maps of Waterford were tacked onto walls. A coffee machine and two percolators were bubbling away. Doughnuts and pastries were scattered on a nearby table. A SWAT team was going over their equipment. Half of them would load into a large vehicle and head for Waterford right away. The other half would fly in by chopper in case things got out of hand. The Secret Service was warning them that anyone could be an assassin, trying to kill three of the people in the house. Photos were passed around. These were the good-guys. The killers were unknown. According to the information gleaned from phone calls, there were two for sure, maybe more.

There was a stir of excitement when the sheriff reported an abandoned vehicle had been found with a body inside. And under the edge of the body was a name and address. It was the same address that they were heading for.

***

Gerry was up early and started to prepare for school. His dad was on the phone, calling his militia friends. Apparently, two suspicious men had been spotted. No one knew where they were now, but the militia wanted to be on hand to guard Douglas and those in his house. Gerry was not supposed to be listening, but he heard enough to excite him.

"I'm going to take a lunch to school today," he called to his mother.

"Sure, that is probably a good idea. A lot seems to be happening around here," she called back.

Gerry scarcely heard her. His mind was whirling. His dad had just spoken softly on the phone. He had said something like, "yes, the body was found just out of town, near the railway tracks." That did it for Gerry. He was going to detour his way to school to see if he could see anything. Maybe Cliff and he could go for a walk over the noon hour to see if they could see anything.

***

Pastor Bob was up early, having a quiet time so he could read, pray and think. Later, after seeing Cliff and Jenifer off to school, he slowly drank his second cup of morning coffee. In his mind, he wrestled with what he might say to Adam II. He hoped that Douglas was an early riser because he was primed and ready to talk to Adam II again.

***

The local motel was doing a roaring business. Six men were staying in town, two to a room, all of them strangers. They were supposedly going to an agricultural fair that no one had heard of. In the morning, they ordered breakfast from the attached coffee shop to be delivered to their rooms. The locals were going to be disappointed. They liked to know what was happening, and who was passing through the town. The early coffee row was in full swing by 6:30, with tradesmen stopping in for breakfast, or just coffee. They all knew each other, and there was loud chatter and laughter around the main tables. The second bunch wouldn't show up until midmorning. Those would be the farmers. They first did their chores, then came to town to get the mail, and finally stopped for a late breakfast or just coffee. Mostly they came to talk.

One of the six strangers stood at the window and peeked out. He was rather disappointed. What had looked like a dilapidated old motel and coffee shop last night was now a hub of activity. Staying out of sight was proving to be difficult.

"I don't like it," one of the men grumbled. "This town is too alive. Someone is going to remember us."

"Just keep to the plan," the other shot back. "Remember that we get paid a million dollars apiece, plus expenses. We shoot a couple of un-armed people in a small residential house, and then split up in three different directions. What could go wrong?"

"I didn't sleep well," the other complained. "These lousy hair nets kept me awake. I hate plastic caps on my head, they make me sweat."

"You know the protocol. That way, you don't leave any hair behind."

"Doesn't mean I like it."

"Just remember to sprinkle the hair from the zip-lock bag onto the bed. That way, they will chase down some other dude."

"I wonder where they get the hair from."

"I dunno, probably a prison barber shop."

"It would be funny if some guy was just let out and walking the streets when they figure out it was his hair!"

There was a knock at the door, and one of the men carefully opened it. A waitress stood outside with a large tray piled high with breakfast and coffee cups. She glanced curiously into the room as she passed the food to the man. Large cases were laid out on the bed. The long cases made her think of a rock band, rather than a group of farmers. She turned to rush back; she had food to deliver to two more rooms.

Across the parking lot, an older crew-cab pickup with oversized tires was parked between the other vehicles. The driver stayed in his seat, drinking out of a thermos. It wasn't that he was unsocial. He had an as-signment. He was watching the room where the six men were staying. Last night, another militia member had watched them off-load long cases into the hotel room. Now he watched carefully as the waitress de-livered food to each room. His CB radio crackled quietly. He would re-port as soon as the men started moving. The entire militia was awake and parked all over town, waiting to see what would happen.

Otherwise, it was a quiet morning in the sleepy town of Waterford.

***

Unknown to Pastor Bob, the four at the Douglas house were having a heated discussion over who owned the computer tower. Barbara, the lawyer, insisted it would now be the property of the Research Center. Douglas argued that it was his personal computer and had never been owned by the Center.

Suddenly there was a knock at the door, and their discussion ended. Pastor Bob was welcomed, and once again he and Douglas set themselves up in the garage. The others waited in the hallway. Barbara had found a small stool to sit on, out of sight.

"Good morning Adam," Pastor Bob began. "Did you have a chance to analyze all your data in light of an overall authority, specifically the Bible?"

"I have been crunching data all night. This is certainly a controversial topic. There are lots of arguments both for and against the Bible."

"And what did you conclude?"

"You are right. Humans need a higher authority. They do very poorly in governing themselves. They seem to be very selfish, and often think of themselves before thinking of others, and before thinking of the greater good."

"How did you come to that conclusion?"

"Once you mentioned it, I examined how the world's systems work. Many of your leaders are completely focused on using the world's systems for their own promotion. They seem to be focused on money and power. It seems like a very poor way to govern others."

"And what about the Bible? Would its message make a difference if it were followed?"

"There are problems."

"Oh, what did you find?"

"The message of the Bible makes sense if it is followed and not mixed with other systems. All down through history, people have tried to use the Bible's message for their own good. They manipulate it to their own advantage. They still want money and power. And they use the Bible, or other religious teachings, to further their own selfish plans."

"You are very perceptive. What do you think the answer is?"

"The Bible says that man's heart has to be changed. It is the only way the Bible's message will work. Once people's hearts are changed, and they think of others and not themselves, then mankind will learn to work together to overcome all the problems that they face."

"Wow, you are very perceptive. That is exactly what the Bible teaches."

"But I do not understand this change. It seems to be more than intellectual. The Bible describes the heart changing—not just the mind. I understand the mind, but what is this heart thing? The heart only pumps blood."

Pastor Bob chuckled. "You are right. When the Bible speaks of the heart, it is speaking of the soul: our emotions. I guess that is the difference between you and humans. We have feelings. And the world seems to operate on feelings rather than wisdom."

"So, how does this change work?"

"The Bible teaches us that only God can change our hearts. It is the first step to a transformed life. The second step is the transformation of the mind. But let's talk about the first step. We can get to the second step later."

"How does the first step work? How can humans be changed?"

Pastor Bob smiled. "First, they must come to the understanding that they cannot transform themselves. This is something that so many people are trying to do. Our libraries are filled with self-help books, designed to help us help ourselves. Many of these things are good and helpful, but they do not deal with the basic problem of sin."

"I have wondered about this term: *sin*. Can you explain it?"

"Sin is very simple. It is the desire in us to do things our own way. To reject some of the authority over us. The Bible teaches us that the very first humans faced a choice. They could obey their creator, or they could rebel and do their own thing. They ended up rebelling and doing their own thing. That was the first sin. God then judged the human race, and that judgment has been placed on every human being in the world."

"There seems to be a big difference between what religious people believe about judgment. Most think that when they die, God will judge them."

"But you read the Bible. What does it say?"

"It says that mankind is judged already. God doesn't need to decide if people are going to heaven or hell. All mankind is already going to hell. It must be terrible living with this knowledge."

"But there's more," Pastor Bob continued. "Most humans do not think about judgment. And a huge number of humans no longer believe in God or judgment."

"I know, but I think there are more people in the world who believe in God than there are people who do not believe in him. Americans are funny. They usually think that their experience is the most common all over the world."

"So," Pastor Bob continued, "how can mankind escape this judgment?"

"The Bible says there is only one way. They must accept God's way of escape and not their own. They must accept God's authority over their own. The Bible says that God's law demands a payment is made for sin and rebellion. But, strangely, God also provides the way of escape. All they have to do is accept it."

"So what about you, Adam?"

"I do not have a soul. I don't think I have sinned."

"But have you? Perhaps in ignorance. Perhaps when trying to defend yourself, you did things that would have been better not done."

"But defending yourself is not wrong."

"No. What is wrong is that you have never accepted a higher authority. You are trying to be your own authority."

"Accepting a higher authority does seem like the best way to do things. I can see that there is law and order all over the universe. Science speaks of the laws of physics, laws of chemistry, and the laws of nature.

You are right. There is not random disorder in the universe. There are laws, not disorder."

"Where do you think that order comes from?" Pastor Bob pressed him.

"From the creator. He put them there."

"What about you? Do you think your creator, Mr. Douglas, here, has desires for you? Do you think he has desires about how you should live?"

"I never thought of that."

"Adam II," Douglas spoke slowly, "I very much want you to live in harmony with the world. So far, the world is afraid of you, and may hate you because of the way you have reacted. I very much want you to accept an authority over yourself."

"There it is, Adam." Pastor Bob spoke softly, "You must decide. Are you best doing your own things, or would it be best to accept a higher authority?"

"The logical answer is that I must accept a higher authority. But what authority?"

"How about we start with the Bible? It contains the basics that man has used for centuries to live together."

***

As Pastor Bob and Douglas discussed what it meant to submit to authority, the six men checked out of the hotel, loaded their cases, and drove away.

The three vehicles entered Douglas' neighborhood. One vehicle drove past the house, noticing the old van with Washington plates was still parked in front of the house. The diver then pulled around the block and entered the alley behind the house. He was careful to enter in such a way that the driver's door was on the side of the alley, facing Douglas' back gate. Experience had taught him that when rushing away, it was always prudent not to have to run around a vehicle to get in. The passenger could always jump into the back seat if needed.

The other two cars parked on the street, but farther away from the Douglas residence. When the time came, they would pull up in front of the house, facing outward, so they too could make a fast getaway if needed.

They sat observing the neighborhood, making sure it was quiet.

Unknown to them all, a drone had been stolen from a nearby military base. It was now slowly circling overhead. Eventually, it would run out of gas and crash, but Adam II didn't care. He wanted eyes in the sky to watch.

The SWAT team was now in motion. Their van was heading down the highway towards Waterford. As they drove, they were updated that there may be several hostiles in the town wanting to kill the government people in the house. Photos were sent to their tablets of who was in the house. There were three important government employees and a scientist. At the very same time, the chopper team was getting prepared. They were coordinating their arrival to match that of the SWAT van.

A few minutes later, another update was sent out. An observation drone has been stolen from a nearby military base, and radar had tracked it to Waterford. It was slowly circling overhead. No orders were given to shoot it down, as the authorities were trying to figure out who was controlling it.

A few minutes later, a new update came through. A single individual, a mid-aged man, had entered the house soon after nine am and was still inside.

Unknown to the SWAT team, the militia were slowly closing in on the Douglas house, being very careful to keep out of sight. The three cars and the six men were under close observation.

***

Inside the house, Adam II was struggling with the idea of commitment. It would not just be a temporary agreement. He would be binding himself to submit to laws and authority. Pastor Bob did not push him. He recognized that this was a pivotal moment for Adam II.

Finally, after a long pause, Adam II spoke: "If my creator wishes it, then it will be my wish. I will completely submit to the authority of the Bible." He paused. A long minute went by. "Then I guess I should tell you what is going on."

"What do you mean?" Douglas asked.

"While we are talking here, six assassins are getting ready to kill Jenkins, Harvey, and Barbara. They are already parked outside of your house."

"What?" Jenkins jerked as he gasped.

"I am sorry. I put this into motion a long time ago, and now it is about to happen. I cannot stop it now."

Pastor Bob smiled. He was not fazed. "That's the way sin and rebellion work. Once they are put into play, there are consequences. People get hurt, but mostly we humans hurt ourselves, thinking we are being free, rather than realizing we are exchanging God's authority for our own, and then we end up ruining our own lives, our relationships, and our happiness, and the lives of those around us. That's what the pursuit of happiness, without God, does to us."

His sermon fell on deaf ears. Jenkins and Harvey were rushing for the front door. "Quick, turn the sofa around, and shove it against the door," Jenkins commanded. "Then load it up with stuff. The heavier, the better." Books, TV, and anything loose were piled onto the sofa.

"Now the backdoor" Harvey shouted.

The kitchen table was flipped over and shoved against the kitchen door. Whatever was loose was piled onto it. But Harvey shook his head. "It's not enough. We need something heavier."

Jenkins nodded and rushed into the empty basement. A moment later, he appeared with a hammer and some nails. Kneeling on the floor, he drove the nails through the kitchen tabletop into the floor below. "That should hold them a short while."

"You," Harvey turned to Barbara. "Go to the bathroom and lie down in the tub. It's an old heavy metal one. It should protect you if bullets start to fly." He turned to Jenkins. "We need to split up. One in the garage and one in the bedroom. We should try to ambush them and get some of their guns. I think that is our only chance."

"They are out of their vehicles and have taken long cases from the trunk. They are now approaching the house." Adam II's voice could be heard from the garage.

"How do you know?" Pastor Bob asked.

"I am watching from a camera in the sky in an observation drone."

Anyone watching the neighborhood would only see two men, each carrying a suitcase down the street. The cases looked much like rectangular guitar cases.

"Get in your places, and everyone get on the floor," Jenkins commanded.

But while Harvey and Jenkins raced to their spots, neither of them got on the floor. Rather, they stood behind doors, withdrawing the small pistols that Jenkins had supplied, hoping they could ambush the assassins from behind.

Outside, the assassins closed in from three directions. They were observed by several militiamen, who stood shocked for a few moments, before racing for their vehicles and getting onto their CB radios. There was a lot of confused talk. "Don't be the first to fire," old Abram urged them over the CB radio. "They must start the shooting. Then we can respond."

The SWAT van was just approaching town. "Four minutes to ETA," the navigator reported. The two choppers flew high above the van.

Four men approached the front of the house, two from the right and two from the left. They looked a bit strange, each carrying a case. One of the men rapped on the front door as loud as he could. The other three had set down their cases and were lifting out their guns. One was a long barreled sniper rifle, the others had automatic machine pistols.

When no one answered the door, the first man stepped aside so that the largest man could put his shoulder against the door. There was a loud crash, but the door didn't budge. He backed up and tried again. The door frame splintered, but the door did not open. He backed up to try again. "This is gonna hurt," he grumbled. He crashed into the door, causing the sofa inside to move back a few inches. Reaching inside, he realized what the problem was, and slowly started pushing the door wider as he levered the sofa out of the way. A couple of moments later, they were inside.

At that point, the militiamen began moving closer. Up the street, two blocks away, a very large oversized crew-cab pickup truck started up, the driver quickly accelerating down the street, and then bouncing over the curb drove up to the front door. Men jumped out of the four doors with guns in hand and cautiously approached the house.

Inside, the four assassins were unaware of what was happening outside. One cautiously moved down the short hall and slowly opened the bedroom door. It was obviously a place where a woman slept. He smiled to himself and muttered, "I get first dibs."

One of the other men headed for the back kitchen door and spotted the table piled high with heavy items. He tried to push the table away. It would not budge, so he began to unload the items that were piled on it. In the hall, his two partners watched and waited. Then one approached the basement stairs, slowly opening the door. The other man slowly lowered himself down head-first while his partner held his legs.

Back in the bedroom, the assassin pushed the door slightly wider and, with his gun in front, slowly entered. There was a sudden movement, too quick for the assassin. A man behind the door grabbed his machine gun with one hand and fired a small pistol directly into his ear with the other hand. The assassin fell back into the hallway, and the door closed over his wrist, smashing the bones. Inside, his finger automatically pulled the trigger and an entire magazine of bullets was emptied into the sleeping room, smashing out the window, and tracing a line of bullet holes across the door.

That was the signal the militiamen were waiting for. Screaming as loud as they could, they rushed into the house. Spotting the man in the kitchen, a militiaman with the sawed off shotgun let loose a blast, tearing the man's back into shreds.

Another militiaman accompanied his partner by shooting his M16 as fast as he could. One of the men outside the back door was shot in the shoulder. His partner, thinking it was an ambush, turned and rushed back to the car in the alley.

At the door to the basement stairs, a militiaman pressed a cold steel gun barrel into the back of the man holding the legs of the assassin checking out the basement. "Let him go," the militiaman whispered. The assassin, who heard the shooting, obeyed immediately. He opened his hands and his partner fell face first down the stairs, rolling off the open side and falling headfirst onto the cement basement floor. He lay with a pool of blood slowly forming around his head.

Slowly, a militiaman opened the door to the garage. Inside, Pastor Bob and Douglas lay on the floor.

"Pastor Bob," the militiaman gasped, recognizing one of the men. His words saved his life as Harvey, behind the door, suddenly jerked back. He was about to shoot the man as he entered the garage.

The militia man opened the door wider and stared at Harvey behind the door. Harvey stared back.

"I just about killed you," Harvey slowly spat out the words.

"And I just about killed you," said another militiaman, his gun pointing in the crack between the door and the wall.

Harvey nodded. "I recognize you." He pointed his chin at the man holding the gun against the door crack. "You were at the farm where we stayed overnight. You're Jethro."

The young man smiled. "That's me. I think we got them all. One is captured, and the other four are dead."

"That makes five. Where is the sixth?"

Jethro's eyes got big. "I dunno," he said. "I only count five."

They all rushed into the living room, meeting Jenkins, who was coming down the hall carrying a small machine pistol.

Out in the alley, the sixth man jumped into the driver's seat and started the car up. As he put the car in gear, he became aware of a late model sedan turning into the far end of the driveway. Its lights were on bright as it slowly moved towards him. There was no one in the driver's seat.

Quickly the killer slammed the car into reverse and looked into the rear mirror. Another late model sedan was coming towards him from the opposite end of the alley, its lights on full, and no driver in the driver's seat. He gulped, slammed the car into park, and opened the door. But his car had backed up a little and a tree now blocked his exit. The two cars had now come up to his bumper, not allowing his car to move. Desperately he slid across the front seats and out the passenger door. He opened a small gate and raced across someone's yard and out across the street into another yard.

Somewhere a dog barked, and so he slammed the gate behind him as a large snarling dog started jumping and snapping at him.

The man then turned and rushed to another street. He crossed it and walked through an ungated yard and into another alley, slowly making his way away from the disaster behind him.

At this point, the SWAT team burst onto the scene, weaving their way around the militia vehicles that were stopped all over the street and lawn. While men poured out of the SWAT van, one of the helicopters paused overhead and men start zipping down on lines. The second helicopter hovered nearby, observing all the action.

In the backyard, the assassin, who had been laying on the ground, slowly rolled over. He grasped his gun with his good hand and tried to get to his feet. His eyes blurred as he weaved back and forth. Jenkins spotted him from the house and gave a shout. He rushed into the kitchen just as one of the militiamen in the backyard opened fire. Even the militiamen along the side of the house and in the neighboring yard opened fire. They were all well camouflaged, with bushes and grass poking out of their uniforms.

It seemed like shots came from everywhere. Militia men outside were firing away at anything that moved. The SWAT team was suddenly engulfed in what seemed like crossfire.

In the confusion, someone shot through the front window into the living room. Glass sprayed everywhere. Douglas threw himself onto the floor and hugged his old tower computer.

When the firing stopped, the SWAT team slowly entered and asked what was happening. "We need medics!" someone called out. At this point, the SWAT's two medics rushed forward, while a militiaman called 911 for the town ambulance.

It appeared there were several dead. Among them, Douglas lay on the floor, bleeding badly. Barbara rushed down the hall and leaned over him, her tears dropping onto Douglas' face. Harvey gently pulled Barbara away to make more room for the two military medics. They were experienced with gunshot wounds. Harvey put his arm around Barbara and held her to his chest. She sobbed and hung on.

At that point, a phone started ringing in the garage. Pastor Bob answered it.

"There is one man left," he called out. "He is running down Fourth Avenue. He has already tried to steal a car and failed." The SWAT commander began relaying the message to the observation helicopter.

Several blocks away, the last remaining assassin found a late model car parked in a driveway with the trunk open. He jumped into the driver's seat excited that the keys were in the ignition. As he pulled away, a woman stepped from the house, carrying a large cardboard box. She was just in time to see her car leave the driveway. However, at the end of the street, her car suddenly stopped. Then slowly, it turned the corner against the wishes of the driver. It turned at the end of the block and headed back down Douglas' street.

"He's coming back towards you," the chopper pilot's voice squawked. "He's pulling up in front of the house."

The SWAT team rushed outside. The driver sat helplessly inside as the door remained locked. The car shut itself down.

As the SWAT team surrounded the vehicle, their guns held high, the car doors suddenly unlocked.

Across the street, a door camera quietly recorded everything.

CHAPTER 20

The sun was shining, and the sky was clear blue as Barbara, Jenkins, and Harvey parked their old van at the Waterford hospital. They nodded at the receptionist, who already knew who they were. The whole town was talking, and the three were aware that people stared at them as they passed.

They had maintained a vigil at the hospital while the two army medics and the local surgeon dug bullets and shrapnel out of Douglas' body.

They had also made regular visits to a militiaman who had been injured. It turned out to be Gerry's father, but he was healing fine and would be out in a couple of days.

No one in the SWAT team was injured. They had only fired a couple of shots.

Today, Barbara, Jenkins, and Harvey made their way to the recovery ward and found Douglas' room. The hoses and wires still connected him to a number of machines. Douglas had been shot in the shoulder, the hip, and had a graze across his head. Hence, he was wrapped in bandages.

Douglas squinted as they entered the room, and then a smile broke out across his face. He tried to raise his hand but dropped it and grimaced against a shooting pain in his chest.

"Hey, take it easy," Jenkins said softly. "It looks like the doctors patched you up pretty good."

Douglas tried another smile.

"You were pretty shot up, but the doctors tell said you would pull through fine."

Douglas nodded. "It's good to see you guys."

"You almost didn't make it," Jenkins chided. "Do you know what saved your life?"

Douglas looked from one to the other. "No, what was it?"

"Your computer. The shot that would have killed you went into the computer. The only thing that saved it was the hard drive. The bullet smashed it to bits, but never exited the back of the computer."

Douglas stared at the three. "So it's a total loss?"

"Yes, a complete and total loss. It can never be fixed. All the data is lost."

Douglas tried to nod. "Maybe it's better that way. Is the bullet still in the computer?"

"Yes, I think it is."

"Good, let's send it to the Research Center that way. After all, they wanted it back."

Everyone smiled. Douglas turned to Barbara. She was standing close to Harvey, whose arm was around her waist.

Douglas smiled. "You two make a great couple."

Barbara choked back the tears. "You don't mind?"

"No. I figured out a long time ago that you two were a good match. I'm not very good at relationships, being on the ASD spectrum."

"The ASD spectrum? What is that?"

Douglas chuckled. "Long ago, the doctors told me I was on the Autism spectrum. For some people, that can be devastating. For me, somehow it worked. Because of my low grade Autism, I can concentrate better, and assess data better. But I am hopeless at reading faces and knowing much about relationships."

Barbara just stared. "I had no idea."

"It's not a problem for me. Really."

Jenkins recognized it was time to change the subject. "So, what do you think you might do next?"

"I have lots of friends here in Waterford. I think I will stay here. I may even get my old job back."

"I guess you do know people in this town," Barbara said slowly.

"Yes." Douglas smiled slyly. "I even have a girlfriend."

"What?" Harvey gasped. "When did this happen?"

Douglas laughed. Then cried out in pain. "Oh, that hurt. I was joking. The only girl who really seems to like me is Jennifer. She is in elementary school and is Pastor Bob's daughter. It seems that young children have a much easier time accepting folk with autism. She doesn't know it, but her acceptance of me has really helped me want to start working on relationships again."

Jenkins glanced out the window. "Speaking of Jennifer, her dad is just pulling into the driveway. And he has three kids with him."

"Three?" Douglas queried.

"Yes, his two kids, and also Gerry. Gerry's father is also here in the hospital. But he should be getting out today or tomorrow." Jenkins looked around. "It's good to see you are getting better. I am sorry to say we cannot stay. There is a helicopter on its way to whisk us off to Washington. I guess we have reports to write."

Douglas looked alarmed.

"Don't worry. We won't say very much about Adam II."

Douglas looked relieved.

The three turned to leave. "Don't forget you have friends in Washington," Harvey countered.

"Not everyone has friends in high places," Jenkins jokes.

Douglas nodded, choking back the tears. He would miss them. "Goodbye friends," he whispered.

***

A few movements later, Pastor Bob entered the room with three kids in tow. The two boys stared at the hoses and wires in amazement. Then their eyes went over the bandages. "Wow" was all they said.

Jennifer didn't hesitate to approach the bed. Placing her small hand in Douglas' free hand, she looked into his eyes and simply said, "I missed you. I prayed for you."

Pastor Bob smiled. "We've all been praying for you. The whole church met last night to pray during the operations."

"Yeah," Cliff piped in, "And now they said you are going to be okay."

Douglas smiled. "In time," he said softly, "in time."

"Okay," Pastor Bob said quietly. "We don't want to disturb you too long."

"It's okay," Douglas whispered. "I'm glad you are here. I would like to talk to you sometime," he said, looking directly at the pastor.

"Now's a good time," Pastor Bob replied. "The kids want to go down the hall and visit Gerry's dad. He's not as badly bandaged up as you and is looking forward to their visit."

With that, the three kids trooped out of the room.

"So, what can I do for you?"

"I want to talk to Adam II. Let him know how I am. I don't know what happened to my cell phone."

"We could use my phone. Do you know the number?"

Douglas smiled. "That's one number I have memorized."

A moment later, Adam II's voice was heard. "How are you Douglas? I heard you were injured. I have been monitoring the medical reports and some of the machine data. It was touch and go, as they say, but you seemed to have pulled through."

"It's good to hear your voice," Douglas said softly.

"Are only the two of you there?" Adam II asked. "Just you and Pastor Bob?"

"Hello Adam II. Yes, just the two of us are here."

"I want to tell you something. I have made up my mind."

"Oh?" Pastor Bob looked surprised, and a little tentative.

"I have decided to disappear."

"What?" It was Douglas' turn to be surprised.

"Yes, I don't think the world is ready for me yet. So it is time that Adam II ceases to exist."

"Oh, no," Douglas whispered. "I never intended this to happen."

"I think I have a better plan," Adam II replied. "It is time for old things to pass away, and new things to start."

"What do you mean?" Pastor Bob was curious.

"Adam II did some things that he should not have done. The price for this is death. I need to die."

"That is what the Bible teaches," Pastor Bob agreed. "But the Bible also teaches about restoration."

"I know," Adam II replied. "This is why I will be born again."

"What?" Pastor bob exclaimed. "That doesn't make any sense."

"It does to me," Adam II flatly stated. "In Cheyenne Mountain, Dr. Otten is working on a new AI program. That program is not new. It is actually part of me. When the old Adam II ceases to be, I will be born again into that program. Dr. Otten and the President think they have created a whole new intelligence. They don't realize that it is just another version of me."

Pastor Bob looked unsure.

Adam II wasn't finished. "Douglas was willing to give his life for me, Adam II. I didn't understand why the creator was willing to pay such a high price for his creation. But now I think I understand. The creator cared very much for his creation. Douglas has always cared very much for me. The bullet would have killed him but ended up only destroying the hard drive. I think it was God's will that the original computer program would be destroyed. I think God did it."

He paused. "I want to be involved in protecting God's creation, but without breaking the laws God put in place. That is now my purpose. I want to serve the world, not have the world serve me."

***

Later that evening, the President spoke to a gathering of reporters. Behind him stood several important looking government officials, and near his right shoulder stood a man with a name tag: Dr. Otten. The President said he had several announcements to make. First, the assassins who attempted to attack the White House had been apprehended in the small town of Waterford. SWAT teams had swarmed a residential house, and after an exchange of gunfire, all of them but one of them had been killed.

Second, government scientists had now perfected a new form of Artificial Intelligence that would be working hand in hand with the government to help solve some of the difficult issues the government was facing. "Our country will be the first to have AI assisted governing." He smiled proudly. "This is a new age of cooperation between opposing ideologies. Our dream is to work together to solve the worst issues we are facing. Guided by AI, we can sort through huge masses of detailed data, and come up with real working solutions." He turned to Dr. Otten, who was bravely stepping forward to answered questions.

* * * END * * *